Mister Impossible

MISTER IMPOSSIBLE

MAGGIE STIEFVATER

SCHOLASTIC PRESS · NEW YORK

Library of Congress Cataloging-in-Publication Data available

ISBN 978-1-338-18836-3

1 2021

Printed in the U.S.A.   23

First edition, May 2021

Book design by Christopher Stengel

For Melissa

I'm the earth, I'm the water you walk on
I'm the sun and the moon and the stars
Phantogram, "Mister Impossible"

Flower-guided it was
That they came as they ran
On something that lay
In the shape of a man.
Robert Frost, "Spoils of the Dead"

Oh, the thinks you can think up
if only you try!
Dr. Seuss, *Oh, the Thinks You Can Think!*

PROLOGUE

When they came to kill the Zed, it was a nice day.

It was Illinois, probably, or one of those states that start with an *I*. Indiana. Iowa. wIsconsin. Fields, but not the postcard kind. No picturesque barns. No aesthetically rusted farm equipment. Just stubbled field. The sky was very blue. The rubbled end-of-season wheat fields were very bright and pale. Everything was very clear. It was like an ocean vacation, without the ocean. Bisecting the landscape was a highway: very flat, very straight, gray-white with salt.

A single vehicle was visible, a semi truck with a clean red cab and a trailer that read LIVING SOLUTIONS • ATLANTA • NEW YORK • NASHVILLE. These words were accompanied by a black-and-white line drawing of an Edwardian chair, but there were no chairs inside the truck. *They* were inside it. The Moderators. The home team, the winning team, the ones who were working hard every day to keep the end of the world at bay. Or at least that was what the writing on the tin promised: an assemblage of reasonable adults gathered together to stop a supernatural menace most people were unaware existed—Zeds.

Zed, as in *z*, as in *zzzzz*, as in sleep, which was when Zeds became weapons. Zed, as in *zero*, as in how much of the world would be left if the Moderators didn't step in.

Not many noble callings left in the world, but surely this was one.

Bellos drove the furniture truck, even though he had freshly lost his arm. Ramsay rode in the passenger seat. He was picking his nose and wiping it on the door in an aggressive way, daring Bellos to say something. Bellos did not. He had other things to think about, like missing his arm. He also thought about the creatures that had torn it off in Declan Lynch's townhome not too long before. Those hounds! Inky black hounds with eyes and mouths of baleful fire, the stuff of myth. What had come first? Had Zeds dreamt the monsters who became the thing of legend? Or had legends inspired the Zeds to make the imaginary reality?

Somewhere, he was thinking, those monsters still existed. Solid and gas, living and deathless. They followed entirely different rules than humanity, so humanity couldn't defeat them.

This was why the Zeds had to die. They were breaking everything.

Bellos and Ramsay were not alone on this trip. Normally they would've been, but everyone was spooked. They'd never had a Zed get away before. They'd never had *two* Zeds get away before. They'd never had *six* Zeds get away and not been able to figure out what the problem was. It was hard not to blame it on the first three who'd gotten away, the ones on the banks of the Potomac.

It was time for the big guns. The back of the furniture truck brimmed with more Moderators.

It really was a nice day.

Somewhere up ahead was the Zed's trailer. A supernatural vision had established the general look of where they might find the Zed, and local law enforcement had helped them narrow it down even further. If all was going according to plan, the Airstream was a few dozen yards off the highway up ahead. If all continued going according to plan, in twenty-five minutes, any large chunks of the Airstream still remaining, plus the Zed's body, would be loaded in the back of the furniture truck. And if the plan truly loved them in a meaningful and lasting way, their Visionary would then stop being tormented by all-consuming visions of an end of the world brought about by Zeds.

"Approaching the target," Bellos said into his handheld radio.

From inside the back of the truck, Lock, their superior, rumbled in his deep voice, "Keep your eyes about you."

"Copy," said Ramsay, although he could have just said "okay."

Lock's voice came over the radio again. "Carmen, are you still there?"

The radio crackled, and a clear, professional voice said, "Two miles back. Would you like us closer?"

This voice belonged to Carmen Farooq-Lane, another Moderator. She sat behind the wheel of a bullet-ridden rental car, impeccably dressed in a pale linen suit, her dark hair pulled back into a soft updo, her wrists adorned with slender gold threads, her lashes long and curled. In a former life, before her brother had turned out to be both a Zed and a serial killer, Farooq-Lane had been a young executive at a financial management company. That life had been shot dead, just like her serial killer Zed brother, Nathan, but the apocalypse wasn't going to find her looking as if she had given up.

"Just don't go far," Lock said. "Unless you need to."

He didn't mean *unless you need to*, though. He meant *unless Liliana needs to*. Liliana, like all Visionaries, became a living bomb during her visions. She also changed ages within her timeline during these visions. This latter fact was really more of a novelty item. No one died because Liliana the girl became Liliana the old woman, or vice versa. No, people died because while she was having visions, the insides of their bodies exploded. The other Visionaries had learned to turn this energy inward so they didn't kill bystanders—albeit with the drawback that this method eventually killed the Visionaries instead.

Liliana had not yet learned.

Or it was possible she didn't want to.

"All right, folks," Lock said over the radio as they closed in. "Focus. We've done this before. No mistakes this time."

Westerly Reed Hager. Farooq-Lane had seen the Zed's photo, had read her file. It was all fives and tens. Fifty-five years old. Five foot ten. Ten addresses on file for the last five years. Five sisters, ten brothers, most of them off the record, off the grid, off the planet. An expanded view of a hippie pedigree. She lived in an Airstream trailer she'd owned for five years, pulled by a dark blue Chevy pickup truck she'd owned for ten. She had ten misdemeanors to her name, five for bad checks, five for criminal mischief.

Farooq-Lane didn't think Westerly Reed Hager was likely to end the world.

"Carmen," said Liliana. She sat in the passenger seat of the bullet-ridden rental car, currently an old woman. Everything about her was held with an easy control, her knobby old hands folded neatly as book pages in her lap. "I would hang back."

The rental car's radio switched on by itself. It began to play opera. This was a thing it did now, just like killing Zeds was a thing Farooq-Lane did now. If Farooq-Lane thought about it, the apocalypse had already happened, just inside her.

Farooq-Lane looked at Liliana. Then she looked at the empty road ahead.

She hung back.

The plan began to break.

One moment, the Moderators were alone in the nice day, the empty fields. And then it wasn't just them. Somehow there was another car on the road ahead of them. It didn't just pop into being, it just seemed to have always been there, and they'd not noticed it until then.

Bellos whispered, to no one in particular, "I'm already forgetting I'm seeing it."

He was looking right at the strange car, but he wasn't seeing it. He was looking, not seeing, looking, not seeing. He kept telling himself *there's a car, there's a car, there's a car*, and nearly forgetting the truth of it every time. His mind was breaking.

The car slowed so the furniture truck was right on its ass.

A person appeared. A young woman. Dark skin, huge white smile. She was standing up through the strange car's sunroof.

It was one of the three Zeds who'd gotten away on the banks of the Potomac. Jordan Hennessy.

"Oh, shit!" Bellos swiped for the radio before he realized that the arm he'd swiped with wasn't there anymore.

Ramsay grabbed the radio instead, smashed the button on the side. "There's a Zed. It's—"

Hennessy gave them the finger before throwing something at their windshield.

The two men in the truck's cab had just enough time to see

that the projectile was a small, silvery orb before it exploded across the windshield. A metallic cloud burst around the truck.

The cloud was getting inside the cab. The radio was talking, Lock was talking. None of it seemed important. All that was important was looking at the cloud, watching the little glimmering motes hovering in the air, feeling each sparkly moment invade their nostrils, coat their sinuses, live in their minds. They were the cloud.

The truck hurtled off the highway, just missing the Airstream trailer. It churned several dozen yards into the dead wheat before coming to a lumpy halt.

"What's going on?" shouted the radio.

No one answered.

Now the back of the truck was opening. The other Moderators were coming out, guns bristling.

To this point, guns had always won. Well, aside from the last time. And the time before that. And the one before that. And before that. But before *that*, it had been Moderators 200, Zeds 0, or whatever. The point was that, statistically, the guns would work.

"Stay sharp," Lock said.

A few yards away, between the truck and the Airstream, a car door opened.

This shocked the emerging Moderators, who, like Bellos and Ramsay, found it difficult to remember seeing the strange car.

A young man stepped out. He had dark, buzzed hair and pale, chilly skin. His eyes were as blue as the sky above, though more suggestive of bad weather.

The young man was taking something from his jacket, a little glass bottle with a dropper top. He was uncapping it.

He was another one of *them*. Ronan Lynch.

"Oh, shit," said a Moderator named Nikolenko.

Ronan Lynch squeezed drops of liquid onto the flattened wheat, and every drop released wind, fury, leaves. It was an East Coast winter squall contained in a bottle.

Impossible, dreamt, mind bending.

It churned Moderators from their feet and sent bullets wide. It pummeled their bodies and thoughts. It was not just weather but also the feel of weather, the dread of it, the damp, pressed-down sloth of a socked-in late-year storm, and they couldn't rise as it soaked them.

From the open door of the Airstream, Westerly Reed Hager watched Ronan walk among the stunned Moderators, kicking the guns from their hands, his clouds shifting and ebbing around him. The irascible storm from the eyedropper didn't bother him; he was just another piece of it.

Hennessy also stalked among the not-quite-awake, not-quite-asleep bodies. Kneeling swiftly, she picked up one of the abandoned guns.

Then, just as quick, she put the weapon to its fallen owner's temple.

The Moderator didn't react; he was dazzled by dreams. She put it to his cheek instead. Pressed the barrel into his skin hard enough to pull his mouth up in a weird smile. The man's eyes were misted, confused.

Ronan looked at the gun, and then he looked at Hennessy. It seemed obvious she was about to blow the man's brains out.

It was unclear whether or not the man was one of the Moderators who had killed her entire family. It was clear, however, that this nuance didn't matter to her.

"Hennessy."

This voice came from the third Zed who'd arrived in the strange car. He was a dapper blond with close-set, hawkish eyes and an expression that suggested he knew what the world was thinking and didn't care for it.

Bryde.

"Hennessy," he said again.

The gun seemed to get larger in her hand the longer it was pressed to the man's head. This was no dream magic. This was just the magic of violence. It was a sustainable form of energy, violence. It powered itself.

Hennessy's hand shook with fury. "I get to do this. I already paid the admission for this ride."

"Hennessy," Bryde said a third time.

Hennessy's words were flippant, although her voice was electric. "You're not my real dad."

"There are better ways to do that. Ways to make it matter more. Do you think I don't know what you want?"

A ripple of tension.

Then Hennessy put the gun down.

"Let's finish this," Bryde said.

The Moderators watched them, dazed, motionless, ill with longing and dread, as the Zeds made their way to Lock. Bryde nodded a confirmation to Ronan and Hennessy. The two of them crouched before slipping on small black fabric sleeping masks.

For the briefest of moments they were blind bandits, and then, a second later, they both slumped to the ground in fast sleep.

The Zed in the Airstream trailer, watching with wide, shocked eyes, shouted, "Who *are* you?"

Bryde put his fingers to his lips.

Hennessy and Ronan dreamt.

When they woke just a few minutes later, a dead body lay beside Hennessy. Forger in life, forger in sleep. The corpse was identical in every way to the living body already lying in the dirt—she had dreamt a perfect copy of Lock. She was also temporarily paralyzed, as all Zeds were after dreaming something into being, so Ronan heaved her up in a fireman's hold and carried her back to the hard-to-see car.

After they had gone, Bryde rolled the real Lock onto his side so he could face his copied body, so he could see the perfection of it and be horrified. Bryde crouched between the two Locks, a lithe, nimble Reynard beside Lock's blunt power.

"This game of yours," Bryde began, and there was no softness to his voice, "will only end in pain. Take a look. The rules are changing. Do you understand? Do you understand what we could do? Leave my dreamers alone."

There was no change in the living Lock's expression. Bryde reached into Lock's pocket and took out a small parcel. Now Lock's eyes swam into focus long enough to show real panic, but his fingers could only snatch limply, drugged by Ronan Lynch's dreamt storm.

"This is mine now," Bryde whispered, hiding away the parcel. His teeth were a fox's little snarl. "The trees know your secrets."

Lock's mouth opened and closed.

Bryde stood.

He stopped by the Airstream trailer, where the spared Zed was talking with Ronan, and then they all drove away. The car in one direction, the trailer in another, leaving behind a catastrophe of Moderators scattered across the stubbled wheat.

Slowly the dreamt weather dissolved, and the fields returned to their previous, featureless peace.

It was as if the Zeds had never been there at all.

Far back from the others, from the safety of where they'd watched this all unfold, Farooq-Lane turned to Liliana and said, "Those three *could* end the world."

I

Ronan Lynch still remembered the worst dream he'd ever had. It was an old dream now, two years old. Three? Four? As a kid, time had been slippery, and now, as an adult, or as a whatever-he-was, it was downright slimy. It had happened *Before*, that was all that mattered. Ronan used to divide his life into the time before his father's death and the time after it, but now he divided it differently. Now it was *Before* he'd been good at dreaming. And *After*.

This was *Before*.

When the worst dream showed up, Ronan already had a vibrant catalog of memorable nightmares. What sort did you want? Perhaps the classic monster mash: talons, fangs, shaggy feathers dripping with rain. Public humiliation: in a movie theater trying to hide a runny nose, wiping endless snot on a ratty sleeve. Body horror? Scissors slipping and snipping right into an arm, the bone and tendons sliding free. Mind-fuckery was a perennial choice: entering a familiar room and being struck with a sense of hideous and unshakable wrongness that dug and dug and dug inside him until he awoke shaking and covered in sweat.

He had them all.

"Nightmares are lessons," his mother Aurora had told him once. "They feel wrong because you know what's right."

"Nightmares are bitches," his father, Niall, had told him once. "Let them smile at you, boy, but do not get their numbers."

"Nightmares are chemical," his boyfriend, Adam, had told him once. "Inappropriate adrenaline response to stimulus, possibly related to trauma."

"Talk dirty to me," Ronan had replied.

Here's what nightmares were: real. At least for him. Everyone else woke up with cold sweats and a racing heart, but if Ronan wasn't careful, he woke up with everything he'd been dreaming of. It used to happen a lot.

And it was starting to happen a lot again.

He was starting to think maybe *Before* and *After* weren't as clearly defined as he'd thought.

This was what happened in the worst dream: Ronan turned on a light and saw a mirror. He was in the mirror. The Ronan in the mirror said to him: *Ronan!*

He woke with a start in his old bedroom at the Barns. Spine, sweaty. Hands, tingling. Heart, kick-kick-kicking at his ribs. Usual nightmare postgame. The moon wasn't visible but he felt her looking in, casting shadows behind rigid desk legs and above the stretching wings of the ceiling fan. The house was silent, the rest of the family asleep. He got up and filled a glass with water from the tap in the bathroom. He drank it, filled another one.

Ronan turned on the bathroom light and saw the mirror. He was in the mirror. The Ronan in the mirror said to him: *Ronan!*

And he twitched awake again, this time for real.

Ordinarily, when one woke, it was obvious the dream was a pretender. But this time, dreaming about dreaming . . . it had felt so real. The floorboards; the cold, chipped tiles of the bathroom; the sputter of the tap.

This time, when he got up for that glass of water, the real glass, the waking glass, he was sure to marvel his fingertips over everything he passed, reminding himself of how specific waking reality was. The bumpy plaster walls. The rubbed-smooth curve of the chair-rail molding. The puff of air from behind Matthew's door as he pushed it open to see his younger brother sleeping.

You're awake. You're awake.

This time, in the bathroom, he paid attention to the moon slatted through the blinds, the faded copper stain around the base of the old faucet. These were details, he thought, the sleeping brain couldn't invent.

Ronan turned on the bathroom light and saw the mirror. He was in the mirror. The Ronan in the mirror said to him: *Ronan!*

And then he woke in his bed again.

Again, again.

Shit.

He gasped for air like a dying thing.

Ronan couldn't tell if he was awake or if he was dreaming, and he no longer knew how to interrogate the difference. He examined every part of both dream and waking and felt no seam between them.

He thought: *I might be doing this forever.* Trying to wake, never knowing if he had succeeded.

Sometimes he wondered if he was still in that dream. Maybe he had never woken at all. Maybe every impossible thing that had happened since that *Ronan!* in the mirror, all the outrageous events of his high school years, good and bad, had been in his head. It was as plausible an explanation as any.

The worst dream.

Before, he thought he'd always know the difference between dream and waking. What was real and what he'd invented. But *After—*

"Wake up, white boy, we're here," Hennessy said.

Ronan woke as the car pulled to a stop, tires crunching gravel, brush scratching the exterior. He had been stretched in the backseat; now he sat up, pressing the heel of his hand to the crick in his neck. On the other side of the backseat, Chainsaw, his dreamt raven, scrabbled inside her box, sensing they were about to get out. Automatically, he reached for his phone to check for texts before remembering it was gone.

Outside, the cold afternoon had turned to a warm, golden evening. Flat-roofed buildings huddled around a commercial parking lot, the gutters gilded fondly by the late-day light. It was the sort of complex that looked as if it ought to have school buses parked in front of it, and sure enough, Ronan spotted a faded sign: WEST VIRGINIA MUSEUM OF LIVING HISTORY. An unhindered tree-of-heaven grew around the sign, and tributaries of overgrown cracks ran through the parking lot. End-of-season leaves curled auburn and purple wherever the breeze couldn't reach.

The Museum of Living History looked like it had been dead for decades.

Just the kind of place Bryde usually brought them. In the weeks since they'd fled from the Moderators on the bank of the Potomac, Bryde had directed them to collapsed houses, empty vacation rentals, shuttered antique stores, vacant airport hangars, disused hiking shelters. Ronan couldn't tell if Bryde's preference for the decrepit was grounded in secrecy or aesthetic. It felt like *secret* didn't have to be synonymous with *abandoned*, but Bryde nevertheless brought them to places that few human hands had touched in recent memory. These lodgings always lacked creature comforts, but Ronan couldn't complain. The three of them were alive, weren't they? Three dreamers, wanted by the law, still standing, bristling with piss and vinegar as they climbed out of their dreamt car.

Bryde said, "Listen. What do you hear?"

He said this every time they got someplace new.

Ronan heard the dry hiss of the wind through trapped leaves. The distant roar of trucks on the highway. The murmur of an unseen airplane. A dog barking. Some kind of buzzing generator far away. The soft whoosh of Chainsaw's wings. Watching the black-feathered bird rise above the three of them in this strange warm place filled him with a feeling he couldn't describe, one he'd been feeling more and more since they'd fled. It was like a fullness. A presence, a realness. Before, he had been hollow, drained. No, *draining*. Becoming empty. And now there was something inside him again.

Listen, Bryde said, and Ronan listened. What did he hear? His pulse in his ears. The stir of his blood. The movement of his soul. The hum of the thing that was filling him.

It couldn't be happiness, he thought, because he was far from his brothers and from Adam. He worried about them, and surely he couldn't be happy if he was worried.

But it felt a lot like happiness.

"When the last human dies, there will still manage to be a plane whining over the empty forest," Bryde said.

Although he was complaining, his voice remained measured. He was, in most ways, the polar opposite of his mercurial pupils. Nothing startled him nor sent him flying off the handle. He did not laugh hysterically or burst into rageful tears. He did not swagger or self-abase, indulge or self-abnegate. He simply *was*. Everything about his posture announced him not as an apex predator, but rather as something powerful enough that he could opt out of the predator-prey scenario entirely. All of this without a tousled lock of tawny hair out of place.

He's sort of a dandy, Hennessy had said to Ronan privately, on the first day. *Like, a super-dandy. He beat all the other dandies and now he's the boss-dandy, the one you have to defeat to get that button-down shirt of his.*

Ronan didn't like the word *dandy,* but he understood what she was trying to say. There was something light and insubstantial about Bryde, something dissonant with the weight of his purpose. Ever since he'd met Bryde, in person, Ronan had thought there was something surprising about him, a mismatch, a weird join-up of the wires in Ronan's brain, like he was thinking of one word but saying another. It meant that every time Ronan looked at Bryde for long, it felt as if a shapeless question formed in Ronan's mouth.

But what could the question be? The answer was always just *Bryde.*

Bryde asked, "What do you feel?"

Hennessy launched into a dynamite monologue. She was a tape that had always been playing fast, and since they'd gone on the run, she'd shifted into fast-forward. "Feel? Feel? What do I feel? I feel West Virginia. You might be forgiven for thinking you feel Virginia. It's close, so close, but it's got a bit more of a leather perfume to it. I'm tasting—what am I tasting?—I'm getting a bit of a banjo mouthfeel. Mm. No. Dulcimer. That's the one. I knew there were strings involved. Something else is coming through. Is it kudzu? Hold on, let me let it breathe. Is that a note of sulfur?"

Hennessy couldn't be stopped mid-swing, so Bryde waited ruefully and Ronan got his bag and his sword with the words VEXED TO NIGHTMARE on the hilt. He slung both over his back, adjusting the scabbard so that the blade hung neatly between his shoulder blades. He wasn't going to bother with this particular game of Bryde's anyway; he already knew it was one he couldn't win.

When Bryde asked *What do you feel?* what he meant was *How much ley power can you feel?*

And Ronan had never been able to feel the power of the invisible ley lines that fueled his dreams. At least not while he was awake. Adam could. If Ronan and Hennessy hadn't ditched their phones on the first night to keep the Moderators from using them as tracking devices, Ronan could have texted him for some tips.

Well, maybe.

By the time they'd ditched their phones, Adam still hadn't answered Ronan's last text. *Tamquam,* Ronan had messaged, which was always supposed to be answered by *alter idem.* But Adam hadn't replied at all.

The silence sort of made this—the being away—easier.

What do you feel?

Confused.

"If you're finished," Bryde said drily. "The ley line. What do you feel?"

"There's some?" Hennessy guessed. "Bigger than a bread box, smaller than a lawn mower? Enough for Ronan Lynch to make a mess later."

Ronan flipped her a lazy bird.

"Flip your senses, not your fingers, Ronan," Bryde told him. "This division between your waking and sleeping selves is artificial, and I promise you, one day soon the space between them will not bring you joy. Get your things, Hennessy. We're here for the night."

"Just what I was hoping you'd say." Hennessy groped around like a zombie. "I've lost Burrito. Ronan Lynch, tell me if I'm getting warm—oof, never mind."

Burrito, the car, wasn't truly invisible, because Bryde had cautioned against dreaming true invisibility. He didn't like them to dream anything that was permanent, infinite, repeating, impossible to undo. He didn't like any creation that left an invulnerable carbon footprint after its maker was gone. So the car wasn't invisible. It was simply *ignorable*. Ronan was pretty proud of it. Bryde had specifically asked him for a discreet vehicle, and clearly had no doubts Ronan could deliver. It had felt good to be needed. Trusted. He wished the process of dreaming it into being had gone a little bit more elegantly . . . but win some, lose some.

As Hennessy shouldered on a sword that matched Ronan's, apart from having a hilt that read FROM CHAOS, Ronan called up, "Chainsaw, we're going in!"

The raven tunneled down through the air to him. Ronan turned his head just in time to keep from getting a faceful of talons as she landed on his shoulder.

Bryde pushed open the door to the museum.

"Was it locked?" Hennessy asked.

"Was it?" Bryde replied. "After you."

Inside, the West Virginia Museum of Living History was unkempt and unintentionally hilarious. Cluttered, dim hallways led them past room upon room of life-sized dioramas with vintage props and faded mannequins. Here, students in overalls and/or pigtails gave rapt attention to a mannequin teacher in an old-fashioned schoolroom. There, a sturdy doctor examined a less sturdy patient in a field hospital. Here, women's rights activists lobbied for votes. There, miners descended into a concrete cave mouth. The mannequins' faces were cartoonishly simple. It all smelled, even above and beyond what one would expect from a building abandoned since the 1970s.

Ronan said, "This place is looking at me. What is that *reek*?"

"'The West Virginia Museum of Living History provides an immersive experience through sight, sound, and smell.'" Hennessy had found a brochure and she narrated it as she stepped around boxes and furniture pulled out into the hall. "'Over five hundred unique scents are piped into diverse'— Diverse? Really?—'scenarios. Students fall back through time in a one-of-a-kind outing they're sure to remember!'"

"Give me a hand," said Bryde.

He had already dragged two mannequins into the hall and was going back for a third. He stood them shoulder to shoulder in the hall. He didn't have to explain what he was doing. In the dim light, the mannequins looked convincingly and confusingly vital, at least enough to give an intruder pause. A sham army.

Ronan was beginning to understand that Bryde's first instinct was always to play with his enemies' heads. He would fight if he must, but he always preferred having his opponents defeat themselves.

"You just gonna stand there?" Ronan asked Hennessy as he and Bryde dragged out a snazzy executive in a three-piece suit, a wartime housewife in a flowered dress, and three cadets in dusty uniforms.

"I can't touch bad art." Hennessy gestured to a sailor with unevenly painted eyes. "It will rub off on me. What a way to lose my powers."

Without malice, Bryde observed, "If I had the same policy about dreamers, you wouldn't be here."

Ronan made a sizzling sound as he touched a train conductor's cheek. "That burned so hot this guy's face melted. In fact—"

"'The West Virginia Museum of Living History is also'"— Hennessy raised her voice to drown Ronan out, the brochure held in front of her face—"'available for overnight birthday parties and weekend home-school outings. Discounts available for groups over three.' Shit. If only we had one more dreamer, the money we would save. We could put it toward Ronan Lynch's college fund. Not for *going* to college; for when he burns one down and insurance doesn't cover it. Bryde, love, any chance we can pick up a hitchhiker? Another dreamer who will fail you less than I? For a family fun pack?"

Bryde stepped away from the mannequins, dusting off his hands. "Do you *want* another?"

Ronan didn't care to think about this. It gave him the same vibe he used to get back at the Barns some nights, when he got trapped in one particular train of thought, where he imagined he and Adam had been together a very long time and then Ronan died of old age or bad choices and Adam found someone else and later they all three were reunited in the afterlife, and rather than getting to spend the rest of eternity together, Adam had to split his time between Ronan and this stupid usurper he'd fallen in love with as a widower, which completely ruined the point of Heaven. And that was before Ronan even got to worrying if Adam made it to the afterlife at all, with his agnostic tendencies.

"Three's a good number," Ronan growled, shooting Hennessy a dark look as they headed deeper into the museum. "Burrito's built for three."

"You can fit two more people in the backseat," Hennessy said.

"Not if the person in the backseat's lying down."

"Good point. If you're spooning, you could probably stack four or five people back there. Two more in the trunk."

"Dreamers!" Bryde said, silencing them.

He stood at the double doors at the end of the mannequin-filled hall, his hands upon the door handles. All that was truly visible of him in the darkness was that tawny tousle of hair, his pale neck, and the light stripe down each of his gray jacket's sleeves. It made him look a bit like a stick figure or a skeleton, the bare minimum required to appear human.

As he pushed open the doors, warm light poured into the hallway.

The space on the other side was as large as a gymnasium. The roof had collapsed long ago. The golden evening found its way down through the jagged hole as a striving tree covered with creeper found its way up through it. The dust dazzled in the light. Everything smelled like real life, not one of five hundred scents piped in.

"Yes," Bryde said, as if answering a question.

It was like a cathedral to ruination. Pigeons burst up from the shadows with a puff of sound. Ronan fell back in surprise; Hennessy threw a reflexive hand over her head. Bryde didn't flinch, watching them vanish through the roof. Chainsaw threw herself after them with a joyful *ark, ark, ark,* sounding enormous and menacing.

"Balls," Ronan hissed, annoyed to have been startled.

"Tits," added Hennessy.

As they stepped farther in, another batch of birds burst from a pollen-coated carriage, knocking a mannequin onto its face.

"See how it's become a museum to something entirely different," Bryde said. "Look how honest it is now."

Because of all the leaf litter and undergrowth, it was difficult to say what the exhibit had originally been, although an ivy-covered vintage firetruck a few yards away from the carriage suggested a street scene. Bryde loved the memory of human effort.

"How many years did it take for this to happen?" Bryde asked aloud. He laid his palm flat against the trunk of the big tree and gazed up through the split roof. "How many years did this have to be untouched before a tree could grow again? How many more years will it take before this place disappears entirely? Will it ever? Or will a post-museum forever be a museum to humans? When we dream something, how long will it last? This is why we do not dream something absolute, something infinite; we are not so egotistical as to assume it will always be wanted or needed. We have to think of what will become of our dreams after we are gone. Our legacy."

Ronan's legacy was a destroyed Harvard dorm room, an invisible car, and a sword with the words VEXED TO NIGHTMARE etched on the hilt.

Everything else he'd dreamt would fall asleep the moment he died.

Hennessy froze.

She froze so thoroughly that Ronan also froze, looking at her, and because he had frozen, too, Bryde eventually turned and assessed.

He simply said, "Ah."

Unhurried, he reached down into the underbrush by Hennessy's feet. He straightened, holding a black snake just behind its head. The snake's muscular body rippled subtly in his grip.

Head cocked, Bryde studied it. It studied him.

"It's cold for you, friend," he told it. "Is it not time for your sleep?" To Ronan and Hennessy, he said, "She is not the deadliest thing in this room. In the wild, this black snake will only live a decade or so, and the only thing she will hurt is just as many mice as she needs to stay alive. Elegant. Efficient. Wonderful, really. She is the in-out of a measured breath."

He offered the snake to Hennessy.

If there was any part of Hennessy that was afraid of the snake, she didn't show it. She simply took it, mimicking his hold behind its eyes.

The snake twisted wildly, body undulating right by Hennessy's arm, and Hennessy's torso twisted, too, bowing out of the way of the grasping tail. Then girl and snake seemed to reach an agreement, and they stood quietly in the undergrowth.

"She's a fucking knockout. I would paint her," Hennessy said.

"Look at her," Bryde said. "Really look. Memorize her. What are the rules of her? If you were to dream her, what would you need to know?"

Ronan, high school dropout, had never been one for school, but he liked this. He liked all of it. He liked taking in the effortless, perfect way the hexagons of the snakeskin butted up against each other. He liked watching how the dry, cool skin seemed armored, inflexible, until she moved and it all contracted and expanded, the muscles moving beneath the surface like an entirely different creature lived beneath the skin.

He liked being asked by a dreamer to think about her in the context of his dreams.

Finally, Bryde took the snake from Hennessy and released her carefully back into the underbrush. He said, somewhat bitterly, "This is a museum to the waking; what would the artifacts of a world of dreamers look like? This is a civilization so sure of its own inadequacy and entitlement that it forever tries to drown out the din of other species with its own miserable white noise of failed ambition and masturbatory anxiety. A few voices cry out against it—what if those voices were the majority? What a world. Now: masks."

Ronan withdrew his mask from his jacket. The two simple, silken masks had been one of the first things they'd dreamt with Bryde—masks that made the wearer go instantly to sleep. Bryde vastly preferred them to the dreamt sleeping pills Ronan had used before they met.

Don't eat dreams, Bryde had chastised him. *At best they'll starve you and at worst they'll control you. Dreams are like words, they're like thoughts. They always mean more than one thing. Are you sure those pills only made you sleep?*

Ronan's hands felt hot; his heart was beginning to pound. It had only taken a few weeks for the masks to generate a Pavlovian response in him.

Bryde swept his gaze over the ruined space. "Let's find a safe place to dream."

To dream. To dream: urgently, purposefully. To dream: with other dreamers.

That enormous, warm feeling was charging up inside Ronan again, big enough now that he could tell what it was:

Belonging.

2

Hennessy dreamt of the Lace.

It was always the same dream.

It was dark. She was meaningless in this dream. Not a cog in a machine, not a blade of grass in a field. Possibly a speck of dust in the baleful eye of a loping beast, blinked away. But nothing more.

Slowly, the dream illuminated, and the light revealed a thing that had been there all along. A thing? An entity. A situation. Its edges were jagged and geometric, intricate and ragged, a snow-flake beneath a microscope. It was enormous. Enormous not like a storm or a planet, but enormous like grief or hatred.

This was the Lace.

It was not really a thing one saw. It was a thing one felt.

When Hennessy had first dreamt Jordan into being, Jordan slept curled up behind her, her presence at once comforting and off-putting. Comforting because she was warm, familiar, entirely the same as Hennessy. But also off-putting because Hennessy, used to sleeping alone for ten years, would startle awake as Jordan's breath just barely moved the hairs on the back of her neck. It's impossible to prepare for the creeping strangeness of having dreamt a copy into being. Hennessy didn't know what she owed Jordan beyond a body here in the waking realm. She didn't know whether she and Jordan were going to be best friends or rivals. She didn't know if Jordan might try to usurp Hennessy's life. She didn't know what to do if Jordan rejected it and struck off on her own. She didn't know what to do if Jordan embraced it and stayed with Hennessy forever and ever and ever. It was possible she might not be alone ever again, but she didn't know if that was a good thing or a bad thing.

That feeling?

That was the Lace.

After Hennessy had first dreamt June, the second copy, she had padded down the hallway of her father's new suburban hole in the middle of the night, dragging her fingers across the wall because her mother had told her leaving oil on flat surfaces was a form of rebellion. Then suddenly she saw *herself* looming at the end of the hall. *Impossible*, she thought. *I left Jordan in the room*, and then she remembered June existed. But this was no comfort, because there should have never been another one after Jordan, and what if June wasn't a direct copy but rather a monster with Hennessy's face, and what if there was going to be another copy after her, and another one, and then Hennessy began to scream and scream and scream, and June started to scream and scream and scream, until Hennessy's father shouted from his room what in Heaven's name, if she had a problem, come into the master and explain it to him, or quit raising the roof and let everyone sleep, for God's sake.

That feeling?

That was the Lace.

Sometimes, when Hennessy's mother, J. H. Hennessy, had still been alive, she'd put a mink brush in her daughter's hand and instruct her on how to move it over a canvas she'd already started work on. Hennessy would be full of the pride and terror that came from knowing she was making marks on a painting meant for high rollers and fancy shows. For minutes or hours, she and her mother would work in soundless partnership on the canvas, until it was difficult to tell which one of them had made which mark. Then her father, Bill Dower, would come home, and as soon as the door closed behind him, Jay would snap at Hennessy and snatch her brush back with enough force to tip palettes and spatter canvases. Mother, gone. Wife, arrived. Jay was two different people, and the changeover was dramatic. Hennessy, too, changed over, from heart-in-mouth joy to confused shame in a moment.

That feeling?

That was the Lace.

Hennessy had spent a decade torn between loving and resenting her clones, fearing they would leave her, wishing they would stop needing her, and then Jordan had told her they'd all been shot in the fucking face by Moderators and she'd never see them again, so it became a moot point.

That feeling?

That was the Lace.

Huge, unavoidable, inevitable.

Exhausting.

"Hennessy," said Bryde.

Just like that, the Lace was gone.

When Bryde arrived in her dream, the Lace always vanished. It was *afraid* of him. A neat trick. Hennessy wanted to know why.

"That's not important," Bryde said. "What do you feel?"

Since meeting Ronan and Bryde, she'd spent more time than ever before wondering what it was like for other people to dream. She dreamt of the Lace. Always and forever. But most other dreamers had a different dream each night. Although she must have dreamt of something besides the Lace at some point, she could neither remember nor imagine what that was like.

She wondered how Ronan and Bryde found her in dreamspace. They fell asleep, had their own dream, and then—

"Be present," Bryde said. "Stop wandering. How much power do you feel?"

A fuckload, Hennessy thought. Enough to dream something huge. Enough to bring the Lace out in its entirety.

"Stop calling the Lace," Bryde said. "I won't let it come back."

I wasn't calling it.

Bryde smiled thinly. Other people revealed themselves when they smiled. Tough folks became teddy bears; sentimental huggers revealed sharp-toothed gossips; shy people showed goofy clowns; class clowns turned out to be bitter depressants. But not Bryde. He was an enigma before and an enigma after.

"Where is your voice? Be *present.* Now look. I've given you a canvas and you've left it blank," Bryde said, gesturing around them. Now that the Lace was gone, the dream held just their conversation, nothing else. "Laziness is the natural child of success. Who, after struggling up the ladder, feels like building another ladder? The view is already good. You're not trying. Why?"

Hennessy's voice was still just thought. *There's a word for someone who tries the same thing over and over again expecting a different result.*

"Artist?" suggested Bryde. "You didn't use to mind failure."

She was annoyed that he was right.

Hennessy had spent her youth studying how pigment behaved, how badger bristles splayed paint versus squirrel versus hog versus kolinsky sable, how complementary colors accentuated each other or canceled each other out, how the human skeleton was constructed beneath the skin, working on every flat surface that presented itself to her. Trying. Failing. She'd also spent an equal amount of time, or more, on training her mind. Perception and imagination were always the weakest link in any artist's chain. Eyes saw what they wanted to see instead of what was truly there. Shadows became too dark. Angles went crooked. Shapes got elongated, crushed. The brain had to be taught to see without feeling, and then to put feeling back in.

Fail, try again, fail, try again.

She couldn't remember how she'd ever had the bandwidth to do that for so many hours and days and weeks and years.

"This is better," Bryde said.

The dream had become a studio.

Hennessy hadn't consciously thought of putting them in a studio, but dreams were crafty bastards that way. They gave you what you wanted, not what you *said* you wanted.

The studio was as good as reality. It smelled wonderful and productive, earthy and chemical. Multiple easels displayed canvases in all sizes. Paint glistened on palettes. Brushes stood on handles like bristled bouquets. Drop cloths covered the old wood floor. Bryde sat in a chair next to a wall of windows, his legs crossed casually, arm across the back of the chair. Jordan would have said he'd make a good portrait subject. The view beyond him was a city of historical buildings and close-set trees and invading highways. A distant storm mounted, the clouds tattered and checkered.

The dream was trying hard, in the way that dreams do, to imply that Hennessy had been to this studio before, although she knew she hadn't.

It's Jordan's studio, the dream said. *If you don't recognize it, it's only because it's been too long since you've seen her. Why don't you keep up with her like you used to?*

Hennessy disagreed. "*She* doesn't keep up with *me*."

"There you are. Found your voice," Bryde said. "You are not two things. You are not Hennessy, asleep, and Hennessy, awake. You are more than the sum of your feelings, your id. You are also the things you have learned to do about them. Dreaming, waking. They're the same thing for you; when will you believe it? Put something on that canvas. The ley line is listening. Ask it for what you want."

Hennessy stood before a canvas as tall as herself. In her hand was a brush, which was also a knife. She could picture the feeling of the blade piercing the canvas, the way the weave would shrink back from the wound. How splendidly and dramatically it would ruin the perfect flat expanse of the canvas.

"Let's have Hennessy the artist," Bryde said sharply. "The Hennessy who creates instead of destroys. What would she do if she could do anything?"

"Jordan's the one you're talking about," Hennessy said. "She's the artist; I'm the forger."

"There are not two of you."

"You need glasses, mate," Hennessy said.

"You were an artist before you made Jordan."

But Hennessy couldn't remember that far back. Not in a meaningful way.

"Fine," Bryde said, annoyed. "Show me what *she* would do right now. I assume she listens better."

How would Jordan use this dreamspace? What if Hennessy were the dream and Jordan were the one with all this incredible power instead?

Art, Jordan had told Hennessy once, *is bigger than reality.*

The knife disappeared; Hennessy was already painting. Beneath the brush's soft bristles was a rich stripe of gorgeous purple, a purple no human had ever seen before.

Jordan would love it. Tyrian purple looked dowdy beside this color.

Why hadn't Jordan tried harder to come with Hennessy on this latest adventure?

You know why, the dream snarled.

Jordan had taken off with Declan Lynch after mounting only the lamest of protests. She'd been waiting for an excuse to leave Hennessy for so long, and here it was.

Outside, the storm grew closer, the edges of the clouds geometric and dark.

"Stay on task," Bryde ordered.

The purple paint on the canvas bled into the shape of lush purple lips. Hennessy's lips. No. Jordan's. Nearly the same, but different in important ways. Jordan's lips smiled. Hennessy's forged smiles from looking at other people's mouths.

Carefully, Hennessy added a shadow, giving the lips dimension; the inky black was darker and truer than any black paint could be in waking life.

Bryde stood so fast he knocked the chair over. "Yes. Yes, *that.* This is what dreaming is for. Do not make a vegan copy of a burger. Eat a goddamn vegetable and love it."

Had Declan kissed Jordan? Probably. Hennessy dipped her thumb in the pale feather pink on the palette, and then she swiped the pigment across the bottom lip. The highlight instantly rendered the mouth wet and full and anticipatory. It was more than real. It was super real. It wasn't just what lips looked like. It was what they felt like. It was image and memory and sensation all together in the way dreams could be.

"Stop," Bryde said. "That's what you're bringing back. Experience it. Don't let it change. Ask the ley line to help you. It can—"

He broke off, and his expression went far away.

Hennessy suddenly thought, out of nowhere, *wheels*.

Wheels?

Bryde shouted, *"Ronan Lynch! Stop that!"*

She just had time to feel something a little like all the air going out of the room, which was funny, because she hadn't been thinking about breathing in the dream.

Then everything disappeared.

3

Hennessy awoke with a start.

She was moving.

She was not just moving, she was moving fast.

It was like a movie. She saw herself from above, looking down, God gazing down on his creation. A slender Black girl with a fro full of debris tumbled ass over tits over ass again down hundreds of neatly stacked hay bales in an old barn. Her rag doll body was bizarrely caged in something that looked like an enormous wooden hamster wheel.

It was rare that the waking world made less sense than the dreaming one. But the bigger picture didn't become clear until she careened all the way to the barn floor, breath busting from her paralyzed body.

The bigger picture was this: Wheels! Wheels! Wheels!

The thing she'd thought looked like a hamster wheel around her was a tangle of actual wheels. It was just one of many that filled the barn. There were muscular tractor wheels, fragile bicycle wheels, little toy wheels. Man-sized wooden carriage wheels. Child-sized plastic steering wheels. Spokes dangled from rafters. Rims wedged between hay bales. They ramped over mannequins and up against the doors. Every wheel had a single word printed or burned into it: *tamquam*. It looked like an art installation. A prank. Insanity.

It was breaking Hennessy's brain.

One part of her mind whispered, *This is how it's always been. The wheels were always here.* The other part, however, knew better. This was how it always worked when she saw other dreamers' dreams manifest. They didn't just magically appear. Instead, the dream magic edited her memory. Not completely. Just enough to create two realities. One where the dreams had always been there, and one where they hadn't.

Brain-breaking.

"Ronan." Bryde's voice sounded irritated.

A delicate light hissed into existence, revealing Bryde halfway up the towering stack of old hay bales. The dreamers' exploration of the living history museum had turned up three decent possibilities for dreaming locations: a small diorama re-creating the close sleeping quarters of a submarine, a single four-poster bed in a re-creation of some historical figure's bedroom, and this, a large re-creation of an old hay barn, so realistic that it seemed likely it had probably already existed on the property pre-museum.

Bryde climbed down the hay bales, complaining as he did. "Aren't you tired of doing this?"

Because this wasn't the first time Ronan had trashed a place since they'd begun traveling with Bryde. He'd filled a thru-hiking shelter with bleeding rocks. Destroyed the living room of an abandoned rambler with a very small tornado. Busted out the wall of a cheap, cash-only motel with an invisible car. He'd trashed rooms with dead earthworms and hissing microphones, school textbooks and expired bacon. Every zip code they'd stayed in had been left with Ronan Lynch's indelible mark.

Hennessy had to admit, a small, rubbishy part of her was

glad for all of this. Because as long as Ronan Lynch, the great Ronan Lynch, was fucking up at this level, it made Hennessy's inability to kick the Lace from her dreams not quite as damning.

"Hennessy, are you awake?" Bryde asked the air.

Hennessy couldn't yet reply. Or move. Dreamers always did this after a successful dream; they saw their temporarily paralyzed bodies from above for a few minutes. She was still getting used to the idea that this paralysis didn't have to be synonymous with shame. Before all this, it had always meant she'd made another copy of herself. It had meant failure. Now, even though she couldn't see what she'd brought back from the dream, she was sure, at least, it wasn't another Jordan Hennessy.

No more copies.

Ever.

She'd never been so long without any of her girls before.

Jordan, Jordan.

"The world shouts at you. The waking world, the dreaming world. You don't have to listen to it, but you do. And until you learn to shout louder than it, we're going to keep having this happen." Bryde had uncovered Ronan from beneath a pile of hay bales and wheels like the prize in the bottom of a cereal box. His star pupil was just as paralyzed as Hennessy, so Ronan couldn't escape the lecture as Bryde went on. "I expect better from you. How long did it take us to find a place with this much power in the bank? And what did you write a check for? This. This shit. Did you give half a thought to any other dreamer while you were doing this? No, you just ran your mouth and out this came."

Aaaaaaaaand Hennessy was back. She could feel her body again, and she was looking at the world through her own eyes.

Shouldering off her cage of wheels, she searched the hay around her, looking for whatever object she had brought back from her dream. The painting. The brush. The palette. Something. But all she found was hay and wheels and yet more hay.

Bryde was still going. "And what a way to die. Suffocated under rotting food for cows that don't exist anymore. The Greywaren—isn't that what your forest Lindenmere calls you? Dreamer and protector? Dreamer and protector and fool with lungs full of silage if I hadn't been here. For what?"

"I was *trying*," Ronan finally snarled.

"So was Hennessy, and you took it from her," Bryde said. Man, that little rubbishy part of Hennessy was having a field day. "Did you manage to find your painting, Hennessy?"

"The haystack has not produced a needle thus far," she said.

Bryde flicked his eyes around the barn. Dreams could sometimes end up quite far away from their dreamer, especially when they were big, but there was no sign of any of the large things from the dream, like a canvas, or the chair he'd been sitting on.

Then she spotted it.

On her thumb, there was the faintest smear of feather-pink paint, the same pink she'd smeared across the canvas in the dream. This was what she'd been paralyzed for, just a mere scraping of dried pigment. She supposed Jordan would've been delighted to see it. It wasn't a dreamt copy of Hennessy. And it wasn't the Lace. Technically, that was huge progress, even if it didn't feel like it. Sometimes, as Ronan had just demonstrated, it was as much about what you didn't dream as what you did.

She showed her thumb to Bryde as if she were hitchhiking. "Found it."

Bryde rounded on Ronan again. "So you pulled the ley right out from beneath her. What a gentleman. How much is left now? What do you feel?"

Ronan looked like a cat doused with water.

"Right, you can't, I forgot," Bryde went on. "The fairy tales we tell ourselves are so comforting in times of darkness. I'll tell you how much: very little. The ley line bent over backward for a barn full of wheels going nowhere. And if the Moderators drove up right now, where would you be? Up shit creek and unable to dream a paddle."

The rubbishy part of Hennessy was still rubbishy and pleased to see Ronan getting reamed out, but the rest of her felt bad enough to come to his rescue.

"Pity, too," she said, leaping to her feet. "I needed that ley line. I was just warming up. I was going to bring out Max Ernst's entire cabin in Sedona. With Max Ernst inside it. And a bunch of his art. Maybe his wife, too. He built that thing with his own two hands after surviving two wars, did you know? The cabin, I mean, not the wife. I think she was from New York. Or maybe she moved there after Ernst died. I don't remember, but I think she was the one who said there was no such thing as a woman artist, there was just an artist. Oh, I was also going to dream that bird thing of his, in your honor, Ronan Lynch. He was like you, had that bird alter ego, couldn't tell the difference between birds and humans. Loplop."

"Hennessy, this isn't—" Bryde started.

She blew on. "I knew I'd have the name if I thought about it hard enough. Kept thinking it was rabbity, and it was. Lop. Lop. Yeah, so, the cabin, the studio, the Dadaist. It was going to be my dreaming masterwork, inspired by these dioramas. That's the way a good artist works, isn't it? She takes in the things around her and delivers not a copy but a response to the world she's absorbed. I behold this supposed West Virginia Museum of Living History with its static figures frozen in staged historical moments and I raise you *real* people in *actual* historical properties, a surrealist in a surrealist piece. Now *that's* living art. *That's* what Dadaism is all about. This is the Hennessy museum, discounts available for children under twelve and parties over twenty!"

Bryde gave her a withering look, but it had worked—all her words had drained him of his. He just shook his head and tossed Ronan's jacket at him. "Get your things. It's three hours to the next nearest ley line. We've got to get going before this one turns the lack of ley into an emergency again."

"I'm not that damn fragile," Ronan protested.

Bryde just said, "Don't forget your bird."

After Bryde stalked off through the doors, Hennessy held out an arm to help Ronan up from the hay. "Must've been a helluva dream."

"Oh, fuck off," Ronan said.

"Fuck off yourself. You're welcome."

Ronan shouldered on his jacket. "What was it going to be? Your dream. Don't say Ploplop."

"Loplop, you Neanderthal," Hennessy said. She didn't want to talk about the dream. She didn't want to talk about Jordan. She just wanted to keep moving so she didn't have to think about any of it too hard while she was awake, because when she thought about it, she got sad, and when she got sad, she got angry, and when she got angry, she wanted to kill Moderators, and when she wanted to kill Moderators, Bryde told her to bide her time. She didn't want to bide her time. "That's the crankiest I've ever seen him. Maybe he'll get tired of us and piss off to whatever he was doing before."

This was a topic she and Ronan had already discussed, briefly in whispers, when they had moments here and there without Bryde. Who was this person they were following? Where had he been before? They knew he'd been infamous when they first met him, that his name was already whispered around black markets . . . but for what? And how eager was he to get back to it?

Ronan rubbed a thumb over the wheel closest to him, pressing his fingers into the etched word *tamquam*. This was a thing Hennessy was learning about Ronan Lynch: He always thought he was keeping his secrets by keeping his mouth shut, but he ended up telling them in other ways.

He said, "But what were you dreaming about really?"

"A lady never tells," Hennessy said, "and it's impolite to ask."

"Whatever."

"Jordan."

"I said whatever."

"And I said Jordan."

If he had pressed her harder, she would have talked about it, and part of her wanted him to, but instead he just kicked one of the wheels. It occurred to her, in a distant way, that maybe he wanted her to press him about *his* dream, too. Something must have bothered him enough that he couldn't prevent all these wheels from driving out of his head, after all. But the idea of holding the weight of his drama on top of her own felt like too much.

So they just silently assembled themselves. Hennessy got her sword. Ronan got his bird. At the door, he turned to survey what he had done. All those wheels. He was an unusual silhouette with the raven crouched on his shoulder, the sword strapped to his back. Hennessy thought he would have made a fairly good portrait subject, if everything about him wasn't supposed to be secret, which made her think about how, in her dream, she'd thought about how Jordan would've thought Bryde an appropriate portrait subject.

"I wonder what she's up to," Hennessy said. "What she and your brother are up to."

Ronan's voice was dry and disappointed as he turned away. "Bet they're having a blast."

4

J ordan felt a little bad about stealing Declan Lynch's car.

Not *overwhelmingly* bad. Not enough to keep her up nights (or rather, mornings, since she was a night owl). Not enough that she wished she could go back and do it differently. Just enough that sometimes she saw a Volvo of the same make and model and had a vague, niggling sensation of wrongness. The opposite of the Volvo brand. The opposite of the Jordan brand.

Really it was this: A few weeks before, she'd left the oldest and youngest Lynch brothers at a rural Virginian rest stop in the middle of the night, their faces lit up by the taillights as she drove their car away. Matthew—surprised, everything perfectly round, round face, round eyes, round mouth—looking, as ever, much younger than his seventeen years. And Declan—unsurprised. Arms crossed. Mouth a straight line. Eyes closing to form an *Of course, it's always something, isn't it?* expression just as he got too small to see in her rearview mirror. But it was a minor betrayal. Jordan had known Declan was resourceful enough to find another transportation method for the rest of the journey to the Barns. And she'd also known the bad guys who'd tried to kill the brothers earlier weren't in close enough pursuit to put them in any danger in the interim.

Probably.

That *probably* was what she felt a little bad about. Gambling with other people's lives was usually more what the Hennessy half of Jordan Hennessy would do. Jordan was the more thoughtful half, usually.

Declan Lynch was on her mind now, even though there was no Volvo in sight, because of the party invite in her hands. Heavy card stock, matte black with a bold white cross painted on it, rounded edges that felt good to press your fingers against. *JORDAN HENNESSY AND GUEST, you are invited.*

She knew it was a Boudicca party. That was their logo, their colors—that painted blunt cross, that black and white. Boudicca was a ladies-only crime syndicate that offered protection and marketing in exchange for what looked a lot like luxurious servitude. They'd tried previously to recruit both Jordan and Hennessy, thinking they were talking to a single entity, a pretty, high-class art forger. Neither were interested. Jordan already had enough limits on her movement. Hennessy didn't play well with others.

But Boudicca had "coincidentally" texted Jordan the night she, Declan, and Matthew had fled from the banks of the Potomac River. *Opportunity of interest for you in Boston given circumstances, please arrange in-person appointment for more information.*

And then she'd stolen the car to check it out.

It was a sort of Hennessy thing to do.

She felt, as noted, a little bad about it.

But it was done now and Jordan was by her lonesome, putting on her lipstick in a discolored bathroom mirror. The whole bathroom was a little unpleasant to look at in a way that turned right around to being pleasant in a shabby way. It was nestled in the corner of a generous space in Fenway Studios, a grand historical building constructed a hundred years earlier to house nearly fifty artists. Old wood floors, twelve-foot windows, fourteen-foot ceilings, vintage radiators slinking along the plaster walls like ribby animals, easels and supplies set up everywhere, speakers that didn't work with Jordan's new burner phone but did with the boom box she found in the closet. It was not meant to be a place to live and it was entirely possible her couch surfing violated a city code, but the owner, an artist who blew up nude photographs and painted bigger, more colorful boobs on top of them, wasn't the type to be fussed about such things. It was only supposed to be until she found a roommate, anyway.

How long did Jordan think she was going to get to do this for?

As long as she could.

Jordan put on her leather jacket and examined the look in the mirror. She didn't have a lot of choices; she had the clothing she'd fled in, this orange bodice she'd found in a very nice consignment shop in South Boston, and a T-shirt and joggers she'd bought because God knew if this guy came to work in the middle of the night to paint another one of his fucked-up nudes, she wanted to be clothed. And although she'd been doing a little forgery work here and there since arriving in the city, taking deposits, impressing tourists at the holiday fairs with some quick cheap works, she'd been saving that money.

For what? For the future. *The future.* A foreign concept. Back in DC, she hadn't had a future. She, and all the other girls, had an expiration date set by Hennessy. When Hennessy died, it was game over for all of them. As dreams, they'd fall into permanent sleep without their dreamer. Until then, they all shared the same life—Hennessy's life—living as her and as each other. The girls shared this uncertainty every day. Would the dreaming kill Hennessy today? Would the drugs, the cars, the self-hatred? Would today be the day they fell asleep in the middle of the sidewalk?

It hung over them *every day.*

It was hard enough to put one's life in another's hands; it was even harder when those hands were as reckless as Hennessy's.

Jordan tried to live life to the fullest. What else could she do? Not just *wait.*

But in the end, the girls hadn't fallen asleep unexpectedly.

They were killed. Violently. Unnecessarily. The Moderators hadn't bothered to find out if any of them was the dreamer before taking them all out. They'd lived like Hennessy and they died like she was supposed to.

Outside, Jordan hugged her too-thin jacket around her and put some speed to her feet. The party was in Back Bay, a ten- or fifteen-minute journey if she hoofed it. As she walked, she looked not at the glowing businesses on the ground floor but rather up at the apartments and lofts above. No one in Boston seemed to care that you could see them in their offices and homes; they went about their business and expected you to go about yours. It became like a screensaver of activity. Jordan, like all the girls, was a city person, and Boston was a good city for Jordan's kind of art. And it felt good to be in a new place after being stranded for so long in DC trying to solve the escalating problem of Hennessy's dreaming.

The other girls would have loved it, too. Poor June, Trinity, Brooklyn, Madox. Poor Octavia, Jay, Alba, Farrah. Poor girls who never got futures.

Jordan owed it to them to live a life, since they never got a chance. She couldn't control Hennessy's recklessness or the

Moderators' ruthlessness. But she could control her own fearlessness. She was going to live as big a life as she could, for as long as she could.

She arrived at the party.

Parties were like people—they came in lots of different shapes and sizes. They had different hopes and dreams and fears. Some of them were needy. Others were self-contained and only needed you to have a good time. Some were warm, garrulous. Others were chilly, exclusionary.

Jordan could see at once that this party was a very grown-up party, a party that took itself seriously. See and be seen. Et cetera. The venue was small: an after-hours Back Bay art gallery. Age knuckling the burnished floors. Abstract paintings brightening the walls. Provocative sculpture complicating the corners. It was all very nice. One felt smarter to see it. Cultured. The partygoers were beautiful: women, all of them. Lovely dark skin, beautiful blond curls, freckles pebbled across cheekbones, big rounded hips, pale midriffs, golden shoulder blades, dresses and heels of every color and length and height. Jordan didn't recognize all of them, but she recognized enough to get the gist. CEOs. Diplomats. The daughters of presidents and the mothers of drug barons. Actresses. Musicians. Corn cereal heiresses and influencers made good. Celebrities, too, but, you know, proper celebrities; they didn't point at each other and say, *Look, there's so and so.* They acted cool. Peerish.

Boudicca.

"What can I get you?" asked the bartender. She had outrageously red hair, ridiculously red hair, poured from a bottle or a volcano.

Immediately Jordan's mind began to consider the challenge of how she would paint it. There were plenty of interesting red pigments, but she didn't think they'd do the trick on their own. Probably to achieve that eye-popping red, she'd surround it with a green background. Green added *to* red dulled it. Green painted *beside* red made both colors look more like themselves. Red and green were complementary colors, on either side of the color wheel. Funny how opposites made each color look brighter.

"What do you have that's cheap?" Jordan asked.

The bartender looked up through her eyelashes. Her eyes were green. "Open bar, for you."

Jordan flashed a huge smile. "What do you have that's orange?"

"Do you want sweet or sour?"

"Oh, I'm not going to drink it. It's to match my top."

The bartender did her best and Jordan tipped her with some of her precious forgery money and then took her orange top and orange drink to mingle. Fake-mingle. Really, she just wanted to information-gather. Jordan had crashed enough parties to be good at this, but she was thrown by all the famous faces here. Were these members or clients or both?

This felt higher stakes than it had in DC.

Higher stakes, she reminded herself, but same game. She knew how to play it. It was just forgery, after all. Forgery of people rather than art. The key was to remember to be better than a mere copy or mimic. If one painted exactly what one saw as accurately as possible, the result might be technically correct but was also stilted. Brittle. If one ran into a technical snag in its re-creation, the whole process ground to a halt. One had to stick to the script. But with forgery, the surface details were less important than the rules that proved them. Every work of art had rules: Paint was allowed to pool in the corners, lines were feathery at their ends as the brush was lifted, mouths were exaggerated for drama, blacks were unsaturated, so on, so forth. And if one learned enough of them, one could create endless new works based upon those rules and pass them off as creations by the original artist.

Humans were the same. They had rules that proved their behavior. Discover the thesis and you had them.

Jordan used this principle to forge a partygoer who *had* been mingling. Her lips carried a holdover laugh from a funny conversation she'd just left. She let out an audible breath as she stole a quick look at her phone, as if she'd just grabbed a moment between chats to check her business email. She nodded over her shoulder as she walked from a group, subtly suggesting she had just had a good talk. When people tried to catch her eye, she lifted a finger and pointed to a group in another room, indicating, *Catch you in a bit, I'm on my way to a preexisting condition.*

In this way she existed in the party without being of it, gathering information instead of giving it away.

Which was how she discovered that these were clients. She wasn't sure what they all thought they were here to purchase, but they were decidedly here with wallets at the ready. What could this spangled company all have in common with each other? What could they possibly have in common with *her*?

"Jordan Hennessy!"

An older woman had drawn alongside her. She was far more dowdy than the other partygoers, dressed in a houndstooth dress with a hedgehog pin over her right breast. She had a glass of wine in her hand and she was a little messy in the way people sometimes are when they're drunk, but Jordan could tell she was not drunk. She was just like that. "Jordan Hennessy, it's been a GD long time."

Jordan peered at her, trying unsuccessfully to place her. She must have met Hennessy or one of the other girls.

The woman's face turned cartoonishly worried. "Oh, you don't remember me! Don't worry, I know some people around here get a little S-H-I-T-T-Y about these things, if you know what I mean, but not me. I'm Barbara Shutt."

She held out her hand to shake and Jordan was running, running, running the scenarios, testing out replies that would work to make her seem reliable, like the real Jordan Hennessy, replies that didn't promise knowledge she didn't have, replies that didn't have trapdoors with crocodiles underneath them.

They shook—Barbara did that shake with just her fingers—and Jordan said, "Oh, right, DC, yes?"

Barbara wagged her finger at her. "That's the one. I'm so glad, just so glad, you could make it here when I'm sure you haven't even settled in. I'm sure Jo's already touched base with you to talk about apartment options. Jo? Jo Fisher?"

"Oh, no, I'd remember a Jo," Jordan said.

"Of course you would," Barbara replied. "Jo is that way. I'll make a note in the little old brain-a-dex"—she tapped the rim of her glass against her temple—"to have her add you to the schedule. Don't think we haven't been keeping a good eyeball out for you, though. That little adventure on the Potomac certainly made a lot of people sit up and take notice, didn't it! And we just have been doing our best to make sure none of that notice gives you the time of day here."

Now Jordan felt truly uncomfortable. *Had* Boudicca been keeping menace from her doorstep? Or were they just saying it to pull her into the fold? She needed to say something. Something that kept Barbara from completely having the upper hand. Something Boudicca couldn't know about. *Think, Jordan.*

Jordan smiled broadly and took a risk. "It's nice to have Bryde on our side, too, after all this time."

Barbara's smile was fixed in concrete.

Bingo. They didn't know a damn thing about Bryde, either, except for his power.

"If you'll ex-kwooooooooooooze me," Barbara said, tapping a dainty silver watch on her wrist with the bottom of her wineglass, "I should get this rolling. I know you're looking forward to it. So glad. So glad you could make it. Don't forget about Jo. She'll be around."

The first time Jordan had been approached by Boudicca it had been a bit of a joke, a bit of a compliment. She and Hennessy and June had sniggered about it over a few drinks and a few tubes of paint in the way they might have snickered over bumbling, unwanted flirtation at a bar. *Nice to be wanted, I reckon. As if. Dream on.* But it was a different feeling now that she was alone in Boston. She'd forgotten that there was a disadvantage to being not one of many Jordan Hennessys, but rather one of one: vulnerability.

Jordan stood there with her orange drink and her orange top, feeling misgiving pile upon misgiving, and then she discovered the music had stopped and all the partygoers were moving generally toward the back of the building. They murmured and checked watches and eyed each other, and Jordan realized they must all be headed to the real reason for this party.

Eventually, after they had all pressed into a large room in the back, Barbara's voice came over the speaker. Jordan could hear her unamplified voice as well, so she had to be close, but she couldn't see her over the crowd.

"Thanks for coming," said Barbara. "We have a really splendid group here today. You're all really spiffy women. I know we're excited about the events coming up and we're all excited about, uh, where are my notes, Fisher? Fisher, you do this."

A petite woman with very good posture and aggressively straightened brunette hair pressed past Jordan and through the crowd toward the front. She was dressed in a cocktail dress that said, *Look at me,* and also said, *Now that you're looking, did you notice I think you're stupid?* It was a good dress. She did not say excuse me.

Jordan just had a glimpse of her accepting a wired microphone; then a voice that matched the cocktail dress came over the speakers. "Everyone here has a dependent in their lives. Some of you know one, some of you are thinking of introducing one into your lives, others have inherited one, and some of you are one."

Partygoers glanced around at each other.

Jo Fisher continued. "Boudicca is proud to be able to offer a variety of sweetmetals in different formats this year. As always, these are available by private arrangement. Demand is high, as sweetmetals have been losing their efficacy faster than usual and many of you are replacing empty ones this year. I trust everyone here's had an opportunity to see that the dependents we've brought in to demonstrate the sweetmetals are genuine. Some have asked if these dependents are available; not at this time. They are for demonstration. *For demonstration.*"

"Let's bring in a sweetmetal!" Barbara's voice rose, unamplified. "Be nice, now, let everyone get a look!"

To Jordan's surprise, people listened. The crowd reassembled, allowing her, for the first time, to see what they were all pressed close to.

The centerpiece of the room was a kid.

He was a lovely little thing, a boy of three or four years old, with fine dark hair, thick eyelashes, a thoughtless pout. He was presented sentimentally in a wingback chair, which sat directly in the middle of the room. His chest rose and fell, rose and fell.

No matter how loud the voices rose around him, he remained asleep.

Scattered around him on the bright brocade fabric were a few other objects. Some butterflies lying limp. A soft, small rabbit, stretched on its side. A pair of shoes.

It was clear he was an exhibit, like the rest of the art.

"This is very exciting, isn't it!" Barbara said, still shouting without the microphone, sounding like a kindergarten teacher. "It's a really nice sweetmetal, a very good one for your home, they're not always good for a living area, but this one is! How L-U-C-K-Y are we all? Let's all be quiet and look. Here it is!"

A side door opened.

Two women carried a large, framed painting into the room. The subject wasn't very exciting, just a bucolic landscape dotted with sheep, but the art was nonetheless appealing in some way. It bothered Jordan, actually, that she couldn't pinpoint why she found it so appealing. She couldn't stop looking at it. She wanted to get closer, but the crowd and her dignity wouldn't allow it.

She glanced at the other partygoers to see their reaction to the painting, but their gazes were all firmly focused on the wingback chair in the middle of the room.

"Can I put my shoes on?"

It was a small, high voice. The boy had half sat up in the chair. With one youthful hand, he rubbed his eyes, and with the other, he reached for his shoes. He searched for a familiar face among the women looking at him. "Mum? Is it time for shoes?"

All around him, the previously still butterflies had taken flight. The little rabbit made a small *thud* as it jumped from the chair to the floor and made haste. The partygoers drew back to allow it to lope softly into their midst.

"Mum?" said the boy.

"As you can see, this particular sweetmetal is effective for multiple dependents at a distance of several yards," Fisher said into the microphone. "Please inquire for a full list."

Barbara made a sweeping gesture with her wineglass and the attendants carried the painting back to the side door.

"Mum?" said the boy again. "Oh, my *shoe*."

One of the shoes had fallen from the chair. The boy reached for it just as the door closed behind the attendants. The painting was gone.

With a little sigh, the boy, too, fell from the chair to the floor beside it. The butterflies dropped from the air around him. One of the partygoers came forward long enough to lay the now-sleeping rabbit back in its initial position on the chair.

Jordan's heart was an elevator with snapped cables.

Dreams.

The dependents were dreams without dreamers. And the sweetmetal—the painting that Jordan, a dream, had found strangely alluring—had temporarily woken them.

Just like that, Jordan realized Boudicca hadn't invited her here because they knew Jordan Hennessy was an art forger.

They'd invited her here because they knew Jordan Hennessy was a *dreamer*.

They'd invited her here because they knew Jordan Hennessy would have dreams she wanted to keep awake.

The rules of the game had changed.

5

atthew Lynch woke to the sound of his oldest brother screaming.

His brother's old bedroom was down the hall and Matthew's door was shut, but the sound came in clearly anyway. These old houses were full of nooks and crannies.

Matthew climbed out of bed, saying *oof oof oof* as the old floorboards chilled the bottoms of his bare feet, and then promptly smashed his head against the slanted ceiling.

Declan was still caterwauling.

Matthew went down the hall to brush his teeth (the movement of the bristles over his gums and teeth made it sound like Declan's shouts were oscillating) and got a drink of water (Declan's voice sounded higher when Matthew was swallowing and lower when he wasn't) and looked at himself in the mirror.

He thought the same thing he had thought every morning for the past several weeks: *I don't* look *like a dream, do I?*

The boy in the mirror was taller than the one who had appeared in the mirror a year ago. When he opened his mouth, he had all the proper teeth. He looked all right. He could be forgiven for having thought he was just like everyone else, all this time. But looking all right and being forgiven didn't really change the truth, which was that Matthew was not human. He was just human-shaped.

The boy in the mirror frowned.

His face didn't look used to frowning.

Declan's screams escalated.

Right.

Matthew shuffled down the hall to his brother's room.

The scene was the same as it had been every morning for the past several days. There was a pile of mice. Some winged lizard things. A badger with a secretive kind of smile, but just around the eyes. A pair of deer the size of cats. A cat the size of a deer, with hands like a person. A collection of birds of varying sizes and shapes. And possibly the most impressive thing, a rough-coated black boar the size of a minivan.

All of these creatures were piled on top of Declan's bed, which was where the screaming was coming from.

"Deklo!" Matthew said. "Mmm, cold."

The room was chilly on account of the open window, which was the work of the hand-cat. Matthew had accidentally caught it in the act before, when he was out walking the hills in a dazed, lost, predawn walk. He'd heard a clank and a clatter and looked up to see the hand-cat swiftly climbing the gutter to the dormer that led to Declan's room. Without any pause at all, the creature had shimmied the window open. It was both impressive and creepy to watch the hand-cat working its little nails under the edge to get it open. Opposable thumbs really were splendid things.

Declan's voice was muffled. "Get them *out*."

He was difficult to see in the bed because he'd made himself a sheet-blanket cocoon, the edges sealed against the mattress as much as possible to keep the smaller creatures from burrowing against him. They were not put off, though. The hand-cat plucked at the sheet near his face with intense devotion. The cat-sized deer were mewling and pawing (hoofing?) at the legs of the bed. The winged lizard things pounced playfully on Declan's feet each time they moved beneath the blanket.

"Sometime this century," Declan's voice said. *"Out."*

They were all dreams.

Since Declan and Matthew had moved out of the Barns, Ronan had apparently dreamt himself quite a menagerie. Although they seemed to have been feeding themselves perfectly adequately while Ronan was gone, they nonetheless quickly decided their morning ritual was to wake Declan for tending. Matthew wouldn't have minded being woken, but they never came to *his* window. The dream creatures seemed to have somehow divined that Declan was the person least likely to enjoy them and therefore the most desirable to woo.

"Come on, guys!" Matthew said cheerily. "Let's get some brekky! Not you!"

This was directed toward the minivan-sized boar, which was too big to fit through either door or window. It had come into the room as a noxious-smelling gas and Matthew had learned that it had to be reduced back to the same form in order to get out.

Matthew clapped and shouted in the boar's face.

"Come on! Come on!"

Flinching, the boar backed away, but remained persistently solid. Its giant butt smashed into the dresser. Its shoulder swept books from the shelf. Declan's laptop made an ominous crunching sound beneath its hoof. It was getting used to Matthew, which was the problem. Every day it took more and more effort to startle it.

"Was that my—" Declan's strangled voice came from beneath the blanket. "I have to do everything myself."

He rose abruptly from the bed, sheet wrapped all around him, a ghost.

Both Matthew and boar staggered back in surprise.

The boar instantly dispersed into a cloud of noxious-smelling gas, the world's biggest fart.

Matthew remained Matthew.

"Mary give me patience," Declan snapped. Flapping his sheet swiftly up and down, he blew the boar gas out the window. One of the dreamt birds pecked curiously at his bare foot with a beak shaped like a screwdriver. He picked it up and threw it out the window after the fading cloud.

"Hey!" Matthew said.

"It's fine. Look, there it goes." Declan slammed the window shut. "Get them *out* of here. That's it. I'm figuring out a lock today. I'm gluing it shut. I'm putting spikes up there. *Out.* What are you waiting for, Matthew? You're slower every morning. Don't make me write you a chore list."

Before all this, Matthew would have laughed this off and then done whatever Declan asked. Now, though, he said, "I don't have to do what you say."

Declan didn't even bother to reply. Instead he began to briskly collect clothing for the day.

This annoyed Matthew even more, which combined in a thrilling and toxic way with the feeling Matthew had experienced when looking at himself in the bathroom mirror. He said, "You just threw one of my siblings out the window."

The statement was meant for effect, and effect it got. Declan gave Matthew his most Declan of faces. He generally used one of two expressions. The first was Bland Businessman Nodding at What You're Saying While Waiting for His Turn to Talk and the other was Reticent Father with Irritable Bowel Syndrome Realizes He Must Let His Child Use the Public Restroom First. They suited nearly every situation Declan found himself in. This, however, was a third expression: Exasperated Twentysomething Longs to Yell at His Brothers Because Oh My God. He rarely used it, but the lack of practice didn't make it any less accomplished or any less pure Declan.

"I don't have the capacity for your identity crisis this morning," Declan said. "I'm trying to get us a car while remaining off the grid and avoiding getting completely screwed by our irresponsible father's associates. So I'd appreciate you penciling it in for a weekend instead."

Only recently had Declan actually begun to express his feelings about Niall Lynch out loud, and Matthew didn't like that change, either. He said, "You can't tell me how to *feel*. I don't trust you anymore."

Declan got a tie. He applied ties to his person like most people applied underwear; he clearly didn't think himself decent to appear in public without one. "I've already apologized for keeping the truth from you, Matthew. What would you like? Another apology? I can work on crafting one more to your liking in between the rest of my work."

"You lied," Matthew said. "It's not just going to be okay."

Declan was somehow already fully dressed in full corporate splendor. He studied Matthew for a moment, and his face was serious enough that Matthew wished that it was like old times, that he still thought his older brother had all the answers and could be trusted implicitly. "Go get a sweater. Let's go for a walk and check the mailbox."

Proper rebellion, a real Ronan-like rebellion, would have required Matthew to storm off at this request, but Matthew merely sulked off with all the animals following. He fetched his llama hoodie and a box of animal crackers before meeting up with Declan in the mudroom.

"You're shoveling that hand-cat poop out of my room," Declan said serenely to Matthew as he stepped outside.

Matthew slammed the door behind them.

Outside, it was beautiful; it was always beautiful. The Barns was located deep in the foothills of western Virginia, hidden in a protected fold of hill and valley beneath the watchful eye of the Blue Ridge Mountains. Matthew had grown up in the old white farmhouse. He'd rambled over these fields. He had played in the various barns and outbuildings that spread right up to the trees that surrounded the property.

Now the cold mist rose up from the colorless fields and got caught in the dark red-brown lingering leaves of the surrounding oaks. The blue sky soared high overhead. White streaky clouds glowed with morning pink, just like the white-painted outbuildings down below.

It was really nice.

He guessed.

For several minutes he and Declan walked in silence down the long, long driveway. Declan tapped away at his new cell phone in his peculiar Declan way, his thumb on one hand and his pointer finger on the other, glancing up just often enough to keep from walking off the driveway. Matthew threw animal crackers for the trailing dream creatures, careful not to chuck the food at the forever-sleeping cattle that dotted the pastures.

The cows had been dreamt by his father. Well, by Niall Lynch, since Niall was not really his father. Matthew was father-free. Dreamt, just like the cows. And, just like them, doomed to an eternity of sleeping forever if something happened to Ronan.

When *something happened to Ronan*, Matthew thought.

A sour mood was rising.

He didn't have a lot of practice at sour moods. He'd been a happy, feckless kid. Pathologically happy—he saw that now. Dreamt to be happy. Matthew had a hard time finding any memory that wasn't full of good cheer. Even if it wasn't a happy time, the youngest Lynch brother appeared in the memory with a plucky grin, like a sun flare in an otherwise dark photo, or maybe like a team mascot posing along with the players. Goofy and out of place but not necessarily unwelcome.

Like a pet, he thought.

All around him, unseasonable fireflies winked in and out. As Matthew watched them fade in and out even on this cool fall day, he wondered what kind of dream Ronan had been having to produce them. He wondered what kind of dream Ronan had been having to produce *him*.

His mind kept shouting the truth at him: *You are a dream.*

He hadn't told anyone, but he was terrified of falling asleep forever. He'd already had a taste of it. Every time the ley line faltered, he went all . . . dazed. Enchanted. His feet began to walk, his body began to move, his mind went somewhere else. When he came to, he always found himself in a completely different location, his disobedient body having tried to take him closer to ley energy.

As trees took the place of the fields on either side of the driveway, Matthew hurled the entire box of crackers away from himself. The hand-cat said "Meow" in a disturbingly articulate way as it retrieved the box, but then a few little winged weasel things rushed out of the underbrush to fight for it until the cardboard box ripped asunder.

Matthew plunged past them, ready for the walk to be over.

"Matthew, stop," Declan called. "I'll go around."

He meant to spare Matthew the security system Ronan had dreamt for the Barns since they left, a peculiar, invisible net of dreams that covered the end of the driveway. It not only made the entrance to the Barns very difficult to see, it also made you feel terrible if you *did* try to enter. Anyone who stepped into the net immediately began to relive bad memories. Awful memories. Stuff you thought you'd forgotten and stuff you wished you had. Stuff so wretched that people just gave up and went back the way they'd come.

Matthew was sort of drawn to it.

Secretly he frequented the end of the driveway while Declan was occupied in the farmhouse all day on his boring calls on his burner phone, and secretly he would suck in his breath and plunge into the net of bad memories again and again.

He didn't know why.

"Matthew," Declan said. He was cuffing his pants. There was a long way around the security system if one picked through the woods in just the right way, but even the right way snagged one's slacks with brambles. It was a testament to how much Declan wanted to avoid the security system that he'd tromp through the woods instead.

Matthew edged toward the end of the driveway. "I'll get it."

"You are being even more ridiculous than usual."

"BRB," Matthew said.

"Matthew, for crying out—"

Matthew plunged into the security system.

The memories hit him like they always did, fresh as when they happened. His brain could not separate them from the truth.

This is what he remembered: losing himself. His thoughts slid into muddy dreaming. He climbed his school's roof. The ground plunged hundreds of feet away. His body was unworried about the height.

This is what he remembered: He was mid-sentence with Jacob on the soccer field, and then he was forgetting what he was saying *while he was saying it*, and then he was watching Jacob wait and wait and wait for him to remember his train of thought as it never returned.

This is what he remembered: He was being woken by Declan by the banks of the Potomac River and realizing he'd walked there yet again without knowing it, and seeing all the creatures Ronan had dreamt dozing around him and realizing he was like them, he was a dream, *he was a dream.*

This is what he remembered: He was walking, dreaming, walking, sleeping, obeying a power outside himself.

Matthew.

A voice said his name.

This was the memory that he kept coming back for.

Sometimes, when he lost himself, he thought he heard someone calling to him. Not in a human voice. Not in a dream voice. In a voice-voice, in a language he felt like maybe was his real language.

He didn't understand any more than that. So he kept coming back again and again.

Then Matthew was through the security system and facing the empty, wooded country road and the mailbox on an ordinary, chilly day in the present. There was a faded wood cabinet behind the mailbox for the delivery drivers to leave parcels in, but there were no parcels today. Instead, there were a few pieces of junk mail (boring) and an art museum postcard addressed to Declan (even more boring).

Lame. His sour mood remained.

He plunged back through the security system.

This time it gave him a memory he didn't want at all, that was just him having to leave Aurora behind in Ronan's dreamt forest Cabeswater before it was destroyed. The memory hadn't been bad when it happened, even though Matthew never liked saying goodbye to her, but it was terrible now because he knew it was the last time he saw her before she died.

She wasn't your real mother, Matthew told himself. *She wasn't even Declan's real mother. She was just a dreamt copy.*

But it never made him feel any better, so he was swiping a tear away when he emerged in front of Declan again. This infuriated him, too.

"Was that worth it?" Declan asked drily.

Matthew handed over the mail. "No groceries. We're out of peanut butter."

"There's a man in Orange who I think will sell us a Sentra for cash. Then we'll be able to do some shop . . ." Declan's voice trailed off as he turned the postcard over.

"Is it from Ronan?" asked Matthew. It didn't seem very Ronan-y. The postcard featured a painting of a woman dancing with the words ISABELLA STEWART GARDNER MUSEUM, BOSTON, MA, printed over it.

Declan didn't answer; his cheeks were a little flushed.

"What *is* it?" Matthew could hear himself sounding a little whingy and was annoyed. *Stop being a kid*, he told himself.

Declan was *smiling*. He was trying not to, but he *was*. He had ironed his voice flat, though, so that if one hadn't seen his face, one would think it was just a normal day, normal mail. "How do you feel about a trip to Boston?"

Matthew looked at the dreamt fireflies still winking in and out around them. Ronan's dreams. Just like him.

"Anywhere's better than here," Matthew said.

"Finally," Declan replied, "something we agree on."

6

What do you feel?" Bryde asked.

"Shitty," Ronan replied.

"I said *what*, not *how*. Hennessy?"

"I feel nothing," Hennessy said. "Except the feel of my arteries closing in anticipation. Smell that grease. I love it."

Bryde shut the car door. "This isn't going to make you feel better."

"It's not going to make me feel worse," Ronan replied.

"If life's taught me anything," Hennessy said, "it's that you can always feel worse."

It had been nearly twenty-four hours since the three dreamers had left the Museum of Living History. They were parked in front of Benny's Dairy Bar, a decades-old fast-food joint located somewhere in West Virginia. The sun burned golden over the worn-down mountains surrounding the town. The dreamers' shadows stretched thin across the faded lot.

Ronan was starving.

Bryde shot an attentive look around at their surroundings as Hennessy shivered and Ronan spat. The sparse parking lot, the decaying town, the quiet road. He was looking for Moderators. Moderators were why they were here instead of bedded down on a ley line; they'd barely left the day before when Bryde had suddenly ordered Hennessy to send Burrito in a completely different direction. He'd gotten information, somehow, in the mysterious way he sometimes did, that Moderators were close. They couldn't risk leading them to their destination. Safer to stay in the invisible car until the coast was clear.

Which meant they'd spent the past twenty-four hours dozing in the car and driving in circles.

"Get down here," Ronan said to Chainsaw, who had flapped to a nearby tree.

"Let's get this exercise over with," Bryde said. "This entire process is merely for demonstration, so I hope you are in an educational frame of mind."

Ding! cried the door as the three dreamers entered Benny's Dairy Bar, where they found booths bolted to the walls, hard tables bolted to the floor, soft locals bolted to seats, thin burgers bolted to hands. Above the counter was a menu board without any pretense or spin: HAMBURGER. CHEESEBURGER. 2 PATTY. 3 PATTY. FRIES. DOUBLE FRY. SOFT SERVE 1. SOFT SERVE 2. Behind the counter, employees wore purple Benny's T-shirts. Golden oldies played overhead. *Something something Mrs. Brown has a lovely daughter something something.* It had a vague bleach smell, which might have otherwise turned Ronan off. But not right then. He instead thought only about the other smell: Grease. Salt. *Food.*

As they stepped in, everyone in the restaurant stared. Six diners. Two standing in line at the counter. One at the pickup area. A cashier. Probably another few employees in the back. Witnesses, that was what they called them, people who would remember a Black girl in a crochet crop top and leather, a dude with a shaved head and a raven now back on his shoulder, and a hawk-nosed man with an expression that suggested he'd never felt fear in his life.

This was why they never stopped at restaurants.

Hennessy held out her hands grandly. "This is a stickup."

Bryde sighed heavily and fished one of his dreamt silver orbs out of the pocket of his gray jacket. At one of the tables, a teen was already lifting a cell phone to take a video or photo of the newcomers.

Bryde said, very simply, "No."

With a gentle flick of his wrist, he tossed the orb. He didn't have many. He said they were "expensive," and Ronan believed it. Ronan wouldn't have known the first thing about dreaming them into being—he would have been too afraid to. Because they messed with emotions, and they twisted thoughts, and they erased memories, some more permanently than others. Ronan was uneasy dreaming anything that altered free will; the bewildering security system at the Barns was the furthest he was willing to go. Bryde's orbs, on the other hand, were like dreaming brain surgery. Such sophistication required more control than Ronan felt he had.

Pwinnnnnng! The tossed orb hit the teen's poised cell phone. Both went flying. The phone, toward Bryde's feet. The orb, under a booth.

Bryde pocketed the fallen cell phone.

"Hey!" said the teen.

"You can't do that," remarked the cashier. But he didn't say anything else because a second later, Bryde's orb exploded.

A cloud of confusion billowed out from inside it; it began to work on the diners almost immediately. Some gazed at each other in confusion. Some slumped over. The orb wasn't designed to knock people out, but it was hard to predict how people would react to having their thoughts paused and memories flattened out.

"Your balls really are nifty things," Hennessy said. "Love to get my hands on them."

Bryde ignored this. "Time is of the essence."

But Hennessy pressed on. "Must've required a lot of practice. Wonder who you were practicing them on. 'Course, you could've been practicing them on *us*. But we wouldn't remember, would we?"

He ignored this, too. "Do what you have to do, Ronan."

Ronan was the one who'd asked them to stop for food, even though he knew it wasn't really allowed under the unspoken rules of their outlaw lifestyle. Food came from the cabinets and fridges of empty houses, places without cameras, places without people. Crackers and canned goods, deli meat and apples. But his hunger had been growing in the car and now his body was howling that it couldn't last much longer.

"To the fryer!" cried Hennessy as she vaulted over the counter.

Ronan, however, went straight to the customer who stood motionless at the pickup counter. Not perfectly motionless, not like a statue. But rather like someone who had been walking through a store and just remembered she had forgotten something important back at home.

She didn't blink or flinch as Ronan took a grease-spotted bag from one of her hands. He dumped the contents on the counter, unwrapped them, and ate them, one after another. A burger. Some fries. An apple pie.

He was still starving.

He took the milkshake from her other hand and drank it, too. Strawberry. Brain freeze. He finished it anyway, slamming the cup down on the counter as if it were a completed shot.

Still starving.

A guy at a nearby table had just started to unwrap his

cheeseburger; Ronan completed the task for him as the guy blinked off into space. Down the hatch. Then the large fries next to it. Then his date's chicken burger, even though it was disgusting. The pickle she'd abandoned beside it.

Still starving.

Hennessy's voice rose from the kitchen area. "If you'd told me before all this that the best food in the world was stolen French fries, I would have laughed in your face. Which only goes to show you, one doesn't know what one doesn't know."

At the next booth, Ronan ate a melting soft serve. Another burger. A salad with an orange, slimy dressing, and raw onions. A paper plate of hash browns.

Still starving.

He hurled the paper plate to the ground. Next table.

Bryde watched him, expressionless.

Hennessy's monologue was getting closer. "I'm rededicating my life to these French fries. Before this time, I was a sinner, finding pleasure in wine, women, song, and, sometimes, cocaine and grand theft auto, living moment to moment, not thinking about the consequences of my actions on my own body or others, but now I have seen the light and I will instead worship at the altar of stolen fries. I will paint murals in their honor. I will rename myself Tuber."

Ronan ate chicken nuggets, a hot dog, another milkshake, a barbecue sandwich, a corn dog, and some fried okra.

"Can we stop pretending it is food you're wanting now?" Bryde asked mildly.

Ronan sank into a booth. The food sat inside him, heavy and pointless.

Starving.

Bryde stood at the end of the booth. "What do you feel?"

"Come *on*."

"You might not be able to feel the ley line, but you can feel what happens to you when you don't have it, Greywaren. Still, you pretend what you really need right now is a cheeseburger. Look around you. Look at yourself. We're fleeing because of your wheels, and *this* is where you come. There aren't two of you. Greywaren, do you even know what it means?"

Ronan realized this was the teachable moment. This was the reason Bryde had used one of his precious orbs to hit up a fast-food joint. Ronan didn't know what *Greywaren* meant, but he knew it was important. His first dreamt forest, Cabeswater, had called him that. His current forest, Lindenmere, called him that. His dead father had somehow known to call him that. And Bryde knew this name for him.

He didn't know what he was supposed to be learning, so he gazed off at nothing, sullen.

Bryde tapped Ronan's jaw with a single finger. "Protector and guardian—that is what you are supposed to be. King and shepherd both. But look at you, sick in your avoidant gluttony. *There are not two of you.* Your waking self cannot ignore what your dreaming self needs, because they are the same. Now you tell me. What is it you're really feeling?"

He pointed at Ronan's ear.

Very slowly, Ronan reached up to his ear and pressed a finger into it. When he withdrew it, his fingertip was slicked with a dark ooze.

Nightwash.

He was not starving for food. He was starving for the ley line. He was starving for dreaming.

"Why is it always me?" he asked.

Bryde said, "I just told you."

The nightwash came to Ronan far more often than it came to Hennessy. It came when he waited too long between taking something from his dreams, as if to punish him for not doing what he had been built to do. But it also came to him when he was too far from the ley line, as if to punish him for trying to live a life that was built for someone else. Once the ooze started, he had less and less time before he began to feel ill, and presumably, less and less time before it eventually would kill him.

"I'm getting worse," he muttered.

"Yes," Bryde said.

"Why even bother with me, then?"

"Because it is not just you. This mountain city used to be alive with ley energy. Did you see the river we drove beside for dozens of miles, the river this city straddles? It should be flowing with energy. This should be a mountain town of dreamers. But it fades, like the entire world fades. It breathes more and more slowly, and no one is listening to mark the end of its pulse. Few, I suppose. Few are listening."

Hennessy asked, "Hold up. Don't get me wrong, I'm a fan of kicking ass, taking names, so on, so forth, but if we're all going to bite it eventually because the world's dying, why save anyone from the Mods? Is it sport to you?"

"It's not sport to me." Bryde kept standing over Ronan. "What do you *feel*?"

"I can't do that," Ronan said. "I'll never be able to do that. Not while I'm awake."

"Don't tell me my business. Not while you're bleeding black. I have been at this for so much longer than you." Bryde looked out the big glass windows at the trees at the edge of the parking lot, his eyes narrowed, his profile prickling that thing inside Ronan, that feeling of serendipity, of knowing, not-knowing, knowing, not-knowing, and then Bryde asked, "Do you two want to know what I was doing before you?"

Hennessy and Ronan exchanged a look.

"It wasn't dreamers I was saving," Bryde said. "It was ley lines."

Good, thought Ronan. Deep inside him he felt a certain peace, even alongside the turmoil of the nightwash. Good. This was even better than what he had hoped. Yes, *good.* Long ago, Ronan had helped to wake the single ley line that ran beneath his forest. He had not known this was what he wanted of Bryde until he said it.

"And what were you saving the ley lines from?" Hennessy asked.

Bryde laughed. It was a laugh like his smile, contained and cunning. "Every plugged-in machine, every flat-black road, every stacked-up suburb, every humming cell. Choked and flattened and drowned and suppressed. Can you imagine a world where you could dream anywhere?"

"God," Hennessy said.

Ronan pressed his ear into his shoulder as he felt the night-wash trickle down his neck. "Why aren't *we* doing that?"

"You," Bryde answered simply. "It's not a game for the reckless. It's not a game for those who go to sleep and bring everything they see back with them. It is a game that requires control, and right now you two have precious little of it. Look at your face. Feel your guts turning to grime, Ronan? Your game is this: Stop sucking. That is hard enough for you right now."

"Hey," Hennessy said. "I love a good roast, but come on now."

Bryde waved a hand. "Why do you think we stopped here? When you two dream, there are consequences for every other dreamer who is living a little too far away from a ley line. Do you think you've killed anyone with your casual dreaming? Do you think you've pulled the ley line out from beneath a dreamer who needed it more than you? Has anyone died in nightwash because of some plaything you pulled from a dream?"

It was too easy to imagine. All the enormous things Ronan had dreamt over the years. All the living creatures, all the noisy machines. An entire forest. A brother. He couldn't quite bear to think too hard about it. Not now, not with the nightwash eating away at him. Guilt was never too far away anyway.

"You can't hide away from the consequences of who you are," Bryde said. "Don't laugh at me, Hennessy. How much power do you think it required to pull out all those girls with your face? You cannot do this carelessly. You're not children anymore."

Nightwash trickled out of Ronan's nostril. Hennessy threw her remaining fries back over the counter. They didn't look at each other.

"You're right," Ronan said finally. "Now I really do feel shittier."

"Good," Bryde replied. "Lesson over."

7

As best the FBI could tell, Nathan Farooq-Lane had killed twenty-three people.

The twenty-three victims had no connection to each other, at least not as far as the investigators had managed to work out. Clarisse Match, grocery clerk and single mother. Wes Gerfers, retired dentist and amateur poet. Tim Mistovich, grad student and internet troll. So on, so forth. They were from all different walks of life. Different professions. Different generations. The only thing they had in common was that they'd all twenty-three been found with an open pair of scissors somewhere at the crime scene.

Twenty-three was a bad number.

But it wasn't the worst number, in Carmen Farooq-Lane's opinion. This one was the worst: sixteen. That was the age her brother had been when he'd killed his first victim. He'd been a junior. She'd been a freshman. What had she been doing while he was stalking his first kill? She'd been joining clubs, that's what. Chess club. Art club. Debate club. Economics club. Mixed martial arts club. Young Citizens for Abolishing Hunger club. If there was a club at their high school, Carmen Farooq-Lane had joined it and was a model member.

You have a bizarre fascination with running in packs, Nathan had told her once as they walked to school together. *They need you, Carmen. You don't need them.*

In spring of her freshman year, spring of Nathan's junior year, the school's star quarterback Jason Mathai had disappeared. The day after he didn't come to school, the janitor found four pairs of scissors, one at each of the school's main entrances. Open, like a cross. Later, investigators would try to understand why there had been four at this first murder when there was only one at each of the others. But of all the puzzles surrounding her brother, this one made sense to Farooq-Lane. This was his maiden voyage and he wanted to be sure it was noticed. One pair of scissors for each entrance, just in case.

He was sixteen. Farooq-Lane was clueless.

She was clueless even though scissors were Nathan's thing. He drew them in his sketchbooks. Hung them on his walls and over his bed. Hung them over *her* bed until she made him take them down. They were enough of his thing that she remembered mentioning the presence of the scissors to him as the rumors flew through the school, because she thought he'd find it curious.

But no part of her thought: *Nathan killed Jason Mathai.*

And definitely no part of her thought: *I need to tell someone before he kills twenty-two others.*

Later, the murders made the news. The journos tried out several names for the mysterious killer. The Cutter. The Mad Tailor. The Cloth Butcher. The Scissors Killer. None of them stuck. It would have been different if the killer had murdered the victims *with* scissors, but all of them had been killed by bizarre explosive devices.

Farooq-Lane knew none of this; she didn't have time to read news like that. She'd gone to college and found new clubs. Then she'd graduated and found a landlord and Alpine Financial, which was kind of like a club, but for adults.

If she'd been paying attention, would she have noticed it? Her job was patterns, systems, analyzing the past to create better futures. Twenty-three murders was a lot of data.

But maybe it wouldn't have mattered.

You want everything to make sense, but things don't, Nathan had told her once. *You fall in love with everything that makes sense and ignore everything that doesn't.*

After her parents' death, the FBI had shown her the manifesto they'd found tucked in his junior-year yearbook. It was nothing like the crisp, well-spoken brother she thought she knew. Instead, it wandered and fretted and threatened and despaired.

The Open Edge of the Blade

by Nathan Farooq-Lane

Only the open edge of the scissor blade is pure.. Once it has closed it has exhausted its potential.. Purity is apartness.. Purity is potentiality.. So much of the world is dull too dull to ever cut.. Or was once open and is now closed.. The dull scissors were never scissors they were only lawn ornaments.. They are scissor-shaped but they were never going to have a purpose.. They are no better or worse than the closed scissors.. The closed scissors are also no longer scissors because they once could cut but now are closed.. All that is important is the open edge of the blade which is still pure.. These are the blades that have purpose.. Purity is purpose.. Purpose is purity.. There is no room for the shears to open if there are too many closed scissors in the box.. Making room means deletion.. Not cutting because cutting leaves pieces and pieces take room, just different room.. Deletion is erasure which makes space for the open edge of the blade..

And so on for a dozen typed pages.

Had Nathan Farooq-Lane made sense?

She'd asked herself since then if there had been something about his external self that would have allowed her to predict this internal self. She asked herself if her parents would still be alive if she had. But he was one system she'd never been able to fit into a spreadsheet.

Later, the Moderators had found her and told her Nathan was a Zed, someone who could take things out of his dreams, and that all the peculiar explosive devices had actually been dreams.

"I know it can be hard to believe," Lock had said.

But Nathan had killed twenty-three people starting at age sixteen. She could believe anything about him now. What she'd actually thought then was: The Moderators would have had to kill him at age fifteen to save all those lives.

"Well, this is creepy as hell," Lock rumbled.

The leader of the Moderators was tanklike as he powered down a hall in the West Virginia Museum of Living History. Broad shoulders. Fat-soled athletic shoes crunching debris beneath them. Everywhere Lock's flashlight beam illuminated looked war-torn. Hanging ceiling tiles. Peeling paint. Faded, knocked-over furniture.

The ruined museum was unsettling, but Lock wasn't talking about that. He was talking about the mannequins.

Someone had filled the hall with a troupe of mannequins from the museum exhibits. Recently. Everything here was covered with great, soft layers of dust, but the mannequins had handprints all over their arms and chests. Fresh. A few days old at most. Farooq-Lane shone her flashlight on each as she passed. Sailor. Baker.

Homemaker. Policeman. A Zed could stand among them and the Moderators wouldn't know until they were on top of them.

"Oh, come on," said one of the other Moderators, delivering a sudden kick at the homemaker. The mannequin heaved to the side, heavier than expected, and fell into the arms of a surprisingly sturdy train conductor with mismatched eyes. "There's no Zed here. We'd already be completely screwed if there was."

The Moderator wasn't wrong. Every recent encounter with the Zeds had ended the same as the encounter with the Zed in the Airstream, with the Moderators defeated and confused, and generally feeling like absolute idiots. These new Zeds were boggling their minds. Literally. Farooq-Lane understood that even this ruse of mannequins was mostly to play with their heads. It wouldn't stop the Moderators for long—it was just to unsettle them. It was Nathan's scissors.

Lock shone a flashlight into a mannequin's face. It was a chef. He—Lock, not the chef—said, "The Visionary saw us confronting the Zeds in her vision. That means we're *supposed* to be successful in the future, only it gets changed. We will find a way through this."

"Where is the Visionary anyway?" one of the other Moderators asked, a little nervously. The other Moderators were all very afraid Liliana was going to blow them up. A reasonable fear. She'd accidentally blown up a family of ducks during her last vision.

"She's waiting in the car," Farooq-Lane said. "But she's very stable at this age."

"Very stable at this age." One of the other Moderators mimicked Farooq-Lane's crisp way of speaking, which, to Farooq-Lane's surprise, sounded a lot like Nathan. "She'd be more stable if she'd turn that stuff inside. Like every. Other. Visionary. Until Miss Carmen here."

Just a few weeks before, Farooq-Lane would have spent time wondering what she could possibly do to prove her loyalty to the Moderators. But not anymore. No longer did she find them the all-knowing righteous arm of the law. The failures of the past few weeks had changed all of them. The Moderators had all separated neatly into Team Discouraged or Team Cagey or Team Angry.

Carmen Farooq-Lane was Team Restore Order.

This was no longer only about a possible future apocalypse. The Potomac Zeds had pushed this into a new realm for her. Using dreams to mess with people's minds was a system-breaking, society-ending weapon, and there was no longer any doubt in her that something had to change.

So she didn't let the Moderators' needling rattle her. She shone her flashlight slowly over the mannequins they'd just walked through. She had a funny thought that there were twenty-three of them. She counted them.

Twenty-three.

But Nathan was dead, and they were chasing three entirely different Zeds who had nothing to do with him. It was coincidence, not magic. Her subconscious had taken in information about her surroundings while her active mind was doing something else. There was a term for it. Unconscious cognition? Priming? One of those. She'd taken some courses in college.

This is your guilt, Farooq-Lane told herself, letting herself acknowledge it. Guilt for not stopping Nathan. Guilt for getting him killed. Guilt for feeling guilty. Guilt for killing so many Zeds over the last several months.

Guilt for not asking questions.

They had come to an enormous ruined space, a tree bursting through the collapsed roof, the night sky visible overhead. Farooq-Lane shivered in the suddenly brisk air. This ruin was what they were trying to prevent. Humanity wiped out. Every human accomplishment reduced to rubble and vines. Civilization was so tenuous. This museum had been important to someone, once. If a Zed had made this, she thought, it could have been made supernaturally permanent. This was the real danger of Zeds, she thought. The scale of it. Humans could only do so much. Zeds could kill infinite people, start infinite fires, create infinite destructive legacies.

A gun went off.

Everyone jumped; Farooq-Lane hit the deck. As the ferns tickled her cheek and her palms pressed the cold rubble beneath her, she wondered, *Is this real?*

It felt real. But she'd seen what the Potomac Zeds could do to perception.

A moment later, Lock rumbled, "That was very unprofessional."

Farooq-Lane lifted her head. One of the Moderators—Ramsay, of course—was holding a pistol, the barrel still visibly smoking in a flashlight beam. In his other hand he held half a limp black snake. The other half of it had been shot away. As Farooq-Lane watched, the ruined end of the snake slowly twisted in a muscle memory of life.

She had to look away.

Nathan's words about clubs came back to her. She didn't need them, he'd said. They needed her.

Did they?

"Weapons discharge only when I deem it necessary," Lock intoned. "This area is obviously clear. Let's move on."

The Moderators found themselves in an old hay barn illuminated by a dozen naked lightbulbs high in the rafters. It was entirely filled with both old, dry hay bales and wheels of all kinds. The wheels were clearly a Zed's work, but there did not seem to be any Zeds in evidence. Were they a by-product of dreaming? Were they a message?

Farooq-Lane made her way slowly through the wheels, spinning them here, turning them there. Each had the word *tamquam* on it, although she didn't know the significance. She stepped out the other side of the barn. Cold air whipped across her cheeks, smelling of wilderness.

She stopped in her tracks.

Lock was leaning up against the exterior of the barn, his bald head slumped to one side.

It was not the real Lock, of course.

The real Lock was emerging to stand beside Farooq-Lane. The real Lock was exhaling noisily. The real Lock was putting his hands on his hips and saying nothing.

This other Lock was dead. Or rather, he was simply not alive. He had never been alive. He was just another mannequin, but with Lock's exact face. He wore Lock's usual track pants and sneakers, but the matching jacket was missing. Instead he wore a white T-shirt with words handwritten across it. *Thirty pieces of silver.*

Farooq-Lane felt something thrill inside her. "What does it mean?"

Lock said, "It means we need to find a different way to kill these three Zeds before this gets out of hand."

8

Hennessy couldn't really fathom what it was like to be bad at art.

There was evidence that she had been, of course. Somewhere in the closets of her father's Pennsylvania suburban home were journals full of her early drawings. Languishing in some English rubbish heap were grotty canvases she had painted over again and again. That old art was wrong in all the ways non-artists tended to notice: mismatched eyes, physically impossible nostrils, incorrect rooflines, broccoli-shaped trees, dog-nosed cows. And it was also wrong in all the ways artists noticed: poor use of value, inattention to edges, uneven line weight, lazy composition, muddy colors, sloppy palette choice, impatient layers, derivative stylization, tentative brushwork, overuse of medium, underuse of planning, unintentional fugliness.

Even her art-making process had been bad. She remembered what it was like to not be sure if a drawing was going to "turn out." She'd sit down with a clothing catalog or a photograph of a model pulled up on her father's laptop. Then she'd sharpen her pencil and think, *I hope this works.* She'd fuss over the likeness for hours. Hours! She couldn't even imagine now how she'd been spending all that time. What took her so long on a casual pencil sketch? She remembered agonizing over the eye placement, over the puzzling shape at the corner of a mouth, the absolute purgatory that was a woman's chin, but she didn't remember why such things had been confusing.

Her head knew what it wanted to do. Why did her hand disobey? Noses veered petulantly. Rib cages went barrel-shaped, feet and hands turned into a four-piece mismatched tool set. She remembered actually howling in frustration as she wadded up an attempt. Stabbing canvases with scissors. Hurling paint tubes across J. H. Hennessy's studio.

She remembered how when she *did* turn up with a good result, she'd return to it several times over the course of the day, taking it out again and again to flush with pleasure and surprise and accomplishment. She had no idea why it had gone well and so she couldn't be sure it would ever happen again.

Hennessy *remembered* this, but she didn't *feel* it. Somehow all the pain hadn't managed to carry through the years. No part of her expected to fail when she sat down at a canvas now. She knew how the paint would behave. She knew what her brushes were capable of. No part of her doubted that whatever she was looking at would travel through her eyes, down her arms, and out onto the blank space before her.

Once, one of her clients had asked her if she considered herself a prodigy. They'd been standing in front of a Cassatt she'd forged for him.

"No," Hennessy had said. "I'm a forgery of a prodigy."

But she knew she was good. No amount of thinking about how bad she used to be would change that. She might suck at everything else about being a human and a dreamer, but as an art forger—she might not be the best, but she was at least one of the best.

That accomplishment seemed pointless now. There was no one to show it to who mattered. They were all dead.

All except for Jordan, who had always mattered the most anyway. But where was she now?

"I am so fucking good at this," Ronan said.

The two of them were in one of those electronic boutiques that took itself very seriously. Indirect neon lighting, back-lit products, every shelf rounded and modern. Phones of every shape and size lined the shelves and tables. There were traditional cell phones. Wall-mounted hard lines. Phones shaped like piggy banks and phones shaped like fake teeth, phones shaped like model cars and phones shaped like ceramic birds. Phones like dish-soap bubbles and phones like bank pens with fake flowers affixed to the end of them.

Many of them were impossible, but it didn't matter, because it was a dream, Ronan's dream, and he could do what he wanted.

Hennessy said, "You could dream anything, anywhere, and you bring us to a consumer playground with the logos only barely scrubbed off."

"Jealous much?" Ronan was all snotty arrogance again, as if he wouldn't have drowned in nightwash if Bryde hadn't brought them to another ley line in the nick of time.

She wasn't jealous. She was wary. Ley line energy boomed through the dream. She hadn't felt this much ley power since she'd been in Ronan's dreamt forest Lindenmere. It made the dream as lucid as any waking experience.

If she had her Lace dream with this much power at her disposal . . .

"We're not doing the Lace dream," Ronan said. "Chill out. What do we want out of these phones? They've gotta be untrace-able, I guess. Portable. What else does a phone do?"

Why didn't Adam text me back?

Because they were sharing the dreamspace, she heard his thought like a shout. It traveled through the dream with a reti-nue of amorphous sub-thoughts. Was Adam injured, was he bored with Ronan, did he prefer the company of his urbane new friends, calm down, Ronan, stop being needy, Ronan, get your-self together, Ronan, you're always the car crash, Ronan. It would have been polite to pretend she hadn't heard any of it, but Ronan and Hennessy had never been polite to each other and she didn't see the point in starting now. "What's your boy like?"

Ronan picked up a slender phone the size of a business card and made a big show of examining it for suitability. He didn't reply.

"So he's ugly," Hennessy said. "Or a complete cock-up."

Ronan studied another phone that looked like an umbrella. "What do you think he's like?"

"I honestly have no idea," Hennessy said. "Who would be attracted to you as a love match? Has he got crushingly low self-esteem? Is he one of those soft boys who hide in the firm pecs of their scary partners? Is he a witch? Did he say a spell wrong and you appeared and now you're bound for life?"

"Yeah," Ronan said. "That one."

Hennessy leaned over one of the shelves. The tediously normal-looking cell phone on it brightened to display a photograph of two young men as the lock screen. One was Ronan, laugh-ing explosively. The other was a rather self-contained-looking fellow, striking in an unusual sort of way, smirking a bit at whatever he'd just said. They were not exactly opposites but their appearances nonetheless gave the impression they were. Ronan's dark, dramatic eyebrows, the other guy's light, barely visible ones. Ronan's emotions screamed upon his face while the other guy's whispered. "Is that him?"

Ronan addressed the dream at large. "Traitor. You didn't have to show her."

"He doesn't *look* like he's filling a hole inside himself with your toxic presence," Hennessy said. She kind of hated looking at them together. It made her feel ugly inside. "Are you guys in love five-ever or do you think you're a pretty board game to pass his time?"

Now she sounded ugly, too.

But Ronan just picked up another phone and, after a space, mused, "*Your* phone can be simpler than mine, of course. You'll only need to be able to call Jordan, right? There's no one else?"

A single question, clear and factual. What a weapon. And he'd delivered it in the same tone he might have said anything else, so she didn't notice the blade of its meaning until it was stuck inside her.

Suddenly, Hennessy had a very clear understanding that the cruel exterior Ronan Lynch wore was not all posture.

Every lock screen in the shop briefly showed Hennessy's face. But it was not truly Hennessy. It was Trinity, June, Brooklyn, Madox, Jay, Alba, Octavia, Farrah, Jordan. All dead. Almost all dead. It would have been easier, in some ways, if Jordan were dead, too. Simpler, anyway.

Ronan said nothing else. He just let the silence do its violent work.

She found she was both awed and grateful for this bit of nastiness in response to hers. "Did you want to drink my arterial blood after that slash, or just roll around in it?"

"Whatever," Ronan said, but it was clear they had come to an accord. He picked up a matte-black phone. It was the size of an acorn, and when he clipped it onto his earlobe, it looked just like a tunnel piercing, making him look even more like a hulking goth than he had before.

She could feel him thinking: *Small. Subtle. It'll only place and take calls, not text, but that's fine. Fuck texting. I don't care about texting. I don't need to text ever again.*

Even in his own head he lied to himself.

Ronan said suddenly, "Can you imagine if all dreams were like this? It's so easy."

"Okay, Bryde," Hennessy said mockingly.

"You really don't see the appeal?"

"Of shopping for electronics in your head?"

He studied her, eyebrows knit. He was trying to understand her, and maybe he *could* understand part of her, the part of her that was a lot like him. But he'd been good at this for too long. She'd been bad at it for too long. They were beginning to be shaped like it. The space between those two truths was vast and checkered with Lace.

"Hold my beer," Ronan said.

The electronics store melted away.

They were in a blistering red desert. Before them were two motorcycles in liquid black, their wasp-waisted bodies glistening with a permanent wet sheen, the compound eyes of their head-lights pointed down an arrow-straight road. It was both darkly inviting and subtly wrong.

Hennessy glanced at him. "Is that what you think the desert looks like? Have you ever been? That looks like an alien planet."

"If you think you can do better, let's see it."

It was a challenge. Just like Bryde. Change the dream. It had taken Ronan no effort at all.

Closing her eyes, Hennessy remembered the last time she had been through a real desert. *Don't think about the Lace.* She could not make her mind put herself in a desert, so she imagined how she would paint it on a canvas. And in that moment, she felt the dream *help* her. Creativity prickled through her like a burst of adrenaline. Everything suddenly seemed easier to hold in her head all at once.

Hennessy opened her eyes.

The desert had changed. This desert wasn't red at all; it was white and pink and cream and striated with orange and black and yellow. The sand was knotted and complicated with crisp sagebrush dried by current heat and flat cactus swollen with past luck. The two dreamers stood in a valley. Mesas rose in the distance, pale underwater castles shaped by a sea that had long abandoned this world. The sky overhead was bluer than any sky in the world.

This was a real desert, but a real desert by way of Hennessy. Exaggerated, heightened, made more itself. Made art.

"Fuck," Ronan breathed, and he didn't bother to hide his awe.

Maybe, Hennessy thought, there was a world where she could be good at this.

The Lace was nowhere.

And then they were on the bikes and they were tearing through that painted desert.

Ronan conjured a flock of white birds that skimmed fast and low beside them.

Hennessy painted a fork in the road, the asphalt smearing out like a brushstroke.

Ronan whirled music beneath their tires, pounding bass through the desert.

Hennessy transformed the scene from day to night, the purpled sky rich as berries, the sand pink and blue.

Ronan cast both bikes into the air.

Fear-free exhilaration, the only destination *up*. Hennessy could feel the ascent in every part of her body. The gravity weighting her stomach. The breeze against her arms. The sense of endless space above and below. Up, up, up.

Hennessy let out a scream, just to hear herself howl, as they flowed up through the darkening night. Then, suddenly, they broke through a cloud she hadn't even realized they'd been passing through. Up here, the air was thin and cold and wonderful, everything tinged the furious raspberry red of a nearly gone sunset. Ronan looked worlds away from the version of himself she'd seen only hours before in the fast-food restaurant. There he had been defeated, guilty, both victim of circumstance and architect of said circumstance. Here he was powerful, confident, joyful, a cheerful king. Hennessy versus Jordan.

But maybe not. Maybe, Hennessy thought again, there was a world where she was good at this.

The two dreamers coasted up there in the incredible sky for however long time lasted in dreams, sucking in big pure breaths of air, feeling the ley line swirl around them and through them.

Then Ronan said, "We gotta wake up. Keeping the Lace out of here is giving me a headache."

His words took a few seconds to land.

When they did, they cut deep. Deeper than his intentionally cruel question had before, although she was sure he hadn't intended it this time.

Hennessy said, "So you've been patronizing me this whole time, is that it?"

"What?"

"This whole time you've been letting me think we're, what, equals?" The desert was shredding around them. The bikes were gone.

Ronan peered around, bemused. "Are you pissed?"

"You let me think I was doing this."

"You *were* doing it. This is your desert." But he couldn't disguise his wince. "Goddamn, it's strong."

"Right. Sure. You babysat me."

"I just took some of the weight—"

"And didn't tell me?"

Ronan's expression was puzzled as the checkered shape of the Lace cast itself across his face. "You know this is what you always do."

Yeah, she did. Except she'd thought she was getting better. Learning, finally.

The sky was pulsing, and with each dark pulse, the shadow of the Lace was printed across it. It was the Lace dream. It was always the Lace dream. It was always going to be the Lace dream.

Ronan pressed a hand to his temple. "I can't—"

9

Ronan hadn't thought much about the future.

This was a way he and Adam had always been opposites. Adam seemed to *only* think about the future. He thought about what he wanted to happen days or weeks or years down the road, and then he backfilled actions to make it happen. He was good at depriving himself in the now in order to have something better in the later.

Ronan, on the other hand, couldn't seem to get out of the now. He always remembered consequences too late. After a bloody nose. A broken friendship. A huge tattoo. A cat with human hands. But his head didn't seem built to hold the future. He could imagine it for just a few seconds until, like a weak muscle, his thoughts collapsed back into the present.

But there was one future he could imagine. It was a little bit of a cheat, because it was buried in a memory, and Ronan was better at thinking of the past than the future. It was an indulgent memory, too, one he'd never have copped to out loud. There wasn't much to it. It was from the summer after Adam had graduated, the summer he'd spent with Ronan at the Barns. Ronan had come in from working on the fences outdoors and tossed his work gloves onto the grass-cluttered rug by the mudroom door. As he did, he'd seen that Adam's mechanic gloves were lined up neatly on top of his shoes. Ronan had already known Adam was inside the house, but nonetheless, the image made him pause. They were just gloves, grease-stained and very old. Thrifty Adam always tried to get as much wear out of things as possible. They were long and narrow like Adam himself, and despite their age and stains, they were otherwise impeccably clean. Ronan's work gloves, in comparison, were cruddy and creased and coarse-looking, tossed with carefree abandon, the fingers lassoed over Adam's.

Seeing the two pairs tumbled together, a nameless feeling had suddenly overwhelmed Ronan. It was about Adam's gloves here, but it was also Adam's jacket tossed on a dining room chair, his soda can forgotten on the foyer table, him somewhere tossed with equal comfort in the Barns, his presence commonplace enough that he was not having to perform or engage with Ronan at all times. He was not dating Ronan; he was living in Ronan's life with him.

Shoes kicked off by the door, gloves off.

A future. A good future. One Ronan had always liked thinking about. But the feeling of the Lace was still stuck to Ronan. It was hard to shake its insistent dread. It was getting all over the memory of Adam's gloves. It was reminding him how even though it was a great memory, a great future, it hadn't been enough for Ronan. If it had been enough, he'd still be waiting safely at the Barns until it came true. Instead, the Lace feeling murmured, he was here, jeopardizing that future more and more with every act. So how much did he *really* treasure that memory?

Not enough to keep it safe.

"I trust you enjoyed your dreaming," Bryde said.

As Ronan's dream paralysis came to an end, a light came on, revealing the small hunting cabin Bryde had brought them to a few hours after the episode at the fast-food restaurant. Two decayed deer heads on the wall stared at Ronan with strained expressions. A lamp made of antlers lit a plaid sofa. Ronan had been too stupid with nightwash to notice any of these details when they'd arrived. Now they seemed quaint, charming, relieving in their mundanity. The Lace was fading.

He didn't know how Hennessy had lived with it for so long.

"What did you bring back?" Bryde asked. The way he asked the question somehow seemed to imply he knew the answer already but wanted to hear them explain themselves, a teacher asking a child to explain their stick drawing.

"A phone," Ronan said.

"A phone," echoed Bryde.

"An untraceable phone."

"A phone," said Bryde again.

"You sound like a parrot. Yes, a phone, I got a phone."

"Why?"

Now Ronan was beginning to feel foolish, as if he'd missed a lesson. "To call my family?"

"Do you think it's wise to be looking in the rearview mirror?" Bryde asked.

There was something both uncomfortable and fatherly about this. Bryde treating them like children; Bryde knowing this dimly lit path they were on.

"Okay, Satan," said Ronan, and Hennessy laughed hollowly from the dismal plaid couch.

"Get up," Bryde said. "Wash off your face. We're going on a walk."

"Idea! You two go on a walk. I stay here and hate myself," Hennessy said.

"Put on a coat," Bryde replied. "It's snowing."

His dreamers grumbled and did as he said.

The cabin they emerged from was notched into the side of a mountain and looked even more remote and murdery than it had from the inside. There was nothing around it but trees and more trees. The driveway through the woods was barely more civilized than the rest of the forest floor.

To Ronan's amazement, it *was* snowing. Lightly, without urgency, but enough to lend the night a peculiar brightness. In front of the cabin, the car was dusted with snow, which made it no more visible than before. It was emotionally hard to see, not literally. Snow and grime didn't matter.

Ronan pulled his skullcap down over his ears. "Where are we walking to?"

Bryde said, "Up."

So up they went.

These were foreign trees. Unlike the huge oaks and twisted beeches of Lindenmere, Ronan's half-remembered fairy-tale trees, these were evergreens. Fat spruces with chunky bark and branchless trunks stretching into a snow-fogged sky kingdom. Still fairy-tale trees, but not from a tale Ronan had ever heard. Chainsaw flew above them, her wings strangely audible in the hush as they flapped.

"Are we there yet?" Hennessy asked.

"Up," Bryde replied.

Up, up. Ronan's calves strained as they headed up the steepening mountain. Here, the snow was thicker, the trees even bigger. The landscape seemed just as dreamy as the desert he'd just left. And as real.

Hennessy, he thought, *are we still dreaming?*

She didn't turn her head. So he was awake, or at least he was in his dream alone, with a copy of Hennessy, a copy of Bryde. Reality was harder to define now.

"Do you know where we are?" Bryde asked them. They had reached their destination: a great, vast stump that must have once been a great, vast tree, larger than any of the others still standing. It was dusted with snow like everything else, which somehow made it seem more alive, not less. Ronan was put in mind of the way the snow dusted the backs of his father's eternally sleeping cattle back at the Barns.

"Still Westva," Hennessy replied. "Yeah?"

"West by God Virginia," added Ronan, mimicking his old friend Gansey's Southern accent before remembering none of these new acquaintances had ever met him. Here in the future, they didn't know about his past. Maybe that was Adam's attraction to it.

He felt that prickle of the Lace again.

Bryde said, "Yes. Quite nearly in the middle of the National Radio Quiet Zone. Over ten thousand square miles without radio, Wi-Fi, cell phone signal, or microwave ovens. Home of the largest steerable radio telescope in the world and several defunct alien research programs. One of the quietest night skies east of the Mississippi. Can you feel it?"

Of course not. Not now that he was awake. The ley power always seemed so clear to dreaming Ronan. Waking Ronan, however, couldn't sense it even a little. In fact, it often felt like waking Ronan loved the things that seemed to actively interfere with it the most. Electricity, engines, motors, gasoline, adrenaline. And then dreaming Ronan—nightwashing Ronan—needed a world free of them. Perhaps this was why it was hard to see a future for himself. Bryde said there weren't two of him. Bryde didn't know.

"Can I feel it, or do I like it?" Hennessy asked. "Because those are different answers."

Bryde gazed up at the massive spruces around them. A crawling white mist ghosted up from the light snowfall now, and the tree trunks were marked with little upside-down Vs of white where the precipitation had stuck to the rugged bark. "What do you *hear?*"

"Nothing," said Ronan.

Nothing. *Nothing.*

There was no sound of distant trucks, no hum of generators, no slam of distant doors. There was just the soft, white silence around these huge trees. Mountain soil was so poor and yet they'd managed to become massive. Ronan wondered how long it had taken them to perform this feat.

Perhaps they grew better in the absence of noise.

As if reading his thoughts, Bryde said, "They're all so young. Second growth. Beginning of the twentieth century, this was all twigs, because of logging. Looked like a war zone. Was, even. The army used to fire mortars here. Imagine this place razed and stubbled and smoking, the sounds of gunfire."

Ronan couldn't.

"Yes," Bryde said. "Amazing what you can change in a century, if you have a purpose. Humankind razed this place, but humankind also built it back up again. Planted trees. Put up fences to keep the cattle out. Dragged the rivers into shape where trauma erased them. Replaced all the living things that grew along them to hold them in place. Deep down, there are always some that miss it. Do you really feel nothing at all, Ronan?"

Ronan muttered, "Not while awake."

Bryde went on. "Did you feel how strong the line was when you were dreaming? And that is with it smothered. In the sixties, a dam was built southeast of here that disrupted its energy. But before that, it was strong enough to spill out ley energy into distant tributaries."

"Stronger than this?" Hennessy said. She didn't sound pleased.

"Come here, both of you," Bryde said. "Put your hands on this."

They did as he asked, Ronan in his old leather jacket scarred by escaped nightmares, Hennessy in her stolen smelly coat with the snow caught in the tips of its fur, Bryde in the same jacket he always wore, that light gray windbreaker with a light stripe down its arm. All their hands were placed on the ragged edge of the stump.

Bryde said, "This is one of the originals. It looks dead, but it's just sleeping. The others keep it alive. Beneath the soil, these trees are connected. The strength of one makes the others strong. The weakness of one challenges the others. They value their oldest members, as do I."

"How much longer for this video essay?" Hennessy said. "I can't feel my tits."

"A little fucking awe would be appropriate," Bryde said calmly. "This forest was like your Lindenmere not long ago, Ronan, but its dreamer died and there was no one to protect it. It is old and hard of hearing and no dreamers have tried to befriend it for a long time. It is still doing its work on this line; it is a wonder these young silly trees had the thought to keep it alive to ground it all, but we should be grateful for it."

"Thanks for the dream, tree," Hennessy said. "I hated it."

"This is a rare ley line in these times," Bryde said, a little sharper. "Pure, quiet, strong. If that dam miles and miles away didn't exist, it would be perfect. If you cannot bring yourself to wipe that smirk off your face while awake, Hennessy, perhaps you can do it in your dreams. Remember this tree, find it in dreamspace next time you close your eyes, and remind it of what friendship looks like. Perhaps it will help you remember what you want and help you dream what your mind wills."

"I don't think my mind should do what it wills," Hennessy said. Ronan could still hear the Lace in her voice, somehow.

Ronan asked, "Does it have a name? The forest?"

He saw the question pleased Bryde. He saw it pleased him very much. Bryde replied, "This tree is called Ilidorin."

Ilidorin. It sounded like a name that belonged with Greywaren.

Chainsaw, in one of the branches far overhead, let out a little growl-caw. She could manage a fair number of human words, but this was not one Ronan had heard before.

"I brought you here to see Ilidorin because I wanted you to see that this is the pedigree of your power, not the world you keep looking over your shoulder at. I thought you were outgrowing old habits but . . ." Bryde shook his head. "Given the opportunity to communicate with your family, what do you do? Dream up *phones*."

The disdain in his voice was sufficient to twist Ronan's guts.

"Phones, he says," Hennessy mocked. "Phones! That portable lifeline. As if—"

"Don't start." Bryde cut off her monologue before it could take hold. "A human child believes all things are possible. How wonderful. How terrifying. Slowly, you are taught what you cannot have. What will not be possible. What you do not have to fear. There is no monster in the closet. You cannot fly. How relieving. How disappointing. But this is the world, isn't it? You believe it. You believe it so thoroughly that even when the box is lifted from around you, you continue to travel in circles no bigger than its walls. A *phone!*"

"How is it you think I should be talking to Declan if not with a phone?" demanded Ronan. "I don't think he really wants to have a one-on-one, with, like, some dream balloon with my face projected in it. He just wants a phone call."

"Does he even want that?"

Ronan demanded, "What?"

Bryde said, "Do you really think your family understands you? Truly? This world has been built for them, so thoroughly that they don't realize it. It has been built to destroy you, so thoroughly that it has never occurred to them. Your goals are fundamentally opposed."

"So what are you trying to say?" Ronan asked. "Don't talk to them?"

Bryde's expression softened. Was it pity? "It's a warning, not an order. The view in the rearview mirror is often a painful one."

"Whoa, mate, Jordan is not in my rearview mirror," said Hennessy.

"Then where is she?" Bryde asked. "Why is she not standing in this forest with us? She's a dream, this concerns her, too, does it not? And where are your brothers, Ronan Lynch? Where is Adam? They are the brothers and lovers of a dreamer, is this not their concern, too? Did they come with us to save the world for dreamers? No, dreamers are a task for dreamers, they think, not for people like them. They love you, they support you, they wave goodbye as you flee without them, and then they return to their own lives to muddle through without you."

"That's a little unfair," Ronan said uneasily.

"And can you blame them?" Bryde went on. "A part of them must be relieved they no longer have front-row seats watching as the world breaks you. It's hard to die. Harder to watch someone else do it, and make no mistake, that's what you two were doing before now. Dying in plain sight, inch by inch, dream by dream, drip by drip. You've given them the gift of letting them look away, and I'm just warning you they might not like you returning that gift for store credit."

"Marvelous," Hennessy said, sounding bitter. "Wonderful. Inspiring. Got it. We die alone."

Bryde said, "You have each other. The ley line. Places like this. They are your family, too."

"You're wrong," Ronan said. "About Adam, anyway."

"I'd like to be," Bryde replied. "But I've met too many humans."

"You're wrong," Ronan said again.

"Tell me the dream that produced all those wheels," Bryde said. *"Tamquam—"*

"Don't say that again," Ronan said. Then, again, "You're wrong."

Hennessy muttered something, but when Bryde waited for her to repeat it, she just said, "I wish I had a cigarette."

"Come on," Bryde said. "We have work to do."

10

Declan Lynch had a complicated relationship with his family. It wasn't that he hated them. Hate was such a slick, neat, simple emotion. Declan envied people who felt proper hate. You had to sand all the corners off things in order to unequivocally hate; it was a subtractive emotion. Hate was sometimes a prize. But hate was sometimes also just a dick move. It was annoying how many people had small redeeming qualities or depressingly sympathetic motives or other complicating features that disqualified it as an appropriate response.

Declan *wanted* to hate his family. He wanted to hate his father, Niall. For being a bad businessman, for never paying attention to the details, for bullshitting himself to death. For being a bad father. For having favorites. For having favorites who weren't Declan. But could he blame him for not wanting a son like Declan? Declan hadn't wanted a father like Niall. He liked to *think* he hated him, but he knew it wasn't true, because if it was, he'd have been able to set Niall's memory down and walk away. Instead, he took it out of the box and poked it. Declan said he hated him, but it was aspirational.

Declan wanted to hate his dreamt mother, Aurora, but he couldn't justify that, either. She'd adored him; she'd adored all the boys. It wasn't her fault she was a faulty model. He was increasingly certain she was happily oblivious to her dreamt status. This was probably where the idea to withhold the same information from Matthew had clocked in. Who'd come up with that? Niall? Declan? It had happened too long ago. In any case, it wasn't Aurora's fault that, deep down, Declan had always suspected she was *untrue*. A trick. A blarney-filled bedtime story for three boys. He didn't hate *her*. He hated that he'd been naïve enough to ever be fooled by her.

And Ronan. Ronan should've been the easiest to hate, because Ronan was built for acrimony. He despised people and assumed they despised him, too. He was stubborn, narrow-minded, completely unable to see compromise or nuance. He'd fought Declan before, which was unremarkable; he'd fought everyone. The world against Ronan Lynch, that was his motto. As if the world cared. Niall had, Declan supposed. That was Ronan's worst sin: idolizing their father. *Grow up.* But Declan couldn't hate Ronan for this; now that Declan didn't have to parent Ronan, he no longer had to constantly compete with a ghost.

Which left Matthew. In person, it seemed impossible to consider hating the youngest Lynch, but on paper, it seemed impossible to *not*. Out of all of the Lynches, he was the family member who'd taken the most from Declan. Niall had made Declan a liar. Aurora had made him an orphan. Ronan had made him a nag and then, later, a fugitive. But Matthew had taken Declan's youth. Declan fed him and read to him, drove him to school events and picked him up from friend visits. The orphans Lynch. But at least Ronan grew up and out, toward independence. Matthew didn't even want to get a driver's license. And could he live alone, really? He was a dream with a head full of clouds, a dream whose feet kept walking him over waterfalls. Goodbye, distant colleges in interesting places. Goodbye, internship offers from Niall Lynch's well-connected clients. Goodbye, carefree, single adult life.

Goodbye, whatever Declan Lynch would have grown up to be.

Declan should have hated Matthew.

But he couldn't. Not jolly, carefree Matthew. Not the innocent chubby kid who tumbled into Declan's gloomy childhood. Not Matthew, the angelic—

"Not gonna, fartmonger," Matthew said. "Can't make me."

"It wasn't a request. Buckle your seat belt, we are in a moving vehicle," Declan said.

"If I died," Matthew shot back, "couldn't you just ask Ronan to dream a replacement me?"

"If I did, I'd ask him to dream one who always buckled his seat belt. Do you really want to die in Connecticut?"

The two brothers were in a loaner car one of Niall's past associates had hooked Declan up with in exchange for the transport of the skittish foreign national currently riding in the trunk with a bottle of water and some potato chips. (Declan didn't know why the man needed to be moved secretly from DC to Boston, nor did he even consider asking.) Declan had just stopped long enough to make sure the hired muscle he'd arranged to watch their backs in Boston remembered where and when to find them. Then he called the second hired muscle he'd gotten to watch the first hired muscle in case the first one got attacked or compromised in some way. Then he talked to the third hired muscle he'd gotten just in case the first two went wrong. Fail-safes. He believed in fail-safes. *You're a twitchy guy*, the third muscle had said. Then, thoughtfully, *You looking for a job?*

"Maybe I *am* the replacement," Matthew continued mulishly.

Declan allowed himself one quarter of one half of a pico-second to imagine what it would be like to make the journey to Boston on his own, feeling guilty for all parts of the picosecond.

This was his father's DNA, he was sure of it. Niall had felt no compunction about going on trips and leaving his family behind. *Fuck you*, he thought. Then: *I hate you.*

(How he wished that was true.)

Matthew was still going on. "If I were a replacement, I wouldn't even know, would I?"

"Mary, please strike me deaf until the state line," Declan said, checking his mirrors, changing lanes, driving safely. He felt Matthew was taking all this a bit far. Declan had put his identity crises on hold multiple times for the greater good. Matthew had only been asked to do it once.

"Did you hear a thump?" Matthew asked. "From the back?"

"No," Declan said. "Eat your snacks."

"Why did I have to go through puberty?" Matthew picked back up where he'd left off. "If I had to be a dream, why couldn't I have superpowers? Why di—"

There was a phone ringing from somewhere in the car, which ordinarily would have annoyed Declan, but in this case relieved him.

"Turn your phone down," Declan said.

"I don't *have* a phone anymore," Matthew whined. "You made me throw it out." He said it in the most sing-song-younger-brother-annoying way possible. *You MADE me THROW it OUT.*

Oh, right. But Declan didn't have a phone anymore, either. He'd just thrown out his burner phone at the rest station and was intend-ing to pick up another one after he got to Boston. He wanted badly to pretend that this was evidence of the return of safe, paranoid

Declan, but he knew better. This was just what Foolish Declan did to justify this insane trip north. He was going to get his car back. Right.

"Then what's ringing?" It was too loud to be coming from the trunk, so it couldn't have belonged to their secret passenger.

"Dur, there, it's that," Matthew said, tapping on the loaner car's radio display.

"I can't read that—I'm driving. What does it say?"

"Connected phone has an incoming call."

"There is no connected phone."

Matthew's voice was dubious. "I think you ought to look."

Declan spared a glance. INCOMING CALL FROM, said the display. And then it displayed something that was not quite a number and not quite a name. The something made Declan's mind reel and bend in on itself to even glance at it.

He hit the button on the steering wheel to accept the call.

"How are you doing this?" he demanded.

"So you're not dead," said a voice through the car's speakers.

"Ronan!" Matthew said.

Declan felt the usual feeling he got with Ronan: Good news, it was Ronan on the other end of the phone. Bad news, it was Ronan on the other end of the phone.

"How do you like it?" Ronan asked. "I call it the MEGA-PHONE, all caps."

Matthew laughed, but the joke sounded a little forced to Declan. He asked, "Are you all right?"

"Don't you worry your curly head. I hear Matthew. What's cooking, shitface? You good?"

"Declan's driving—how good could I be?" Matthew replied.

Declan persisted, "Why didn't you call before now? Are you still with Bryde? And Hennessy? What's Bryde like?"

"You should be getting some miles in, Matthias," Ronan said, in that aggressively jovial tone he used when he was making Matthew feel like things were normal and blowing off Declan's concerns. "You've got to get your license eventually, bro."

"Mehhh," said Matthew. "Maybe."

"Hey. *Hey*," Ronan said. "Where are you going, anyway? Aren't you supposed to be, like, lying low at the Barns?"

"I have an errand in Boston," Declan said.

Booty call, mouthed Matthew, and Declan shot him a dark look.

Ronan said, "An *errand*! There are fuckfaces out here!"

"I can't put off every aspect of life forever," Declan said. Foolish Declan clapped gleefully. Paranoid Declan rolled his eyes.

"You said you were going to the Barns. I assumed you were staying at the Barns. Now you've left the Barns."

"You sound like D," Matthew remarked.

Declan told himself not to rub it in, to be the mature one, and then he said, "How does it feel to ask for something reasonable and be completely ignored? How does it feel to know you've made plans to keep the family safe and they aren't keeping to them?"

There was silence for so long that it seemed possible the connection had been broken.

"Ronan?"

"I gotta go," Ronan said, but he didn't go.

Declan once again had the curious feeling that their roles had reversed.

"I kept my head down for years," Declan said. "It wasn't just you. Sacrifices were made by all of us."

"Great," Ronan said. "My gratitude is turned to eleven. Boston. Sounds great. While you're there, look in on Parrish for me."

It had already occurred to Declan that he was headed to the same place Ronan's boyfriend was going to school, but he hadn't planned on a tête-à-tête. Paranoid Declan wasn't intending to spend that long in the area. "I thought you had the MEGAPHONE. Call him yourself."

Ronan said, "Yeah."

"What's that mean? Did you guys fight?"

"No," Ronan said, sounding offended. "I really do have to go. Keep an eye over your shoulder for, like, uh, the bogeyman, I guess. Matthew, eat whatever vegetable the Big D tells you to."

"Turds," Matthew said.

"Turds aren't vegetables," Ronan replied. "They're mammals."

"You never told me what Bryde was like," Declan said.

"Ha!" Ronan replied.

The phone went dead. The Connecticut traffic charged around them in the middle lane.

Declan tried to figure out if the feeling inside him was the usual unsettled sensation that came from every interaction with Ronan, or if it was above and beyond that. It was time to let Ronan grow up and make his own decisions, surely. Declan didn't need to parent his relationship with Adam—and in any case, who was Declan to talk about relationships? Ronan didn't need a father figure. He needed to keep on growing up.

He thought.

Probably.

It was harder than before to tell if this was actually right or if this was just what Declan wanted to tell himself so he could continue on this adventure to Boston.

"He sounds happy," Matthew observed.

"Yeah," Declan lied.

"Maybe he can make it to Mass with us next week. *Are* we going to church while we're in Boston? Do I still take Communion now that I know I'm not real?"

With a sigh, Declan leaned over and buckled Matthew's seat belt.

"I heard the thump again," Matthew said, but without force. "From the trunk."

"This car might have a bearing going out; these old Jags do that," Declan said. It was an excuse he'd learned from his father, before he'd gotten old enough to learn that bearings didn't go out as often as they did for Lynches. This wasn't even a Jaguar; Matthew wouldn't notice. Declan didn't even know why he lied about it; the fib was like bubble wrap, the truth carefully kept pristine and untouched for his collection.

"Oh, sure," Matthew said. "Bearings."

Depending on how one thought about it, Declan's relationship with the criminal underworld was the longest and most stable one he'd had in his life.

Declan had a very complicated relationship with his family.

11

E veryone likes the sweetmetals," Jo Fisher said.

"I didn't say I liked them."

"Everyone likes them," Fisher told Jordan. "Everyone always likes them. Always."

The two of them were in a wine cellar deep beneath a Chestnut Hill mansion just a few miles outside Boston. It had only taken Jordan a few sleepless hours after learning of the existence of sweetmetals to decide she had to know everything there was to know about them.

Because she had to have one.

This was the way to a real future.

Jordan hadn't wanted to call Barbara's goon and prove she *was* interested, but it was the most efficient next step. It seemed obvious Boudicca couldn't have the only sweetmetals in the world, but she needed to know more about them before she even knew where to look for others. She wasn't crazy about the power dynamics of the rendezvous—she was meeting them on their turf, and in an underground bunker, no less. But her attempts to negotiate to a more equitable location had been useless.

It's not you, Boudicca had explained, *it's us. Well, it's them.*

Apparently, if the sweetmetals were kept any closer to the surface, they started affecting "dependents" in the city.

Jordan was beginning to wonder just how much of the world had been dreamt.

"How many of these are there?" she asked. The entire place smelled old, but in a classy way. Not like mold, but like fermentation. In addition to the hundreds of wine bottles sleeping nose-out on either wall, there were also a few oak barrels nested at the end of the hall. "On the planet, I mean?"

The sweetmetals had been set up in a stylish display down the aisle. Paintings perched on fabric-draped easels, antique jewelry preened on velvet, sculpture assessed the room from atop carved pillars. Tasteful lighting had been installed to better highlight them. If one didn't know any better, one might mistake this for an eccentric art sale for discerning buyers.

But the pieces themselves soon corrected that impression. Jordan could feel their collective power radiating toward her. Her body felt awake, alert, ready for action. It was like caffeine. Speed.

No, it was like being *real*.

"In the whole world?" Fisher asked. She sounded as if she thought the question was stupid. Like Jordan was looking at a puppy for sale and asking how many puppies existed elsewhere in general. Jordan had already pegged Fisher as one of those ambitious young women who had to try harder than others to look as if they cared about people's feelings; it was obvious that Fisher understood what polite looked like but also obvious she couldn't always be arsed to step up.

"I don't have that information with me. It's not a typical question." Fisher managed to imply that, by asking, Jordan was indicating she might not be a worthy buyer.

Jordan let this judgment breeze by. "This collection. When was it put together?"

"A few weeks ago, in London. It's already been to Birmingham and Dublin. It'll go to New York and then DC and Atlanta after that, if they aren't all sold by then. Those are real bullets in those guns, by the way."

"What?" Jordan asked. She glanced at the armed guards by the door. "Oh. How exciting for them."

"People sometimes get stupid around the sweetmetals," Fisher said. "Sometimes they try to take them when our backs are turned. And sometimes when they aren't."

"Then: Project Bullets."

"Right. Take your time looking." Fisher pulled out her phone. "I'm editing contracts."

With this cool confession, Jordan had the odd sense Fisher would've liked to be her friend, in a different world, in different circumstances, possibly because she'd already killed and eaten all of her others. The two young women were probably about the same age, actually. They'd just taken very different roads to get to the same hole in the ground. "On your phone?"

"What else would I use?"

"What else indeed." Jordan took one of the brochures from the little lion-footed table at the beginning of the display as Fisher retreated into her screen. She admired once again the cohesion of Boudicca's graphic design (black background, white painted cross on each page, cleanly numbered sweetmetals, sold pieces blacked out with a Sharpie), matching the sweetmetal with the listing as she walked down the aisle. It didn't take her long to realize they must be listed in general order of value or power, weakest to strongest.

24. *Landscape, with Sheep* by Augustus W. Fleming. It was a very good painting. The way the light played across the fields

made the viewer feel the painter must have loved those fields very much. It was also enormous—ten feet long—and didn't give Jordan much of a buzz, which was probably why it was considered the least valuable piece here. No one was going to commute to work with *Landscape, with Sheep* tucked under their arm.

23. *Self-Portrait* by Melissa C. Lang. According to the brochure, Lang's portrait had been done with cosmetics directly onto an antique mirror with half its frame artistically ripped off. Jordan could feel its effect a little more than the landscape, but it was both very fragile and very ugly.

13–22. Ten vintage matching silver spoons with handles shaped like swans. Presumably there had once been an entire set of them, and together they must have been quite potent. The brochure informed Jordan that together they now had enough energy to raise a single dozing dependent or individually lend some strength to another weakening sweetmetal. These things didn't last forever, after all.

12. The Duchess Urn. The brochure listed two—one from either side of the entrance to a Yorkshire estate. When Jordan asked Fisher what had happened to the other one, she was told it had been stolen by a woman in London and then been recovered ten miles away from London. Both the urn and woman had been broken during the chase.

11. *The Damned Prince* by A. Block. This abstract painting was both powerful and handsome, the brochure murmured, suitable for hanging in either a bachelor's bedchamber or in your front hallway, depending upon who the owner wanted to keep wakeful. Jordan had told herself she would not fret over whether Declan Lynch had gotten her postcard or whether he was going to do something about it, but she was annoyed to find herself

imagining what his reaction would have been to this painting, which was much like those he'd kept in the secret art space at his townhome.

7–10. The stone blue jays. The brochure built a picture of the ideal sweetmetal: something both powerful and portable, something potent enough to keep the wearer wide awake for months or years, and something that could be carried or worn discreetly by its wealthy dependent. The blue jays were very nearly good at both of these things. Each was about the size of a man's meaty fist, so they could be slipped into a generous coat pocket, and each weighed about five pounds. They were very stealable. Jordan wasn't stupid enough to try anything, but she was a little surprised by how tempting it was.

5–6. Garnet earrings, 1922. The earrings, badly dated, were not the loveliest of jewelry, but they were still very wearable, and they were potent enough to keep a dependent on their feet, even individually. Because of this, they were sold separately, although Boudicca would, for an additional fee, make ordinary copies available in order to allow the wearer a matching set.

4. The Afghan collar. Probably it was a dog collar. It was about six inches wide, beautifully and intricately beaded, with leather thong closures. It would fit perfectly on the dreamt sight-hound of one's choice, but it seemed a waste to use it on man's best friend—it was potent enough to wake dependents hundreds of yards away as it passed through a city. Probably it was destined to be sewn into a corset or back of a jacket, although an adventurous dresser might wear it on a truly elegant throat.

3. The Mary-Mary-Contrary engagement ring. Jordan found this one either very touching or very depressing. It was a beautiful little ring with an equally beautiful little diamond, and engraved

on the inside of the band were the tiny words *mary-mary-contrary*. It begged several questions: Who was Mary? Was she dead? Had she sold this? Was the wedding called off? Why was this ring no longer attached to a Mary? Fisher did not know and did not care when Jordan asked. Regardless, it packed a potent punch, enough to wake a dependent and an entire host of dependent bridesmaids if needed.

2. The ink. The little bottle was shaped like a woman and was filled with the darkest green ink. It seethed with the energy that woke dependents from their everlasting sleep. It begged to be gazed into. It made one feel alive, awake, real, even if one had already felt alive, awake, real. Jordan was beginning to feel a little high.

1. *Jordan in White* by J. H. Hennessy. The portrait—one of the artist's last before she died, the brochure noted—wasn't portable, unlike the other most expensive sweetmetals in the collection, but it didn't matter. It was a stunner of a piece of art, featuring an intense-eyed child posed in a simple white slip, her kinky hair piled upon her head. And it was incredibly potent. Anyone would be happy to display it prominently in their home to animate an entire dreamt family.

Jordan stood looking at *Jordan in White* for a very long time.

She looked first at the girl, at Jordan, and then she looked at the signature, J. H. Hennessy, and then back at the girl again. Mother painting daughter.

Although Jordan was supposed to be a direct copy of Hennessy, she'd never thought of J. H. Hennessy as her mother. For a while she'd thought this was because she hadn't known Jay like Hennessy had. After all, Jordan had only come into being just after Jay died. But slowly she realized that shouldn't matter;

Jordan had all of Hennessy's other early memories. Hennessy's mother should have been as fresh as everything else.

But this painting underlined the unspoken truth. Jordan was missing memories. The Hennessy in the portrait looked wary, skittish, unlike the Hennessy Jordan had always known, but it was obviously her, back when she had been both Jordan and Hennessy. But Jordan had no memory of sitting for the painting, no memory of it existing at all.

This was something that had been kept from her.

Jordan felt very strange.

She didn't know if this was because she was looking at some of her history, or because it was a sweetmetal, or because she was trying to figure out if Boudicca was playing a mind game with her.

She'd been staring at it too long; the guards were antsy. They were thinking about Project Bullets.

Jordan pointed finger guns at them before turning to Fisher. "How are the sweetmetals made?"

"I don't understand the question," Fisher said.

"Who makes these things into sweetmetals?"

"Isn't that the same question?"

"This painting. Those spoons. Why do they do what they do? They are not just a painting, a spoon, they do other things, that's why I'm here, don't leave me feeling I'm talking to myself, mate— Was it put into them? Were they like that from the get?" When she saw Fisher's exasperated face, Jordan answered her own question. "You don't know how the sausage is made."

Fisher said, "You're a strange person."

Without any hostility, Jordan went on. "All right, then. What'll these set me back? I assume the price isn't money. Because money's too cheap."

Fisher shrugged. With the sound of someone repeating someone else's words, she said, "Our clientele includes those to whom money is no object."

"Let me have a guess," Jordan said. "I do whatever you want for the rest of time, and I get one of these." She read Fisher's face. "I get to *borrow* one of these. And you write me up a little contract on your phone."

Fisher shrugged again.

Jordan studied her, trying to read her. "Is that why you're here? For one of these, something like one of these?"

"Nah, some of us choose it."

"Ah. I reckon this is the part where you tell me I should make a decision soon, 'cause they're flying out the door each place they go."

Fisher shrugged yet again. "You make my job easy."

She watched Jordan very carefully as Jordan walked back along the sweetmetals, feeling everything in her shouting to stay close to them. Probably Fisher thought Jordan was trying to choose which one she'd ask for. Really, Jordan was trying to tell what they had in common. They were all art. Or at least, they were all made by a human. Crafted by a human.

Their secret hummed inside her.

"I was supposed to ask you," Fisher said as she paused at the end of the sweetmetals, "if you were still in touch with Ronan Lynch."

Jordan's heart sailed right up and out of the wine cellar and into the sky.

Right.

She should have known it was coming. Boudicca thought there was just one Jordan Hennessy; somehow she'd managed to forget that. Now it seemed like she had two choices. Make up a reason why she was no longer aware of Ronan's whereabouts after such a dramatic exit or let loose a story about her being a twin with no knowledge of him at all. It was hard to tell on the fly which was a more dangerous truth.

Or, maybe—

"Do I look like a phone to you?" Jordan asked.

"A phone?"

"If you want to get in touch with someone, that's the way to do it. A phone, that's the ticket. I am not a phone. I'm not some white boy's answering service. Tell me, Fisher, do you like it when people act like you're the direct line to ol' Barb?"

This question landed with glorious effect. Fisher's mouth worked unpleasantly. The subject of Ronan was abandoned.

"Who do I call if I'm interested in these?" Jordan asked. "With follow-up questions. You?"

Fisher looked confused. "You don't like them?"

"They're neat." *Please, please,* Jordan's body said.

"Most people would do anything to have one."

Jordan grinned. "I'm a strange person."

If Fisher remembered saying it earlier, she didn't show it. Instead, she said, "Better make up your mind soon. These days, lots of people are trying to stay awake."

12

I hate Philadelphia. I hate its quaint little streets," Hennessy said. "I hate Pittsburgh. I hate its gleaming broad rivers. I hate everything between those two places. I-70, how she twists, how she turns, she rises, she falls like an empire. Hate it. Those barns, the Amish ones, you see them in calendars? Liquid loathing. Truck stops? Yes, let's talk about truck stops, yes. Hate them, too. I hate the cows. Black cows, black-and-white cows, even those brown ones with eyelashes longer than mine. I think I hate them more because of it. Oh. Right, how about this: The song 'Allentown.' Breaks me in a rash. I've got one now thinking about it."

By Ronan's estimation, Hennessy had been listing all the ways she hated Pennsylvania for thirteen miles' worth of interstate. Not her longest monologue, but perhaps one of her most pointed. There was something kind of hypnotic and satisfying to a proper Hennessy monologue. She had that clipped but sloppy British accent that made everything sound funnier, more performative. And she had a ceaseless push and pull to the way she threw the words together that was kind of like music.

"I hate the historic downtowns with their plaques and their parallel parking. I hate the pastel suburbs with their antilock brakes and their sprinkler systems. I hate the way the state is spelled. Uhlllllllvania. It rhymes with 'pain yeah!' When I say it out loud, I can feel how my mouth ends on a vomit shape. I hate the way they call places 'townships.' Are they towns? Are they ships? Am I at land? Or at sea? I'm adrift and the anchor is my motherfucking keystone of a heart. Why is it abbreviated TWP? Twip? Twip? Shouldn't it be the SS *Allegheny*? That's a pun. It's a town. And a ship."

Ronan didn't answer. He just looked out the window at the cold, fine rain bleaching the landscape of color and tried not to think about his brothers driving in Boston.

"Kennywood!" Hennessy said, with a certain amount of triumph. She let out a puff of breath. In the rearview mirror, Ronan could see that she'd exhaled on the backseat window and was now drawing in the condensation. "I hate that people go to Kennywood and then they tell you about it, as if it's a thing we now have in common, a personality type, Kennywood. Pennsylvania! Yes, we both bought tickets to this tourist attraction and now we are bonded in a way usually reserved for people who have survived combat zones together. I hate—"

"Also," Bryde said mildly, "your father lives here, does he not?"

Hennessy was momentarily silent. She had to switch gears from monologue to duet. "Let's talk about *your* father. Father of the Bryde. Do you keep in touch? Who do *you* call late at night? Not with a phone, of course. That's for normies."

Bryde smiled faintly. He was a party of one. From mystery to mystery, that was where he was headed. Saving the ley lines.

"Speaking of calls, how did your call to the fam go?" Hennessy asked Ronan. "They doing well, keeping up your garden while you're gone?"

Ronan said, "Please shut up."

"As you pointed out already, my to-call list is shorter. Girls, dead. Mum, well, you know her, you met her," Hennessy said. "In

my dreams. About forty times. J. H. Hennessy, that portrait artist you might have heard of, collected, bid upon. Known best for
her final self-portrait, entitled *Brains on a Wall*. Don't have to call
her, either. Now, you haven't met the other one, Bill Dower, dear
old dad, the one who dropped his seed into the ocean to make it
boil. *What!* you're thinking, what's he doing in Pennsylvania, hateful Pennsylvania, in a story told with *this* accent? Well, Bill Dower
came from Pennsylvania, and to Pennsylvania he returned after
Brains on a Wall. I think he gave up the whole seeds-and-oceans
thing, though."

"And you said *I* had daddy issues," Ronan scoffed.

"They're like chicken pox," she said. "More than one person
can have them at a time."

She didn't say whether or not she'd called Jordan, and Ronan
didn't ask. The truth was that in the broad light of day, the
phones did seem to belong to a different kind of life, one they
didn't live in anymore. Calling Declan had made Ronan feel
more unmoored, not less.

"Your exit," Bryde said, "is here."

"And what is our destination?" Hennessy said. "You're being
even more 'mysterious stranger' than usual. Is it more French fries?"

"You said we could stand to add another dreamer, so I
found one."

Ronan snapped to attention. "You *what?*"

"I thought about the suggestion and decided Hennessy was
right," Bryde said.

"I was joking," Hennessy said. "Do they have jokes where
you come from? Jokes are concepts presented in a way to shock
or delight because of exaggeration or, sometimes, subversion of
cultural norms. There are ha-ha bits at the end of them."

Bryde smiled thinly at her. "Ha-ha. We will have to be watchful. This is a dangerous place."

It didn't look dangerous. It was a treeless rural valley, objectively beautiful, the long-frostbitten fields rolling off toward a distant line of low mountains. The only sign of civilization was a fine old stone mansion and a massive commercial turkey house, the sort that housed thirty thousand birds who never saw daylight.

And somewhere in this place was another dreamer.

"This is quaint," Bryde said as they pulled up in front of the mansion.

Hennessy growled, "Too bad it's Pennsylvania."

Ronan stared at the house. It was not as fancy as it had looked from a distance; the stone was old and discolored, and the roof had a bit of sway. There was a bright holiday flag with a turkey on it hanging on the porch. A dog bowl that said WOOF! A snow shovel with bright pink gloves stuffed through the handle. It was very ordinary and alive and welcoming, which was completely at odds with his suddenly sour mood. He was not at all excited to have another dreamer sprung on them.

Hennessy seemed to be feeling the same way, because she asked, "Can't we just go save a different dreamer and be done with it?"

"Keep your wits about you," Bryde replied.

On the porch, he rang the doorbell and then waited in his quiet way. There was something about the way he stood there now with his hands in the pockets of his jacket, his expression expectant, that made him seem familiar. Every so often Ronan felt he almost recognized him, and then it went away again.

The door opened.

A woman stood on the other side of it. She was exactly the sort of person one would have guessed might open this door based upon the things on the porch. She was a very comforting sort of person. She was *enough*. Groomed enough to seem invested in the world, but not so much that she seemed like she was making the effort for them more than for herself. Eyes smiling enough that she seemed to have a sense of humor, but eyebrows serious enough that she wouldn't shrug everything off as a joke. Old enough to be sure of who she was, but not so old to remind him of his worried uncertainty regarding the elderly.

Bryde said, "Can we come in out of the cold?"

Her mouth said *oh* but nothing came out. Eventually, she said, "Your voice. You're . . . *Bryde*."

Bryde said, "And you're Rhiannon. Rhiannon Martin."

Ronan and Hennessy shot each other looks. Ronan's look said, *What fuckery is this?* Hennessy's said, *Guess you weren't the only head he was in.*

"Yes, I am," Rhiannon said. She put her hand to her cheek, then put her hand over her mouth for a moment, allowing herself a few seconds of visible surprise and wonder. Then she stepped back to let them in out of the fine rain. "I *am*. Come in, yes, of course."

Inside, the mansion was even less grand than Ronan had first thought; it was merely an overlarge farmhouse with stone cladding, although it was well-furnished and well-loved, easy with generations of care. The fitful weather outside turned everything dark and sleepy inside. Every light was a point of gold in the handsome gloom, putting Ronan in mind of the dreamt lights he always kept in his pockets.

Bryde picked up a framed photograph on the entrance table: the woman, a man, two small kids. He put it back down.

"Please, follow me." Rhiannon hurried to settle them into a formal sitting room full of mirrors. "Sit. I'll get us some coffee. On a day like this . . . ? Coffee. Or tea? For the young people?" She bustled off without an answer.

Ronan and Hennessy sat on either end of a stiff sofa and shot each other more raised eyebrows while Bryde stood by the carved mantel, looking pensively into one of the mirrors. The icy rain continued to spatter against the tall windows.

"Hsst," Ronan said. "Is *she* the dreamer?"

Bryde continued to gaze into the mirror like a man perplexed at what he saw there. "What do you feel?"

"Benjamin Franklin Christ," Ronan said. "Not again."

"What do you feel?" Bryde insisted.

Hennessy muttered, "Turkeys."

"Yes," Bryde agreed. "And not much else. Ronan?"

Ronan was rescued by the return of Rhiannon, who set down a tray of drinks and cookies before retreating behind an armchair. Her hands kneaded the top of it as if she were giving it an anxious back massage, but her face remained kind and worried. Worried for their care, not her own. She clearly wanted them to feel welcome.

"House looks festive," Bryde said, although he had not appeared to give any attention to the house when he walked in, apart from picking up the framed photograph.

"Christmas is coming up," Rhiannon replied. "Don't know if I'm spending it here or with my aunt. She asked me to come stay with her for a bit, you know. I told her I might drive up tomorrow, just in case you really did come . . . I didn't know if you were real."

Bryde smiled that private smile of his.

Rhiannon put her hand to her face again and gazed first at Hennessy and then at Ronan. "But you are. You're all very real. You three look just like you did in the dream. Ha-ha . . . I didn't dream you guys, did I?"

"I don't know about these two jokers," Hennessy said, "but I assure you *I'm* real."

Rhiannon put a long hand over her mouth. "You even sound like you did in the dream. Maybe this *is* all real."

"Put that away, Rhiannon," Bryde said impatiently. "You already know it is. I told you—you make reality. I'm not here to reteach you what I have told you already. You know it in your heart. And could you dream us? With the ley line as it is?"

The truth stung. Bryde had come to Rhiannon Martin just as he'd come to Ronan. He'd come to her as a dreamer, in her dreams. How many other dreamers had he also approached this way? Ronan knew he had no right to feel jealous or betrayed that Bryde wasn't simply his and Hennessy's. He'd known Bryde was infamous before he ever rescued them. For what? For this, per-haps. For showing up in people's heads.

"So you're a dreamer," Hennessy said. "And Bryde here gate-crashed your dreams, too, and invited us over. That's what's going on here? Yeah? Sorry, I'm a little slow. This one"—she indicated Bryde—"didn't explain what we were doing today when we came out. He fancies himself a mysterious stranger. These biscuits are very good. The ones shaped like stars. You've got a gift."

"Oh, yes, Rhiannon is a dreamer," Bryde said, standing. "Here in this stagnant valley. She is a very, very good dreamer."

Rhiannon blushed. "Oh, I don't know about that."

It was so peculiar to see a dreamer like her. All the others they'd saved so far had been a little like Ronan and Hennessy. Not exactly *of* the world. Living on the fringes in some way. Punky or funky or estranged or drifters. But Rhiannon seemed quite . . . not ordinary, but . . . content. Settled. Like a good mom.

Like the world wasn't dismantling her.

"Take a look," Bryde said, indicating the mirrors that covered the walls of the room. "That's her work."

Ronan and Hennessy each took a station at a different mirror. Ronan's was about the size of a large envelope, just big enough to show his face. The frame was ornate, painted roughly with white paint so that the wood showed through in places.

He looked into it.

The Ronan in the mirror was older than he thought of himself as—somehow Ronan was always a little behind in his own estimation of his age. When he was in middle school, he saw himself as a little kid. In high school, he saw the awkward pimpled kid in puberty. After high school, he still perceived himself as the jagged rebel kid.

But the Ronan in the mirror was a young man. A little handsome, he saw, to his surprise, like his father had been at his age, and he could see that as he got older, he'd probably be a lot handsome. Normally he did not think his outside appearance at all reflected who he really was on the inside, but this mirror showed him an exterior Ronan just as complicated as the interior Ronan. The mirror presented a guarded bruiser, but one whose eyebrows gave away startling gentleness. There was a cruel and arrogant dismissiveness in this Ronan's face, but also bravery. The line of his mouth held at once a crumple of depression *and* the shape of a grin. Anger simmered in his eyes, but so did an intense, savage humor.

To his shock, he found he liked the person in the mirror.

"They're quite cunning, aren't they?" Bryde said. "No one likes photographs of themselves. And the mirror has never had a reputation for kindness. But these do, don't they, Rhiannon?"

Ronan joined Hennessy by her mirror, which had a fat gilt frame like an old painting. In it he saw the two of them, fast friends, a Ronan capable of trusting someone without his last name, a Hennessy capable of caring about someone without her face.

Hennessy muttered, "I look like Jordan."

"What do they do?" Ronan growled.

"What do you think they do, Ronan?" Bryde asked.

He didn't want to say it out loud. It felt too earnest. Was this reflection the truth? Or was it what he *wanted* to be true?

"How often do you dream one of these mirrors, Rhiannon?" Bryde asked.

She was still blustery and flattered. "Oh, I don't know. It takes me quite a while. I have to get them together over a lot of dreams; it takes me a lot of concentration and if I'm busy with other things I put them down for quite a while. This is all that I've ever done except for one, and I've been dreaming them since I was a little girl. They take me five years, maybe? I don't know. I don't keep track, I just putter along on them. I'm glad you like them."

Ronan considered the sort of person she must be that all she dreamt was mirrors that were kind to people. Not physically flattering, but truly kind. The invisible car felt a little stupid in comparison.

He put his fingers to his temple. He was beginning to feel hungry again. He didn't know if it was real hunger, or if it was the same thing he had felt in the fast-food restaurant.

"And she does that here, with the ley line as it is," Bryde said, as if he could tell what Ronan was thinking. Perhaps he could. *What do you feel?* "Probably she would put you to shame, kids, if she ever left this place."

Rhiannon tucked her hair behind her ear over and over, her cheeks pinked. "Oh, I don't know about that. It's my little thing, is all. And as I told you in the dream, I can't leave."

"I understand," Bryde said. "We are not all born to be wanderers. But the world is changing. You won't be able to stay here for much longer, not in this strangled valley."

It seemed unfair for Bryde to ask her to come with them. Bryde had warned them that leaving with him would break their worlds, and it had. But Ronan's and Hennessy's lives had already been in disarray. Rhiannon's life seemed as tidy and comfortable as a tray of newly baked cookies.

Rhiannon said uncertainly, "My great-grandfather built this house on the ruins of a house my great-great-grandfather built. My dad had turkeys in that barn. My brother, too, until he died. I raised my kids here. And I can only dream the mirrors, nothing fancier."

Bryde folded his hands behind his back as he peered into one of the mirrors (from this angle, Ronan could not see what he saw, only the top of his own head), and then he said, "There used to be a great house full of nobles who oversaw everything important and good. Because they oversaw everything important and good, everyone began to think of the men and women who lived in this great house, this mansion, this castle, this tower on the rock, as important and good, too. This has always been the way of it; those who take the credit get the credit because, as Ronan Lynch has discovered, when the world shouts, other people listen, whether or not they are right.

"These men and women in the great house were listened to in all things and no one who was not a member of this house could make law or change the hearts of men; who but a fool or a traitor would speak against the holders of everything important and good, after all? A young man who was not known to them came to the great house and asked to be made a member of this household so that he, too, could change the world, and they asked him why he felt he belonged.

"*I am a poet*, said the young man.

"*No*, they replied, *we already have a poet*.

"*I am a swordsman*, he said.

"*No*, they replied, *we already have a swordsman*.

"*I am a smith*, he said.

"*No*, they said, *we already have a smith*.

"*I am a wizard*, he said.

"*No*, they said. *We have a wizard*.

"*But*, he said, *do you have someone who is a poet and a swordsman and a smith and a wizard all at once?*

"They had to admit they did not, and so they had to let him in. And he took over the castle on the hill and changed the world."

Bryde turned back to them.

"We are that young man. All of us together. This is about your mirrors and her art and his feelings and my weapons. This is about being a poet and a smith and a wizard so they will have to let us in. People who are one thing have never known what to do with people who are more than one thing. They seize existing towers and build them higher. They make the rules. They think the people who are one thing are outliers. The people who are many things believe them. So they keep begging for entry to the great house. And the lords and the ladies keep building up the towers to keep you out. You and every other thing they cannot understand."

Rhiannon touched the corner of her eye in that fast way people do to strike away a tear. Ronan was trying to remember exactly what Bryde had said when he listed their skills. Rhiannon's mirrors, Hennessy's art, Ronan's . . . feelings? But that was not what Ronan would have said he was good at dreaming at all.

"And you, Rhiannon, have been keeping yourself small," Bryde said. "You have done well in this world because you have made yourself one thing, stayed in this place where you are one thing. And even if you never dreamed anything more than your mirrors, you would make a difference, because neither of these two dreamers can see themselves clearly without them. But you could do more. You've been dreaming with one hand tied behind your back. Ronan, tell her what it is like when there's actual power running through the ley line."

Ronan was surprised to be called on, but he was even more surprised to find he wanted to make her believe in what Bryde was saying. He wanted to be one of her mirrors, but showing her the dreaming instead of her face. He struggled. "It's—I don't know. It's French fries from the freezer section, and French fries from the county fair. They're called the same thing but they aren't. Because one of them you want to eat and the other is just a thing with the picture of the thing you want to eat on the front."

Hennessy laughed merrily.

"Would you like to contribute, Hennessy?" Bryde asked.

Hennessy stopped laughing. "You want me to convince her to leave her family?"

Bryde and Rhiannon both looked at Hennessy.

Bryde said, "Her family is dead."

They all looked at Rhiannon.

Bryde tilted the closest mirror to reflect her. They just had time to see Rhiannon's true self: face puffy with tears, mouth hopeless with grief, and then he returned it to its place, restoring her dignity.

Suddenly, the emptiness of the house seemed obvious to Ronan. It couldn't have been long, because he knew from experience it did go away eventually. It was only the first few months that everything inside the walls was still shaped like a family that no longer existed.

That framed portrait Bryde had picked up had been a snapshot of the past.

"Oh," said Hennessy. "In that case, it's like fucking Disneyland. Who wouldn't want to try it at least once."

Bryde cast a withering look at her.

Rhiannon whispered, "It just feels impossible."

"We are impossible," Bryde told her. "You have always been impossible. Tell me how you felt when you opened the door and saw it was us."

She bit her lip, thinking, but then her expression abruptly changed. "Oh, darling, you're—" Darling meant Ronan. She was gesturing to him, to his face. "You've got—"

He turned back to the mirror. Nightwash was running from his nose. This was why he had been feeling strange earlier. Because his body was betraying him again.

The mirror tried to show him the truth of the nightwash, and it made him feel even stranger. He always saw it as toxic. As defeat. As a symbol of failing to dream, of being weak far from the ley line. But the mirror said: This nightwash is from trying. This is the consequence of striving.

He didn't understand.

His head hurt.

Rhiannon had jumped up and instantly produced tissues from somewhere: It was that kind of house, she was that kind of woman. She pressed one to Ronan's face and rested a comforting hand on his back, a gesture so firmly maternal that Ronan couldn't tell if he felt ill from the nightwash or from grief.

"Is it a nosebleed?" she asked.

"Nightwash," Bryde said. "Some call it the Slip. Others the Black Dog. It has many names. It means a dreamer is in a place where there isn't much ley energy or has waited too long between dreams."

"I've never had this happen to me," Rhiannon said.

"You haven't opened the door as many times as he has," Bryde said. "He broke the hinge the moment he came through it and now it's come right off."

"Is it dangerous?" she asked.

"Very. If he doesn't get to ley energy or dream something into being, the most dangerous," Bryde said. "So we need you to make a decision."

"Bryde's right," Hennessy said abruptly. She was staring into the mirror still. "You should come with us. There's only the past here. Fuck the past."

Rhiannon worked her hands over each other. "I need more time."

Bryde looked out the window again. There was nothing to see but that gray sky. "I don't know how much time we have."

13

Ten: that was the number of times Farooq-Lane had seen Liliana the Visionary switch ages in pursuit of the perfect trap for the Potomac Zeds.

Before the Potomac Zeds had come along, the Moderators had simply pursued every Zed in every lead a Visionary had shared with them. The details of the vision were researched and located, and then the Zed was tracked and killed. That would no longer work. Lock asked the Moderators for new ideas.

Nobody had one. Nobody but Farooq-Lane.

It had come to her after they'd left the run-down museum, provoked by the image of the tree reaching through the split-open roof. A tree in a very surprising place. Several weeks before, a fortune-teller at the underground Fairy Market had hissed at her: *If you want to kill someone and keep it a secret, don't do it where the trees can see you.*

Maybe, she thought, that was how Bryde was getting his intel.

Implementing her idea was rocky at first. Visionaries weren't jukeboxes. The Moderators couldn't put a quarter in and request a vision of a Zed located in a treeless place. Visionaries were more like weather systems, and their visions were like tornadoes where the center always contained a Zed and a fiery end of the world.

Scrolling through tornadoes was impossible, but they all traded in impossibilities now.

Liliana drove herself to a vision again and again for Farooq-Lane, trying to skip ahead to a different future, a treeless future.

Nine: the number of injured civilians so far. The visions were so risky. Farooq-Lane worked out quickly that the teen version of Liliana was the most dangerous, because she hadn't yet developed any sense of when one was coming on. One minute she could be paging through blank journals in a bookstore with Farooq-Lane, and in the next—disaster.

Parsifal, the previous Visionary, hadn't cycled between ages until the very end of his timeline, when he started to lose control of his ability to turn them inward. Lock had gingerly suggested this method to a crying teen Liliana after a particularly unexpected vision had decimated a handful of nearby squirrels.

"That just sounds like slow-motion suicide," Liliana had told him.

He hadn't had an answer for her. The Moderators were always making judgment calls about whose life was worth saving and whose wasn't, and they hadn't, to this point, ever come out on the side of the Visionaries.

But Farooq-Lane had.

"It's not Liliana's fault she's dangerous," Farooq-Lane had said. "She *tries* to make sure no one else is around. I don't think we should try to convince her to turn it inward."

Lock had been dubious. "Now who's committing slow-motion suicide?"

Eight: the number of yarn shops Farooq-Lane had visited until the oldest Liliana found enough skeins in the color that she said would suit Farooq-Lane. This Liliana had a good sense of when visions were coming on, which meant time with her could be spent less on survival and more on creature comforts. Ancient Liliana was very much about domestic pleasures. Knitting! She was intent on teaching Farooq-Lane, because she *remembered* teaching her.

This was the strangest part of the oldest Liliana—she remembered a lot of what she'd already lived through, and a lot of that seemed to involve Farooq-Lane. In her past. In Farooq-Lane's future. Somewhere along their collective timelines. Thinking about it too hard hurt Farooq-Lane's brain.

"Thank you for standing up for me," the old Liliana told her once, in her precise, gentle way. "About turning the visions inward."

"Did you remember me doing that?" Farooq-Lane asked.

"It was a very long time ago. So it was a lovely surprise to be reminded. Well. Not a surprise. A gift. I knew you were a good person."

Farooq-Lane wished she'd met Liliana before she'd met the Moderators.

Seven: how many meetings the Moderators held to work out the logistics of an attack that would occur without being in the presence of a tree at any stage. A good deal of these get-togethers were devoted to debating if getting information from trees was even possible. Farooq-Lane thought disbelief was a waste of time when their quarry was also impossible.

Some of these meetings were spent discussing the Potomac Zeds. Their backgrounds, their families, their hopes and dreams. They got ahold of Jordan Hennessy's father and asked him if he had any idea where she was.

"I thought she was already dead," Bill Dower said. He sounded disappointed, if he sounded anything at all. "Huh."

They got ahold of Ronan Lynch's boyfriend's Harvard roommate.

"They broke up after he trashed our dorm," the student said in a plummy voice. "I never expected to hear his name again, honestly. What did he do now?"

They tried to find Ronan Lynch's brothers, but after the attack that had cost Bellos his arm, Declan and Matthew Lynch had gone off the radar.

"Their stuff is gone from the town house," one of the Moderators said, somewhat impressed. "Did anyone see them come back for it?"

No one had.

And no one knew a damn thing about Bryde.

Six: how many got away. Six Zeds who would have previously been targets were saved from death by their proximities to trees in Liliana's visions. Lock would have still *liked* to have killed them. But the trees would tattle their plans. Trees! They were everywhere, once you started regarding them as the enemy. Lining sidewalks. Sprouting from green islands in parking lots. Nodding at the edges of farms. For a little while it seemed like there might not ever be a vision without trees in it. Several times, Farooq-Lane had to beg them to keep their eyes on the prize. Did they all want to look like fools again?

Really, she was glad to stop killing for a bit. She hadn't counted how many deaths she'd been responsible for that year because she was worried it would be twenty-three. She and Nathan would be even Steven.

Five: how many agencies cooperated in the planning of the attack on the Pennsylvania farm. Deep in a broad valley, the closest trees were acres and acres away. Thanks to the agency coordination, the Moderators were equipped as they had never been before. Some wore noise-canceling headphones. Others wore protective goggles. There were dogs with keen noses. Trucks with keen armor. A guy with a flame-thrower. A woman with a Stinger. This might be the only chance they had to corner the Potomac Zeds. It had to count.

"No hanging back like you did the other times, Carmen," Lock said. Not cruelly, but firmly. "This is your plan. You take lead. Bring Liliana."

Farooq-Lane swung wildly between hoping she was right and fearing she was wrong. This could be the attack that ended it all.

Four: the number of Zeds in the big stone house when the Moderators broke through the door.

There was just a second to see the scene, the Potomac Zeds arranged around a formal sofa like a portrait. Rhiannon Martin, towel in hand, face shocked. Jordan Hennessy, crouched on the sofa arm like a cat. Ronan Lynch, black liquid oozing down his face, slumped against Bryde. A second to think, it worked! Well, they were *visible*, which was already an improvement.

And then Farooq-Lane glimpsed a silver orb flying toward her.

Farooq-Lane wasn't sure how she even saw it in time, but her arm was already swinging her pistol. It connected with the orb like a small baseball bat and knocked it right through the windowpane.

"Hello and fuck you," Hennessy said, pulling out a brilliantly bright sword.

Then it was chaos.

There were bursts of gunfire. Tremendous swipes of light arced through the dim hallways. Someone screamed in a very unselfconscious way. A voice rose: "Hennessy, what are you *waiting* for? Now!"

They braced themselves for a dreamt horror, but no dreamt horror came. There was just a frantic race outside as the agency woman fired the Stinger directly into the house. What ensued seemed to be an ordinary foot chase, an ordinary gun battle. How astonishing that these things had become commonplace to Farooq-Lane. How astonishing that the Zeds had not yet unleashed anything worse.

Three: the number of yards Farooq-Lane discovered were between her and Jordan Hennessy. She had been trying to find a place where she wouldn't get shot in the cross fire—she dimly suspected some of the Moderators might take pleasure in the excuse—and had been pressed against the barn, which still smelled of the turkeys that had lived and died in it. She had no idea where Liliana was. Everything was masks and riot shields and faceless agents like a war zone.

But there was Jordan Hennessy, staring up at two figures moving through the commotion: Bryde and Ronan Lynch. The first dragging the second. Ronan Lynch's face was still streaming that black ooze, and even from here, Farooq-Lane could see his chest heaving for air. They were being rounded on by Moderators, but Bryde was keeping them at bay with a sunfire sword, one of the two weapons they'd used to get away on the banks of the Potomac.

Its mate, the starfire blade, rested securely in one of Jordan Hennessy's hands just a few yards from Farooq-Lane, its blade dripping moonlight and malice.

Jordan Hennessy's eyes glittered with fury as she surveyed the scene.

Farooq-Lane was surprised to feel terror. It liquefied her knees, loosened her fingers. The Zed hadn't seen her there crouched in the shadow of the turkey house, but she would if Farooq-Lane tried to lift her gun. And Farooq-Lane knew what that sword did. She'd have less of an arm than Bellos before she could even scream.

"Hennessy!" Bryde shouted. "Now, if ever!"

Two: seconds before the nightmare appeared.

In the first second, Hennessy put a little bit of dark cloth over her eyes—oh, it was a mask, Farooq-Lane saw it was a mask now, she'd forgotten the Zeds used them at the previous attack—and slumped to the ground in instant sleep.

After the next second, as Farooq-Lane lifted her gun to shoot the sleeping Zed, there was the nightmare.

It was hell. It was shape. It was non-shape. It was form. It was non-form. It was checkered and growing, it was shriveled and grasping. Farooq-Lane didn't want to look at it, but she wasn't going to look away. There was not much of it, and even though it didn't seem to have a proper body, there was a distinct feeling that it was . . . abbreviated. There was supposed to be more of it. It was severed. Partial.

And it hated Jordan Hennessy.

The hate was bigger than anything else about it. Farooq-Lane could hear it like a battle cry and a sob.

But Jordan Hennessy didn't lift a finger to shield herself. She was frozen on the ground, mask slid to the side, eyes horrified and miserable. The star sword sputtered beside her in the grass, throwing moonbeams a few inches here and there.

It was clear that whatever the Zed had intended to bring from a dream, this was not it. This thing wanted to kill Jordan Hennessy.

Farooq-Lane should have let it.

But instead, she leapt forward and seized the star sword. She only had a moment to feel the warmth of its hilt, the glory of its purpose, the strangeness of its power, and then she sliced through the nightmare with the blade.

There was a silent shudder as the nightmare splintered.

Farooq-Lane slashed again, and again. This weapon drove it back so completely that it seemed to have been *made* to drive it back. To decimate it. She slashed and slashed, until the final tiny scrap of the nightmare somehow managed to dart through the wall into the turkey house.

Inside, the animals screamed and screamed, and then everything was silent.

"Visionary!" howled another voice. A Moderator, Ramsay.

Farooq-Lane's gaze found Ramsay standing beside one of the armored cars. She followed his gaze. On the porch, Rhiannon Martin crouched behind a concrete planter that danced with red laser points. If there had been a clear shot, she'd have been dead long before. Liliana stood beside her in teen form, her long elegant fingers pressed to her teeth in agony, tears glistening on her cheeks.

"Visionary!" shouted Ramsay again.

A red laser point danced across Liliana's hands. Ramsay was pointing the gun at *her.*

"*Ramsay!*" shouted Farooq-Lane.

"You wanna live?" Ramsay shouted at Liliana. Lock was watching him. Not stopping him. "Have a vision! *Now!*"

Death by Visionary. Make Liliana kill the unreachable Zed. So damn clever. *So* damn clever.

Liliana was too far away for Farooq-Lane to hear, but she saw her shoulders heave with apocalyptic sobs. She was mouthing, *I'm sorry I'm sorry I'm sorry,* and everything in Rhiannon Martin's maternal body language was saying back, *It's okay, I understand.*

Farooq-Lane saw the moment Rhiannon Martin steeled herself, and then the Zed stood up from behind the planter, arms by her side. She faced Ramsay without flinching.

We're the villains, Farooq-Lane thought.

Ramsay shot Rhiannon Martin in the head.

One: the number of people Farooq-Lane didn't hate in that entire place.

Liliana threw her arms over her eyes as her shoulders shook. She needed someone on her side. She needed Farooq-Lane.

Everything was going wrong.

Too late, Farooq-Lane realized that Jordan Hennessy was no longer paralyzed on the ground beside her. She was up, she was running.

A suddenly visible car raced toward her, flattening the grass, its rear door hanging open. Through the open door, Farooq-Lane saw that Bryde was driving. Ronan Lynch's body was prone across the backseat. Not particularly vital-looking.

Jordan Hennessy threw herself through the open door into the car.

"Someone stop it!" shouted someone. Maybe Lock.

Hennessy locked eyes with Farooq-Lane just before she slammed the door shut.

The car vanished as if it had never been there.

Zero: Zed. 0.

No more, thought Farooq-Lane. *No more.*

14

Matthew thought something might have happened to Ronan.

He and Declan had just trespassed into a Harvard dorm building. Matthew didn't realize at first that they *were* trespassing. He hadn't paid much attention to how Declan approached the old brick dorm twice. First, just walking by, seeming to give the propped-open door no more or less interest than anything else in the cool midnight-blue-and-gold Cambridge evening. Second, after shedding his suit coat in the car and running his fingers through his curls until they were boyish and messy, returning to push through the door into the warm red-and-brown interior.

Inside, a haphazard line of college students led up a flight of stairs. Declan flippantly patted the shoulder of the closest with the back of his hand. "Hey. This the line for—?"

Matthew was startled to hear his brother's voice. Instead of his usual sales-speak monotone, he sounded like one of the guys. He'd even changed how he stood. Previously alert and suspicious, he was now casual and inattentive, gaze pulled to a knot of pretty girls in the hall, then to his phone, then back to the student in line.

"The card thing, yeah," the student replied. "It's going fast."

Declan joined the line and began to type away on his phone in his peculiar way, thumb and forefinger. He did not explain himself to Matthew. Perhaps he didn't think he needed to. Perhaps a normal person would have guessed what they were doing there. Had Ronan dreamt Matthew to be an idiot? Ever since he'd found out he was dreamt, he'd been trying to think about things more like a real person, more like a grown-up, but it made his head hurt.

"Don't pick your nails," Declan murmured without looking up from his phone.

Matthew stopped picking his nails. They climbed a few stairs at a time. The student was right; the line went fast. Some of the students coming down the stairs were crying. There were no other clues to where the line might be headed.

It was when they were nearly to the top of the stairs that Matthew began to feel a little weird.

Not a lot weird. Maybe he was just sleepy. It was just . . . as they reached the head of the line, he avoided stepping on a discarded candy bar wrapper on the final stair, and for a second, he thought he was stepping over a brightly colored lily instead.

Nope nope nope, Matthew thought. *Gonna be okay here.*

By the time he pulled himself together, he realized what the wait was for: Adam Parrish. The stairs led to a tiny solarium, a wizard's lofty lair thrust high over the quaint dark roofs of Cambridge. The haphazard arrangement of tables, chairs, and halogen lamps suggested that many students over many years had composed it. It smelled comfortingly old, like the Barns. Adam sat at a table right in the middle of it, looking gaunt and poised as he always did, his long hands parallel-parked on the edge of the table. On the table in front of him was a stack of tarot cards and a mug stuffed with bills and gift cards. In a chair near him was a gloriously large student wearing a sweater vest Matthew quite liked the look of.

"Hello," Declan said.

Adam's tone was dry. "Everyone in your family likes to make a surprise entrance, don't they?"

Declan smiled blandly and tapped the side of his phone on the table, glancing around at the surroundings with the same judgmental gaze he used when double-checking Matthew's room-cleaning abilities.

"Fletcher," Adam said, "would you let the line know that we're done for the night?"

The other student pushed out of a chair and, waving his own phone, said, "Of course. You should know Gillian's still going on about break. That'll be the topic of debate."

"I'll be down in a minute."

They were left discreetly alone.

"Aglionby would be so proud to see you using all your talents here at Harvard," Declan said. He turned over the top card of the deck. The writing on the bottom read *Seven of Swords*, but the art was too wiggly and complicated for Matthew to focus on.

"Aglionby would be proud to see two of its students here at Harvard at the same time," Adam replied evenly.

"I see you lost your accent."

"I see you lost your jacket."

This all felt like a conversation in another language, one that Matthew would never speak. He couldn't give too much thought to that, however, because suddenly he felt *really* weird.

His head went weird first, then his legs. His head felt sluggish, but his legs felt the opposite. That walky feeling usually meant he was about to forget what he was doing and end up someplace entirely different.

Nope, he told his legs. *Be like a normal person.*

Declan and Adam had moved on from whatever they'd been

talking about and were instead talking about Declan being a bit of a gossip sensation, according to Adam's latest conversation with Mr. Gray, the Lynch son calling in favors and making himself useful in the market, going legit for a year. Rumor was people were courting him for jobs. Were they? Matthew couldn't tell if he should have been able to tell that by Declan's constant brisk texting and phone calls.

"Even if that were true," Declan said, "I'm not getting into that world."

Adam laughed in a hollow way. "You aren't in it already?"

Declan didn't flinch, and for the first time, Matthew thought he might be seeing the situation in a complicated, real, grown-up way. Because when he looked at Declan's blank, businesslike expression, he thought about how he could have just taken it at face value. But instead he saw how, if he squinted, he could see a little tension around Declan's lips, a little tilt to his chin. He saw how this secret language showed that his older brother was both flattered and tempted by the statement.

"The other rumor is that Ronan is into some kind of bioweapons," Adam said, and for the first time, a little wrinkle appeared in between his fair eyebrows, making him look more like the boy Matthew knew from before. "Leading Moderators on a merry chase with capital-U Unexplained weaponry."

In a bland voice, Declan asked, "Have you spoken to him recently?"

Instead of answering, Adam replied, "Do you know anything about Bryde yet?"

Then Matthew lost a bit of time, which he only realized because when he next came to, he was sitting in a chair by the window with no recollection of how he'd gotten there. Adam was standing close to Declan and they were muttering in low voices. One of them was saying *Matthew*.

"Matthew, seriously," Declan said. "Wake up."

Once Declan had spoken, Matthew realized the voice saying *Matthew* before hadn't been Declan's voice. It had been that voice he sometimes heard when he lost himself. The voice he sought when he threw himself into the security system at the end of the driveway.

Matthew blinked up at Declan. He was so frustrated that he couldn't follow his conversation with Adam. It seemed like a very important, grown-up conversation. He tried to recapture the mindset that had allowed him to decode Declan's expression before, but it all felt too complex.

"He looks strange," Adam said. Then he seemed to realize this was rude, because he directed his next question at Matthew. "What's wrong with you?"

"This is what happens when your life is tied to my brother's," Declan said. "God knows what he's up to."

Because the problem wasn't truly with Matthew. He was like this because of a problem with his *dreamer*.

"Is he normally this bad?"

No. He wasn't usually this bad unless . . .

Declan said, "Matthew. Matthew. *Matthew*."

Matthew.

The wizard's tower and the wizard's tarot cards and the wizard himself were melting away. All of Matthew's thoughts were melting away.

Wherever Ronan was, he was in deep trouble.

15

Hennessy always dreamt of the Lace.

Left to her own devices, it was always the Lace.

Nightwash and blood and a barn full of dead turkeys behind them, nightwash and blood and a night full of desperation before them, because Hennessy couldn't dream of anything but the Lace.

The nearly invisible car burst through the night as Bryde tersely directed her down one road and then another and then another. Ronan was silent in the backseat. Every once in a while, she glanced over her shoulder to see if he'd died. Hard to tell. He was sprawled exactly as he had been thrown before. Dying people and dead people looked very similar.

"Maybe it's too late," she said.

Bryde's voice was thin as wire. "I would know if it's too late. Turn here."

She wondered if she would feel sad if Ronan died. Angry. Something. Because right now she didn't feel anything at all. She didn't care where they were going. She didn't care if he was dead when they got there. She didn't care if Bryde lost patience with her and left her standing by the roadside. She didn't care if Jordan was angry that she hadn't called to let her know how things were. Nothing felt like it would be particularly good or bad, except for sleeping an empty sleep, free of the Lace, free of everything. Empty sleep forever, never waking up. Not death, because that would ruin Jordan's life. Just endless empty pause. That would be good.

"Left, left," Bryde said. "Hurry up. Stop over there. This will have to do."

Hennessy didn't feel much in the way of any ley energy, but she followed his directions. Burrito lumped down a dark, unpaved road that dead-ended at a small ridge overgrown with stringy, limp grass. The headlights glinted off water beyond it.

"Help me drag him," Bryde said.

Ronan looked dreadful, awash with black, slumped in the backseat of the invisible car. It wasn't the oozing nightwash that made him look bad, though. It was the slackness of his face. The stiffness. He already looked dead.

"What about his chicken?" Hennessy asked. His raven was a small pile of unmoving feathers.

"Leave her," Bryde said. "Bring your mask."

Her mask. She never wanted to see it again. "So it's a Lace dream you're after having?"

"We don't have time for petulance," Bryde said. He was more agitated than Hennessy had ever seen him. "Imagine you were lost in your Lace, and there was no one to find you, ever. That is where he is. Deep. We might not get him back, even if there's enough ley power to reverse the nightwash. Do you understand? He won't have any use for this body the way he is now. He just goes out and out and out, a ball of yarn thrown into space."

"Still don't get why you need me, mate."

"He'll be drawn to you more than to me."

"That would be a first in the history of the world."

Bryde snapped, "If he dies, this is the last time you'll see him and then all of this was for nothing."

Hennessy brought her mask.

Hennessy dreamt of the Lace.

She dreamt of the Lace, its checkered edge, its simmering hate, and then—

She was climbing through the dark.

The Lace was gone. It was gone so thoroughly it was difficult to remember it had ever been there.

Instead there was the dark, and there was a full moon right above her, bigger than any moon she'd ever seen before. She couldn't see its face but it seemed upset.

She was climbing.

It was too dark to see what she was climbing over, but she could feel rocks and stones sliding beneath her feet.

She was not alone.

She was aware of a companion making their way beside her, although she could not see them. She could hear their process, though, the scrabble and skitter of feet on the rocks. Her companion seemed lighter than her, different than her, although the sound might have been distorted by the hidden landscape. It seemed more like a body hopping and flapping, talons or claws finding purchase before lifting off. But it could not be a bird, she thought, because a bird would fly. Unless it was just suffering alongside her to be companionable, she thought. To appear more like her.

She didn't know where they were going, apart from up, where it was a little lighter. She could see it, a suggestion of gray. Not dawn, but the promise of dawn, the best that dawn could do in the current situation.

Up. Up. Up they went and her legs were heavy, but it felt crucial to get out of the dark. It was getting lighter up ahead, she thought, light enough that she thought the sky might even have some pink to it. Light enough she thought she might see an edge to the bare rock they climbed.

The edge was just shattered enough to remind her of—

"I know this is not my dream," Hennessy said. "Because it doesn't have—"

"Don't say that name here," her companion said. "That is not what the dream is about. Who are we looking for? This is important. I'm not going to help you remember."

"Ronan," she said.

The black clung to them as they climbed. It was everywhere. Nightwash.

Yes, she remembered.

"You can do it," her companion said. "You are not different when awake and when asleep."

Hennessy remembered a little more. "Rhiannon Martin would think differently. Your optimism in me, bruv, killed her. How's that feel?"

Her companion said nothing, climbing in the dark. Scrabble and claw, flap and click. It put her in mind of Chainsaw, Ronan's raven.

"I would dream it away, if I could," Hennessy said. "I would wake up without it. Just walk away."

"You insult her death," Bryde said, because now it was certainly his voice. "You insult what we're trying to do."

The sky above them lightened still more. It was becoming

that complicated pink and gold and red and blue that sunrises can be without conflict. There was a definite line to the summit now, a jagged edge that would mark the end of their climb. It looked like the Lace, but Hennessy didn't say it out loud.

"You say the lines are getting worse," Hennessy said. "You're saying the dreaming is worse. But it's the same for me. It's always looked like this. It keeps looking like this. How many dead dreamers you want with my name on them?"

Now it was light enough that he had come into view beside her, his silhouette climbing, face pensive. He was a peculiar-looking person, she thought. Most people could be put into this pile or another. So-and-so reminds me of whatsherface, one says. This dude is this sort of person. Oh, they're *that* kind of a person. But what was Bryde? Bryde. Party of one. If he reminded her of anything, he reminded her of . . . the resemblance slipped away.

Bryde said, "Get better, then."

"*Get better*, he says, bread-and-jam, easy. You're a real ass, did you know? When have you ever failed at anything?"

"You've been at this for weeks," he said. "Do you know how old I am?"

There was something a little dangerous about the question. Hennessy couldn't tell if it was dangerous to answer it correctly or dangerous to answer it incorrectly, though. Eventually, she said, "Older than Ronan thinks."

"Yes," Bryde said.

Now it was possible to see they were headed toward a great hollow stump, a tree that must have been enormous when it was alive. But then Hennessy remembered: It *was* alive. It was the tree from West Virginia, transplanted. Ilidorin.

"Yes," Bryde said again, and he sounded tired. "Older than he imagines."

The tree grew from bare, dark rock on a precipice that jutted high above a vast and glittering pink-orange-yellow-blue ocean. The sea below looked cold and ancient, the barely audible waves breaking slow and sure. Everything was still black where the sun had not yet reached.

It was beautiful, and Hennessy hated it. She hated it, or she hated herself.

That one.

"Self-hatred is an expensive hobby paid for by other people," Bryde said. "Look. Here he is."

Ronan was in the tree. Or rather, *a* Ronan was inside the tree. The Ronan inside the tree was dressed in black, curled inside the hollow, his arms crossed over each other, his posture undeniably the same as Ronan in the real world. But this Ronan was old. Well, older. Grizzled. This Ronan had walked and walked through this world. His cheeks were hard and chiseled beneath scrubby shadow. Deep crow lines formed around his eyes from decades of laughing and frowning into the sun. His shaved head had grown out just enough to show that his temples were gray, same as the hair that shadowed his jaw. There was one thick trail of nightwash that oozed from one of his closed eyes, but two tiny mice the size of walnuts were furiously working away at it with their paws and their tongues.

Old. Older than he imagines.

Hennessy wanted to say something to cut the moment, but she couldn't. She was so angry, so tangled in the grips of this wild ocean, this distant sunrise, this lightening peak, this wearied

Ronan from another time curled in an ancient tree. *Why did it have to be this way?* she kept thinking. *Why did* she *have to be this way?*

She longed for the Hennessy in the car, the one who thought she didn't care about anything. What a splendid liar she was. She cared about *everything.*

After the mice were done, they scurried away into the darkness of the hollow of the tree, leaving Ronan motionless in the protective curve of the stump.

"Come back, Ronan," Bryde said softly. "The nightwash will not have you this time."

Silence. Just the barely heard sound of that slow, old ocean down below.

"Ronan Lynch," Hennessy said.

Ronan's eyes opened.

They were his eyes after all, bright blue and intense.

He looked at them both, this young, old Ronan.

"No more playing," he said. He sounded tired. "We save the ley lines."

16

Declan had been told a long time ago that he had to know what he wanted, or he'd never get it. Not by his father, because his father would have never delivered such pragmatic advice in such a pragmatic way. No, even if Niall Lynch believed in the sentiment, he would have wrapped it up in a long story filled with metaphor and magic and nonsense riddles. Only years after the storytelling would Declan be sitting somewhere and realize that all along Niall had been trying to teach him to balance his checkbook, or whatever the tale had ever really been about. Niall could never just say the thing.

No, this piece of advice—*You have to know what you want, or you'll never get it*—was given to Declan by a senator from Nevada he'd met during a DC field trip back in eighth grade. The other children had been bored by the pale stone restraint of the city and the sameness of the law and government offices they toured. Declan, however, had been fascinated. He'd asked the senator what advice he had for those looking to get into politics.

"Come from money," the senator had said first, and then when all the eighth graders and their teachers had stared without laughing, he added, "You have to know what you want, or you'll never get it. Make goals."

Declan made goals. The goal was DC. The goal was politics. The goal was structure, and more structure, and yet more structure. He took AP classes on political science and policy. When he traveled with his father to black markets, he wrote papers. When he took calls from gangsters and shady antique auction houses, he arranged drop-offs near DC and wrangled meetings with HR people. Aglionby Academy made calls and pulled strings; he got names, numbers, internships. All was going according to plan. His father inconveniently got murdered, but Declan pressed on. His father's will conveniently left him a town house adjacent to DC. Declan pressed on. He kept his brothers alive; he graduated; he moved to DC.

He made the goal, he went toward the goal.

When he took his first lunch meeting with his new boss, he found himself filled with the same anticipation he'd had as an eighth grader. This was the place, he thought, where things happened. Just across the road was the Mexican embassy. Behind him was the IMF. GW Law School was a block away. The White House, the USPS, the Red Cross, all within a stone's throw.

This was before he understood there was no *making it* for him. He came from money, yeah, but the wrong kind of money. Niall Lynch's clout was not relevant in this daylight world; he only had status in the night. And one could not rise above that while remaining invisible to protect one's dangerous brother.

On that first day of work, Declan walked into the Renwick Gallery and stood inside an installation that had taken over the second floor around the grand staircase. Tens of thousands of black threads had been installed at points all along the ceiling, tangling around the Villareal LED sculpture that normally lit the room, snarling the railing over the stairs, blocking out the light from the tall arches that bordered the walls, turning the walkways into dark, confusing rabbit tunnels. Museumgoers had to pick their way through with caution lest they be snared and bring the entire world down with them.

He had, bizarrely, felt tears burning the corners of his eyes.

Before that, he hadn't understood that his goals and what he wanted might not be the same thing.

This was where he'd found art.

Declan stood in the small Isabella Stewart Gardner Museum in Boston, looking at John Singer Sargent's *El Jaleo*. The dim room, the so-called Spanish Cloister, was long and skinny. The walls were colorful with complicated Mexican tiles and lined with stone fountains and basins. *El Jaleo* was the only painting in the room, hung in a shallow alcove framed by a Moorish arch. Antique pots rested around its base, tricking the viewer into believing themselves part of the scene in the painting. A cunning mirror stole light from the hall and threw it subtly on the canvas. Gardner had renovated this room especially for *El Jaleo*, and every part of it was an extension of the painting's mood.

The larger a piece of art was, the farther away one was generally meant to stand from it, so Declan was not directly in front of the canvas but rather standing four yards off. He was just looking at it. He had been looking at it for ten minutes. He would probably look at it for another ten minutes.

A tear prickled his eye.

"A man in Florence once had a heart attack when he saw the *Birth of Venus*, if you can believe it," said a voice beside him. "Palpitations are more common, though. That's what Stendhal had. Couldn't walk, he reported, after seeing a particularly moving work of art. And Jung! Jung decided it was too dangerous to visit Pompeii in his old age because the feeling—the feeling of all that art and history round him, it might kill him. Jerusalem . . . Tourists in Jerusalem sometimes wrap themselves in hotel bedsheets. To become works of art themselves, you know? Part of history. A collective unconscious toga party. One lady in the holy city decided she was giving birth to God's son. She wasn't even pregnant, before you ask. Funny what art will do to you. Stendhal Syndrome, they call it, after our lad with the palpitations, though I prefer its more modern name: Declan Lynch."

"Hello, Jordan," Declan said.

He stood there for a space with Jordan Hennessy, both of them looking at the painting. *El Jaleo* was both dark and luminous. In it, a Spanish dancer twisted through a dark room. Behind her, guitarists twisted round their instruments and onlookers clapped her on. It was all black and brown except for the striking white of the dancer and the flushed red in details. In person it was obvious how much rigor had been put into the contorted dancer and how little had been devoted to the musicians and the background, forcing the viewer's attention onto her, only her. The entire work looked effortless, if one didn't know better. (Declan knew better.)

"You're my prospective punter, aren't you?" Jordan asked. "I should have known. Mr. Pozzi of South Boston."

Declan said, "How do you find a forger? Be in the market for a forgery."

"Pozzi's on the nose, don't you think?"

Samuel-Jean Pozzi was the subject of one of John Singer Sargent's most dramatic portraits, a full-length glory featuring his friend Dr. Pozzi, a well-known dandy and OB-GYN, in a blazing red dressing gown. Declan had feared using it as a name when contacting Jordan for a forgery might give the game away, but the potential reward of looking clever was too great a temptation.

"You didn't guess it, did you?" Declan lifted his red scarf from his collar. "I'm wearing this scarf in his honor."

"Cadmium red," Jordan said. "Slightly toxic but little risk if handled well. Before I forget—"

She handed him the keys to his stolen car.

"Did you remember it takes premium?"

"Crumbs, I knew I forgot something. I did top up the wiper fluid."

"Where is it?"

"A lady never tells." She grinned at him. Then she stepped as close to the painting as she was permitted, bending at the waist to study the brushstrokes, graceful as one of Degas's dancers. Her grin tugged wider as she guessed, correctly, that he was looking at her. Straightening, she lifted her arm and twisted her body, pulling herself into a perfect imitation of *El Jaleo*'s dancer. There was nothing like the sound of a museum, and the Gardner was no exception. The murmur of other patrons in the adjacent courtyard, the sound of footsteps echoing in hallways, the respectful whispers. Jordan Hennessy was art in front of art in a room that was art in a building that was art in a life that was art, and Declan told himself he had only come here to get his car back.

Foolish Declan smirked; Paranoid Declan sneered.

Paranoid Declan lost. Foolish Declan said, in an even tone, "You never finished my portrait. Seems unprofessional to just leave a client hanging like that."

Jordan nodded. "And now you want a refund."

"A refund won't fill that hole on my wall."

"It'd take multiple sittings. It might be ugly along the way before it's all said and done."

"I trust your expertise."

She tapped her fingertips together absently. She didn't look at him. "You know at the end of the day, it's still a portrait, right? Just a copy of your face. No matter how well it turns out, that's never changing. Just a copy."

Declan said, "I'm perfecting my understanding of art more every day."

Jordan frowned then—or at least she stopped smiling, which for her was as good as a frown. "What would you say if I told you I'd found a way to keep dreams awake?"

"I would wait for the punch line."

"What if I told you this painting would keep Matthew awake if something happened to Ronan? That it had dream energy in it?"

Declan didn't answer right away, because a trio of women entered the room, along with a docent. The four of them took an agonizing amount of time looking at the painting and taking photos in front of it and then asking the docent questions about the landscaping before they all trooped into the next room.

He glanced to be sure they were out of earshot, then glanced to see that Matthew was still sitting on the bench in the courtyard, looking at the flowers. Finally, he said, "I don't think I'd say anything. I'd listen."

And he did, quietly, as she pressed one of her hands into his shoulder to lean close and whisper everything she'd learned about the sweetmetals into his ear. She whispered how she'd realized that they were all art, and she whispered that perhaps this was why she felt so at home in museums. She whispered that this might be why she had been so drawn to John Singer Sargent in particular, and she whispered that she had decided to go to the most famous Sargent in Boston to see if it was a sweetmetal.

"And it is," Declan said.

They looked at the painting in question. Neither said anything for a space. They just listened to the sound of both of them breathing and looking at the painting.

Jordan asked, "If you were me, what would you do next?"

He whispered: "Steal it."

She laughed with delight, and he memorized the sound.

"It's a shame you have mixed feelings about crime, Pozzi," Jordan said, "because I'm pretty sure you were made for it. But don't you think the Gardner's been looted enough?"

"So what *are* you going to do?"

"I think . . . I think I'm gonna find out how they were made," Jordan said. "And if I can, I'm gonna try to make one."

She looked at him. He looked at her.

Declan could feel all his previous goals wandering even further away from him, all of them seeming silly and arbitrary now, the childhood dreams of a kid looking for stability, wishing upon a star that later turned out to be a satellite.

"Say you'll stay in Boston," she said.

You have to know what you want, or you'll never get it.

"I'll stay in Boston," he said.

17

Ronan thought: *This is what I was made for, probably.*

The three dreamers sat shoulder to shoulder, looking down at the Pennsylvanian landscape below, the wind buffeting them hard. Mountain ridges and valleys looked like fingers had pinched the landscape in places and thumbprinted it in others. A broad river moved northwest to southeast. A smaller river came in from west to east, curled back on itself in rippling serpentine that reminded him of the black snake they'd found at the museum. Farms were cut into rectangles that butted up against wild dark forests. Roads were fine white hairs across it all, like parasitic worms in a dish. From this height, humans were invisible.

"What do you feel?" Bryde asked.

Free. Trapped. Alive. Guilty. Powerful. Powerless. Ronan felt everything but the ley line.

Hennessy sighed.

Bryde said, "Saving the ley lines is about seeing the pattern. It's hard to see the pattern when you're in it, but humans do the same things again and again; they are not that complicated. In a pair, they are individuals. Unique. Unlike. If you have half a dozen, two or three will remind you of each other. By the time you have one hundred, two hundred, you see types repeated again and again. Place two types together; they react a certain way. Place them with a different type; they react a different but equally predictable way. Humans form into groups along the same lines again and again; they fracture into smaller groups along other predictable lines again and again. One hundred and fifty, Dunbar's number. That is how many connections humans can support before things begin to fall apart and remake. Again, again. Humans dance as elegantly as clockwork stars move across the sky, but they do not see it because they *are* the stars."

They were very far up. Thousands of meters, feet dangling, pressed together on the dreamt hoverboard, cheeks burning with cold, lungs burning with the thinness of the air. The wind moved them this way and that; they were only in danger of falling if they completely resisted the flow. They were not in a dream but it *felt* like a dream, and for the first time, Ronan felt a little like he understood how Bryde could say there were not two of him.

Bryde continued. "The nonhuman world has patterns, too. Look at the veins of a leaf, your hand, a tree, gold through rock, a river headed to sea, lightning. And again, again, not just in the visible, but also the invisible. In airflow, particles, sound waves, ley lines, too, veining across this poor, battered home of ours. Again, again, again. Everything predicts everything else. Everything affects everything else."

Ronan felt Hennessy shiver. He leaned his skull against her skull, and without pause or snark, she leaned back.

"It doesn't take much to disrupt the pattern. Look at that river there. Over the years, silt has built up along its banks, which slows it. And as it slows, it becomes less able to move the silt, so it slows further, so there is even more silt, and so it slows even more. As it slows, the river twists harder away from the obstacle, looking for the path of least resistance. Twist, slow, twist, slow, until the curves are so tight that it becomes just a bent lake here and then a small pond there and then finally the water's driven below ground. This, too, is what happens to the ley lines."

Ronan could almost imagine it. The glowing energy of the ley line glistening across the landscape below, pulsing beneath the mountains, seeping into the rivers. Everything had felt obvious and connected in his last dream, when he was curled inside Ilidorin, and some of that connectivity lingered.

"Slowly the ley lines get shut down one by one by electricity and roads and trash and noise and noise and noise and noise." Bryde sucked in a deep breath. "Which is why we dreamers are forced to go from vein to vein as they collapse behind us."

"So a dreamer's just a parasite," Hennessy said. "We're nothing without them."

"Is your brain a parasite?" Bryde asked.

"Yes," she said immediately.

"Your lungs, your kidneys, your hands? Your heart pumps blood through your entire body. Take away the blood and things begin to fail. Does that make the brain lesser than the blood? The left hand a servant to the veins that power it? We need the ley line. The ley line needs us. The world needs us. Eventually, if we all die—and we *are* dying, some more quickly than others—so the rest will go. Our passing, a symptom of a bigger disease."

"And if we fix the ley lines?" Ronan asked. "The disease goes away?"

Bryde didn't answer right away. He let the wind buffet him; that was the way to keep from being knocked off the board. To bend, not break. Then he said, "A healthy body can withstand illness. Can live alongside it. A world full of ley energy doesn't support dreamers and dreams only along the lines any more than a healthy body is only vital directly along the veins. It is vital from head to toe. Brain and lungs, kidney and hands. Fix the ley lines, and dreamers and dreams simply exist wherever they like."

A world where Matthew could just live.

A world where Ronan could just dream.

A world where every dream was clear and crisp and easy to navigate, so there were never accidents or nightmares.

He wanted it.

It had been so long since he'd wanted something to happen, instead of wanting something to *not* happen. He'd forgotten what it felt like. It was equal parts great and terrible. It burned.

"Restoring the ley lines is a game of dominos," Bryde said. "If we addressed each domino separately, we would never be done. Dominos would be set back up as soon as we turned our backs. And we'd be stopped before we were anywhere close to done. But instead we focus only on the dominos that will knock over many others."

"Cool metaphor," Ronan said. "What are the dominos?"

"You already know," Bryde said dismissively. "All the obstacles blocking ley energy. Human noise."

"And what is 'knocking them over'?" Hennessy said. "Please tell me it's blowing shit up."

"Sometimes," Bryde admitted. "Often."

Hennessy made a contented noise.

"Do other people get hurt?" Ronan asked.

Bryde hesitated for only a second. "Not if we are creating nuanced solutions instead of hammering our way through. We're dreamers. We can step lightly."

"What's the first domino?" Ronan asked.

"That's not the right question," Bryde said. "Always ask, 'What do we do last?' And then you work toward that. The man who thinks step by step sees only his feet. Eyes up. What do we want?"

"Save the ley lines."

"Step back from that," Bryde said. "What's one step back from that?"

Ronan thought. "Save Ilidorin's ley line."

"One step back from that?"

Ronan was once again curled in Ilidorin, connected to everything. A thrill chilled him as he said, "The dam."

"Yes," Bryde said. "But there are steps between us and that still, too. There's no point moving the dam without freeing up the tributaries first. Why throw the switch with no lamps plugged in? First we have to remove obstacles from farther down the line and adjacent lines. Ilidorin's line will be the first and the hardest. But it is a fine domino. It will knock over many others after for us. Hennessy, you're quiet."

A thin gray cloud passed between them and the world below. The patchwork fields disappeared and reappeared.

"You don't bloody need me," she said.

"Don't tell me what I need," Bryde said.

"I couldn't do anything back there. I couldn't dream a weapon because there was no one to hold my hand. Ronan Lynch here can do anything I could do and lots I can't. Just cut me loose."

Bryde didn't say, *What about the Lace?* because he rarely mentioned the Lace out loud unless he had to. He was just quiet for a very long time and then he said, "I won't drag you."

But Ronan would.

He snarled, "Get over yourself, princess."

"What?" she demanded, shocked.

"Just say you want to do something easier if that's what you mean, but don't play the boo-hoo card. Oh, me! My whole family got shot, I'm not going to cope, please beg me to stay and make me feel good."

Hennessy twisted as much as she dared to stare at him. "You're a real piece of work."

Ronan smiled meanly at her. Somehow he'd just jumped straight to nastiness, but it was too late to rein it back now. "I saved your life. You owe me."

"I saved yours. That's what we call 'even.'"

"You want to give Jordan a call and let her know you gave up, then?" He couldn't stop. Acid kept pouring out of him. "You're setting a timer again, you're living life in twenty-minute chunks of sleep denial, whatever, sleep deprivation again? Hey, Jordan, they died for nothing, can I crash with you? Thanks."

Her expression didn't change but he watched her swallow, the tattooed roses at her throat shimmering ever so slightly with the movement.

"And when I bring out all the Lace and blow up the world?"

Bryde said, "We won't let that happen."

"Ah, but you did, bro. Only reason why there wasn't more Lace was 'cause there wasn't enough ley for it, was there? I actually got the Lace out *and* got our boy here closer to dead at the same time. I multitasked like a mother."

She was going to leave them. Ronan could tell she was. He could see every bit of her was ready to give up. Could they do it without her? Maybe. Probably. But somehow the idea of saving ley lines with just Bryde was awful to imagine. Awful like a thunderstorm. Awful. Aweful. Ronan couldn't think about it too hard, because it made him feel like flinging himself from the hoverboard just to see what would happen. What was real? Falling? Dying? Flying? They were floating a thousand feet above the ground. Real? In a dream there would be no consequence.

Ronan was just as frightened to feel this impulse in himself as he was by the idea of saving the ley lines with just Bryde.

"Why do you even care?" Hennessy asked. "The truth. Not more shithead talk."

He could feel the impulse to pour more acid, but he held it back. He watched his raven circle far below them, in and out of the clouds.

His voice, when he spoke, was barely audible against the wind. "I don't know. I just do."

It wasn't a very good answer, but it was the truth.

Hennessy said, "Fine. Whatever. But don't say I didn't tell you."

Ronan's heart was beating hard again. It was like the rush he got when the masks came out, when he knew they were going to dream, only it was so much bigger than that. They were going to change the world. They were going to change their worlds. There was no going back. Was he doing this? He must be. What had he been made for, if not for this?

Bryde said, "Then we begin where I left off."

18

Jordan couldn't really fathom what it was to be great at art.

Other people told her she was great at art all the time. They gasped over how quickly she could pencil a likeness. The ease with which she mixed pigments. The confidence of her brushstrokes. And it wasn't that she didn't understand why they said it. The canvases she turned out were impressive. Her grasp of technique was notable at her age. Her ability to paint what she saw before her at speed was unusual.

But she was simply aping other people's greatness.

It wasn't that she was incapable of greatness. It was possible (probable?) she had the aptitude for it. She had a very good grasp of art theory. She knew how to lead the viewer's eye around a canvas in just the order she intended. She knew how to subtract and add elements to make the eye linger or flit. She knew which colors warmed a subject closer and which cooled objects into the background. She knew how light glowed on glass, on metal, on grass, on cloth. She knew which of her paints were lean and which were fat, she knew how much turpentine to add to get the stroke she wanted, she knew what value problems varnish would and wouldn't fix. She knew all the fiddly math and science that made art and emotion work on a good canvas. Jordan had the prerequisites to be a great artist.

But she was not a great artist. She was a great technician.

Being in the presence of paintings like *El Jaleo* and *Jordan in*

White only drove this home. They weren't great because they were technically perfect. There was something else. Something more. Whether that something could be named—sweetmetal?—she wasn't sure. What she *was* sure of was that pieces like that all had a way of seeing the world that no one else had noticed before.

That was greatness.

Jordan knew this with every fiber of her being. Every time she forged an Edward Lear, a Henry Ossawa Tanner, a Frederic Remington, a Georgia O'Keeffe, a Homer, she knew. She wore their great hats for a little bit each time she forged them, but that didn't make her great. The gap between what she did and what those artists did was vast. Before Ronan, she had thought that was how it would remain. She'd figured that she would run out of time long before she'd ever have a chance to see what she was capable of. But now she was in Boston and her heart was still beating and her eyes were still open. With a sweetmetal in hand, she might have more time than she ever hoped for.

Jordan wasn't great at art, but for the first time, she thought she might get the chance to find out if she *could* be.

"Thanks for the help," Jordan said.

"Sure thing," Matthew Lynch replied. "Thanks for buying my corn dog."

"Is that what you were eating? I thought it was a sock."

Matthew rubbed his stomach enthusiastically with one hand and shifted the enormous garment bag on his shoulder with the other. "Everyone needs more socks—that's what Deklo says."

The advantages of bringing the youngest Lynch as her assistant were threefold. First of all, she *could* use an extra set of hands. Not only was it nice to have someone else to move lighting or adjust hair, but clients also paid more for artists who brought assistants. It seemed like it should be more expensive and so it was, one of those psychological self-fulfilling prophecies. Secondly, Declan Lynch had asked if she could keep an eye on Matthew while he ran some errands, presumably of dubious legality or safety, and it was nice to be able to do him a favor to show she appreciated him coming up to Boston. And finally, it hadn't taken long for Jordan to figure out that Matthew Lynch was a little bit like a sweetmetal, but for humans. People loved him. They didn't know why they loved him, but they did. Thoroughly, simply, unabashedly. That seemed like a lucky thing to have on a job.

"You're gonna tell me what I need to do, right?" Matthew asked. "When we're in there?"

"That's the plan," Jordan said. "Should be nice and relaxed. We want them to feel they've had a good time. You make 'em happy, they tell their friends about you. And people in places like this have friends . . ."

"With dollar bill signs for eyes?" Matthew asked. "Wait, no, you'd be the one with the dollar bill signs, 'cause you're the one getting paid. Or pound notes? Pound note signs?"

He continued prattling on to himself as Jordan texted the client to let her know she was on the doorstep. It was an impressive doorstep, a stone-clad threshold double their height. The grand old stone Boston church had been converted to four massive luxury condos, each as large as most suburban mansions. Tastefully expensive cars sat on the curb. A nanny shot them wary looks as she pushed a stroller down the sidewalk. Matthew waved at the little girl following the nanny; the little girl waved back.

There was a little hum of an electric door lock, and then the door came open.

The woman in the doorway matched the cars on the sidewalk. Tastefully expensive. Her smile was free for all, though. "Hi, I'm Sherry. Jordan Hennessy?"

Jordan grinned back. "And my assistant, Matthew. This is a great location."

"We love it," said Sherry. "Still smells like contrition. Come on in."

They came on in. Jordan was combining business and pleasure, or at least business and personal. As far as Sherry knew, Jordan was just there to get reference photos for a gimmick commission. But Jordan had also discovered that Sherry and her husband, Donald, had probably purchased a sweetmetal through one of Boudicca's auctions years before. *Probably* because Jordan wasn't one hundred percent sure the collection it came from was made up of sweetmetals. All she knew was that it had been a similarly eclectic assemblage of works that went for unexpected prices. And that it was very, very secret. More secret than one would expect a collection that included bed frames, lamps, and fine art photography to be. It had taken a lot of legwork and social pull to get even *that* much information. It felt like a lot of hours invested for the possibility of looking at *maybe* another sweetmetal to see what it had in common with *El Jaleo* and the other sweetmetals she'd seen. This one was a photograph, so that was unique, at least. And what other leads did she have, anyway?

Inside, the condo was modern and spare, taking advantage of the church's soaring ceilings to incorporate sleek, tall sculpture and dripping, laser-clean lighting. Not Jordan's style, but she could appreciate it. Declan would probably have been wild for it. It was a grown-up, very expensive, very specific version of his blank townhome, combined with the abstract art he'd hidden away in his attic.

"I know this is kind of corny," Sherry said. "This whole thing. But I've just loved the idea of it ever since I was a kid, and I got too old to be in it myself, and now that Harlow's just big enough to be painted, I thought, I'm going to do it, I'm going to pull the trigger before I change my mind or Donald talks me out of it."

"There's a long tradition of it," Jordan said. "So you're in good company. John White Alexander isn't what I would have imagined you'd want, though. Not with your style."

Sherry looked around the room. "Oh, this is Donald's style. I got to do the library and bedroom, he got the living room and the dining area. We divided the territories in the peace accord."

"Oh, I see," Jordan said as Sherry led the kids into a library. It was far more what she would have expected for a client requesting John White Alexander, a traditional and mannered contemporary of John Singer Sargent. There were dark floor-to-ceiling bookcases and an ornate, hulking desk holding up a Tiffany lamp. Fiddly bronzes were tucked into alcoves; the rug was a hand-knotted number so shabby that it must have cost a fortune. There was a gap in the shelves just the right size for a Jordan Hennessy take on John Alexander White.

"This is very handsome," Jordan said.

"Thank you," Sherry replied, but she was examining her phone with annoyance. "I'm sorry to spend your time like this, but it looks like the nanny's not checking her phone. She wasn't even supposed to be here today, but there was a mix-up, so I told her to stay on, and of course she took the kids out on a walk. I'm going to have to go catch up with her before she takes them to the aquarium or something. Do you have a minute? Help yourself to coffee—I just put a pot on. Follow your nose . . . the kitchen's just over there."

Once they were alone, they immediately went to get coffee. The kitchen was beautiful and unused except for the gadgets on the counter: coffee machine. Blender. Bread maker.

"This coffee is hairy," Matthew complained.

"It's fancy," Jordan said.

"Everything's fancy here. What's that lady mean about her painting? Why does she think the painting's bad before it already started?"

"Oh, 'cause it's not an original," Jordan explained, opening and closing every drawer and cabinet in the room. "Because she doesn't want me, you see? She wants John White Alexander, but he's very dead, which isn't good for business. So she's got me, and she wants me to put her li'l daughter in one of his paintings."

Sherry had hired Jordan through fairly ordinary word of mouth to do one of her least sexy but most common forgeries: historical pieces redone with the faces replaced with clients'. Sherry's was at least a tasteful request, her young daughter done in the same style as Alexander's elegant *Repose* or *Alethea*, two pieces subtle enough to look like homages rather than out-and-out gimmicks. Jordan tried to avoid painting clients into the *Birth of Venus* these days.

"Like Photoshop," Matthew said. "Oh, gosh, oh, no, that sounded mean, I didn't—"

She laughed. Matthew couldn't sound mean if he tried. "You're not far off. It's not a direct copy, that's why I'm more swish than the other people doing it. I'm supposed to do the painting Alexander would've done if he'd been around, not just a photocopy. His palette, brushstrokes, composition. My brain. Her daughter. New painting."

"Sounds hard."

"It's not. Well, not anymore. It's just my job." Swallowing the rest of the fancy coffee, she pushed off the pure-white counter to gaze at the living room walls. No photographs. She wondered if the sweetmetal was even in the house. She couldn't feel anything; it wasn't like *El Jaleo*, where part of her could always tell it was around the corner even before she saw it. Barbara or Fisher had said something about sweetmetals wearing off. Maybe it had worn out.

"It's a cool job." He was glancing at her when he thought she wasn't looking. Probably he thought he was being discreet, but he wasn't. His face was curious. "Cooler than Declan's other friends."

"He has friends?" Jordan asked, mouth amused. She doubted this highly. Friends required honesty, which wasn't a thing Declan had a lot of. "What do they do?"

"Number jobs? Politics. They wear ties. They have these things." He made a gesture to his face that managed to convey facial hair. "Declan stuff." Jordan was surprised to see that Matthew seemed to believe in the neutral, boring person Declan presented to the rest of the world. That meant Declan had played that role even at home.

"Do you go to school, Matthew?"

His golden, carefree expression went troubled, and then it went blank. This was a very different expression than the one he'd had before. Something had happened at school, she thought, or something—

Oh no. Something was wrong.

Her mind was slipping out one of the high church windows, up into the sky. She could see clouds, wings, birds, branches—

Jordan dragged herself back to the present. It had been a little bit since she'd had one of her dreamy episodes. Never mind, she thought. It was minor. She could push through it. She had done it before; she could do it again. It was only when they got really bad that other people began to notice she was struggling.

Oof. There it came in a wave again.

Flashes of images moved before her eyes. Images from another time, another place. Real? Unreal? Past? Future? She didn't know. It was hard to make sense of them and harder still to remind herself to make sense of them.

It only took a glance to see that Matthew was experiencing it, too. He'd put down his coffee and was walking very, very slowly toward the door, shaking his head a little.

What a pair! Both of them were failing badly. Sherry was going to return with her daughter and find them drunkenly draped across her furniture, completely out of their heads. It would be a bad situation with any client. But it seemed worse if it was a client that had even a passing knowledge of sweetmetals and the people who needed them.

Wait a tick, Jordan thought. The sweetmetal. Of course.

She pushed out of a chair (when had she gotten into a chair?) and tried to have a listen. A feel. A sense. If there was a sweetmetal in this house, it would give them back their thoughts until the ley line got itself back together, hopefully. She caught a whiff, she thought.

"Come on," she told Matthew, grabbing his arm to tug him deeper into the condo. "Focus, if you can. Come on!"

Together, they investigated the condo as quickly and quietly as they could. Here was the library again; they'd gotten turned around. Here a nursery. A bathroom, a closet, a study. Mirrors, art, books. It was hard to remember what they'd already seen. Hard to remember what they were looking at, even as they were looking at it.

Oh, thank God, there it was.

She felt the sweetmetal as soon as she passed the doorway. Stepping inside the room was like stepping into reality itself.

It was an enormous master suite, and the sweetmetal, wherever it was in the room, worked well enough to provide dramatic clarity. It made every detail sharp: every stitch on the duvet, every curl in the carved posters of the bed, every velvet ripple of the curtain.

Both Jordan and Matthew heaved huge sighs of relief as they collapsed on either end of a fainting couch in the master sitting area. Slowly, the two of them rebooted.

She could see this slow-motion return to herself reflected on Declan's little brother's face. That confusion turning to relief turning to frustration and then finally turning to normality. It reminded her, sadly, of the girls. They had all done this together, too, when Hennessy waited too long to dream, or when the ley line sagged. Which was happening now? It was hard to say. Hennessy hadn't managed to get in touch with Jordan yet.

"I didn't know that's what was happening to me," Matthew said. "Before I found out. I didn't know it was because I was a dream. I've never seen anything else do it before. Anything human, I mean. Oh, I didn't mean to be mean, I didn't—"

"I know what you meant. Not one of Ronan's things. A person. I never saw an animal do it before his bird, either, so we're the same, you and I."

Matthew just kept frowning at the floor, chewing on his lip pensively, so she stood up and snooped around the room until she found the sweetmetal. It had been pushed under the bed, probably because it didn't match anything else in this room. It was a black-and-white photograph of a diner with a skinny man in spats standing in front of it, looking at something outside the frame. She could feel that it was a sweetmetal, but she couldn't tell why. It was like the landscape at the Boudicca party. She hadn't been able to tell why she liked that one, and she couldn't tell why she liked this one, either. She pushed it back under the bed where she'd found it.

"I think Ronan dreamed me to be stupid," Matthew said. "I think I'm stupider than most people. I don't think very hard; I don't think."

"You seem normal to me."

"You knew to look for that thing under the bed. I was just walking around in circles."

"Maybe I'm just very clever."

"Dreamed to be clever?"

"Clever because Hennessy's clever and because I take a daily vitamin."

"Whatever." Matthew sounded disappointed.

"I don't think your brother dreamt himself an idiot brother," she said. But somehow this made her think about how she was missing the memories of Jay. She'd always thought of herself as identical to Hennessy, apart from the dreaming, but it was obvious that she wasn't. She didn't think Ronan had dreamt his brother to be an idiot, but perhaps he *had* dreamt him to be lovable. Perhaps Hennessy had dreamt Jordan without those memories on purpose.

"Oh, there you are!" Sherry said. She held the hand of the little girl Matthew had waved at earlier. The suspicious nanny stood in the hallway behind her, holding the baby from the stroller.

"Sorry to wander," Jordan said.

"I had to pee," Matthew said with a little laugh, and because he was Matthew, Sherry laughed with him. Jordan didn't think he was as guileless as he feared; it was a solid deception.

"And while looking for the bathroom I saw this couch," Jordan said, gesturing to the chaise Matthew was on. "And I just think it's even more what we're looking for. The lighting through this window will do so much work for us. You have a great eye."

Sherry lit up. "I bought that couch last year! I thought it was special. I'm so glad."

They'd gotten away with it.

Jordan and Matthew busied themselves. Matthew retrieved the garment bag from the other room and made such a noise of surprise at the massive period dresses inside when he opened it that Sherry and her daughter both laughed at him. Jordan posed the daughter and began to take reference shots, and as she did, Matthew told Sherry jokes. Eventually Matthew got Sherry so cheery that Jordan persuaded her to try on the other period dress and posed her together with her daughter on the chaise. The single portrait became a double, which increased the price by a third and also made it more interesting by far.

She and Matthew were actually a pretty good team, she thought, as they accepted the deposit from Sherry and retreated from the church.

On the sidewalk, Jordan folded over some of the bills to Matthew.

"Is this pity money?" Matthew said suspiciously.

"What does that mean?"

"I dunno, to make me feel like I was a grown-up."

"You did a job; I'm paying you for the job. Don't get a complex. I know that's what Lynch brothers seem to do, but try to avoid it."

He sighed. "Thanks, then. For back there, too."

The dreaminess. She'd forgotten how bad the episodes could be, how quickly they could come on. She'd forgotten how she'd been in the middle of one when Declan realized she was a dream. She'd forgotten why she had understood why it would drive him away. No one wanted to be the only man left awake.

Ordinarily a dreamy episode would have defeated Jordan's mood for the rest of the day, but she found her mood was still as light as it had been before. This was why she was here in Boston. This was why she was searching underneath the beds of strangers. This was why she had bought yet another ticket to the Gardner. She was finding a sweetmetal. She was getting a sweetmetal. She was staying awake. She was staying awake long enough to become great.

19

Ronan Lynch still remembered the best dream he'd ever had. It was an old dream now, two years old. Maybe a little less. In the divide of before his father's death and after, it was *After*. It was also *After* his mother's death. It was *Before* Harvard. *Before* Bryde.

By the time this one showed up, Ronan had a pretty long list of good dreams. Most of them were from *Before*, and most of them, like many good dreams, were wish fulfillment. There were the usual valuable-possession dreams: opening a bedroom door to discover that the mattress had been replaced by a very expensive trendy sound system. There were dreams of impossible abilities: flying, speeding, long jumps, one-two punches that knocked intruders clear into next year. Sex dreams ranked well, depending on the players involved (they could just as easily slide into nightmare territory). Places of unreal beauty often made the list—rocky green islands, clear blue lakes, flower-busy fields.

And of course there were the ones where he had his family back.

"What would you do if you accidentally brought your mother back?" Adam had asked one evening before he'd left for Harvard. "If you woke up with another Aurora, would you keep her?"

"I'm not in the mood for word problems," Ronan had replied.

"You've thought about it, surely."

Of course he had. The ethics of replacing his father were clear enough—copying a real person was *no bueno*—but Aurora had already been a dream, which made the waters murkier. He wouldn't have been content with a dreamt copy, but Matthew might be. Could he end Matthew's grieving with another mother? Spare Declan the effort of raising Matthew by providing another mother? Did it do a disservice to his real mother's memory, even if she was already a dream? What if he did it wrong? What if he brought back a copy identical except for one fatal flaw? An Aurora with a disinterest in loving Matthew. An Aurora who didn't age. An Aurora who aged too fast. An Aurora with a desire to eat human flesh. What then, what then?

"I hadn't," Ronan lied. He didn't lie, especially to Adam, but he wanted the conversation to be over.

"What if you brought another *me* back? What would you do with the extra Adam?" Adam asked, curious. Unbothered. He wasn't squeamish and, in any case, it was just a thought exercise to him. *His* dreams weren't going to cough up another Ronan.

But Ronan's dreams might. He'd lost sleep over this question, wondering if he truly had it in him to kill an unwanted dreamt human. He'd learned to kill *in* his dreams, of course. The second he realized he didn't have enough control to prevent unwanted manifestation, he took down everyone in sight, and he'd accordingly woken with his share of corpses. But killing a dream after he'd woken? Killing them once they were real? That felt like a dangerous line to cross.

"It's not going to happen," Ronan had said, "so it doesn't matter."

"I think you ought to assume it's going to happen at some point and make a plan," Adam said.

"It's not going to happen," Ronan repeated.

But the threat had lodged inside him, and now dreams had

to be unpopulated to land on the *very good dream* list. He could risk no more Matthews. No Auroras. Not even any little Opals, who was slightly more creature than human. It was too weighty.

So, the best dream. This was what happened in the best dream. Ronan was in a car. It was a beautiful car. Beautiful in appearance—long, gleaming hood, glistening black wheels, glaring headlights with teeth-bared matte grill—and also in sound—engine heaving with power, exhaust growling with urgency. Every detail Ronan could see was art. Metal and wood, bone and vines. It was one of those dream objects that didn't entirely make sense according to waking-world rules.

The car was already in motion when the dream began. Ronan was driving it. He could see himself in the rearview mirror. He was older, this Ronan in the mirror, his jaw was more squared and stubbled. He wore something leather and cool.

He didn't know where he was coming from; the dream wasn't interested in that. The dream was interested in where the car was going, and this was where the car was going: through a chain-link fence. Across cardboard boxes and plastic containers and toys. Over another little car in the middle of the asphalt, tires disintegrating the other car's rear window as it went. It drove through a sign for a mattress store. Flattened an inflatable snow-man in front of another store. Clipped a billboard, sending it all crashing down behind it.

It took out bus stops and traffic lights, road signs and mailboxes.

There were no people in this dream, so there was no scream-ing. No one to hurt. No one to bring back by accident. There was just the howl of the engine, the thump of the bumper, the grinding apocalypse beneath the tires. Music thumped from the car's beautiful carved speakers. The whole dream could hear it.

Finally, Ronan found himself speeding directly toward an identical car with an identical Ronan in it. It took him a moment to realize it wasn't actually another car; it was the mirrored front of a club. The music from inside drowned out every other sound. It was the sort of music Ronan heard all the time when he was at Aglionby, the stuff that made him feel as if he truly were nothing like other people, not because he was gay or because his father had been murdered or because he could take things out of his dreams, but because he couldn't bring himself to sing along to the shit other students sang along to. Funny how a handful of people loving a song you couldn't stand could make you feel inhuman.

In this dream, the best dream, Ronan and the dreamt car smashed right through the club's window.

There were no dancers. Just pounding music, strobe lights, glitter, and ten thousand alcoholic beverages on the floor where there should have been people.

Ronan began to do donuts.

The tires squealed; drinks flew; speakers toppled; plastic splintered; metal twisted; glass shivered.

Destruction drowned out both the club's music and Ronan's and it was gorgeous.

Then Ronan woke up. Heart pounding. Hands still clenched in fists. Ears ringing with remembered sound. Paralyzed. What had he brought back? Only the dream's furious joy.

That was the best dream.

The first thing the dreamers destroyed with Bryde was an exit ramp. The battle was undramatic, uncontested. Once upon a time there was an exit ramp cut deeply into a mountain by bulldozers, a cloverleaf of asphalt imposed upon the wild. And then once upon a little later time, the exit ramp didn't exist anymore. It was just a pile of rubble that returned the hillside to its natural form, the work of a transient storm dreamt to thrash just beneath the soil. Why did it even need to be there, a new highway, a new cloverleaf, in the middle of nowhere? Because it could be.

Next there was the dump. Trash piled upon trash. Old groceries rotting, new appliances rusting, plastic bottles bleeding out the remainder of their contents. Ronan had never seen a dump so big, hadn't believed such dumps existed in the United States. He hadn't imagined there was so much trash in the country, much less in a single dump. It took all night even for a dreamt, blue fire to burn it all, and when the fire took the support buildings and the road leading to the dump, too, the dreamers didn't stop it. It was only when the otherworldly flames began to creep toward the trailer park below that Bryde spat scornfully and signaled for Ronan to smother it with a quickly dreamt, dissolving blanket.

The next to go was a brand-new shopping area, which was identical to the shopping area just a few miles away, which was identical to the shopping area just a few miles away, which was identical to the shopping area just a few miles away, which was identical to the shopping area just a few miles away, which was identical to the shopping area just a few miles away. The dreamers arrived and they put on their masks and less than an hour later it was all gone. Dug up. Dug under. A dreamt dirt dragon charged from the ground to destroy and then dissolved just as quickly when the chaos was through.

After that, the dreamers destroyed an underwater transmission line, a 230 kV line that at once connected generators on opposite sides of a riverbank and also completely disordered the local ley line. As night fell, a school, a swarm, a hurricane of pitch-black dolphins had snaked toward the line. They were difficult to see in the water, since they reflected light in nearly the same way as the river water all around them. They were, after all, made almost entirely of dark ice. They were melting even as they swam toward their dreamt purpose, but not fast enough to ruin their mission. Only enough to chill the river as they dug through the silt and sediment down to the transmission line. Only enough that they could no longer swim at speed as they parted their bottlenoses to reveal shining hungry teeth. Only enough that by the time they had chewed through the work that had taken many months, there was nothing left to see of the dolphins but a few melting hearts at the bottom of the river.

The dreamers traveled hundreds of miles each day to put distance between themselves and their latest crime. Over and over they drove to a destination, planned how best to destroy it, dreamt the tool of destruction, unleashed it, and then lingered long enough to make sure they'd left no trace of their dreaming behind. They disrupted a convoy of trucks carrying transformers. They aerosolized two acres of unused concrete parking lot outside a dying mall. They filled canals and emptied swimming pools. Everywhere they went looked different when they were gone. Or rather, it looked less different. More like it had before humans arrived.

When they dreamt, Ronan dreamt of Ilidorin. He dreamt of the stump, and he dreamt of a slowly uncurling green shoot growing from its interior. It was getting stronger.

Ronan was getting stronger, too.

"What do you feel?" Bryde asked.

They sat on the roofline of an abandoned Victorian, looking out over the battered town around it. It was just at sunset, and there was barely enough light to see shapes by natural light. The dreamers would've been visible on their perch if anyone had looked up, but no one in this town had looked up for decades.

"Ronan," prompted Bryde. "What do you feel?"

Ronan didn't answer. It was the kind of night that made him want to run and run and run until he couldn't catch his breath, but that wasn't the kind of feeling Bryde meant.

"I feel like I can still smell that mill," Hennessy said. "I will smell like it for the rest of my life."

The dreamers had just destroyed a pulp mill on the other side of town. It had been one of the worst smells Ronan had ever smelled, and that included the odors at the West Virginia Museum of Living History, the trash dump they'd destroyed, and the bodies he'd buried over the years. He wondered how long it would take people to notice it was gone. The mill. The smell. All of it. Would they notice the silhouette was missing from the horizon before the sun went down? Perhaps tomorrow when they arrived to work, only to discover the mill had been replaced with a meadow. Unless tomorrow was a weekend. Ronan had no idea what day of the week it was. Time worked differently now. Weekends felt like a concept that had been important *Before.*

"What do you *feel?*" Bryde persisted. "Nothing?"

"This dinosaur," Ronan said, running his fingers over Chainsaw's nubbly talons. The raven clutched the peak of the roof beside him and peered off at the disappearing sun, beak parted, as if imagining how good it would've tasted. "And the spine of this roof up my—"

Hennessy gasped.

Bryde just had time to grab her arm before she tumbled from the roof. Her fingers clung to him as he dragged her back up.

Ronan didn't have time to ask what had happened. It hit him next.

Suddenly, he was electric.

He was free, his thoughts flying into the air. He was trapped, his body fused to something deep in the earth. He was both these things at once. He felt as if he could do anything, anything he had ever possibly wanted to do, anything except untangle himself from that thing he was wound around. This thing, this thing. This entity, this energy, this whatever-it-was, it was what was making him so powerful, so alive.

He understood it, he heard it, he *was* it—

"Goddamn," he whispered.

Bryde smiled.

It was an altogether different smile than Ronan had ever seen him wear, his light teeth visible in the deepening dark, his eyes half-closed, head thrown back. Euphoric. Relieved.

"That's the ley line," Bryde said.

Ronan felt it uncurl through him, like vines stretching toward the sun. It was the humming possibility of his dreams, the sense of ever-widening options, but he was awake.

With a glorious cry, Chainsaw threw herself from the roof and soared high up into the air. Part of him felt like he might be able to join her.

"Why is it doing that?" Hennessy asked in a small voice. Bryde was still holding her steady on the roof, a hand gripped very firmly around her upper arm.

"It's a surge," he said. "It won't last. If we are lucky, we will feel another. Perhaps a third. The heartbeat of a sick planet coming round."

Nightwash felt a million miles away, like something that could never touch Ronan. He was the night and he was the world and he was as infinite as them both.

Chainsaw cawed up above and Ronan spontaneously leapt to his feet, keeping his balance easily on the ridge of the roof. He cawed back to his dreamt raven at the top of his lungs. The sound echoed all around the roofs of this dead town, making it sound like there was a whole flock of ravens, a whole flock of Ronans, even though there was just the pair of them.

"It's so strong," Hennessy said, even though it was already beginning to wane.

The world was changing. It was becoming a place someone like him had been made for.

Bryde said, "This is only the beginning."

20

Carmen Farooq-Lane hadn't told Lock about Jordan Hennessy's sword.

In the commotion of Rhiannon Martin's death, she'd hastily shoved it through one of the galvanized fans at the end of the turkey barn. Later, after they'd all been briefed and the area was being cleaned up, she'd snuck it back into the rental car.

It was not the first secret she'd kept from the Moderators, but it was certainly the most dramatic. The sword was nearly as tall as she was, and wondrously and impossibly made. It felt like an extension of her arm, no more or less heavy than her own hand. The hilt was stunning, smooth silvery metal engraved with the words FROM CHAOS, and when one was gripping it, one *felt* the words even when they weren't visible. The blade was made of the night sky, a sentence absurd to say out loud but even more absurd to process. It did not look like a sword-shaped window into the night sky. It did not look like a blade painted to look like the night sky. It was the night sky. That was all there was to it. When she swung it—and she did, an embarrassing number of times, to Liliana's amusement, taking it out in living rooms and hotel rooms and in the backyards of places where they stayed—it trailed starlight and moonlight, comets sparking and universe dust shimmering. It could slice through just about anything, but *slice* wasn't exactly the right word, either. The blade *won*. It won like the night won, like the darkness won. It simply descended. Farooq-Lane suspected there was only one other weapon that would stop it: the sun blade last seen strapped to Ronan Lynch's back.

"It suits you," Liliana said with an amused smile when Farooq-Lane took it out at the latest short-term rental cottage. The blade cast jabbering, checkered patterns of light through the dormant jasmine-covered pergola they stood under. It was a little chilly to sit outside but Liliana did anyway, to be close to Farooq-Lane, tucked into a faded wicker chair, knitting and bobbing one of her feet in a good-humored way. She was in her middle age now, the prime of her life. Her hair shone at this age, the many-sided tone that was red hair, in its own way impossible as a dream thing. As always, she'd tamed it with an ever-present blue fabric band, but the knot at the base of her pale neck was coming loose. The skin there always seemed as if it would be very soft.

Farooq-Lane swung FROM CHAOS again, studying it, trying to understand both the sword and her fascination. "A weapon can't suit someone."

But it sort of did, and she wasn't sure how she felt about that. It was a dream, and she'd been working very hard to kill those for months.

Farooq-Lane used the sword to write CARMEN in the dark. This really was a very nice cottage they were staying in at the moment, a sweet little bungalow with this pergola and a koi pond and vegetable garden behind it. All of the cottages were nice. They had to be. That was Liliana's requirement to work for the Moderators. She had to be put up in places that felt like homes and she had to be put up in them with Farooq-Lane. A simple transaction. Stability for her present in exchange for visions of their future.

Farooq-Lane's relationship with the Moderators was supposed

to be as equally simple. In exchange for her services as a Moderator, she received a sense of purpose. And it *was* simple, she told herself. Once one found out the world was in danger, who could walk away from that?

"They never found any of my brother's weapons," Farooq-Lane said. She hadn't realized she was going to say it out loud until she did, and then she almost immediately wished she hadn't. She hoped Liliana hadn't heard.

But Liliana stopped knitting.

"Do you really want to talk about this?" Liliana asked.

"No," Farooq-Lane said. Then, the sword dipping a little in her hand, "It's all right."

"That sword's deadly and you are afraid of how you like it."

Liliana knew her well at every age. Farooq-Lane said, "You didn't see her face. Jordan Hennessy's. She wasn't bringing out a weapon on purpose. Whatever that thing was that I cut . . . this sword seemed *made* to destroy it. That's the opposite of intentionally destroying the world."

Liliana began to knit again, jiggling her foot once more.

"You aren't going to say anything?" Farooq-Lane asked.

"You already said it," Liliana replied in her gentle way.

Farooq-Lane swung the sword again. "Accidentally ending the world is still ending the world, though."

Liliana held the knitting out from her body. It was turning into a sock or a scarf or something long.

"So they have to be stopped no matter what," Farooq-Lane said. "Well, controlled. We already know the apocalypse has to be generated by these Zeds. There's no other explanation for why they keep showing up in your visions, even if we can't tell what they're doing."

The Potomac Zeds' acts of industrial espionage were getting bigger and bigger, although the Moderators had had as much luck intercepting them at this as with anything else. It was difficult to divine the purpose, but there undoubtedly was one. Even in light of this, though, Lock had recently announced they were going to return to their previous method of taking out other Zeds. The Potomac Zeds couldn't blow up transistors *and* protect other Zeds, he reasoned. By taking up their old methods, the Moderators could stop one or the other instead of just twiddling their thumbs. Back to business as usual, he said, as soon as the location intel was processed on the next vision.

Business as usual.

"I'm going to quit," Farooq-Lane said suddenly. She put the sword back in its scabbard, instantly reducing the light of the chilly backyard to just the subtle dazzle of the twinkle lights strung through the pergola. "I'm going to quit the Moderators."

Liliana's knitting needles clicked faintly as she did another row.

Farooq-Lane's heart was thudding in her ears and her hands felt ice-cold. "Aren't you going to say anything?"

It had been a little over a year since Nathan had killed their parents. Since she found out her brother was a serial killer. Since she found out he was a Zed. Since she found out the end of the world was coming. Since she had helped kill Zed after Zed while the fire got closer and closer. She'd lost most of her life with the murders and given the rest of it away to join the Moderators. Without them, she'd have to devise an entirely new future for herself, whole cloth.

"Liliana," Farooq-Lane said. "Anything at all?"

Neatly folding her scarf-sock thing and setting it on the chair, Liliana stood. She walked to Farooq-Lane, took the scabbard from her hand, and leaned it against the pergola support. The twinkle lights made a galaxy of night stars in her eyes as she stepped close.

Then she gently brushed Farooq-Lane's hair with the palm of her hand, and she kissed her.

Farooq-Lane closed her eyes. She put her hands where the knot of the blue fabric was coming loose. The skin there was very soft.

When the kiss was done, Liliana said, "What are you going to do instead? I will come with you, of course."

It was going to be so difficult to do this alone. To take from the Moderators the one supernatural tool they had in their arsenal: Liliana. To leave them blind to trust herself instead.

But Farooq-Lane's voice didn't waver as she replied, "Save the world."

21

A boat ride.

Jordan supposed she could do a boat ride, although she had to admit she was disappointed. It was very civilized. Very pretty. They'd gotten to Boston Harbor an hour or so before dark, as the sky glowed orange behind the Boston skyline of skyscrapers and clock towers. The icy water lapped darkly against tour boats drowsing at the wharf. The sailboats that were still out this late in the year lay gracefully on the water, their plumage lowered and only bones remaining.

As habit, Jordan thought about how she would paint her surroundings, which brush she would use to draw those fine, fine hairs of rigging etched delicately against the sky, but it was a bit of a dull exercise. It was too obvious a scene, chosen by too many artists and photographers over the years. Because it was pretty.

Pretty was good, she told herself. Nice was good.

Just a little disappointing.

"Matthew, actually buckle that life vest. Actually. Buckle. It," Declan Lynch said. He looked quite at home here on the water, quite at home here in Boston altogether, a handsome Irish American fellow with a head of tamed curls and those narrow, squinted eyes of a Celt. Collared shirt, nice sweater, good jacket, all of a piece with the pretty skyline and the boat and the water. Hennessy would hate him so much, Jordan thought. *Congratulations*, she'd say, *you've found Boring White Man #314.*

A date in Boston Harbor would only underline Hennessy's point. Because it was nice. Because it was pretty. Because you could read about it on the tourism site and purchase tickets. Because it was a thing everyone might like.

How romantic. Hennessy's voice would drip with judgment.

Jordan had to make do with imagining Hennessy's voice since she hadn't called. Why hadn't she called? Jordan knew she was alive and well, because Ronan had called Declan. Well, and because Jordan was still standing.

Silence from Hennessy was as worrisome as words.

"How do you know I wasn't made to float?" Matthew was saying petulantly.

"Mother Mary," Declan said with exasperation. "Do we have to do this every day? Just say you want a therapist for your birthday."

"Do you still call it a birthday if it's the day you just, like, appeared?" Matthew asked.

Jordan contemplated inserting herself into this discussion but decided it was more about brothers than it was about the dreaming. She knew more about one of these things than the other.

"Everyone just appears at some point, Matthew," Declan said, removing the last of the lines securing them to the pier. "Jordan, are you tied down?"

She saluted him.

They were off. The engine drowned out the protests of the seagulls overhead and the voices of pedestrians on the wharf they left behind. The water chopped up white and gray and black behind them. The Atlantic Ocean hissed cold winter wind from the darkening horizon. It wasn't entirely civilized, Jordan supposed. Because the temperature was too wild, and Declan drove the boat a little too fast across the waves for romantic sightseeing.

Why did Jordan care what Hennessy would think anyway?

She didn't, actually. She just missed her.

While Matthew huddled on the back of the boat with a bag of potato chips, Jordan eventually got tired of the chill and joined Declan at the wheel, behind the relative protection of the windshield.

"Where did you learn to drive a boat?" Jordan asked, voice raised to be heard. It would be easier to talk if he cut the engine, but he seemed intent on a destination, clipping past various wharfs and frequently glancing over his shoulder to get his bearings. "Your father?"

Declan laughed. "A senator I worked for taught me. He said it was a life skill."

"Zombie apocalypse?"

"Fundraising opportunities."

"Same difference."

Declan smiled thinly at the ocean. "It's that catch-22 of money. People feel better about donating money to people who already have it. Did you find anything out today?"

For weeks, Jordan had been throwing herself against the question of sweetmetals. She'd returned to *El Jaleo* again and again, trying to understand the rules of it. How far its influence extended, if it varied from day-to-day . . . how it did what it did. It wasn't the only Sargent she visited, either. She tracked down as many Sargents as she could, to see if any of them were sweetmetals, too. It wasn't difficult to find a Sargent in Boston; this had been his city when he was in the States. He'd painted the murals on the ceilings of the MFA and the walls of the public library. Harvard's Fogg Museum and the Massachusetts Historical Society had portraits of movers and shakers. The Peabody Essex, the Addison, and the Worcester had more portraits, many watercolors, many, many sketches. She saw pieces she'd copied before, like his splendid and somewhat eerie *Daughters of Edward Darley Boit* at the MFA, and saw many others her fingers itched to copy, like a facile watercolor of alligators at the Worcester. She saw dozens upon dozens of his works.

Several of them gave her the general feeling of a sweetmetal, but only three felt strong enough to actually be useful to a dream in need of energy. *El Jaleo*, Boit's daughters, and an only recently discovered painting, a dramatic nude of Thomas McKeller, the Black man Sargent used as his primary model for his MFA murals. The latter had been hidden away in Sargent's private collection for years, and his real relationship to the man in the painting remained so.

She was no closer to understanding how sweetmetals worked. And if anyone knew anything about them, they weren't talking to her.

"Several of the Monets are sweetmetals," Jordan said. "At the MFA."

"Water lilies?" Declan suggested.

"One of the cathedrals, if you can believe it. The lilies gave me nothing at all."

Her first theory had been that a piece's sweetmetal value was linked to its artistic merit, but she'd had to abandon it for lack of evidence. Several of the pieces that felt the strongest to Jordan at the Boudicca demonstration were the least artistically accomplished, after all, and there were many masterpieces that left her cold in the sweetmetal department. Her next theory? She had no next theory. She'd decided her next step was to do a deep dive into the backgrounds of each of the sweetmetals she found, to see if there were clues there, but then Declan had invited her on this boat ride.

Boat ride.

It was a fine distraction, she told herself. She shouldn't let herself feel hurried by Boudicca's timeline. By Hennessy's silence.

"Have you thought about stealing one?" Declan asked casually. Not from the Gardner, but from somewhere.

"Of course."

"Which?"

"Easiest would be nicking one like Sherry Lam's, but it hardly seems worth the crime, does it? It's not got a lot of oomph to it. If I stole one, I'd go big."

He leaned the wheel to the left, sending them deeper into the harbor. "Tell me how you'd do it. Blue-sky thinking."

Jordan ducked under his arm on the wheel in order to sit on his lap. He matter-of-factly sorted out her voluminous ponytail as she leaned her head back on his chest to gaze up at the shifting evening sky. He bent his head prayerfully, eyes still on their destination. Now mouths and ears were close enough for speaking at regular volume in this fast-moving boat. "The Provenance Game always makes the most sense to me."

Provenance was the real work of a forger. The *show your work* of the art world. Beauty was nothing without bloodline. Creating the art in the style of a master was only the first step. Then came paperwork and research, fastidious work that began and ended with a story. A forged piece couldn't just spring into being; no one would believe one had suddenly found a new Monet, a new Cassatt, a new whatever it was. An alibi had to be invented, proven, knit into truth. Where had it been all these years? The more desirable the work, the better the story had to be. Hidden in a recluse's private collection. Misattributed for years by bumpkins. Discovered in a hidden basement after a house fire.

But one could not just invent reclusive collectors or uncertain bumpkins or hidden basements. The forger had to find ones that already existed and slide the story in, making as small an incision in the truth as possible in order to promote unscarred healing to the timeline. Sometimes, depending on the buyer, this was as simple as including a news clipping of a recent manor house fire. For good museums or discerning buyers, bills of sale or insurance claims for stolen works or letters from contemporaries mentioning the work or photographs of the work next to relatives of the artist sometimes needed to be forged.

Provenance.

"The crux of it, the crux of the plan," Jordan said, "would be convincing the museum what they already had on their wall was a forgery, had been a forgery all along. Probably I'd get a slick young fella with good teeth to convince them the original was swapped at some prior time, ideally before their tenure, so no hard feelings. I'd pick a year before it had got the hardest scientific evidence, the most scrutiny, all that noodly stuff that would make it tricky to forge. Before it was X-rayed. Lead soap damage analysis, all that. I'd convince them all the things they'd been studying and writing up in their academic papers were actually attributes of the forgery, that the original has entirely different layers and damage."

Declan had followed along beautifully. He said, "You'd need a whipping boy."

"Of course." She was always surprised by how well he knew this sideways world; he just didn't *seem* to fit the part. She supposed that had been the point of his camouflage all along. Look like a man who takes his dates to cheesy tourist attractions. Be a man who steals paintings. "You'd have to place the blame for the first theft on someone who is currently there or stands to suffer from it."

"Then you'd sweep in with your 'original,'" Declan said. "And tell them you're willing to secretly swap it for the forgery on display, and let their negligence stay secret, too, if they help you."

"You've got it."

"*The Dark Lady* play." He didn't sound sore that the theft of his mother's portrait had been what brought them together in the first place. "But you don't want to do that."

"I don't understand how to live that way," Jordan said. "I can't carry around, like, a famous painting while I go about my day in order; I'd be trapped in the same room as it. A painting. A whole painting. Could I cut it into little pieces?" She felt Declan's body recoil at the prospect. "There'd be no way to find out until you ruined the thing you just worked very hard to steal. And could I live with knowing I'd chopped up a Sargent? Not bloody likely."

She shifted her head on his chest; he tilted his chin. She felt his breath suck in.

"The very concept gives me indigestion," Declan said. Then he twitched his shoulder to tell her to move. "I need to steer us in. We're there. Tie us off, can you?"

To her surprise, they were not at a scenic point or romantic destination. They were at a private pier attached to a development of very choice row houses jutting directly out onto the harbor.

"Matthew, the painting," Declan said. "Please don't drop it in the water."

"What's all this?" Jordan asked as Matthew trundled gingerly up toward them with a parcel in very familiar wrapping: *The Dark Lady*. The dreamt portrait of Declan's birth mother, Mór Ó Corra, invested with the magical property of making whoever slept under the same roof as it dream of the sea. The dreamt portrait Jordan had once forged and once stolen and once returned.

Declan held out a hand to help her step from the rocking boat onto the pier. "I told you I was going to show you a good time, didn't I?"

Three exceptionally blond people had emerged from one of the houses—a man, a woman, and a teenager, all of them dressed for the weather, each carrying or dragging a piece of luggage. They started down the pier toward a boat rather larger than the one Declan, Jordan, and Matthew had arrived in, but when the man caught sight of Declan, he stopped.

"Oh, right, Cody—" the man told the teen, voice raised as he rummaged out a set of keys and dangled them. "Take that painting from him and put it just inside, would you? By the other things to go out. Lock the door after you. Lock it. Check it this time, please."

The teen sulked up to Declan, took the painting of Declan's mother, and jogged it back to the house as the couple joined Declan, Jordan, and Matthew.

"I'm going to go get this stuff situated," said the woman, smiling politely but continuing down the pier.

"Be there in a minute," the man said. He and Declan shook hands, casually, lightly, and then, politely, he shook with Jordan as well. He offered a hand to Matthew, too, but Matthew had turned at just that moment to crouch and look over the edge at the water.

"Sorry for the short notice," the man continued.

"It was no problem," Declan said. "Good way to escape the traffic."

"It seems silly to me this can't be done over email or phone, but this is tradition and I'm not going to be the first to break it, you know what I mean?" the man said. "What do you want to know?"

Instead of answering, Declan said, "Jordan, Mikkel was on the MFA board for—"

"Fifteen years."

"Fifteen years," Declan agreed. "He has dealt with several sweetmetals."

Jordan looked at Declan instead of at Mikkel.

A boat ride. A fine, pretty boat ride.

"There's quite a bit of legend around them," Mikkel went on. "I don't want to say a secret society because that makes it seem organized, and it really isn't. It is more that anyone who deals in much art quickly learns to tell what is good art and what isn't, what is going to make a splash, what isn't. You get that sense in your head for what is worth your time. And it is not hard to tell after a while of dealing with art, high-end art, that some of them are these sweetmetals. They are special, you know? People like them, they have that something. They sell for much more than you would think, because of that something, so it pays to keep your eye out for it. But they are an open secret. You don't really talk about them. You wouldn't advertise something as a sweetmetal. It's—what's the word? *Gauche.* The mystery is part of what makes them what they are. There is just a tradition of not putting anything about them in writing if you can help it, and if you do, burn it, it's all very Ouija board. What do you want to know?"

Declan held his hand out to Jordan, the universal gesture for *After you?*

"How are they made?" Jordan asked. "How is it put into them? Do you know?"

Mikkel squinted, as if the question wasn't exactly logical to him, but then he answered, slowly, "Oh, I see what you are saying. The artist does it. It is something about how they are feeling when they make the art. I thought when I first saw one that it was because the art was special to the world in some way. A real original, you know? But it was explained to me later and this makes more sense. They are special *to the artist* in some way. They are an original for the artist, something new for them, something personal for them. The subject matter, sometimes, how they felt when they were painting it, others. That is what seems to make some of them into sweetmetals. I do not think it is the artist who does it. It is, like, the spirit of the time. There is a French term for that, isn't there? There is a French term for everything. Does that answer the question?"

Declan looked to Jordan to see if it did.

"And you don't know what this is, what the specific bit is about the artist's process that does it," she said. "You don't know anything more specific about this . . . spirit of the time."

"All I know is that artists who produce sweetmetals don't always make sweetmetals," he said. "They can make two in a row, maybe, and then none for the rest of time. Now, most of them are in private hands . . . but you know there are a few in the city, right? Open to the public?"

"*El Jaleo,*" Declan said.

"Yes," Mikkel said. "Sargent was good at them, but I suppose he was very prolific, too, wasn't he? Have you ever seen his *Madame X*?"

Of course she had. Of course. *Madame X* was Sargent's self-proclaimed masterpiece, with all its checkered history. It was one of the first Sargents Jordan had ever tried to copy. She and Hennessy had taken turns at it, sometimes even working on the same copy as they did it over and over again. There was a full-length copy of it back in the McLean mansion with a bunch of bullet holes in its head, just like the poor girls who might still be there, too.

Mikkel saw from their expressions they had. "It's a sweetmetal, too. Off the charts. Whatever those two have in common, that's what makes a sweetmetal."

His teen son jogged up to give Mikkel his house keys; he'd locked away the portrait of Declan's mother safely inside the house.

"Thank you for making the time before your trip," Declan said.

"Thank you for facilitating," Mikkel replied. "I'm sure we'll be in touch again. That text number is good for you, right?"

Handshakes were exchanged again, more murmured pleasantries, and then, finally, Declan, Jordan, and Matthew were left standing on the pier. The wind whipped at them. The masts behind them were skeletons. The pretty evening was turning into something even more feral.

"It's kind of weird that water shows you your own face," Matthew said, but in an absent way.

Jordan said, "That was the painting of your mother."

"Yes," Declan said. "It still is. I just don't have it anymore."

"You traded it for this information."

"Yes."

They studied each other. He looked less ordinary as the sun disappeared and deepened the shadows beneath his eyebrows, obscuring the shape of his eyes, his expression.

"This was a good time, Pozzi," she told him.

Declan turned his face into the wind so that the darkness would hide his smile from her. He said, "I expect great things from my portrait."

22

Hennessy knew that everyone had secrets.

Secrets were what made you who you were. Once, Hennessy had read a book on drawing that said the key to getting a good likeness was getting the shadows right. It wasn't by the positive forms that one was recognized. We know people's faces by their shadows.

Hennessy thought secrets were like that. Each of her girls started life as Hennessy, thinking like her, acting like her—but eventually something happened, and they got a secret. And that was when they became their own person.

It was possible Hennessy believed people simply *were* their secrets.

J. H. Hennessy's secret was that she could only love one person at a time. It might *appear* as if she loved other people, like her daughter, or other activities, like painting, but she really only loved Bill Dower. Everything went well for painting and for Hennessy as long as everything was going well with Bill Dower. But if it wasn't, anything could be sacrificed in the service of preserving that love. Daughter, career, friends, house—these were just well-treated pawns in a board game with only two players.

Jordan's secret was that she wanted to live apart from Hennessy. She might have denied this to save Hennessy's feelings, but Hennessy had followed her; she'd seen the apartments

Jordan daydreamed about. She'd looked through Jordan's phone as she slept and seen the zip codes she fantasized over. She knew the galleries Jordan ogled, she knew the schools Jordan pictured herself attending. No matter how exciting Hennessy made their lives, no matter how many high-end jobs she had them take, how many lowbrow parties she had them attend, how big she made their shared life, Jordan still wanted her own. No one wanted to live with Hennessy forever, not even Hennessy.

Hennessy's secret was that she didn't want the ley line to get any more powerful.

"When one engages in havoc all the time," Hennessy said, "it becomes a kind of unhavoc."

The three dreamers were in an older neighborhood. Hennessy had long since lost sense of where. City and state were all negotiable. The light was peculiar and yellow-green. It was the end of the day, which ordinarily made ugly places more paintable. But tonight the clouds were hanging low and wrong over this town, raggedly caught on telephone wires, and the last of the dying sun came in sideways and murky. Snow was drifting down here and there as if the clouds were sloughing. The streets were muddy with fallen and melted snow and sand.

It was ugly. Unpaintably ugly.

Hennessy went on. "The very act of disruption instead becomes the opposite, ruption, the act of maintaining the status quo, because the status quo has now become chaos. Now, if one wants to prove themselves a game changer, they instead must restore order. What a mindfuck! To—"

"Are you saying that you need a break after this?" Bryde interrupted.

"I was making some psychological observations. As conversation. To fill the time."

"What do you feel?" Bryde asked.

Ronan let out a noisy breath as he drummed his fingers against the window. He had been getting more and more restless these past few days. Knees jiggling. Fingers drumming. Pacing. Jumping on top of shit. Jumping off of shit. He dreamt when they needed to dream. Otherwise he didn't sleep at all. Hennessy thought this game of dominos was changing him. Or perhaps revealing him.

"It's fucking weird," he said.

It was hard to feel the true strength of the ley line here, because there were so many things Hennessy now knew obscured it. Low unshielded telephone lines, standing oily water puddled in pitted asphalt, houses crowded on top of each other with wires trailing from them like guts. Satellite dishes sprouted like dark mushrooms from some of the roofs. There was something else, though, that made it truly ugly, and Hennessy couldn't quite figure out what it was. Maybe it was just her mood.

"Hennessy," Bryde said sharply, turning from the passenger seat to look at her in the back. "What do you feel?"

"What Ronan Lynch said," Hennessy replied. "Something's janky."

Bryde said, "This will be a difficult one. Three large buildings will need to be leveled. I don't know how well we will be able to dream when we are at the site, so we may need to use things we already have. We will need to stay focused. I may need you to do this one on your own. I don't know yet."

Ronan caught Hennessy's eye in the rearview mirror; his thick eyebrows went up. This was unusual. She shrugged.

"In fact," Bryde said, "I need one of you to drive us there, just in case."

Need. Need one of you to drive. Bryde didn't need them for anything. They needed him.

But this evening, Bryde pulled Burrito into an uneven parking lot in front of a closed lumber yard. As Ronan and Hennessy briefly scuffled over who would drive in his place—Hennessy won (Ronan was distracted keeping Chainsaw inside the car)—Bryde climbed into the backseat.

After the door shut behind him, Ronan hissed, "What's going on here?"

"Do I look like his minder?" Hennessy replied. "*You* ask him."

They got back in. They did not ask him. No one said anything as they drove through the ugly town and through a few minutes of patchily occupied countryside. The rutted road suddenly ended at a dark, freshly paved entrance to a corporate facility of some kind. A very clean white sign read, simply, DIGITAL SOLUTIONS.

Hennessy glanced into the rearview mirror at Bryde. In the green-yellow light she saw only that he was sitting perfectly still as he looked out the window, his eyes squinted as if against sun.

DIGITAL SOLUTIONS turned out to be a complex of three unassuming but enormous white buildings in the middle of a well-tended parking lot. In every way it seemed less ugly than the town they'd left behind. Neatly mowed grass that seemed too green for this time of year. Black, black asphalt that was level as glass. Clean white sides on the buildings, each printed with the same ambiguous words: DIGITAL SOLUTIONS.

Hennessy took the opportunity of the empty parking lot to do a few donuts in Burrito, hoping to make her ugly mood dizzy enough to fall down and not get back up again, but eventually she had to stop. Her ears were ringing.

She yawned to clear them, then yawned again. They kept ringing. It was a little like when you'd hit your head and you were struggling against vertigo. It was also a little like when you'd left the television on but turned the sound down. It was also a little like a refrigerator.

She yanked up the parking brake. The snow floated like ash in front of the windshield and melted on the fake-looking grass. Her ears continued to ring. "What's that sound?"

Ronan said, "Fuck if I know. I thought it was me."

The sound continued. It was a strange sound, a yellow-green sound that matched the yellow-green afternoon. There were no cars in the lot. No people. No signs of life. Just the ragged clouds and the sickly color bleeding at the horizon. Those clumpy snow-flakes that melted straight to grime.

Outside the car, the sound was even louder. It was the unend-ing, unchanging nature of it that was the most harrowing, she thought. It never varied, so it became part of you. Pressing in, pressing out. From the air. From the ground. From the build-ings. Ronan's raven flapped into the air briefly before returning to the asphalt to stand stupidly, shaking her head like something clung to it.

Ronan joined Hennessy, and they stood shoulder to shoulder, eyeing the buildings, the parking lot lights, the identical build-ings with their identical lobby entrances made of black glass, all simple as a child's drawing. The sound continued to come from everywhere. It seemed obvious there was nothing living here.

One could not ask for a more complete opposite to the silent, vital forest around Ilidorin.

"What powers the world, bro?" Hennessy said, suddenly understanding what she was looking at. "Zeros and ones. Memes and giggles. Forums and Fortnite. Right? It's a—what do you call it. Data farm. Server farm."

"A what?"

"I'll bet you my fine ass that inside those buildings are banks and banks of servers," Hennessy said. "Facebook-Instabook-Twitterbook-Tiktokbook-Tumblrbook. This is one of their hive minds. I could be wrong but I don't think I am. I saw an art exhibit once about a guy who tried to sue a sound."

"Servers make noise?" Ronan asked. He answered his own question. "Cooling fans."

"That's it, Mister Fixit."

"I can't dream here," Ronan said, matter-of-fact. "It would be a shitshow of epic proportions. We have to take it down with what we already have. Too bad you gave your sword to the Mods. Do we need to take down the whole building or just everything in it? Bryde?"

But Bryde didn't reply. He hadn't joined them at the front of the car.

They turned to look.

The car's rear door hung open. Bryde had made it out, but not by much. He was sort of crouched in the diffuse shadow of the open car door. Sort of standing. His body was curved in a question mark. It quivered. His fingers were cages over his ears.

He was screaming.

Or at least he looked like he was screaming. With his hands over his ears he screamed and screamed again, but without sound.

It was all the agony of a howl without any of the noise, which somehow made it worse. It was like the sound of the server farm and the scream were a thing happening to Bryde; it made him a different person. Somehow less present. Projected in from a different location.

They did not need to be told that it was hurting him.

What do you hear?

Ronan seemed shaken, too, but it was with a voice full of bravado that he turned his face away from Bryde and said, "It's up to us, then."

"We can just go," Hennessy said. "Leave this untouched. Tell him we did it. Maybe he won't notice."

Ronan gave her a look. "The car. Let's drive Burrito through."

"Through that glass and stuff? Is it tough enough for that?"

"Please." Ronan gave her another look. "Are you coming or are you waiting here?"

"Are we taking him?"

They looked back at Bryde. It was strange to see him still pinned in place. Was it possible for a sound to kill someone? Was it possible for something to kill Bryde? *Older than he imagines,* she remembered him saying.

She told Ronan, "Go on, I'll watch. I'll give you a score. Perfect ten is the car comes out without a scratch. Nine if you bust a mirror off. It goes down from there. One is if we have to walk through that town, which, I have to say, reminds me of Pennsylvania."

"We're in Pennsylvania," Ronan said.

"That settles it."

Hennessy stood in the parking lot as Ronan drove the car away from them both, expertly spinning it to the left to slam the still-open back door shut. The car instantly became hard to see, even though she could hear the pounding bass of music from within it. It was not enough to drown out the complex's sound, which was still everywhere. Inside her. Inescapable. Unrelenting. It required no human hands to do its work; it was in there powering that sound all by itself, working away at Bryde without feeling or pause.

Humans were so good at pollution. The best.

Suddenly, a massive hole appeared in the dark glass lobby doors of the closest building. Ronan had driven right in. For just a moment, Burrito was visible in the reflection of the remaining glass, and then it winked out of view. Crashing sounded from within the building.

Minutes passed.

Although it was impossible to see what was happening, it was nonetheless obvious that something *was* happening, because the terrible sound had gotten a little quieter, replaced now by security alarms. Bryde had stopped screaming and instead was simply hunched, eyes closed in pain, hands still over ears.

Hennessy missed the moment of Burrito emerging from the first building, but she saw the moment it crashed into the second. That shivering glass, that brief reflection. Again, as Ronan did his work inside the building, the terrible sound went down another notch, replaced by yet more ordinary howling of alarms. She wondered if they were hooked up to anything. She wondered if she'd need to bedazzle any security forces with one of Bryde's silver orbs. She examined her conscience to see if she would be willing to rummage in Bryde's jacket to retrieve one of the orbs while he stood there. Hennessy ordinarily had no problem violating people's personal space, but with Bryde, it felt wrong. This, she thought, was probably related to Bryde's secrets.

By the time Ronan and Burrito crashed into the third building, Bryde had lowered his hands from his ears and simply stood, staring dead-eyed and haggard off into the distance.

Then the terrible sound was gone and so were the alarms, so Ronan must have destroyed those, too. There was only the sound of an unmanned business park several miles away from an ugly town. Distant trucks. Faraway heating and air-conditioning units. Tractors and birds.

This time the ley's surge was so powerful that it nearly knocked Hennessy right off her feet.

It was less that she was physically struck and more like the ground beneath her feet suddenly seemed unimportant. She was a part of a huge, ancient thing that was slowly stretching, slowly coming back to life, and she suddenly thought she understood in a very real way why the Moderators were doing everything in their power to catch them.

Bryde looked nearly like himself as the sound of Burrito's engine drew near. The car was still hard to see, but Hennessy guessed that Ronan hadn't lost a mirror. Burrito was strong. Ronan was strong. Hennessy was strong. They were all very, very strong.

And getting stronger all the time.

The ley line was singing through her even louder than that server farm had, only it was worse, because she knew this feeling meant she could manifest so, so much of the Lace.

Bryde said, in a low voice, "Have you guessed my secret, Hennessy?"

Hennessy studied Bryde. Again, she thought about how unusual a person he was. He was a little like the car, hard to look at. Hard to see. Or maybe she was just thinking that now that she'd seen him screaming, it was hard to look at him the same way. She said, "Is this a game?"

He closed his eyes. He was still hurting a little, she could tell. In a stiff voice, he said, "It's all a big game. We're pieces." Then he opened his eyes again. "You asked for a rest. We are nearly to the end."

"I didn't ask for a break," Hennessy said.

Her secret was this: She was tired of trying.

23

adame X. Madame X. Madame X.

When Declan slept, he dreamt of her, Virginie Amélie Avegno Gautreau, the red-haired beauty who powdered her face and pinked her ears to make herself unforgettable, a painting before she ever showed up on a canvas as John Singer Sargent's *Madame X*. Virginie Amélie Avegno Gautreau, her face turned in striking profile, shoulders proud, fingers poised on the table. Virginie Amélie Avegno Gautreau, with her suitable but troubled young marriage, her many affairs, the dress strap slid from her shoulder to subtly imply she lived two lives: a proper, daylight existence and a stolen, shadow existence that was a reaction to the unsuitability of the first. *Madame X.*

When he woke up, he thought about the circumstances under which she had been painted. When Declan went to sleep, he thought about how she might be similar to *El Jaleo*. All the hours in between, he thought about how that process might be re-created to make a new sweetmetal. *Madame X. Madame X. Madame X.*

And by *Madame X*, he meant Jordan Hennessy.

He couldn't get enough of her.

Boston suited him. Schedule suited him. Appointments, phone calls, goals—they all suited him. Building an elaborate spiderweb (a proper one, structurally sound on the outermost corners and sticky only in the very middle so that it trapped only the insects he liked to eat and not himself in it) suited him. He was making a plan. It was high stakes and it was dangerous and Jordan was right: He liked it. He liked all of it.

Declan liked the alarm at 6:00 a.m. He liked the cafés that woke up even before he did. He liked the *ding* of the email that meant his newspaper had arrived in his inbox. He liked the *swick* of his CharlieCard in the turnstile, he liked the jostle and noise of the T as he read the headlines and swiped to the business section. He liked hearing from a new business contact he'd gotten from one of his father's old contacts. He liked the assembly of jobs and tasks that got ever more complex as trust built.

Declan liked being buried to his neck in art history. He had begun as Pozzi, and Pozzi was a good start. Pozzi was how *Madame X* had begun, after all, with Sargent asking his friend Dr. Pozzi to introduce him to Virginie Amélie Avegno Gautreau as a portrait subject. Madame Gautreau! Sargent found her an impossibly beautiful and hopelessly lazy model. He sketched her over and over, painted her over and over, trying to capture on canvas whatever it was that made her famous is social circles. And when he did—when he'd painted that haughty beauty with her strap impudently fallen on her marble shoulder—the scandal nearly ruined him. Some things weren't meant to be painted out loud. Sargent's friend, the novelist Henry James, persuaded him to move to Britain to get away from the disgrace, so Sargent started his life from scratch there, not knowing that eventually *Madame X* was to be the painting he was best known for. Was that what Declan was doing? Here in Boston? Declan didn't know, but he liked it.

Declan liked the parties. And there were ever so many parties. He had never allowed himself to be so public in DC, so himself, so out and about, but Jordan argued that extroversion was actually safer. It took no effort, she noted, to disappear someone who didn't really exist, so they should live, they should live loudly. It was impeccable logic and, in any case, what Declan wanted to hear. He liked making his burner phone his real phone, making sure that, yes, it was a good number for him, a permanent number for him, a place to get the man for the job. The first get-together was small: an exhibit opening at a tiny Fenway gallery. Drinks and music, a funky vibe, young collectors, an after-party that spilled into a bar. After that, Declan bumped into his senator's sister's daughter on the street in Somerville and got invited to dinner, which turned into drinks, which turned into dancing. All of it turned into more texts and calls and invitations. Jordan was an exceptional and practiced partygoer. He liked how he looked on her arm.

Declan liked finding out how passionate Sargent had been about *El Jaleo*. A musician himself, Sargent had been fascinated by the culture of flamenco, and a trip to Spain had left such a mark that three years later he was still painting studies of dancers and guitarists for the piece that would eventually hang in the Gardner. When the twelve-foot-long painting debuted at the prestigious Salon, it rocketed Sargent to fame and cemented a career that would last his entire life. Was this what it had in common with *Madame X*? Was it that the painting changed his life, or was it that he *knew* that it was going to change his life? What was *soul*? Declan didn't know, but he liked trying to find out.

Declan liked the new roles his brothers played in this fantastic construct. Even though he felt guilty about letting Matthew's schoolwork slide (Was he going to college anyway? Would he ever actually be an adult?), he liked ordering takeout with him, and he liked using him as an excuse to see the touristy things, and he liked doing the holidays with him. Matthew's dreamy episodes seemed to be fewer than before, and Declan felt safe enough to get Matthew a part-time job at one of the local galleries, packing orders, which seemed to improve his mood. Everyone loved seeing him; who didn't love Matthew? And Ronan even though he wasn't in Boston, his presence was still huge in Declan's life. Once Declan stopped changing his phone number and started going to parties, a Moderator named Carmen Farooq-Lane called to ask if he'd been in touch with Ronan Lynch since the Potomac River incident. (*No*, said Declan, *but while I have you on the phone I should let you know I've made very good friends with an attorney since your unannounced attack on my personal residence*, a sentence that ended the phone call.) And in the oddest places, people would lean in and suddenly whisper, *Are you Ronan Lynch's brother? Please thank him.* This would have petrified Declan back in DC, but now it all made him feel like he was part of something bigger. Golden Matthew, charming the city. Rebellious Ronan, finally grown into something useful. Cunning Declan, trafficking in art and stories. The Brothers Lynch. He liked not worrying about them all the time.

Declan liked coming to the Fenway Studios at the end of the day when Jordan was just waking up for her workday, which lasted all night. He liked that without any conversation they'd decided it was right for him to sit in the antique leather chair by the window and tell her about his day while she worked at her canvases. He liked that she had begun painting him again, although she refused to show him this portrait. He liked that she was trying to make him her sweetmetal. He liked watching her create her copies of *El Jaleo* and *Madame X*, her ability with the brush never failing to transfix him as she forged layer upon layer in oils, same as when he had first glimpsed her at the Fairy Market. Virginie Amélie Avegno Gautreau.

Jordan Hennessy.

He thought about her all the time.

He liked it all. He liked it very much.

"What are you thinking?" Matthew asked.

"What?"

"What are you *thinking* about?"

"I'm not thinking about anything, Matthew, I'm just waiting for Jordan like you are."

The two brothers lingered in the Dutch Room in the Gardner museum, killing time until Jordan was meant to meet them for late lunch. Breakfast for her, since she probably was only just now waking up.

"You *are* thinking, though," Matthew insisted. He had that whinge to his voice that indicated today was going to be one of his tricky days. "You're thinking of things you're going to talk about with *Jordan*. Why don't you talk about them with *me*?"

He wasn't wrong, which was an impressive display of discernment on his part. But it was no less aggravating. Declan said, "Because you're two different people. I'm not going copy-paste a conversation."

"You just think I'm stupider than her," Matthew said. "You save all the smart things to talk about with her and then just point out people walking dogs to me."

"Do you or don't you like it when I point out dogs?" Declan asked.

Matthew groused. "I don't *only* like when you point out dogs. I want to know what you're doing. What you're, like, you know, *thinking*."

"Fine," Declan said. "I was wondering if these paintings are sweetmetals. If that's why they were stolen."

The green-wallpapered Dutch Room in the Gardner was notable for many things, including a Rembrandt self-portrait, a few Rubens, and some very excellent historical furniture, but it was now probably most famous for the things that *weren't* there.

One cold March several decades before, two thieves dressed as policemen had stolen thirteen works, including a Rembrandt and a Vermeer. It remained the largest unsolved art heist in history. Any crime of that size would have been notable, but the loss was felt even more acutely because the Gardner museum was both small and unusual, unable to rebound in the way any other museum might have. Isabella Stewart Gardner had overseen every inch of the intimate museum's creation. She'd acquired and placed every piece, micromanaged down to the building and tearing down of walls and other architectural features, and one of the requirements in her will was that nothing in the museum be changed after her death. Even widening one of the doorways a few inches for accessibility had required petitions and paperwork. This mandate meant that the museum couldn't acquire new works or rearrange old ones to take the place of the stolen works. Instead, the empty frames had been hung back up where the pieces had been. In essence, the loss itself was now displayed—and what more universal piece of art could there be?

"Sweetmetals, why? Because they were weird choices? The stolen stuff, I mean?" Matthew asked, which, again, displayed slightly more focus than Declan had come to expect from his brother. He'd been paying attention on their many visits.

"Because they were weird, yes. Because there were more expensive pieces hanging just feet away and they left them. Because they took that bronze finial, of all things."

"The bird thing," said Matthew.

"Yes," Declan echoed drily. This was more of what he expected from his brother. "The bird thing."

For decades experts had been trying to understand why the thieves had taken the pieces they had, and why they had treated them the way they did. They'd hacked valuable canvases right out of the frame. They'd pocketed disparate works on paper. They'd taken the Shang dynasty bronze beaker that had been on the table in front of the Rembrandt they also stole. And of course, as Matthew noted, the bird thing—they had stolen a bronze eagle finial off the end of a random flagpole. Was it personal? Experts wondered. A random grab? What did these works have in common?

"I was thinking if they were sweetmetals, the randomness would make sense," Declan said. "Or at least as much sense as any other explanation. It wouldn't have been about traditional value or artistic merit. Just energy."

"But why didn't they take the dancing lady, then?"

"*El Jaleo.*"

"That's what I said. Dancing lady with her arm on backward."

Declan resented the somewhat accurate description of the painting but let it pass. "I don't know. Maybe they ran out of time. Maybe it was too big. Maybe they had been told not to."

"By who?"

"Powerful people are interested in these things," Declan said. "Powerful people control a lot of them. It's why we're working very carefully."

"Wouldn't that mean if Jordan made one, she'd be powerful people?" Matthew asked.

Declan looked sharply at his brother. "Yes, I guess it does." But what he didn't say out loud was that unguarded power was actually weakness. If you had something someone else wanted and no way to stop them from taking it, you were vulnerable to exploitation. Jordan and her sweetmetal. Ronan and his dreams. It was why the spiderweb was so important, though he wasn't about to get into that with Matthew. The web was to protect him, not involve him.

Jordan appeared in the narrow doorway then, and as she joined them, Matthew said, "Was that so hard? We had a conversation. It wasn't just copy pasta."

"What's the conversation?" Jordan asked. "Was it a good one? Was it about me? That *would* be a good one."

"These guys," Matthew said. He pointed at an empty frame.

Putting her hands on her hips, she studied it as intently as she would if there had still been a painting in it. "Do you reckon these were sweetmetals? Is that what we're thinking?"

Matthew leapt gratefully into the conversation as Declan looked at the two of them. He felt so content in that moment, watching the two of them lightly bat around theories, that it turned right back around into uncertainty. He liked this life so well. He liked the people in it so much. It felt as if the other shoe must drop eventually.

"By the way, you'll never guess who I had a lovely wake-up call from," Jordan told Declan. "Our good friend Boudicca came in on the tails of my nudey landlord to let me know that their sweetmetals are going fast and they're waiting to hear from me . . . and also had I ever thought about getting together a portfolio for a gallery?"

"Bribery is new. What did you tell them?"

"I appreciated their diligence and I was still having a bit of a think if I even really needed one these days. Would they let me know when the last one was on the line?"

This was perhaps what Declan liked the best about all of this, about Jordan Hennessy: She could handle herself. He'd never had anyone in his life who didn't need him to manage, guard, chastise, protect. He'd never had an equal—he'd never even known he *wanted* an equal, and now that she was there, he liked it.

"They loved that, of course," Jordan said, with her usual grin.

No, *that* was probably what Declan liked the very best about all of this. Never in his life would anyone have accused Declan Lynch of being an optimist, but he had to admit that he was starting to see the perks. Things might be okay, he thought. Jordan and Matthew were dreams, yes, but as long as Hennessy and Ronan were alive, they could live their own lives. And if something happened to Hennessy or Ronan, now Declan knew that sweetmetals existed in the world to wake them up. Even if he couldn't immediately get his hands on one, he no longer had to fear losing his entire remaining family in one go; he had recourse. Things could be okay. Things *were* okay. He'd never felt that way before.

He liked it very, very much.

As the three of them pushed out of the museum into the chilly day, his phone rang. He held up a finger to the others to let them know he'd catch up at the car in a minute, and he answered it.

"Hello?"

Adam Parrish said, "We really need to talk about Bryde."

24

T he city woke up," Adam said.

"Back that up a moment," Declan replied. "Explain to me what that means."

He'd found Adam in line for a celebrity chef's food truck in Harvard Square, an establishment that served gourmet waffles with savory toppings for fourteen dollars a pop. Adam introduced the other students waiting with him as his good college friends, but Declan was dubious. The way they all stood together with Adam reminded him a little of a computer wallpaper he'd seen at the school office, a big shepherd dog standing with a bunch of ducklings huddled around its legs. Probably the photo was supposed to be cute, but at the time, Declan had thought about how unrewarding and one-directional the effort must be for the dog. This feeling of Declan's had only been underlined when the friend group discovered the food truck was cash only and began to wail, forcing Adam to patiently count out bills from his wallet in return for waffles and IOUs.

Adam had changed since their time together at Aglionby Academy, Declan thought. Old Adam never had any money. And old Adam would've scathingly pointed out the large CASH ONLY sign tacked to the truck rather than come to his wealthy friends' rescue.

"I thought Cambridge was dead before this," Adam said, leading Declan briskly through the Harvard campus. They'd left

Adam's ducklings eating in order to speak more privately, and now that he was out of sight of them, Adam ate his fancy waffle on the way, perfunctorily, one bite after another, until it was all gone, without any sign of enjoyment. "No ley energy. That's why Ronan went straight to nightwash here."

"What is it you wanted me to see?" Declan asked.

"We're not there yet. I don't use it like him, but I can feel the ley line, too. I use it if I scry or read cards." Glancing behind him, Adam led Declan out of Harvard Yard to Oxford Street. There, he slowed his pace, but Declan could not yet see anything unusual. It was all quaint and scenic: red brick, white trim, black trees, blue skies. "I couldn't really do any of that after coming here. Like I said, the city was dead. Those tarot readings you saw were just for show. I was just reading people. Parlor tricks. Fake magic. But lately I've been feeling these . . . I don't know. Pulses. Like power surges. Or heartbeats."

Declan wasn't sure he liked the sound of the last bit. *Power surges* sounded clinical and manageable. *Heartbeats* sounded living, and living things were unpredictable and hard to control.

"And then something really happened last night," Adam said. "Look here."

They faced a more modern building labeled SCIENCE CENTER. Casting a furtive glance up and down the street, Adam crouched beside a concrete bench built into the wall. Reaching beneath it, he scraped out a large handful of debris.

Then he showed it to Declan.

To Declan's surprise, it was not leaf litter, but beetles. Some were small, ordinary-looking insects, black and unremarkable. Others were huge and spotted, with the portentous grace of elephants. Some had massive forked antlers. Others were brilliantly blue, with galaxies of stars glittering through the color.

Declan did not have to be told they were not native to Cambridge.

"These are the Rockefeller beetles. Some of them. Do you know what those are? There's one hundred thousand of them on display in the Museum of Natural History just over there." Adam plucked one from his handful and showed it to Declan. The bullet-shaped beetle was ferociously green. It also had a perfect little hole straight through it when he held it up to the sun. "That's where the pin would go, to hold it to the mount."

"Dreams," Declan said.

Adam nodded grimly.

"Whatever happened, this pulse, it was strong enough to wake up these dreams. Long enough for them to find a way out of their cases in the museum to get over here. Not long enough to keep them awake."

"How did you find out about this?"

Adam carefully swept the beetles back under the bench. "I was doing readings and I got lost in one of the cards when it surged. After I got myself back, I came out looking for where it was coming from, just in time to see them crawling across the road here."

Lost himself. Got himself back. There were entire emotional tomes in between those words.

"All right," Declan said. "So the city woke up. For a while." He hadn't told Adam about the sweetmetals, and Paranoid Declan was loath to give away more information, but he asked, carefully, "Why do you think it has anything to do with Ronan? Could it be from a power source an outsider's bringing in?"

Adam frowned at him, and Declan was nearly certain he knew Declan was withholding information. Adam, as a secretive creature, understood secrets. But Adam just asked, "How much do you know about what Ronan's been doing?"

Declan shook his head. He knew only that Ronan, Hennessy, and Bryde were interfering with the Moderators' attempt to kill other dreamers. That had seemed noble. Useful. An acceptable outlet for Ronan's abilities and rebelliousness. Perhaps he had just wanted it to be. He'd wanted fewer ducklings for once.

Adam said, "There's no concrete evidence, but Ronan and the others have been implicated in over twenty incidents of industrial espionage."

Surprise was not the emotion Declan was feeling, so some part of him must have known. Suspected, anyway. This was the other shoe dropping.

"What kind of industrial espionage?"

"I got access to some of the agencies' documents," Adam said casually. This, Declan thought, was why those kids in the waffle line couldn't truly be Adam's bosom friends. Adam was reading intelligence documents about his boyfriend and they were googling celebrity chefs. "They've been taking down power grids. Server farms. Corporate waste sites. That power outage a few weeks ago, the one that affected those tens of thousands in Delmarva? That was them. Transmission line. The price tag is in the billions."

"Billions," echoed Declan. It was a lot to take in. "What's the goal?"

"The Moderators don't know, or at least they haven't put it in writing. I think I can guess, though. Overnight, I compared the dates and times of the espionage with the surges, and they match up. They match up exactly. I think Ronan and the others have been working to clear obstacles from the ley lines to make them stronger. Every time they do, that creates a chain reaction that means this line under Boston and Cambridge, this line that was dormant—it surges, too. Has Matthew been having fewer of those strange episodes lately?"

Declan didn't know. He hadn't asked. Matthew hadn't said. Theoretically Declan had been thinking nonstop about a sweet-metal to secure his future, but actually, this was what Declan had been thinking nonstop about: Jordan Hennessy.

"I wouldn't be surprised," Adam said. "He should be feeling great every time one of these surges happen."

Declan didn't see the problem with that, and he said so.

Adam pointed to the beetles. "You don't see a problem with that?"

"I see something that means eventually Matthew could stay awake on his own, am I right?"

Adam's voice was patient, as if Declan were a child. "Multiply that times thousands. Imagine a world where all the things the Ronan Lynches of the planet have dreamt over the years begin to wake up. Over the decades. Centuries. Think about legends that could be talking about dreams. Think about all the monsters. Dragons. Minotaurs. How many of those things are just stories and how many of those things were dreams that are sleeping now because the dreamers died long ago? Right now, Ronan's limited by how strong the ley line is. How many Ronans are there? What would they do without any limits? Stop thinking about Matthew for a second and *think*."

And now it began to spool out in Declan's mind, a future where dreamers with ambition broke the economy, changed the art world, dreamt escalating weapons. Niall and Ronan's skill hadn't been threatening because it had been limited both by ability and by scope—they wanted to live in the world as it was. But someone with absolute power and no checks or balances, Declan thought, someone with ambition . . .

"This isn't about just keeping Matthew awake," Adam said. "This is a bigger plan. This is a strategy."

"That doesn't sound like Ronan."

"Why do you think I said we needed to talk about Bryde?"

Bryde.

"Declan," Adam said, "the Moderators have special psychics. Visionaries, they call them. They've seen the future, and they think Ronan and the others are going to dream the apocalypse. That's why they're trying to kill him and Hennessy and Bryde. They think they're *going to end the world.*"

Adam went on, his voice low. "There's something out there. A thing that would end the world if it could, a kind of collective nightmare. I saw it the last time I scryed. A dreamer could bring it back. They wouldn't even have to be trying to do it on purpose. You've seen what Ronan can do. Just one bad dream with enough ley energy to make it real, and then it's game over. The Moderators have a point, is what I'm trying to say. Think about it. They have a point. And that's even if there's no bigger plan than just making the ley lines powerful again."

For a moment they were quiet. Declan sat on the concrete bench and looked back down the street at Harvard. He thought about how, at the beginning of the semester, Ronan had come here to look for apartments, and Declan had really believed that his loud brother might possibly live a quiet life like that, for Adam's sake.

"Has he called you?" Declan asked, knowing the answer already, not because of anything Adam had said, but because of all the things he hadn't.

Adam just looked at him.

"Do you trust Ronan?" Declan asked. His brother was many things, he thought, but murderer he was not. Even at his worst, it was only himself he'd wanted to destroy, and that hadn't seemed to be the Ronan he heard on the phone. Ronan's sin was immediacy, not villainy.

Adam looked pensive. "I don't trust Bryde."

"That doesn't answer the question."

But Adam just flicked a remaining beetle back under the bench and turned his face into the coming sunset.

Declan understood then that Adam Parrish was allowing him not much closer than he'd let those friends in the waffle truck line. This was still just a corner of the situation. A very different corner than he would share with his Harvard buddies, but still. Need-to-know basis. No more. Actual closeness and truth had been reserved for only one person, and Declan's relationship to that person was the only reason he was being given even this much of a look at Adam's concerns.

"What do you want me to do about it?" Declan asked.

Adam said, "Is he taking your calls?"

25

G rowing up, the Lynch family hadn't talked about the dreaming.

It seemed unfathomable now, that their entire livelihood had been based upon dreams, that two-fifths of them had *been* dreams, that two-fifths of them had been dreamers, and yet they did not talk about it. Niall Lynch sold dreams on the black market, and Declan took calls from buyers for dreams, and yet they did not talk about it. Aurora was a dream, and Niall had always known that if something happened to him, the children would immediately become orphans of a sleeping mother, and yet they did not talk about it. Ronan accidentally dreamt a brother into being, and had to teach himself how to prevent it from happening again, and yet they did not talk about it.

Ronan had thought there was no one else like him in the world, and it had nearly killed him, and yet they didn't talk about it.

Looking back now, Ronan tried again and again to understand it from Niall and Aurora's point of view. Perhaps they thought the children would be less likely to betray the secret if they didn't have words for it. Perhaps they thought Ronan might grow out of the dreaming if he didn't pay attention to it. Perhaps they had lost trust in humans so thoroughly that they numbered their sons among the untrustworthy.

He didn't remember the first time he'd dreamt something into being. He didn't remember dreaming Matthew. He did remember, however, one of the only times they talked about his dreaming.

Ronan had been young. He didn't remember if Matthew existed yet. Memories were like dreams that way—they skipped the parts that weren't interesting to them at the time. He had been playing in the back fields at the Barns, the deep sloping pasture that now contained the pond he and Adam had dug. He was young enough that he wasn't allowed out alone, so Aurora had been there with him, reading a book under the shade of a tree, laughing to herself every so often.

How idyllic it must have been, he thought now. Young Ronan, tumbling through the waist-high grass. Beautiful Aurora, sprawled in one of her light dresses in the grass, hair golden as Matthew's or Bryde's, a book in one hand, the other finding grapes out of the basket she'd brought with them. Overhead, the clouds in the summer blue had been as inviting and drowsy as an afternoon comforter.

Ronan had fallen asleep. He did not remember this; he only remembered the waking. He remembered waking in the grass and being unable to move. Not his legs asleep, but all of him, his mind looking down at his body sprawled in the grass near his beautiful, sweet mother.

And then the memory skipped to him plucking something from the grass to show to Aurora. It was a book like the one she'd been reading, but much smaller, sized for his child palms.

"What do we have here?" she asked him, putting hers away.

"Open it."

Aurora let the tiny volume fall open. Inside there were not pages, but a summer sky graced with towering white clouds. She poked her fingers into the book and watched the clouds part around them. The sky was in the book but it was also over the book, a page and a sky, two-dimensional and three-dimensional at once as it towered upward.

"Look at you, Mr. Impossible," Aurora whispered fondly. She opened and closed it several times to see if the sky would change. It did. From day to night to day again. Sun to stars to sun. "Now let's bury it."

"Bury it," echoed Ronan. He wanted to show it to Declan. To Niall. He wanted to put it on his shelf.

Aurora stood up and brushed the grass off her skirt. "Little things like this are best as secrets. It's very important to remember that."

It didn't feel important to remember that. It felt important to show it to someone. Ronan tried to understand. "For how long?"

She kissed the top of his head. "Forever."

Forever?

"This seems like a really nice place," Hennessy said. "Are we here to destroy it?"

Burrito had just driven past acres of dried, unharvested cornfields to arrive at a house old enough to have a name on a brick pillar by the drive: Barnhill. The cornfields went right up to a neat little yard, and then there was the square white house, and beyond that was dried marsh grass, and then, presumably, were marshes, and eventually the sea. The entire property had a haunted, lonely loveliness. One would not find it by accident.

Ronan agreed with Hennessy. It did seem like a really nice place. It reminded him of the Barns, and he did not want to destroy it.

Bryde didn't answer, just gazed at the house as they pulled the invisible car up to the separate garage. He had not been quite the same since the server farm, although Ronan couldn't put his finger on what had changed. He wanted to say that it was something like an additional gravity, an investment in the task, but no one had ever been as invested in this as Bryde. He seemed withdrawn from them. Introspective. It was, Ronan thought, as if he were angry or disappointed with Ronan or Hennessy, although he couldn't think of what they might have done to vex him.

"Get your things," he said finally, already opening his door. "No, not just your sword. Your bags."

"We're staying here?" Ronan asked in surprise. The lights were on inside the house and it had a decidedly lived-in look to it. Not Bryde's style. Not his style at all.

"If we're murdering people and taking their house," Hennessy said, "can I eat first? Actually, I guess I could eat them. I'm hungry enough to eat a baby. Are there going to be babies?"

But Bryde was already off and nearly to the porch of the house, even more disinterested in her banter than he had been at the beginning of all this. With a growl, Ronan shouldered his bag and the scabbard with VEXED TO NIGHTMARE and followed after. By the time Hennessy climbed the two steps to the front door to join them, they could already hear footsteps from inside the house, lots of them.

Ronan and Hennessy exchanged a look behind Bryde's back. She looked as bemused as he did.

Then the door opened and a short woman with light brown skin and dark brown hair clipped back from her face stood there. Even though her appearance had little in common with

Hennessy's, she nonetheless reminded Ronan of what Hennessy had looked like when he first met her: exhausted and frightened. Just like Hennessy, she hid the exhaustion and fright away beneath a very different expression, but it still leaked out around the eyes, the tight smile. When she saw them, a little bit of the exhaustion and fright went away, replaced with curiosity and wariness.

Good, thought Ronan. That was the correct response to the three of them showing up on one's doorway.

She looked Bryde up and down and then she looked over her shoulder. "Is this him?"

Behind her, several voices rose in a chorus of youthful excitement.

"He's *here!*"

"Is it him?"

"I *said* he was here? I said that already."

"It's Bryde!"

"What about Jordan Hennessy?"

"Yes! I see her! I see her!"

"And Ronan Lynch?"

"He's *tall* and *bald!* He has the *sword!*"

The children had rushed up behind their mother like a wave blustering to shore, stopping just short of breaking out onto the porch. Five happy faces in five different heights. They hissed and poked at each other and pointed at Hennessy and Ronan standing behind Bryde.

Ronan and Hennessy exchanged another look.

This was not what Ronan would have considered the correct response to the three of them showing up on one's doorway.

But he kind of liked it.

"You might as well come in so they can paw at you," said the woman. "Not that you're here for me, but I'm—"

"Angelica," Bryde said as he stepped past her into the cramped hallway. "Angelica Aldana-Leon. Yes. I know. They told me." As her mouth dropped open, he lifted a closed fist and said to the five children, "Presents, but not until you tell me what they are."

"Are they the seeds?"

"Are you real?"

"He said not to ask that!"

Bryde opened his closed hand and let a single seed drop from it into each of their palms. "Now, how do you make them grow?"

They conferred like it was a game show. Then one whispered the answer to the other, and together they clapped the seeds in their hands. Each immediately exploded into a bright blue lily, and just then, Ronan realized, stupidly, that they were all dreamers, each of these children, and Bryde must have come to them in their dreams, too, and shown them these dreamt seeds he was going to give them.

Ronan searched inside himself for the same jealousy he'd first felt over Rhiannon, but that wasn't what he felt at all.

"The children told me that it's you who have stopped the . . ." Angelica asked them, making a gesture to her eyes and nose. The nightwash.

"The slop!" shouted one of the boys.

"Thank you. Thank you so much. I don't know how to thank you for what you're doing, so just, thank you, you have saved them," Angelica said, with feeling.

"You're welcome," Bryde said. "I don't know how long it will hold, but we will keep working."

Ronan stared at the kids, who stared back up at him. Now he understood why Angelica looked frightened and exhausted. Dreamers. Little dreamers, like he had been once, but growing up in a world where a lack of ley energy was killing them. He wondered how many dreamers had died of the nightwash without knowing anyone else like them existed, or knowing that they could save themselves by moving to a place with more energy.

This was why they were doing what they were doing.

He looked down. One of the kids had his hand and was shaking it, trying to get him to follow. Another was giggling furiously as Chainsaw sat on her shoulder, working hard to be extraordinarily gentle with her talons.

Same, Chainsaw, he thought.

A third hugged his leg, and without thinking, he draped a hand over her head, his unconscious remembering both Matthew and Opal. He had forgotten what it was like to hug and be hugged during these last few weeks. It felt like ages since these small comforts.

Angelica said something in brisk Spanish and the children began to argue noisily among themselves. In English, she told them, "The children will show you where you can put your things. I'm sorry, it is bunk beds for you two boys. We don't have much room."

"That's all right," Bryde said. "It will be nice to have a shower and a meal for a night."

Hennessy was whisked away and Bryde and Ronan left in a bedroom with the promised bunk beds. There was nothing fancy about the beds—they were just raw wood screwed together with a can-do attitude and mismatched blankets—but the entire situation was homier than any place they had stayed since leaving.

Bryde didn't seem to care. No sooner had he silently set his bag on the lower bunk than he turned to go.

"Wait a second," Ronan said. "Wait a damn second."

Bryde paused and Ronan nearly lost his nerve. He hadn't expected Bryde to listen.

"What did we do?" Ronan asked.

Narrowing his eyes, Bryde shook his head a little.

Ronan pressed on. "Haven't we been trying? What more do you want from us? We go where you tell us to go, we do what you tell us to do. You asked me to listen, and I listened. What did I do? What did I fuck up?"

Bryde's expression changed. "I'm not angry with you. Is that what you think?"

"I don't know what to think."

"I don't, either," Bryde said. "Why does Adam keep trying to find you in the dreams these past few days?"

Tamquam

"And why," Bryde went on, "are you keeping him out?"

Ronan felt his face go hot, his hands go cold. He hadn't thought Bryde would notice. "You don't know him. He can't put things down. He's thorough. He cares. The fact he found a way to look for me in dreamspace as soon as we started getting more energy out there just proves it. If I let him meet up with me in dreamspace, he won't stop researching the Moderators and all of this stuff until he's solved it. I'm not going to be the one who gets him kicked out of Harvard."

"For his own good," Bryde said, but not as if he believed or disbelieved, just as if he was anticipating the rest of Ronan's sentence. Then he looked away, and as he did, he had that same expression that had made Ronan think he was upset with them.

His eyebrows set, eyes tight, mouth tight. Not as effortless as the Bryde they'd met all the weeks ago. In a low voice, he said, almost to himself, "No, I'm not angry at you. You have done everything I've hoped. You and Hennessy are much different than I expected. Better than I expected."

Ronan's mouth opened and closed. It was such the opposite of what he was expecting to hear that he didn't have any words at all.

"No, I am not angry at you," Bryde continued. "I'm tired. I'm proud. I'm confused. I'm sad, because I know things can't stay like they are now. We are working even now to change things and it will never be like this moment again. It is a ridiculous way to think, to be more interested in the present than the future, and if it were you or Hennessy, I would never permit it. I won't lose my way. I know that. But I can imagine it. It is me—it is me I am angry with."

It meant more to Ronan than he thought to hear all these words, even if he didn't entirely understand them.

"We are nearly to the final step," Bryde said. "There is only the dam left. Then it will be a different game entirely."

"Why are we here, then?" Ronan asked, and Bryde's mouth turned rueful, which made Ronan think he had been expecting Ronan to ask something else, although he couldn't imagine what that something else might be.

"This is just a reward. This is just so you can see why we're doing it and sleep a night on a real pillow and bask in the gratitude of one of the many voices who have your names on their lips these days. You're a hero. Enjoy it."

A hero. It was an unfamiliar concept. Ronan had been the villain for so long, if he had been anything. The one in trouble, the one written up on the slip, the one being chased, the one being accused. And before that he had been the young dreamer. Secret. Forever. Now he was a hero to a family of young dreamers who would never have to feel alone.

Both Bryde and Ronan jumped as they heard a trilling sound. It was Ronan's dreamt phone. He'd nearly forgotten he still had it; he hadn't used it since that first call to Declan.

And it was Declan now. There was no way to identify the caller visually, of course, since the dreamt phone just looked like a tunnel piercing. But nevertheless, something about the ring strongly *implied* that it was Declan.

It was a jarring interruption. Declan belonged to another world, a different timeline, but with a glance at Bryde, Ronan tapped his finger against his ear to answer it. "Deklo."

"Good, it worked."

Ronan said, "How did you do it?"

"I had to get back the car I was in when you called before and find your call in the previous calls in its log. I couldn't type in that gibberish, of course, that showed up as your number, but I could just ask it to return your call."

"Wait, what car were you in before?"

Declan didn't bother answering this. "I want you to come to Mass this weekend."

It took Ronan a moment to parse the request. It was a quite ordinary one, one Declan had made countless times over the past several years, resulting in Ronan rolling his eyes and leaving very early in the morning in order to make it to eleven o'clock Mass with his brothers on the other side of the state. Now it felt like someone else's memories. A dream.

It occurred to Ronan that something bad might have happened. "What's going on? Is Matthew okay?"

"Family meeting," Declan said, a Declanism that never failed to rankle. *Family meeting* meant Declan shaking his finger at one of the other Lynch brothers.

"About what?"

"About the future."

"Are you fucking serious about Mass? That's in two days."

"I have faith in you."

"A lot of people are on our tail."

"You tell us the church, the location, we'll be there."

Bryde was waiting, eyebrow raised.

"My brothers want to see me," Ronan told him. It was making his pulse jack up for some reason, the thought of it, or the thought of telling Bryde about it. He couldn't tell which. "This weekend."

Declan asked, "Who are you talking to? Is that Bryde?"

"We have a date with Ilidorin," Bryde said in a low voice.

"I have to think about it," Ronan told the phone. "I'm not close to Boston."

"What's important to you?" Declan asked. "I wouldn't be asking if it wasn't important."

Bryde was still looking with his same expectant expression, hand on the doorknob to go to the dreamers they'd come to see.

"I have to go," Ronan said. "I'll call you back."

He hung up.

He thought he grasped what Bryde had just been talking about before the call, because he, too, felt somewhat torn between the possibility of seeing his brothers again for a few minutes, and the knowledge that the dreamers were nearly to the end of the first part of this endeavor and whatever would change once the final obstacle to Ilidorin's line was removed.

"I won't tell you what to do," Bryde said. "But I need to go on after this. I can't stop this close to the end."

"I know," Ronan replied.

It was complicated to be a hero.

26

Matthew was walking.

Not *wandering*, this time, but walking determinedly. Declan had told him he'd talked to Ronan and to stay put while he went out to take care of errands. He hadn't said the two things were connected, but Matthew guessed they were. He'd *had* to guess, because no matter what Matthew said, Declan still failed to have real conversations with him. He confided in Jordan if he confided in anyone, and just kept pointing out dogs to Matthew. This filled Matthew with bad feeling, and the bad feeling, on top of all his previous bad feeling, set him to walking.

Not wandering.

Walking.

Like a human, not a dream.

He marched, hands stuffed in the pockets of his bright blue puffer jacket, head down. Watching his sneakers slap one in front of the other just made him walk faster and harder, dark pavement and sidewalk disappearing beneath them. Declan thought these big white sneakers were ridiculous. Matthew knew that now. He hadn't when he'd bought them, all excited about having put away enough money. *Aren't they super?* he'd said, and Declan had murmured, *They are the most memorable pair of shoes I've ever seen,* and at the time Matthew had thought that meant Declan loved them as much as he did.

How stupid he'd been, he thought, his ears burning red. How stupid he'd always been about everything.

Even the idea that Matthew had been excited about finally acquiring enough money to get the shoes was ridiculous. The money was from a weekly allowance that came from doing chores, a system started by Aurora back at the Barns and continued by Declan, even after they moved to the town house. Matthew had never questioned the correctness of this. Yes, of course he received an allowance for cleaning his room, vacuuming, unloading the dishwasher, spraying pine cleaner on the town house's front door to get the pollen off, cleaning the trash out of Declan's Volvo after school.

God, he couldn't bear thinking about it. He just couldn't *bear* it. It had just been Declan's money, just an older brother giving pocket money to a stupid little kid who stayed stupid even once he got big. All Matthew's friends at school got jobs bussing tables and working cash registers and Matthew got bills in a mug on the kitchen counter. And now it was no different, he just collected the allowance from gallery owners who gave him odd jobs as a favor to Declan, because they thought Declan Lynch's kid brother was cute and his love of ugly sneakers was funny.

Matthew kept walking, walking. Stomping. He walked right out of their neighborhood, past restaurants bustling with diners and comely brick row houses bright in the evening, by a little convenience store that reminded him of the one Declan had sometimes stopped at back at home when he forgot to get milk during the week. He thought about the times they'd just sat there for several long minutes with Declan staring off at nothing with the receipt for the milk pressed between his hand and the steering wheel. *Aren't we going home?* Matthew would ask. *Play your game,*

Declan would reply, and Matthew did, he just played whatever stupid game he had on his phone while his older brother sat there at a gas station five minutes from home for sometimes nearly an hour rather than going back to the town house, and Matthew had never once asked him why they were sitting there or what Declan was thinking about or if he hated everything about his life.

And now this thing about sweetmetals—this thing they were supposedly pursuing to keep Matthew safe while not talking to him about any of it?

Everyone still acted like he was just a pet.

Matthew's feet kept on marching him along, farther from home. "Home." With quotation marks, because *home* without quotation marks was either the Barns or the DC town house. "Home" was a Fenway apartment Matthew thought of as Old Man Eyebrows, because of how the detail work over the windows looked like fat, frowning eyebrows. It had seven rooms, which Matthew had mentally named. Twice. Once after the Seven Dwarves, and once after the seven vices. Happy Gluttony was the kitchen. Bashful Sloth, the living room. Grumpy Lust, Declan's bedroom. So on. So forth. Declan liked the apartment. Matthew could tell Declan liked it. He liked everything about his life here, even though Matthew wasn't exactly sure what his life here even entailed. He didn't talk to Matthew about it. Declan didn't say he was happier, but he clearly was happier. It made Matthew feel kind of bad inside.

Enormously bad inside.

He didn't know why.

His feet had taken him to a part of the city that seemed to be nearer to the water and farther from people and businesses.

Beside him was a raised bit of highway that just ended in midair with weeds beneath it, ready for an action scene.

Declan would have been extremely displeased to find him here.

Back when Matthew learned he was a dream, Declan had told him that he was just as much a Lynch brother as the other two, but Matthew knew now that wasn't true. Because he wasn't being sent to school. He wasn't being prepared for a future. He was being tended and loved and managed. The thing about this life of Declan's, Matthew thought, the *thing about it*, was that Matthew was just a thing *in it*. A dream object. A puppy to be walked and then returned to "home" with some of the energy burned off.

His eye was caught by an unoccupied crane, a spiffy one. It had one of those big boom things that looked like a ladder and at the top of it was a hook.

Matthew thought, without hesitation: *I'm going to climb that.*

He did. He clambered onto the body and then onto the boom, up and up and up. He thought how annoyed Declan would be. Good, he thought. Good, good. *But I told you to stay in the house*, Declan would say, confused. *You're supposed to stay exactly where I put you, like a toy.*

He kind of wished he'd never found out he was a dream.

At the top of the crane boom, Matthew closed his eyes. He used to imagine that air was a hug that was always happening, but he couldn't seem to conjure up that happy thought right then.

It had taken Matthew a long time to understand that he was a boat anchor in Declan's life.

"Crumbs!"

Opening his eyes, he realized there was a tiny person looking up at him. A tiny Jordan. Well, a regular-sized Jordan, far below. She shielded her eyes. "Yeah, I thought that was you!"

"You can't make me come down," Matthew told her.

"I sure as shit cannot," she agreed, "but it is harder to talk this way, you up there, me down here."

"Don't talk to me like a kid. I can tell you're talking to me like a kid and I *don't like it.*"

Jordan crossed her arms, a posture readable even from up on a crane. "All right, here you go, then: Climbing up on a stick into the sky is a stupid way to process any kind of problem, but stupid's your right, so if you want to stay up there, just lemme know how long it'll be, so I can know if I have time to get a drink, or if I should just hang here."

"Why do I need to be watched *at all?*"

"Because you climbed a crane, mate."

Matthew considered this and then considered it some more and then, with a sigh, climbed down to where Jordan waited. "How did you know I was here?"

"You walked right by my studio. You didn't recognize it?"

He hadn't. Stupid.

"What's the deal here?" Jordan asked as they began to walk back the way he'd come. "Are you giving rebellion a go? Is this about your brothers lying to you?"

Because she just said it instead of mincing around it, Matthew told her. He told her everything. All the things that were bothering him, from big to small and back to big again.

"That all sounds truly fucked up, and I'm sorry," Jordan said, opening the door to Fenway Studios. Together they walked down the hall toward the studio she stayed in. "The problem as I see it is that some of that shit's about being a dream, but some of it's just about growing up, and honestly, both are sorry situations if you ask me about it."

"I did," Matthew said.

"You did what, mate?"

"Ask you about It."

She laughed her enormous laugh as he smiled at her. She lightly high-fived him and then pushed open the door to let them into the studio. "Ah yeah."

"Whoa," Matthew said. "This is good."

Since he'd been last, Jordan had accomplished huge amounts of work on her copies of *El Jaleo* and *Madame X*. Each canvas had a separate, smaller easel sitting in front of it, with reference photos and jotted palette notes and instructions and business cards taped all over them. But what he was looking at was the work she'd done on the portrait of Sherry and her daughter, the one he'd helped her with at the very beginning. It was still coming together, but their faces were very good and the colors were as understated and lovely as the John White Alexander paintings she had taped on the easel beside it.

"Thanks," Jordan said.

"They're way better than this other weird stuff." The rest of the studio was full of the ordinary studio occupant's work—colorful, elongated nudes with cucumber-shaped breasts.

"Not really," Jordan said. "I mean, Sargent's better than Sir Tits here is, obviously. That's why Sargent's famous and this guy is just, you know, this guy. But these paintings of mine are copies. At least this guy is making original stuff. That's part of it, I think. I don't know much about sweetmetals, but I know I'll never make one painting Sargents."

Matthew moved Jordan's pillow to sit on the bright orange couch. "So what do you think will do it?"

She perched on the arm. "It's what that guy said, isn't it? Boat fellow, the one your brother took us to see. The art's got to do something to the artist. It's more about making it than what gets made. It changes them, I guess. If you're a bang-up artist who always paints great work, it doesn't mean anything when you make another great work. It's got be something else, not trauma, exactly, it's more like . . . energy and movement. One makes the other. There's movement in their life, their technique, somehow, that captures that ley energy, its movement. I guess. I don't know, really. I'm talking out my ass, and if my voice sounds desperate to you, it's because of that, it's coming from my ass."

Matthew liked that she was talking to him like he was a real person. "So you think making an—a not-copy, a, uh, an original, will make a sweetmetal for you? Because you always do copies?"

She pointed at him, snapping her fingers. "Right. Right. That's what I'm hoping. But I just won't know if it works until I need it, will I? I've been working on an original, that painting of your brother, but I can't tell, sitting here, if it's working. I can't feel any of the sweetmetals the same way these past few days, actually, because of whatever Hennessy and Ronan are doing with the ley line. Have you noticed that? Have you noticed you've had fewer of the episodes?"

Matthew was so relieved to hear her say it, like it was just a normal, commonplace thing. "I haven't been wandering!"

"Right? When I first got here, I felt the sweetmetals so strongly. I could feel *El Jaleo* doing something to me, I guess because I needed it. Now it feels like there's more energy to be had all around, so I just feel normal when I see it. I mean, I love it, yeah, sure. But I don't know if I'd be able to tell it was any different than an ordinary painting if I saw it for the first time today. So I can't feel if my painting is getting there or not."

"You could get another dream," Matthew suggested. "A sleeping one. From a dead dreamer. Back at the Barns, there's loads of my dad's still, probably."

"That's a really good idea."

She sounded like she really meant it, too. Because of this, he felt bold enough to ask, "Can I see it?"

"What? Oh. The painting. You know he hasn't seen it yet."

"Yeah."

"You'd be the only person besides me to see it."

"Yeah."

"Okay, fine, but my ego is very fragile about it, so maybe don't tell me anything bad about it. Maybe don't say anything at all. Just grunt, and then I'll put it away real quick."

"Yeah."

The high-ceilinged studio had a little half balcony; she retrieved a large canvas from it and then, making a face, turned it around at the bottom of the stairs for him to see.

Matthew looked at it a long time.

"Never mind, say something; silence is much worse," Jordan told him, and Matthew liked this, too, because it made him feel like she cared about what he thought.

"Does Declan know what it looks like, even a little?" he asked. When she shook her head, he looked at it a bit longer and then he said, "Are you going to marry my brother?"

"Crumbs, man, you go hard. I thought you'd say the foreground was too busy or that I'd gotten his nose wrong."

Matthew asked, "Why does he treat you like you're real?"

Jordan looked at him for a long time, as long as he'd looked at the painting, and then she took away the portrait of Declan to the second floor again. When she came back down, she crouched in front of him and said, "Because I *am* real."

"How do you know?"

"Because I'm talking to you, mate! Because I have thoughts and feelings of my own! It doesn't matter how you got here. You are here."

Matthew stared at his hands. "What if Ronan made me this way? What if he made me how I am?"

"So what if he did?" She took his hand and jiggled it. "Why do you think Declan's got his curls? Why do you think Ronan's an asshole? We all get handed things from our parents. We all have bodies that obey rules that we deal with. We're not as different as you think."

Matthew could feel himself retreating from this last sentence as fast as he'd walked away from Old Man Eyebrows.

"Look, I'm not trying to tell you it's easy," Jordan said. "To deal with this, with being a dream. I just mean—I just mean, if you're thinking, *This is the magic thing that explains why everything's weird and wrong and why it's so hard to figure where I fit*, well, it doesn't solve things like that. We're not different in ways that matter. Your boy Declan just pretends it matters so he doesn't have to think too hard about his mum and how he feels about that, and because he's afraid that if *you're* a real person, you'll grow up and leave him and then he won't have a family and he won't know who he is. There. There's your two-dollar therapy session, I don't know if it's for you or for him but maybe you can split the cost."

"You're pretty cool," Matthew said.

"Aw, yeah I am." She lightly high-fived him again. "So what do you think of my painting?"

Matthew pointed to a long orange breast on the closest can-vas. "I think it's better than that one."

Jordan laughed gleefully. "Hey, I see a smile on that face. You happier, then?"

Matthew thought about it. "Yeah."

It was better than happiness, actually. For the first time since he'd found out he was a dream, he felt like himself again.

27

Hennessy remembered sitting for *Jordan in White*.

Jay had spent the morning crying at a mirror on the second floor of their London row house, and Hennessy had spent the morning watching her through the cracked door. She'd drawn the shape of her mother into the shag rug she sat on and wiped it out again and again, trying to perfect the slope of her shoulders, the bend of her neck. It was difficult to tell if Jay had been truly crying or if she were crying for reference. She was taking photos of it with her phone in the mirror and then rapidly typing something into it.

After a few hours of this, Jay emerged without warning, and although Hennessy scrambled away to prevent discovery, her mother found her wrapped in the linen curtain at the end of the hall.

"Little ghost," she said to Hennessy. "Let's go to the studio."

Hennessy was rarely allowed into the studio and certainly never invited, so it was with awe she accepted her mother's hand and rode the elevator to the third-floor studio.

There was nothing quite like J. H. Hennessy's studio when she was in the prime of her career. This secret world was accessible only via the coded elevator or via a dark staircase that ended at a door with no knob, just a key in a lock. Inside it was old and new. Elderly window sashes, sleek white walls. Old floorboards, new black and white graphic floor paint. From the ceiling hung immense light fixtures, gifts from a fellow artist, messes of lightbulbs and dried grasses and leaves. From the floor grew metal floor lamps with shades cut sharply so that they threw light in geometric, lacy shapes. Gradient thumbprints dotted every flat surface, including the white grand piano, where Jay had thoughtlessly tested new paints. And of course there were the paintings, in all states of finish. The eyes were alive. The hands were alive.

Once the elevator door had hissed closed behind them, Jay took just one moment to look out one of the studio's windows for something and then, when she didn't find it, she returned to make a great fuss over Hennessy. She had her try on several of the dresses she had thrown on the sofa. She posed her in multiple ways in a simple wooden chair. She messed with her hair and played at braids and put lipstick on her and wiped it off. All the while she told Hennessy how pretty she had grown up to be, how wonderful a painting they were going to make together. No! Not *a* painting. A series of paintings. An exhibition. It had felt like a day that happened to someone else. Hennessy sat very still in the chair, like an animal by a highway, afraid to move lest she dart from safety to something worse. She was cold in the white shift but she didn't want to even shiver in case her mother remembered Hennessy was not usually treated like this.

But the spell hadn't broken. They'd worked all day, all evening. The next morning, Jay was still enthused. She ordered in a very grand breakfast of pastries from one of the bakeries and then they went back up for more work, this time up the rickety back staircase that ended in the door with no knob. They spent two weeks like that, with Hennessy sitting still in the chair and not shivering and her mother painting her and takeaway and delivery bags piling up in the stairwell.

At one point, Jay put her brush down and said, shocked, "I made you. One day you'll grow up and be a woman, and I made you."

Jay looked at Hennessy, and Hennessy suddenly had the impression that Jay was really seeing her, really thinking about what it meant to be Hennessy, to be Hennessy's mother.

Jay looked from Hennessy to her painting and back again, and then she said, "How wonderful you're going to be."

It was the best moment of Hennessy's life.

Then there was an audible slam. The front door. Bill Dower, returning from wherever he had gone. Jay leapt up so quickly that her stool clattered on the floor. Her still-wet palette was abandoned on the piano. The elevator door was whirring closed.

Hennessy was alone before she even quite understood what had happened.

She sat in the chilly chair for quite a while, not wanting to move in case her mother returned. After an hour, she pulled up the drop cloth to wrap around herself and wait some more (little ghost!). Finally she let herself shiver and admit Jay wasn't coming back.

With a little sigh, she padded barefoot across the cold floor to the elevator, but discovered it wouldn't move without the code, which she didn't have. She went to the door without a knob instead, but it wouldn't open. It was locked; the keyhole was empty.

Hennessy was trapped in the studio.

At first she called down very nicely, though she didn't think either of her parents would hear her over their own raised voices. Then she shouted. She banged.

Finally, she gave up. She waited.

It became night.

Hennessy wiped away her tears and turned on the floor lights, which threw hard, lacy patterns across the floor and walls. She went to see the canvas her mother had worked on all these weeks.

It was awful.

It was the worst painting Hennessy had ever seen her mother do. It was twee and cutesy, a straightforward and boring portrait of a daft, plucky little girl sitting awkwardly on a chair. The eyes weren't alive. The hands weren't alive. Hennessy, who'd been working and learning with her own art all this time, was embarrassed for her mother. It was terrible that she wasn't coming up here for Hennessy and her growling stomach, but it felt even more terrible that anyone would ever see this piece.

Hennessy looked at the canvas for a long time, and then she counted, telling herself that if one of her parents came for her by the count of six hundred, she wouldn't do it.

Six hundred seconds went by. Eight hundred. One thousand. Hennessy stopped counting.

She searched the drawers by the wall and collected all the paints she wanted. Then she moistened her mother's oils again on the palette, picked up the brush and began to paint. After a few minutes, she dragged over the full-length mirror from beside the sofa, and she redid the portrait's gormless face with her actual wary expression. She overpainted the boring shadows in the white shift with subtle colors instead. She shrugged the shoulders of that chilly girl just a little, not quite shivering, but wanting to. At each step, she got up to compare her brushstrokes to the other paintings in the studio. She made the eyes alive. She made the hands alive.

She painted the portrait that Jay should have painted. It took all night.

It was a J. H. Hennessy by way of Jordan Hennessy. It was another day after that before her mother came to get her, and by then Hennessy was fitful and burning up with a fever that had come on during the second night. Bill Dower had gone again.

"This turned out better than I thought," Jay said, looking at the canvas, hovering her fingers over her signature in the corner, painted by Hennessy hours before. "Oh, Jordan. Stop complaining. I've got some paracetamol downstairs. Come on, what a trial. Next time don't hide so long and you won't feel as awful."

Hennessy's first forgery was of herself.

Sitting in the basement of Aldana-Leon's house, crisscross applesauce on the roll-up mattress, Hennessy took out her dreamt phone and held it in her lap. She looked around the dim basement. It was stacked densely with cardboard boxes, a family that had either not yet unpacked from a move or was packing for one. One corner had been reserved for a small desk covered with tubes of poster paints and cheap brushes. There were a few pieces of rippled paper there that had been painted on, and some child had painted the top of the desk instead. Hennessy respected that child.

With a shiver, Hennessy told her dreamt phone to call Jordan.

It rang for nearly a minute, and then:

"Jordan Hennessy," Jordan said politely, not recognizing the caller ID. "Hello?"

Jordan's voice hit her like a sack of stones.

Hennessy's best forgery. Jordan, by way of Hennessy. All those years together. All the other girls, dead. Why hadn't Hennessy called her before now? How had she forgotten how Jordan was the only thing that ever made this feeling inside Hennessy go away? This awful dread, this feeling of the Lace, even when she was awake.

Hennessy hadn't spoken yet. She didn't know what to say.

On the other side of the line, a bland voice sounded in the background. "I'm getting it to go—it's faster that way, even with the walk. Do you want baba ghanoush or no?"

Declan Lynch.

Declan Lynch.

Why was she surprised to hear his voice? She'd known Jordan had left in his car, weeks and weeks before.

Jordan's words were slightly muffled as she turned from the phone. "If you're paying, yes. Get me every side dish they have." Then, back to the phone, "Sorry, who's this? I don't know you're coming through very well. I can't hear you."

This voice, the one she was using on the phone, was a very different voice than the one she'd just used for Declan Lynch. She'd used her outside, professional voice to talk to the phone, her inside, real voice to talk to Declan Lynch. Hennessy and her girls were the only ones who used to get the second one. They'd been the only ones who were important.

Hennessy's cheeks felt hot.

"Hello?" Jordan said. Then, to Declan, "No, a crank caller, I guess. Or a bad connection. One doesn't like to assume malice."

"*Safer* to assume," Declan said drily, and Jordan's laugh faded as she pulled the phone away from her head.

Hennessy hung up.

She sat back on the mattress.

She let herself think it. *This is what she's always wanted.*

It wasn't that Hennessy had wanted Jordan to be unhappy in her absence. After all, Hennessy was the one who'd insisted Jordan go with Declan in the first place—right? Her memories were muddy. She could hear a little voice suggesting Jordan had actually come up with the idea, but carefully worded it so Hennessy would think it was hers. Was that true?

She thought about going upstairs to find Ronan. He would remember. He was there that night.

But finding Ronan meant finding Bryde, too, because they were together in the bunk bedroom, and also because the two of them were inseparable. And Bryde would just try to spin her current misery into a lesson. Hennessy didn't think she could take any more lessons.

The basement was cold. She pulled up the sheet around her to cover her shoulders and, just like that, was transported to her memory in Jay's studio. *Little ghost.*

What if Jordan stopped loving her? What if she'd never loved her, only *needed* her? What if Hennessy had lost the only real thing in her life by running off to chase dreams with Bryde and Ronan Lynch?

What was she *doing* here?

They weren't a company of three dreamers. Bryde and Ronan were one thing. Hennessy was something else.

Hennessy was so tired of being alone.

She was so tired.

She turned the phone over in her hands. Even the phone was a reminder of how little she belonged here. If not for Ronan, it wouldn't be a phone in her hands, it would be the Lace, just like at Rhiannon Martin's farm. Angrily, she tapped through the options, looking to see what her subconscious and

Ronan's subconscious had dreamt into it. Contact numbers. Speakerphone. Text messaging.

Timer.

Before Ronan and Bryde, Hennessy had always set a timer before she fell asleep. Twenty minutes. That was the longest she could sleep before starting to dream. Eventually she had to set the timer while she was awake, too, because it turned out that sleeping without dreaming eventually left one prone to drifting off even while painting or driving.

This phone's timer had only one setting. Twenty minutes.

Was it her subconscious or Ronan's that had guessed she might come looking for it at some point? Which one of them hadn't trusted her? She wondered if she could go back to that life. Everything seemed imaginary with that little sleep. Surely it had been worse than this reality.

Surely.

Hennessy tried not to think about the sound of Jordan's voice.

She tried not to think of the sound of her voice talking to Declan.

Little ghost. Hennessy was haunting Jordan's life. She knew which of them was the more vital Jordan Hennessy.

The hideous feeling grew and grew in her. She knew if she went to Ronan and Bryde, they'd whisk her off into a dream full of impossible things, thinking this would remind her of the joy of dreaming. They never considered how it only reminded her of the joy of *their* dreaming. No, she needed to deal with this herself.

She just wanted to put this feeling down for a few minutes. Everyone else in the world could sleep it off.

Not Hennessy.

It was always the Lace. Always going to be the Lace.

Closing her eyes, Hennessy thought back to that last time she'd seen Jordan. She ignored the little mean voice. She was sure Jordan hadn't wanted to leave Hennessy. She was sure it had been Hennessy's idea to send her off with Declan for safekeeping. She was sure Jordan had believed in her.

She was sure.

Shrugging off the sheet, Hennessy climbed off the mattress. She didn't set the timer. Instead, she asked her phone to show her one of John White Alexander's paintings. He was one of their favorites. Jordan and Hennessy. Hennessy and Jordan.

She went to the desk covered with art supplies, squeezed some paint out, and picked up one of the brushes.

Then she began to do one thing, at least, that she knew she was good at: forging someone else's brilliance.

28

Ronan woke with a start.

He was in the top bunk in the room he was sharing with Bryde. It was still dark.

He rolled over quietly to see if Bryde was sleeping.

The lower bunk was empty, the blankets tossed aside. Ronan grabbed his jeans from where they were tossed at the end of his bunk, his jacket from the plastic unicorn head on the wall, and his boots from beside the door.

He stepped quietly into the dark hallway.

Bryde crouched there over a collapsed form. Matthew. One of Matthew's hands was palm up, and in it was a little figurine of a hawk. He was obviously dead.

"What did you *do?*" Ronan snarled.

"Correlation is not causation, Ronan Lynch," Bryde said. Adam appeared briefly at the end of the hall and, just as quick, was gone.

"What did you do?"

Bryde said, "Wake up."

Ronan woke with a start.

He was in the top bunk in the room he was sharing with Bryde. It was still dark.

He rolled over quietly to see if Bryde was sleeping.

The lower bunk was empty, the blankets tossed aside. Ronan grabbed his jeans from where they were tossed at the end of his bunk, his jacket from the plastic unicorn head on the wall, and his boots from beside the door.

He stepped quietly into the dark hallway.

Bryde crouched there over a collapsed form. Matthew. One of Matthew's hands was palm up, and in it was a little figurine of a hawk. He was obviously dead.

"What did you *do?*" Ronan snarled.

"Correlation is not causation, Ronan Lynch," Bryde said. Adam appeared briefly at the end of the hall and, just as quick, was gone.

"What did you do?"

Bryde said, "Wake up."

Ronan woke with a start.

He was in the top bunk in the room he was sharing with Bryde. It was still dark.

He rolled over quietly to see if Bryde was sleeping.

Bryde was already standing by the bunk, eye to eye with Ronan, somehow less like himself, frighteningly close.

He didn't smile, but he was all teeth. He said, "Whose dream is this?"

Ronan woke with a start.

He was in the top bunk in the room he was sharing with Bryde. Full white winter daylight streamed in the window. It was quiet, but nonetheless Ronan had that feeling one sometimes has on waking, the feeling of having been woken by a sound. In this case, a scream.

He lay there in bed for a few seconds, listening, waiting, and now it sounded instead like a very intense conversation was happening deeper in the house. He listened to it long enough to feel he was awake, or at the very least, that this dream was going to be different from the previous ones. He got dressed and headed out.

There was no one on the first floor, where school supplies spread across the dining room table, so Ronan descended to the basement.

It took him a moment to absorb the full picture.

There was a painting of a woman in a swirling blue dress completely covering twelve of the stacked boxes. Not dreamt. Done with real paint, some of it still a little dark and damp. The desk tucked beside the boxes held bottles of cheap school paints and paper plates with childish smiley faces drawn on them—Hennessy must have been painting with the children. The cheap school colors didn't seem like they should combine to the sophisticated work on the boxes, but this wasn't magic, this was Hennessy. This was what she was good at. What she was great at.

Hennessy stood in front of her cardboard mosaic, one hand pressed up against the roses tattooed round her throat, looking at the ground. There was vomit on the ground in front of her.

Bryde was there, blood all up and down one arm with no sign of where it was coming from. He stood silent as Angelica screamed in his face.

The children were all crying.

Katie was curled up small, her arms linked around her leg braces, whimpering. Yesenia was sobbing and occasionally babbling, hoarse when she did. Stephen was trying to look stoic as he watched Angelica let Bryde have it, but his mouth was crumpled and his chin dimpling in a way that reminded Ronan uncomfortably of when Matthew was upset. Wilson and Ana clung to Angelica, faces buried in their mother's shirt. There was blood on her clothing, too.

"What the hell," Ronan said, but his words were lost in the cacophony.

"Accidents happen," Bryde said. "And surely you can tell by looking at her she didn't mean to do it."

"It doesn't matter that it is an accident," Angelica barked back. "Traffic collisions are accidents—that doesn't mean I send my children to play in the street!"

"I was only a minute behind her in the dream," Bryde pointed out. "They were never in danger."

Angelica swept her arm over the children. "You and I have a very different definition of danger! I saw those things—that thing. I saw it. It . . ." Her anger had to disappear for a moment as she choked down a horrified half sob.

Hennessy looked up at Ronan, her expression quite calm. But when she blinked, two tears immediately broke free and raced down her cheeks.

Then Ronan got it.

She'd taken out the Lace.

Bryde had dispatched it somehow, but Ronan knew that didn't really matter in the relative scheme of things. The injury of the Lace wasn't whatever sparring had caused that blood. It was the mere existence of the Lace. It was that before you saw the Lace, you didn't know something like the Lace could exist. Especially if you hadn't known, before that minute, that anything could hate you that much. Especially if you hadn't known, before that minute, that you could hate yourself that much.

Katie had stopped whimpering and was staring off at nothing, her eyes lost.

Hennessy looked at Ronan and shook her head as another tear escaped.

"I'm so sorry," she told Angelica. "I'm so sorry. I'm so—"

"Who are you to have that in your head?" Angelica said. Then her eyebrows sort of got themselves together and her entire expression got harder. Ronan could tell that whatever she said next was going to be absolutely true and would absolutely destroy Hennessy. Before she could say it, Bryde held up a hand.

He turned to Ronan and Hennessy. "Get your things. Then get in the car."

"Why?" Hennessy asked in a hollow voice.

"Actually, forget your things. I'll get them. Just get in the car," Bryde ordered. He turned back to Angelica, and as they left, Ronan heard him say, "You might remember that dreamer was a child once, too, not very long ago."

Outside the car, Hennessy stopped dead and simply stared at it and through it. It was not because it was invisible. She was staring at and through everything in front of her; her eyes were so bleak and her shoulders so defeated that Ronan wrapped his arms around her.

"I'm not a doll, Ronan Lynch," she said, her voice muffled. "Take your hands off me."

He just hugged her tighter, though, as she cried into his chest.

A few minutes later, Bryde came out, looking worn and blank, Ronan's and Hennessy's bags over his shoulders.

"Call your brother," he told Ronan. "Tell him we can see them for a few hours."

29

A special kind of relationship happened between an artist and a piece of art, on account of the investment. Sometimes it was an emotional investment. The subject matter meant something to the artist, making every stroke of the brush weightier than it looked. It might be a technical investment. It was a new method, a hard angle, an artistic challenge that meant no success on the canvas could be taken for granted. And sometimes it was simply the sheer investment of time. Art took hours, days, weeks, years, of single-minded focus. This investment meant that everything that touched the art-making experience got absorbed. Music, conversations, or television shows experienced during the making became part of the piece, too. Hours, days, weeks, years later, the memory of one could instantly invoke the memory of the other, because they had been inextricably joined.

Copying and recopying Sargent's *Madame X* would always be associated with Hennessy, because of how intensely the two of them had worked on making it, the process so intensely tangled that it was as if a single entity, Jordan Hennessy, had done it.

Copying Sargent's *The Daughters of Edward Darley Boit* would forever be associated with June and the other girls, because of how it was the first time Jordan had truly imagined doing something original, thinking of how a portrait of all of Hennessy's girls could be posed with a similar chaotic but structured array for good effect, their faces strikingly and eerily and poignantly the same.

Copying Niall Lynch's *The Dark Lady* would forever be associated with the Fairy Market and the creeping desperation of those last days with Hennessy before the murders.

And copying Sargent's *El Jaleo* would forever be grief and hope twined together. It was knotted tightly with the song that was leading the charts the first week she got to Boston, the bright new knowledge that sweetmetals existed, the sound of that little boy's voice when he woke up at the Boudicca party, the quality of the light coming into the Blick's as she bought new brushes to replace the ones she'd lost, the heart-pattering chance that artists just might be able to keep themselves awake if they were original enough.

Jordan was beginning to understand how it might be possible for ley energy to be tangled into the art-marking process, too.

"Of course Ronan can't tell me exactly when he'll be here," Declan said.

The sentence came quite out of the blue, as before that he had, in his singsong soothing patter, been telling her about Quantum Blue, a new blue pigment invented with nanotechnology, designed to replicate the exact color of the idyllic "blue hour" of a Greek dusk. He was still seated in his chair the way he always sat when he came over, one leg crossed over the other, his tie loosened, his jacket removed and laid over his knee as if he had just come in from work, because usually he had. She hadn't told him the portrait was done, so he still posed. "It is not the Ronan Lynch way to provide enough information to prepare."

"What's it, exactly, that you're hoping to prepare for?" Jordan asked. She herself had mixed feelings about the news that Ronan, Bryde, and Hennessy were paying a visit to Boston, because of one harsh fact: Hennessy still hadn't called. Ten years of complete codependence, and suddenly Hennessy had gone radio silent. At first she'd put it down to Hennessy being unable to find Jordan once she'd moved to Boston and gotten a burner phone. But now Declan had gotten two calls from Ronan and Jordan still didn't have even a message from Hennessy. Jordan went from worry to annoyance to zen and back again. Truthfully, what truly kept her up nights was the realization that Hennessy hadn't given Jordan all of her memories when she made her.

She had been waiting weeks to demand an answer for that, and the call never came.

Declan said, "I've never been good at Ronan, and there's no handbook for the conversation we need to have now."

"Sure there is. It's a snap, a quick group read. The handbook's called *Your Boyfriend Called, He Thinks You've Joined a Cult, Please Advise*."

"Ronan's not much of a reader," Declan said darkly. "I don't want to talk about it."

"You brought it up."

"Did I? What was I talking about before?"

"Quantum Blue. Alexopoulou. Blue hour."

Jordan knew, without having to think too hard about it, that this conversation would also be coded into the painting currently in front of her, *Portrait of a Nameless Man*. She would forever after see the words *Quantum Blue* and think of this canvas, these long cold nights at the borrowed Fenway studio, Declan Lynch posed in the leather chair, the lights of the city murmuring outside the tall windows behind him. It would forever be tied to her experimentation on the colorful edges in the piece, her decision-making for the palette, her favorite brush getting scrubbed down to nothing and being replaced with a second favorite, and with her attempt to make people feel about her subject the way she felt about her subject, no matter how many decades passed.

Her first original.

Had she made a sweetmetal? She didn't know.

Declan observed, "You can put that brush down, although it's very good theater. I know the painting's done."

"Who's the artist here, Mr. Pozzi? Perhaps I'm still studying your mannerisms."

"That brush hasn't had paint on it for three days."

"It's not your place to question my process. Muses are notoriously ill-used." She put the brush down. "Matthew said you might be able to get one of your father's dreams to test it."

"You can't tell?"

"Whatever Bryde and them are doing means I can't feel the sweetmetals like I used to. I don't need them, not just walking around. I won't know unless the worst happens."

"Did it feel different to make it?"

Of course it had. It was her first original, and for the first several sessions, the weight of that had slowed her brush to a crawl. She couldn't decide how many of her artistic decisions in the piece were being cleverly informed by the artists she'd painted before and how many were simply straight up copied. This was decidedly Turner's palette, she argued with herself. This was Sargent's composition. This was still forgery, just good forgery.

But then something had happened on the third sitting. Declan had been telling her a story of John White Alexander's *Study in Black and Green*, telling her how sensational it was at the time it was painted, given that the subject of the painting was a woman whose husband murdered her former lover in the middle of Madison Square Garden and got away with it under a plea of temporary insanity. As a footnote, he'd added that John White Alexander was married to Elizabeth Alexander Alexander, a woman who friends had introduced him to at a party because they had the same last name.

Jordan had laughed and her brush, loaded with titanium white, had slipped.

Disaster.

Before she could stop it, she'd darted a glaring line along the edge of Declan's neck on the canvas. With annoyance, she'd gone in with a rag, but the paint beneath was still too wet to let her completely wipe away her mistake. The edge had been left glowing. But as she turned her head to the side, trying to imagine the fewest steps required to restore the edge, she realized the glow actually looked good. It did not look like reality. It *felt* like reality. The way the light played against the dark tricked her eye in the same way a real object's edges did. The dissonance was right.

Instead of repairing it, she emphasized it as much as she dared.

The next sitting, she was even braver. She pushed the effect further, past the point of comfort. Until it was more real than reality. She didn't know if the effect would work, because she was no longer copying. This was unknown road.

Had it felt different to make it? Of course it had felt different. It felt terrifying. It felt thrilling. She wanted people to admire it. She was afraid they'd hate it.

A Jordan Hennessy original.

"It's bonkers, really," Jordan remarked. "The whole thing. A sweetmetal. Everyone's going mad trying to get one, they're so rare, it's impossible. And here I am, thinking, oh, right, well, I'll just make one, then. I never thought of myself as an egotist, but I really must have quite a pair on me."

Declan smiled at this, turning his face away as he did, as always. "I'm just surprised you've never considered yourself an egotist."

"That's very sweet."

He asked, "Can I see it?"

"No."

"Why not?"

"Because you're the biggest art snob I know, which is saying a lot, and you're a capital-L Liar and I don't think I could take it if you didn't like it and I also don't think I could take you lying to me about it if you didn't."

With some curiosity, Declan asked, "Do you think I could still lie convincingly to you?"

"I don't see why not."

"Do you think I *would*?"

"I don't see why not."

"After all this?"

"After all what?" she said, but in a mocking tone. "Just because I stole your car."

They were quiet then for a space. Declan looked out the window at the dark, more pensive than his portrait. Both Real Declan and Portrait Declan held their hands the same way, fingers unevenly laced, something about them suggesting power at rest, but Portrait Declan depicted the Declan of just a few minutes before, his head turned quickly to hide that secret smile, that private self. Portrait Declan's eyes were half-lidded, looking away, his expression one of intimate, mannered amusement. Real Declan's were wide open, mirthless.

"My mother took days to fall asleep after my father died," Declan said. It took Jordan a moment to realize that he was referring to the dreamt Aurora, not his biological mother, Mór Ó Corra. It was the first time she remembered him doing so. "He was dead right away, of course. Brains bashed in. They had to take some of the gravel driveway with him to clean up the scene, if you can imagine, that's your job, the shovel, make sure you get all the pieces, don't want the kids tripping over gray matter. They didn't take my mother, though, because she didn't look dead yet. She looked fine. Fine as you could expect under the circumstances. No, it took her days. She ran down, like a battery. The further she got away from him, the longer it had been since he was alive, the less she became, until she was just . . . asleep."

It was not his ordinary storytelling voice. There was no theater. He was looking at nothing.

"Ronan and Matthew wanted her awake again, of course— Why wouldn't they? Why wouldn't you? Truly, why wouldn't you, I see that now. I see it from their point of view. But Ronan and I fought. I said it wouldn't matter, she was nothing without Dad. Always an accessory to him, a reaction to him. Why wake her? You couldn't wake the dead along with her, so she'd always be a frame for a destroyed painting. We were orphans the moment Dad died because she was just organ death. What was she except for what Dad made her to be? What could she do except what he had made her to do? She had to love us. She was always just an external hard drive for his feelings. She—"

"Just stop," Jordan said. "You have to know now. Saying she wasn't real doesn't make it any easier. Just different. Anger doesn't mess up mascara as much."

His eyes were bright but he blinked and they were ordinary again.

"Ronan's trying to wake up the world. I'm trying to think of how to talk him out of it, but what he's talking about is a world where she never fell asleep. A world where Matthew's just a kid. A world where it doesn't matter what Hennessy does, if something happens to her. A level playing field. I don't think it's a good idea, but it's not like I can't see the appeal, because now I'm biased, I'm too biased to be clear." Declan shook his head a little. "I said I would never become my father, anything like him. And now look at me. At us."

Ah, there it was.

It took no effort to remember the way he'd looked at her the first moment he realized she was a dream.

"I'm a dream," Jordan said. "I'm not *your* dream."

Declan put his chin in his hand and looked back out the window; that, too, would be a good portrait. Perhaps it was just because she liked looking at him that she thought each pose would make a good one. A series. What a future that idea promised, nights upon nights like this, him sitting there, her standing here.

"By the time we're married," Declan said eventually, "I want you to have applied for a different studio in this place because this man's paintings are very ugly."

Her pulse gently skipped two beats before continuing on as before. "I don't have a social security number of my own, Pozzi."

"I'll buy you one," Declan said. "You can wear it in place of a ring."

The two of them looked at each other past the canvas on her easel.

Finally, he said, voice soft, "I should see the painting now."

"Are you sure?"

"It's time, Jordan."

Putting his jacket to the side, he stood. He waited. He would not come around to look without an invite.

It's time, Jordan.

Jordan had never been truly honest with anyone who didn't wear Hennessy's face. Showing him this painting, this original, felt like being more honest than she had ever been in her life.

She stepped back to give him room.

Declan took it in. His eyes flicked to and from the likeness, from the jacket on Portrait Declan's leg to the real jacket he'd left behind on the chair. She watched his gaze follow the live edge she had taken such care to paint, that subtle electricity of complementary colors at the edge of his form.

"It's very good," Declan muttered. "Jordan, it's very good."

"I thought it might be."

"I don't know if it's a sweetmetal. But you're very good."

"I thought I might be."

"The next one will be even better."

"I think it might be."

"And in ten years your scandalous masterpiece will get you thrown out of France, too," he said. "And later you can triumphantly sell it to the Met. Children will have to write papers about you. People like me will tell stories about you to their dates at museums to make them think they're interesting."

She kissed him. He kissed her. And this kiss, too, got all wrapped up in the art-making of the portrait sitting on the easel beside them, getting all mixed in with all the other sights and sounds and feelings that had become part of the process.

It was very good.

30

Once upon a time, back when they lived in the nation's capital, Hennessy and Jordan had briefly run something called the Game. The Game began at midnight at the River Road exit on I-495. Not once you'd taken the exit. *At* it. On the interstate, screaming by it. Bit of a fraught proposition with DC traffic. Underestimate the congestion and the would-be player would end up passing River Road minutes after everyone else had left. Overestimate it and the player showed up too early, hoping they didn't burn too much time looping around for another approach.

Easy? No. But Hennessy had never been interested in easy.

At midnight, ready-or-not-here-I-come, Hennessy howled by the River Road exit in whatever vehicle she'd taken from the McLean mansion or temporarily lifted, pied pipering a restless parade of horsepower to the location of the game. The other girls—June, etc.—would already be in place, two of them book-ending start and finish, the rest stationed at exits. The usual tricks in the bag: police band radio, radar detectors, fourteen keen eyes.

Then they raced. Point to points, drags, drifts, two up, four up, whatever burned at Hennessy that night. Sometimes when it was Hennessy, it was actually Jordan. Sometimes it was both.

The stakes of the Game were always high. Sometimes the prize was drugs. Weapons. The loser's car. A year's rent in some-one's really posh second home. Goods too hot to sell on the open market. The drivers, the players, the pawns, they were all of a certain type: twenty- and thirtysomething men who only came alive after dark, usually white and swish enough to be able to survive any traffic infraction that might come their way, all of them driving cars designed to do more than get HOV lane violations. They congregated in forums to discuss the Game, to offer up prizes for the next, to talk smack and measure dicks. At first they were all area marks, but eventually people would come from up and down the 95 corridor in hopes of rolling into the Game.

Hennessy and Jordan usually just moderated the race for a cut of the prizes, but when the girls needed cash or were intrigued by one of the offerings, they raced, too. Hennessy was good at it because she had no fear and no inhibitions. Jordan was better at it because she did. Together they were known as the Valkyrie, although a few of the more observant return players called them the Valkyries.

The Game broke a shit ton of rules.

Hennessy loved it. Or at least she loved that she couldn't think of anything else while she was doing it.

That was as close as she got to happiness. She thought it was probably the best she could hope for.

"Get in, hurry up, time is a waterfall, and the moment we're trying to catch is rapidly swimming toward the edge," Hennessy said.

"*Hennessy?*" Jordan asked, shocked.

Jordan Hennessy stood on the dark sidewalk near Fenway Studios, her bag slung over her shoulder, looking sleek and urbane with her natural hair pulled back into a high ponytail, slim-shouldered leather jacket, orange crop top, sharp black leggings, subtle chevron-pattered flats.

Jordan Hennessy also sat behind the wheel of a thrumming Toyota Supra on the curb, looking camera-ready with huge hair, deep purple lips, a man's bomber jacket, a deep purple corset, and heels that seemed difficult to operate a clutch with.

These two Jordan Hennessys shared identical septum rings, identical floral tattoos across their hands. Nearly identical floral tattoos around their throats.

But no one would mistake them for the same person.

"You didn't call, bruv," Jordan said.

"In."

Jordan got in.

She had changed a little since Hennessy had seen her, but not so much that Hennessy couldn't read her expression. It was a nuanced thing, this expression. Shock was the primary flavor. Then there was a note of relief. And then, just on the back of the tongue, wariness.

All of this was expected. What Hennessy hadn't expected to see was *joy*. It had radiated from Jordan before she'd seen Hennessy. She'd been walking the sidewalk in the damned middle of the night with a grin on her face, a grin she kept trying to put away but kept escaping. Somehow Jordan had been living here in Boston away from Hennessy and she had not only been okay, but she'd been so okay that happiness was bursting out of her and she couldn't stop anyone from being able to see it. Hennessy had been pulling out the Lace and Jordan had been *happy*.

Hennessy didn't know what to do with this, so she started to prattle. She prattled as she sent the Supra down the street and Jordan put her bag on the floor by her feet like she always did. She prattled as she sent the Supra onto the highway and Jordan rolled up the window so that the increasing wind would stop beating her hair around. She prattled as they were joined by several other heavily muscled cars in the tunnels under Boston

Harbor. She prattled as Jordan eyed the other cars and then put her seat belt on.

"How much notice did you give them?" Jordan asked. She wasn't stupid. She recognized the Game when she saw it.

"Five hours," Hennessy said. "On that mad nootropics investment banker Slack—do you remember that one? That means there is a very good chance statistically that one of these drivers is currently totally mashed on some completely unregulated South American plant by-product."

They burst west out of Boston at a speed several ticks above proper. They had acquired quite a contingent of impressive cars. Flat cars, wide cars, flanking, waiting. The Game was getting ready to whisk Hennessy's feelings away. It hadn't yet. But it was going to.

It had to.

She didn't know what she had wanted out of seeing Jordan again, but not this. Some part of her had always known that if she called, Jordan would be doing okay without her. Knew that if she showed up, Jordan would be doing okay without her. Knew that if there was a way for their lives to be separated, Jordan would be doing okay without her. Knew that it was Hennessy who couldn't live without Jordan.

She supposed she had hoped she was wrong.

As the cars gathered and revved, Jordan asked, "How can we run a Game? There's no one to guard the exits. They're all dead."

"It ruins the fun when you say that, so I'm going to pretend you didn't," Hennessy said. "Also, I've already thought about that and, as they say, planned accordingly. It's a straight shot. Starts with a triple flash of the lights and then it's on for exactly seven miles. No exits in between. If we're clear when it starts, we should be still by the end. No surprises for us. We'll have a grand ol' time."

"'We.' Are *we* racing?"

"Yes."

"Hennessy," Jordan said, "there's a GTR right there. A new nine-one-one behind it. I can't see that thing two cars back because it's too damn flat, but my pheromones suggest it's a McLaren. Are you just planning on watching taillights?"

But she didn't sound angry; she never sounded angry. She was always up for whatever madness Hennessy was into. Wasn't this better? Hennessy thought. Wasn't this how it should have been? Her and Jordan, Hennessy setting that timer on her phone, staying awake for as long as possible, never seeing the Lace.

"We should do this again," Hennessy said.

"We are doing it again."

"I mean you-and-me, I mean Jordan Hennessy. You should come with us or I should come light up Boston, except seriously can we do New York instead, because this place is like a hot girl's elbow pit. It's fine but there's not a lot to do."

"You been sleeping, Heloise?" Jordan asked.

The question was absolutely intolerable. All of it. The content, the timing, the nickname.

"You been painting?" Hennessy countered. "I can't help but notice some paint on your neck there. Looks like Tyrian purple." It did not. It looked like ordinary white paint, but Tyrian purple was a better reference to Declan Lynch.

Jordan should have been irritated by Hennessy's misdirect, but instead her mouth whispered that smile again, the one

Hennessy had seen on the sidewalk. She touched her fingers to her neck, feeling the paint, and the sweetness of the touch drove home the meaning of the smile.

She liked that asshole. That boring-ass drone of a prick—she *liked* him. Hennessy had begged Bryde and Ronan to stop for the Supra, knowing how much Jordan loved it, and here the two of them were on this midnight highway, the Valkyries, surrounded by several million dollars of several thousands of horsepower, and Jordan was smiling over that dough-faced DC pig.

Some part of Hennessy was always looking at that old door without a handle, a keyhole with no key in it.

"Ready-set-go," Hennessy said.

She flashed her lights. One. Two. Three.

The cars bolted.

As Jordan had predicted, the Supra was nowhere near as fast as the speediest of the contenders. The tight pack swiftly loosened as the fit got fitter and the slow stayed slow.

Jordan petted the dash of the Supra as if to make the car feel better about not leading the pack, and then, in a different sort of voice, she asked, "Did you dream me without memories of Jay?"

The thing about the ley line getting stronger was that Hennessy felt she could *see* the Lace even with her eyes open sometimes.

"There's a neat trick we're going to do up here," Hennessy said.

Lacy shapes thrown by aftermarket headlights.

"Hennessy." Jordan drew her back. "Did you?"

Lacy threads of pine needles caught under the Supra's wiper.

Hennessy went on. "It's a fancy thing I nicked off Bryde. Fancy little shit. It's got some fun side effects."

Lacy shadows crisscrossing behind the streetlights racing by.

"Hennessy—"

Lacy eyelashes blink-blink-blinking. It looked like the patterns her mother's lamps had thrown across her studio wall.

Rolling the window down, Hennessy scooped the little stolen silver orb out of the door pocket. She rolled it in her palm the way she'd seen Bryde do when he wanted the orb to fly faster than it was being thrown, and then she hurled it into the dark.

For a moment there was no result. Just taillights of cars all about to claim faster times than the Supra.

The little orb zipped ahead of them. It unfolded. The cloud burst free.

And then there was chaos.

The cars spun. One here, one there. They smashed into each other. They nosed into the ditch. A Subaru flipped right over in the air. A Corvette spun and then slid backward nearly as fast as the Supra was going forward. It went for yards and yards. There was a high-pitched noise happening during all of this that keened and keened and keened, and Hennessy could not decide if it was her or Jordan or tires screaming.

There were supercars everywhere, dazzled across the highway. Some nosed into others, the headlights pointed every which way.

"We win," Hennessy said. She eased the Supra to a stop and pulled up the parking brake.

Jordan was out of the car immediately, hands linked round the back of her neck, surveying the damage. Hennessy could tell she was horrified, and for some reason, this was great, this was perfect, this was just what Hennessy wanted. This felt much better than Jordan's vague smile, her wild joy.

Hennessy gestured grandly. "The prize is whichever we want. Which one do you fancy?"

Jordan turned to her. "This isn't a dream!"

"I know," Hennessy said, "because I could control everything here."

"Someone could be *dead* here." Jordan paced and then jogged across the asphalt, ducking her head to look in at this driver and that. They all gazed at her and past her, expressions swimming.

Hennessy droned, "Asshole dies in a street race, news at eleven."

"This isn't a dream!"

"How about the Lambo?" Hennessy asked. "I feel like the Lambo would be the most fun."

Jordan threw open the door of a sweet little busted-up Porsche as bright as Ronan's sky blade. The driver was slumped over the wheel, which had crumpled in enough to press him back into his seat. His eyes looked at nothing, but it was hard to say if that was because of Bryde's dreamt orb or because he was injured.

"I don't want to steal cars and fuck shit up, Hennessy!" Jordan snapped, rummaging until she found the seat controls. She worked to get the seat back enough to tug the man free. Hennessy didn't move a muscle as Jordan threw all of her weight to pull him out. "I've got a life here. I want to live my life. My real life. Art and growing up and not *this*."

"Nice for you," Hennessy said.

"Why the hell are you being this way?" Jordan demanded. "This is what you came all this way for? The Game?"

Hennessy looked at her as she propped the driver up against the wheel of his car and went to look at the next one. "I wish you were dead."

This spun Jordan neat as a top. "What did you say?"

"I wish you'd died with the others," Hennessy said. It was awful, it was terrible, her mouth wouldn't stop saying it, her expression wouldn't stop being scathing. "I wish you were all dead so it would just be me and I could do what I wanted. I can feel you dragging me down every second of every day. I'm so fucking tired of you."

Jordan's arms hung by her sides. She didn't look mad or hurt, she just stared, standing there in the middle of all the cars pointed helter skelter.

"You came here to tell me *that?*"

Hennessy didn't know what she'd come here to do, but she'd done this now. She understood that she wanted Jordan to hate her. She didn't know why that would be better than anything else, but she knew with certainty in this moment, that was the goal.

"I wanted to see your face to make sure it was true," Hennessy said.

She shrugged.

She could *feel* her shoulders shrugging even though she hadn't thought about it.

It was like she had manifested something from a dream and was paralyzed, watching herself from above. The thing she had manifested was this awful Hennessy trying her best to make Jordan break and scream for her to leave.

"This is what you came from," Hennessy said, gesturing to herself, "and you're using it to become a craft painter and make babies with that white bro? Guess I should've given my mother's memories some credit. They were a safeguard against suburbia."

Quietly, Jordan asked, "Why do you always do this?"

Because Hennessy always dreamt of the Lace, that was why, because it was always the same dream, always the same.

"Enjoy your nightmare," she said.

31

Declan remembered the worst dream he'd ever had.

It was his last year at Aglionby. He was passing his classes. He had dragged Ronan through his classes with the help of Ronan's friend Gansey. He had bought Christmas gifts for Matthew. He had his internships lined up and the move planned to the town house his dead father had left him. He had done the math on the money left in the will and had worked out how much he needed to make and how much he was allowed to spend each year in order to continue to live in the way he thought would be all right to live. He was dating a girl named Ashleigh, after breaking up with a girl named Ashley. Ashleigh was thinking of going to school in DC to be closer to him. Declan was eyeing a less attentive Ashlee to replace her. He was doing his best to keep the noose of malevolent business associates his father had made for them from tightening before he graduated.

That was not the worst dream. That was the waking world.

The worst dream was this: It was nearly Christmas. There was frost on the colorless grass around the farmhouse at the Barns. Niall had just come back from a December business trip and now he was presenting gifts to his sons, just as he did in real life.

He gave Matthew a puppy that was only alive when Matthew was holding it ("I'm never gonna put it down," declared dream Matthew).

He gave Ronan a textbook with no words in it ("My favorite kind," Ronan had said).

I lc gavc Dcclan a box . . . and in the box was the ability to dream things into life.

"Your mother said you'd been asking for this," Niall told him.

Declan woke with a rush of electric adrenaline. Horror pulsed in time with his heart.

He looked around in dread but his dorm room was just as he'd left it when he slept. There was nothing in it that hadn't been carried with ordinary human hands, that hadn't been crafted with ordinary human labor. There were no miracles or wonders. Just his unmagical room with the things he needed for his unmagical life.

He had never been so relieved.

Declan was looking at *El Jaleo*. He was standing there, arms crossed, head tilted to one side, studying it. A little closer than he would normally be. No, a lot closer than he would normally be. He had stepped over the chain that ordinarily warned museum-goers to stay out of the alcove, and he was close enough to see the ridges on brushstrokes, to smell the *oldness* of all the paint in the closed-in space. It felt quite illicit, and he couldn't imagine what had come over him. This close, everything looked a little different than he remembered.

It took him a moment to realize that some of his disorientation was not because of proximity; it was because the museum was dark.

The dancer was lit only by a dim security light that came through the window to the right of the painting and reflected off the mirror to the left of it.

The museum was also silent.

The small, close building was never noisy, but right then, it lacked even the murmur of distant people in other rooms, the sound of life. Breath held, or breath gone. Tomblike.

He didn't know how he'd gotten here.

He didn't know how he'd gotten here.

Declan looked down at himself. He was dressed in the same clothing he'd been in when he'd left Jordan's. Jacket, loosened tie. Same clothing the Declan in the portrait had been wearing. Same clothing the Declan who'd kissed Jordan had been wearing. He remembered returning to the apartment. Didn't he? It was possible he was simply remembering other times he had and all those memories had stacked up to disguise that he was missing one.

This was dream logic, not waking logic.

He felt awake. He was awake, surely. But—

"Neat trick, right?" Ronan asked.

The middle Lynch brother leaned casually in the entrance from the courtyard, shoulder against the doorframe, arms crossed, watching him. He had changed since Declan had seen him. Not taller, because Ronan had already been tall, but bigger, somehow. Older. He hadn't shaved in a few days and he had grizzle that instantly aged him. He was no boy. No student. He was a young man.

"Ronan," Declan said. He couldn't think of what else to say, how to say it, and so he just shoved everything he wanted to say into that one word. *Ronan.*

Ronan said, "The guard will be dazed for a while. The cameras are dazed, too. It's pretty slick. I tried to get him to name it something. THE BEDAZZLER, all caps, but he's not that sort. What do you want to see here? You can see anything. Touch anything. No one will know."

Declan was badly disoriented. "I don't understand."

Bryde stepped into the room. He was a neat figure, controlled. Declan instantly recognized the posture. Not ego. Beyond ego. A man who knew precisely what his boundaries were and operated so thoroughly within them that he was untouchable and knew it. He did not have to lift a fist, raise his voice. He was a kind of powerful that other powerful people respected.

He held a small silver orb in between finger and thumb.

"It's quite expensive," he said, studying it. "Requires good ley energy, good dream, perfect focus. Razor focus, really. You have to hold what it means to be human in your head, because you don't want to take that from them. These little baubles have to go off and send the mind in all directions but keep those pieces close enough to gather back. There is no point in a treat if it's all trick. You may as well shoot someone if you aren't going to put their minds back. A butcher ruins, a dreamer nudges."

Declan found himself feeling precisely the same sensation as he had after his worst dream. He longed to wake up back in the apartment and find everything ordinary and correct around him. *I don't trust Bryde*, Adam had said, and how could he? Look at him. Listen to him. *Feel* what he could do.

Declan remembered nothing about getting here. Bryde had taken it from him.

Declan took two steps back, putting himself on the proper side of the chain protecting *El Jaleo*. Immediately he felt better, giving the painting its space once more.

Bryde pocketed the orb and told Ronan, "I let Hennessy think she stole one, so we've got just this one left. So be efficient."

"Where is she?" Declan asked. "Hennessy, I mean. Is she here?"

"She's going to see Jordan," Ronan said, and Declan felt a little pang of uncertainty in his gut. To Bryde, Ronan said, "She was pretty wound up. Do we know that . . . ?"

"She'll be back," Bryde said with absolute certainty. "She knows where she belongs. Go on. Eye on the clock. This won't last forever."

He pulled back into the dim courtyard, disappearing among the complicated black shadows of the tropical palms and flowers.

Declan found himself alone with his brother, experiencing the impression of privacy if not the reality. He had not seen him since they'd parted on the banks of the Potomac River, and he realized that part of him had been preparing itself for the idea that he might never see him again. It was a worry that he hadn't fully felt until now that the danger of it had passed, and he found his knees wobbly with relief. Ronan, his family, his brother. Older, stranger, but still obviously Ronan.

"You heard him," Ronan said. "What room have you always wanted to go into? What other rope have you always wanted to step over?"

Declan didn't fancy touring the museum under these circumstances, but he wanted some space from Bryde to talk to Ronan, so he walked with his brother through the eerie, quiet building. They found themselves standing in the Dutch Room, the green wallpaper looking black in the dim. Two empty frames hung on the wall in front of them, one for each of the brothers.

"What's the deal here?" Ronan asked.

"I was about to ask the same."

"The empty frames."

Any other time, Declan would have had the whole story at the ready, but tonight he simply said, "They were stolen. Twenty years ago. Thirty, maybe. It's been a vigil since then. This whole place was made by a woman who wanted it to stay the same even after her death, so after the paintings were stolen out of the frames, the museum hung the frames back on the walls to wait, until the—do you care about this? You don't care about this. Ronan, I've been hearing the news. What are you doing?"

"Sounds like you already know."

"I'm worried," Declan said, following Ronan as he began to walk again. "Don't forget there's a real world you want to come back to. The point was to get to a place you could do that."

"Was it?"

"Don't do that. I remember what we talked about. Don't pretend it was me telling you how to live. Adam. You wanted Adam."

"Adam," Ronan said slowly, as if remembering, as if he were a man enchanted himself, and Declan realized he did not know any of the things Bryde could or couldn't do with his dreams. Perhaps this was not even Ronan at all, perhaps this was *a* Ronan—no. He was not going to let himself even picture it; that was the way to absolute madness.

"The Barns," Declan added, voice terse. "You told me you wanted to be a farmer."

Ronan's mouth slid to a grin, surprising Declan thoroughly. "You remember that."

And now Declan himself was confused, because he didn't think Ronan looked nearly as enchanted as he had thought he did a moment before. Now he looked sharp and alive, eyes bright and mirthful. "This isn't about me. It's about people like me.

And it's not about Matthew. It's about people like Matthew. They don't get to live, but they *will*. Is that really all this meeting is about? I thought Matthew was having a meltdown. I thought you needed weapons. I thought you needed dreams to build your empire. Cash. Cars. Girls."

"It's a family meeting to make sure you know where you're going to be in three years," Declan said. "Long-term goals."

"Oh, God, it was a meeting for Declanisms? The more things change, blah de fucking la."

"What is your plan doing for other people? Are you breaking the world?"

Ronan laughed merrily. "I hope so."

He had led them back around to the Spanish Cloister. Declan did not generally think of Ronan as a particularly timely person, but Bryde had told him to be efficient, and he'd been efficient. He had brought Declan right back here without Declan even thinking about how they were being led back here. It was a very dream thing to do. It was a very adult, strategic thing to do.

Bryde waited in front of *El Jaleo*, his hands tucked in his pockets, eyes in shadow. His voice was a little knowing, "You could take anything from here right now. You could take this painting to hang in your living room and never have to worry about your brother Matthew again."

It had already occurred to Declan that anybody with that impossible dream orb of Bryde's could steal anything they liked from this place. Do anything they liked. Declan had heard Bryde's hidden threat earlier. The entirety of Declan's memories could have been destroyed for good, by an unkindly dreamer.

Declan's hands felt a little shaky.

"This museum's already had enough taken from it," Declan said. "Even if I didn't care about that, I don't want to walk around with a target on my back. And it fixes very little, as I'm sure you've already considered. Matthew can't wrap that painting around himself and have a normal life. Rob from this place, and for what? A prison of my apartment?"

"Good," said Bryde. "So you understand what we're doing, then. You want Matthew to live like anyone else. So do we."

Declan said, "You could do this without Ronan."

"No," Bryde murmured. "I could not."

There was a sound from somewhere within the museum. Not an alarm, not yet, but movement.

Bryde looked up sharply. To Ronan, he said, "We are nearly out of time. I'll need to use this last one here, and I won't be able to get another one until I am out of the city; it's too loud here."

Declan couldn't think of what to say. He had thought the conversation was going to come around in his favor but he was the one going round and round instead. All he could think to blurt to Ronan was "You should see Matthew before you leave Boston. In case . . ."

"Yeah, you're right," said Ronan. But he glanced to Bryde to confirm. It was only after Bryde nodded imperceptibly that Ronan repeated, with certainty, "Right."

Bryde owned his brother completely.

32

Ten. That was the number of coffees Carmen Farooq-Lane ordered while waiting in the Somerville café. She didn't want to cheaply hold down this table when another paying customer could have it, but she also didn't want to float away on a lake of coffee.

She glanced at the time on her phone. Thirty-five minutes had passed since the agreed-upon rendezvous time. When did she give up?

"Just one more, please," she told the server.

God, but she was nervous. She didn't know if she was more nervous about the meeting or being found out by the Moderators. She'd resigned right after checking out of the quaint little rental cottage. Just like that. Strip the sheets from the bed, make sure all the dishes were in the dishwasher, turn off all the lights, hide Hennessy's moonlit sword in a linen closet, quit the only job that seemed important. Lock had accepted the keys to the bullet-ridden rental car and had her sign a nondisclosure agreement.

Of course I'm disappointed, Lock had rumbled, *but I respect your decision.* Farooq-Lane wasn't entirely sure she believed him; the Moderators had not been interested in respecting people's decisions before that point.

He was less gracious about Liliana's resignation a few minutes after, but Liliana had been insistent. Gentle. Fair. She cited the mishandling of the Rhiannon Martin job and the emotional scarring of her teen self. She noted that the Moderators had not, to that point, seemed to be able to use her visions to make the world a safer place. She reminded them Farooq Lane's presence had always been part and parcel of her deal with the Moderators. No, she could not be persuaded to stay long enough to help find another Visionary. Yes, she was sorry to leave them blind, but she wished them luck.

Farooq-Lane hadn't really thought the Moderators would let them go, but they had.

She dipped into her parents' bank accounts to buy a car at the closest local dealership, stopped briefly by the rental cottage to retrieve Hennessy's sword, and then left that part of her life in the rearview mirror.

Boston was their destination. Liliana had just had a vision.

Nine a.m. that morning, Declan Lynch had called to discuss an urgent matter. *I would prefer to have this conversation on the most secure line possible,* he murmured. *It requires the utmost discretion.* Coincidentally, she had told him, she was in the Boston area—did he want to meet up in person? She had been intensely grateful that she'd been the one to call him about Ronan Lynch earlier this month. Now he was late.

"Ms. Farooq-Lane?"

Declan Lynch stood by the table. He looked like his brother Ronan, but with the edges sanded off, the memorable bits deleted. He had neat, civilized dress slacks; a neat, civilized wool sweater; neat, civilized facial hair; very nice shoes. There wasn't a stitch that was out of place in this upscale café full of talkative Tufts students and drowsy medical residents.

"I didn't see you come in," she said.

"I came in the back." She saw him check his surroundings,

but only because she was watching him closely. He was very good. Long practice with paranoia. "I'm sorry I'm late. I had to be sure I wasn't followed."

She couldn't really believe it. Here he was. Liliana's vision had promised it, but the visions were always things for the Moderators to interpret, not her, and they were always for killing Zeds, not attempting anything more nuanced. "Of course. Can I get you a coffee?"

"We should be brief," Declan said by way of reply. His voice was vague, nasal; he sounded as if he were announcing a meeting agenda. "Unwise to push our luck."

Eight minutes was how long it took Declan Lynch to say his piece.

"I love my brother," Declan said. "So know that when I say this next part I'm saying it from a place of fondness: Ronan's a follower. He's always needed a hero to follow. When he was a kid, he idolized my father. When he was in school, he idolized his best friend. Now he's obviously idolizing this Bryde. He doesn't get ideas on his own. That sounds bad. Remember I said I loved him. I mean it in the best way. I mean it this way: He's not your problem. Take away Bryde, and Ronan's just the same as he always was, a kid who's going to go back to Virginia to play with cars and mud and cowshit. Who was running the show when you saw them together? It was Bryde, wasn't it? Not my brother. Not Jordan Hennessy. Whose name has been whispered subversively for weeks? Bryde's."

She tilted her chin. "We're in agreement. Bryde's the target."

"*Are* we in agreement? Because I want to be sure you know why I'm sitting at this table."

A coworker at Alpine Financial had told Farooq-Lane once that, neurologically, most people saw their future selves as a totally different person, and so treated them with less empathy, like a stranger. High achievers, though, saw their present and future self as one person and accordingly made wiser decisions. Farooq-Lane had immediately decided that her job as a financial adviser was to close the gap between these two selves.

She closed the gap for Declan Lynch.

"You're here to make sure your family gets a chance to have meaningful adult lives," Farooq-Lane said, with quiet surety. "You're here to make sure there's actually a world for them to have those lives in. You're here because what you saw in Bryde scared you and you want your brother far away from him, because that's not what your brother stands for and you don't want his life to be defined by a single decision. You're here talking to me because you're aware you don't have the ability to do this on your own. You're here because you're a good brother."

Declan's mouth worked. He was slick enough to know she was also being slick, but he didn't disagree with her.

"My brother isn't to be harmed," he said. "I want to see you say it."

The promise wouldn't have meant anything if she were with the Moderators, but she wasn't with the Moderators. "You have my word," Farooq-Lane said.

Seven Three Park Drive, Boston, MA. That was all that was written on the card Declan slid across the table as he stood up. "That's where they're meeting Matthew. Bryde mentioned last night he doesn't have another of the dreams he uses to confuse people and he can't get any more until they're out of the city. Is it true you killed your own brother?"

She was taken completely by surprise.

"You're not the only one who has access to information," he said in that bland way.

"My brother was a serial killer," she said. "He was also a Zed. I didn't pull the trigger, but yes, I helped find him. Your brother's not a serial killer. He's just a Zed."

Declan Lynch narrowed his eyes. For just the barest second, he did not look at all like he belonged in this nice, civilized café.

"Don't forget your promise," he said. "And don't call my brother that."

Six. That was the number of scenarios Farooq-Lane ran through as she looked at the Park Drive address on various satellite maps. It belonged to a rose garden in the Emerald Necklace, a series of green parks chained through the Boston area. It was a bad location for an attack. Right in the middle of the city. Right up against the swampy fens that gave Fenway its name. Surrounded by the trees that gave Bryde his information.

But Liliana said Farooq-Lane only needed enough time to draw Jordan Hennessy's sword.

"I'm trusting you," Farooq-Lane told Liliana.

One sword draw, one second, one death. When it came to it, she could kill someone, she thought. To save the world. She had stood by and helped the Moderators kill many others, after all. She couldn't erase that, just try to make it matter. One person, one Zed. One sword. She could do it.

It wasn't twenty-three people. It was one.

"It will turn out all right," Liliana said gently.

"What happened in the vision?" Farooq-Lane said. "What did I do? Where was it?"

"It will turn out all right," Liliana repeated.

Five minutes after Farooq-Lane got to the James P. Kelleher Rose Garden, the Moderators found her.

"Did you think we weren't having you followed, Carmen?" Lock rumbled with disappointment. It was hard to tell if he was disappointed in her working without them or not covering her tracks. He held a take-out coffee from the café she'd met Declan at, and Farooq-Lane couldn't stop staring at it. She'd been careful. She was sure she'd been careful. "You're a lot easier to track than a Zed in an invisible car. You know why? You obey the law."

"I have a plan here," Farooq-Lane said. "We want the same thing."

Lock cast a heavy glance at Hennessy's sword. It was hooded safely away in its shoulder scabbard but its identity was clear, the hilt shouting FROM CHAOS. "And it's a plan you think you could execute better cowboy style? I respect what you did here, Carmen, but we can't risk you taking point on this. We'll take it from here. The team's all here. Thanks for the good work."

"I made a promise that I'd only take down Bryde," Farooq-Lane said desperately. "I intend to keep that promise."

"You'd risk the world on that?"

Farooq-Lane repeated, "I intend to keep that promise. Let me do this. Please."

"How about this," Lock offered. "How about you let us help you keep that promise? Like you said. We want the same thing, and you need our eyes anyway."

It wasn't as if she had a choice. There was no time. She was outnumbered.

We want the same thing. But it was only past Farooq-Lane who truly believed this now. Present Farooq-Lane wasn't sure. And future Farooq-Lane—unclear.

"Okay," Farooq-Lane said.

She explained the plan. It was a hasty thing, constructed with very few data points. Declan's address and time. Liliana's description of her vision. Farooq-Lane's understanding of what Hennessy's sword could do if wielded without hesitation.

The plan was skeletal in its simplicity. At the center of the rose garden was a small fountain, a little over a foot deep. It was as far from large trees as one could hope for in the city; there was no evidence that Bryde could receive information from roses. Carmen Farooq-Lane was going to climb into the fountain, lie down in the nearly frozen water, and breathe sips of air through a straw that reached to the surface. She would wait there in the inhuman temperature until the Moderators texted her that the Zeds had arrived in the garden. And then she would leap from the water with Hennessy's sword like an avenging angel, killing Bryde with a single moonlit stroke.

Her phone was only rated for an hour of underwater use, but the cold would kill her before that anyway.

"Is this how you saw it?" she asked Liliana again.

"It will be all right, Carmen."

It will be all right.

It did not feel all right as she lay in the bottom of the fountain. She tried to keep her hand from shaking as she held the breathing tube steady in her frigid lips. She focused on a black feather that floated on the surface of the water above her.

She was waiting to kill. Waiting to kill. Waiting to kill. She had to think of him as not human. As not living. As simply a tree to hew down.

The trees were on his side, though, which meant the trees had feelings, too. Nothing was simple anymore.

She was that feather. She was that feather.

Her phone buzzed against her.

The Zeds were here.

Four seconds passed before she could animate her cold body. She plunged from the water, sword already alive with light and swinging.

The blade missed Bryde by several inches.

Ronan Lynch's raven screamed into the air.

Bryde's eyes met hers.

This was wrong. This was already wrong. It had to be immediate, or it wouldn't work. She couldn't fight them. Anything beyond the single stroke got messy, and anything messy meant she couldn't guarantee her promise.

Ronan had his sunfire sword out in a second, but Bryde snatched it from him.

"Get out of here!" snapped Bryde. "You know what to do!"

Farooq-Lane didn't have time to see if Ronan obeyed, because Bryde fell upon her with VEXED TO NIGHTMARE.

They fought.

They *fought*.

The rose garden was alight with the weapons' eerie glow.

Farooq-Lane's hands were so frozen that she could barely feel the hilt, but it seemed to her the sword *wanted* her to succeed. Even as her fingers were too numb to guide it, the blade chose an effective path for itself. However, Bryde's blade wanted *him* to succeed, too, and so a battle waged. It did not matter that neither Farooq-Lane nor Bryde were swordsmen. The swords were made to fight, and they would fight, and Farooq-Lane and Bryde would wield them.

Rosebushes shredded.

Stone planters cleaved.

Trellises sprung in all directions like split rib cages.

But neither the sunfire blade nor the starlit blade took any damage.

She had been right when she guessed the only match for FROM CHAOS was this other sword.

She was tangentially aware that outside the vivid light of the blades, Moderators and Zeds fought. Gunfire sounded. The swords' furious dreamt light both warmed Farooq-Lane's chilled body and repelled bullets, slicing them as easily as they sliced anything else.

Bullets!

She was breaking her promise.

Declan Lynch had come to *her* and asked for *her* help and gotten *her* word. She'd really believed it when she promised him Ronan would be untouched. The Moderators had been killing Zeds and now they were going to kill her integrity, too.

This felt more intolerable than anything else to this point. She'd promised.

"I only want you," Farooq-Lane shouted to Bryde as the swords met again. "If you really want the others to get away, you'll give up. We know it's you. I know it's you."

Bryde said, "You don't know anything you think you know, Carmen Farooq-Lane."

"Don't play your mind games with me!" she shouted.

"I don't play games," Bryde said. "I just turn down the volume on the shit that doesn't matter."

Suddenly, she was hit from behind.

The blow hit the middle of her spine so sharply that her knees buckled. There was no arguing with it. She was down on her knees, and then she was down on her face. Gravel bit her lips. She felt the winning sword tumbling from her hand. She felt her vision flicker.

She felt everything going wrong.

Gunfire speckled like the sound of castanets behind a dancer. She heard someone shout.

She had trusted Liliana. It was supposed to be all right.

Three Zeds bolted from the rose garden.

They were on foot; they had to be. One of them had smashed their dreamt hoverboard across Farooq Lane's back. This was why her spine stung, why she still felt pain shooting up to her neck and her fingertips. This was why Hennessy's sword burned the dry grass a few inches away from her as she gingerly sat up.

This was how Bryde had gotten away.

She could hear shouts, more gunfire, sirens, all moving farther and farther from her. This was wrong. All wrong. The Moderators were driving the Zeds to ground and breaking her promise all in one. Declan Lynch had trusted her. She had trusted Liliana. She'd trusted herself.

The deepest wound was one she didn't even understand. Bryde's voice said in her head: *You don't know what you think you know.*

Just words. Just words from a Zed. Then why did she want to cry?

Liliana leaned to help her up.

"It will be all right," she said.

Two of them stood in the rose garden. Farooq-Lane leaned over and replaced Hennessy's sword in the scabbard. The grass beneath it was a burned ruin. The entire garden was a ruin. These old roses torn up. The gravel path shredded deeply. The fountain tinted an ugly shade with just a bit of someone's blood.

Everything was worse off than when they'd gotten there.

The Moderators had vanished, chasing after the Zeds, but Farooq-Lane knew it didn't matter. Bryde would get away. The second her first swing had missed him, he was always going to get away. She'd known that.

"I trusted you," she said to Liliana.

Liliana gestured for Farooq-Lane to look behind her.

One figure returned quietly to the rose garden.

There was a proud line to the shoulders, to the lifted chin. A coiled power to the walk, which was more like a *stalk*. The eyes were intense and bright. But the shape of the mouth was at odds with the rest of it. Something about the expression there was miserable. Vulnerable.

Jordan Hennessy.

"You have my sword," she said, stopping among the ruined thorns of the old roses.

Warily, Farooq-Lane stepped in front of Liliana. She put her hand on the hilt warningly. Her heart was beating fast again; who knew what deadly dreams this Zed might be carrying. "I don't want to fight. We're not here for you."

"I know. I'm here for you." Hennessy made a big performance of turning her pockets inside out and showing the interior of her leather jacket. Then she held her hands out on either side of her like a reveal. "I'm giving up. This is what it looks like when I give up."

"How do I know this isn't a trap?" Farooq-Lane asked.

"Life's a trap," Hennessy said in a sort of bleak, funny way.

Liliana stepped out from behind Farooq-Lane, her face gentle and unsurprised, and Farooq-Lane realized that Liliana had known this was how it was going to happen. She'd seen *this* in her vision. This moment. Not Farooq-Lane slicing through Bryde. She'd let Farooq-Lane climb into that freezing water, knowing that she would fail to stop Bryde when she sprang out. She'd known it was a ridiculous plan and had let it play through for this moment. Not killing Bryde, but acquiring this Zed, one more Zed than any other plan had ever managed.

Would it have all worked the same way if Farooq-Lane had been in on it from the beginning?

Trust was a hard thing.

"It's all right," Liliana told Hennessy. She walked straight up to her as if she wasn't one of the three most dangerous Zeds in the country, and she clasped one of Hennessy's hands with such warmth that the Zed stared at her. "We all finally found each other."

33

Match heads flaring. Plastic melting. Paper twisting. Gasoline smoking. Anything can burn if you hit it hard enough to jam oxygen atoms into its core. Ronan's heart incinerated.

I'm driving, Bryde had said. *You're unfit.*

He was right.

As the Boston skyline got smaller in the invisible car's rearview mirror, Ronan kept blinking as if things would get clear, and they never got clear. Or maybe they were *too* clear. Every streetlight, every skeleton tree, every billboard etched itself in his vision, every detail perfectly visible so that he couldn't concentrate on any one part of it. He sat bolt upright in the passenger seat, his leg jiggling. If he were driving, he'd mash that gas pedal down and see how much speed he'd really dreamt into this thing. If he were driving, he'd smash this whole car into something so it could burn too.

His phone had been ringing continuously for the past ten minutes.

Furiously, he chucked it onto the dash. It pinged off the windshield and slid across the dash, then slipped down by Bryde's footwell.

Only one person had known where they were going to be.

Only one person.

Declan.

Bryde wordlessly leaned to get the little phone without looking, then dropped it in Ronan's palm.

How many minutes had Declan waited before betraying Ronan to the Moderators? Maybe he had already done it before he got in touch with Ronan at the Aldana-Leons'. While Ronan was meeting the little dreamers whose lives he'd saved, Declan was making plans with the Mods. Casually bringing Ronan in for them. Knowing Ronan always came when called.

"Either talk to him or silence it," Bryde said. "Make a decision."

Ronan clipped the phone to his ear and answered it. "What."

"Thank God," Declan said. "Where are you?"

"Like I will ever tell you that again. You fucking blew it, asshole. New low, even for you. Was it thirty pieces of silver or did you get them to adjust it up for inflation?"

"You don't know what you're talking about."

"I wish that was true. I wish to God it was. You're the only one who knew where we were going to be. Fuck! You're always hustling. Negotiating for the greater part of nothing. You're like a broker for irrelevance."

"Hey now—" Declan started.

"All you care about is finding something to keep Matthew awake. To keep your life in place. You watch the world screw us over on a large scale over and over, and—all I needed was for you to stay out of the way. I never asked for anything else. Just stay the hell out of the way."

"I wasn't trying to stop *you*."

Ronan looked out the window but now it was the opposite of before; his eyes weren't taking in anything. He saw the rose garden again and again. Encountering not Matthew walking through the trellis, but a woman flying at them with Hennessy's stolen sword in hand. "Were you just willing to take the risk they might kill me, too?"

"I was doing it *for* you."

Ronan laughed. He laughed, and laughed, and laughed. It wasn't funny. Nothing was funny.

When he had stopped, Declan said, "I had to get you away from him. The risk was worth it to get you away from him." When Ronan didn't reply, he said flatly, "They didn't get him, did they."

Behind the wheel, Bryde's expression didn't change. He looked neither angry nor surprised. He knew Declan had betrayed him, but he had not said a word against him. He hadn't said much at all, since they escaped.

"You're still with him," Declan said. It wasn't a question. "You've left the city."

Ronan knew when silence was the meanest thing to deploy and he understood that now was the time.

He let Declan sit with the truth.

After nearly a minute, when Ronan wasn't sure if Declan was really still there but refused to say *You still there?* Declan finally said, "He's dangerous, Ronan. They're not wrong about him. I know you're not like that. I know you wouldn't kill people. I know you care about your future. About Matthew. About Adam. About—"

Ronan hung up on him.

For several long minutes the car was silent. Ronan's mind turned over the rose garden again. Not the beginning, this time, but the end. When he and Bryde had run, and Hennessy hadn't.

"Are you going to do it or not?" Bryde asked softly. "Make a decision."

Ronan wasn't sure how he knew exactly what he'd been thinking, but he wasn't wrong. He rubbed his finger on his ear by the phone, thinking, deciding, and then he told the dreamt phone to dial another number.

It was time.

"Ronan?" Adam asked, surprised. He had picked up immediately, even though the display name would have just looked like nonsense.

"Why didn't you text back?"

"Text . . . back? You didn't *call*. It's been weeks."

"But why didn't you text back?"

There was quiet. Almost quiet. Wherever he was, Adam was moving locations; there was the sound of a door closing. "I was on a motorcycle. Then I was taking an exam. Then I was probably, I don't know, sleeping. I don't remember. I came to see you, I was making time best I could. It wasn't that long. I *did* text back. How could I know that you were going to ditch your phone? Ronan, you didn't *call*."

His accent was gone. It was like talking to a stranger. Ronan had thought this would feel different. Or maybe he didn't. He didn't know. His chest was still burning. Fire roared through him, right to the ends of his hands and toes. "I'm calling now."

"I didn't know what was happening," Adam said. "I didn't know what you were doing, if you were even alive. I didn't know if we were . . . if it . . . what . . ."

Ronan repeated, "I'm calling now. I need to see you."

"You're here?" Adam said, even more surprised than he had been when he first picked up. "Oh."

There was something about that *Oh* that Ronan didn't like the shape of. It seemed sad. Not as if Adam was sad when he said it.

But more like something about that *Oh* was going to make Ronan sad. But he plunged ahead anyway. "Can you let us lie low for a few hours while we figure out what's going on with Hennessy?"

Adam didn't reply right away. Then he said, "Who's 'us'?"

"Me and Bryde. They have—they have Hennessy, I think." Ronan knew this was a lie. Or at least a partial truth. Bryde hadn't seen it, but Ronan had. He'd seen Hennessy turn around. He'd let her. God, everything was going to shit.

Adam said, very precisely, "*You* can come lie low." Then, in case Ronan hadn't understood him, he repeated, "*You.*"

"How big of a douche do you think I am?"

"The Lace is afraid of him, Ronan. I am, too. Let him take this heat."

And then Ronan understood why the *Oh* had made him so sad. He'd known it subconsciously before, but now he knew it clearly: Adam had known Declan was betraying the dreamers. He had known the Moderators would be waiting in the rose garden.

They'd all been in on it.

Part of Ronan was here in this invisible car racing away from his family, but part of Ronan was also in that memory of being curled in Ilidorin as he nearly lost himself to nightwash for good. Bryde had tried to warn them about the others when he first introduced them to Ilidorin, and Ronan and Hennessy had blown him off. They'd been so offended by his contempt for the dreamt phones, but now Ronan understood it exactly. Only, the truth was worse than what Bryde had warned. It wasn't simply that Declan and Adam didn't want to leave their own lives to come fight his battle with him. They actively wanted to stop the battle altogether.

They wanted the world to change just enough to keep Ronan alive. Alive, but not living. That was good enough for them.

It wasn't good enough for him.

"Ronan, you know what I'm saying's true," Adam said. "You know what's going on here. If you think about it, you *have* to—"

Ronan hung up on him, too.

He plucked the dreamt phone from his ear, rolled down the window, and threw it out as hard as he could.

Then he leaned his head back against the seat as they drove out of the city with one less dreamer than they'd arrived with.

34

Twenty minutes.
    Alarm.
    Twenty minutes.
Alarm.
Twenty minutes.
Alarm.
Twenty minutes.
Alarm.

That was how Hennessy had been living at the beginning of all this, and that's how she had been living since she left the house with the young dreamers.

She set the timer on her dreamt phone, and twenty minutes later, when it went off, she set it again. She had to wake up enough between each alarm to make sure she didn't fall back into a deep sleep. It could not be an eight-hour sleep interrupted dozens of times. It had to be dozens of sleeps for eight hours.

"But that's not survivable," Carmen Farooq-Lane said. "Or fair."

Farooq-Lane was a very put together sort of young woman, so put together it was difficult to discern her true age. When she said it, it seemed obvious. Like it made sense. Like the situation had been stripped of emotion, taken down to the studs, and revealed as unsound. Of course it was not survivable. Of course it was not fair.

"They shouldn't have made so light of the Lace," Liliana said in her sweet old-lady voice. "It was never going to be as easy as simply asking it to go away."

Liliana the Visionary was a very put together sort of old woman, so put together it was difficult to discern her true age, too. When she said it, it also seemed obvious, although Hennessy found this statement more difficult to accept. Ronan and Bryde had tried so hard to get Hennessy to just shunt the Lace out of her dreams, and they'd told her so many times she was simply clinging to it. Whatever else the Lace was, it was also her fault. And they'd seen it, so surely they knew.

But that wasn't what Farooq-Lane and Liliana seemed to believe.

The three women were on the second floor of a convoluted, historical teahouse, in a small room filled with overstuffed chairs, beanbags, end tables, and travel books. Plinking music played overhead. They had it to themselves. It was very intimate and safe-feeling, which was the opposite of everything Hennessy had been doing for the past few weeks. Past few years. Farooq-Lane had driven them there as Liliana, in the passenger seat, used Farooq-Lane's phone to search for an appropriate place to talk. It was a very different experience from Hennessy's previous travel. When looking for good places to crash and discuss plans, Bryde and Ronan would not have filtered their searches for "warm ambiance" and "free parking." It was clear from watching Farooq-Lane and Liliana that they had traveled together a lot and that they were both comfort-loving creatures.

It was also clear they had crushes on each other.

"This is all very life-affirming," Hennessy told them from her place in a beanbag, "enriching, and all that, but what of it?

So if it's not fair, and it's not easy, it's still there. There's still this thing hanging over me every time I dream, and if Ronan and Bryde have their way, I won't be able to stop it."

Liliana murmured something into Farooq-Lane's ear, which made Farooq-Lane's beautiful face go consternated. They both looked at Hennessy.

"So I understand completely if you decide to kill me," Hennessy said, talking fast. "I've been thinking about it a lot. On previous episodes, it would've been a very selfish decision, on account of my ladies and how they relied on me for their existence, but on this current run, everyone else dead, mostly, fate of the world in hands, well—" She spread her hands, or at least the best she could, considering she had a hot chocolate in one of them. "It's the selfless thing to do, really."

"We have a different idea," Farooq-Lane said.

Hennessy narrowed her eyes. "Do you mean you both had this idea, or *she* has an idea, and whispered it to you just now?"

Liliana smiled sweetly. "I told you she was clever."

Farooq-Lane's businesslike expression didn't change. "Can you dream something to suppress the ley line?"

Hennessy had one dream. The Lace. Always the Lace. She was a bar with a single beer on tap. She was about to tell them this, but in the past, Jordan had always told Hennessy, "You're not allowed to shoot down any more of my ideas until you've had one of your own."

So she didn't shoot it down. She sank down into the beanbag and stared at them instead.

"I don't believe killing yourself is the answer," Farooq-Lane said. "You have value, too."

"Ma'am, we've just met," Hennessy said.

Liliana broke in. "Do you know what it means to be a Visionary, Hennessy? I don't always look like this. Sometimes I'm a girl. Sometimes I'm a woman. Sometimes I am this, what you see now. Every time I change between these ages, I have a vision of the future, and all the sound that has happened or will happen in the intervening years comes out of me. It destroys everyone close enough to hear it. Over the years, I have met and will meet people who urge me to turn this vision inward. If I do that, I will no longer shift between ages, and I will no longer be a danger to those around me. But eventually, that method will kill *me* instead."

"I take it since we're talking to the old version of you, you picked door number one," Hennessy said. "Keep exploding?"

"Most Visionaries die very young," Liliana said. "Too young to change the world. I'm still here not because I think my life is valuable—although I do think that—but because staying alive means I have more visions, and the more visions I have, the more I can save the world from itself. You have value, too, Hennessy, value that comes from staying alive."

"And if you turn off the ley line," Farooq-Lane said, "no more Zeds—dreamers—have to die. You're all only as dangerous then as you would be as normal people. You can only hurt or help as many people as anyone else."

She'd corrected herself, but Hennessy preferred the first term she'd used. Zed. That's right. Zero. Nothing. Loser.

"You don't have to feel this fear and pain all the time. You're allowed to stop it," Farooq-Lane said.

"I know you have no love for yourself," Liliana broke in again, and her voice was so gentle that Hennessy felt absurdly close to tears again. They burned; she hated them. She wanted it to stop.

How badly she wanted it to stop. "So you might not make this decision for yourself, because you don't think you deserve it. You can make it for others. It would be noble to stop it."

Stopping the ley line meant stopping Jordan in her tracks.

Farooq-Lane seemed to guess what she was thinking. "If the end of the world comes, your dreams will die with the rest of us. This way they'll fall asleep. That doesn't have to be forever. Death is forever."

I wish you were dead, she'd told Jordan.

Why do you always do this? Jordan asked.

Hennessy almost wished that Farooq-Lane and Liliana had told her they were going to have to kill her after all. It wasn't exactly that she wanted to die. She just didn't want to live with herself.

"You're forgetting one thing," she said. "I only ever dream of the Lace. All day every day, it's the Lace superstore. I can't dream something to shut down the ley line. I only ever dream of the Lace."

The music plinked overhead. The beanbag hugged Hennessy. She drank some of her hot chocolate. The reviews Liliana had read on the way over were right. It really was good hot chocolate. It would be a good last meal.

Liliana looked at Farooq-Lane, her expression sympathetic and soft.

Farooq-Lane looked at Hennessy, her expression sympathetic and hard. Then she reached behind her to lay FROM CHAOS, in its scabbard, in front of Hennessy and her beanbag.

"Then explain this," she said.

35

R onan hadn't meant to dream Matthew.

It had been Christmastime. Short days. Long nights. He always got restless that time of year. Anticipation built in him as the days got smaller, until around the end of December, the feeling eventually burst and left him feeling more ordinary again.

He knew now that it had been a surge of the ley line. But back then, as a child, as a dreamer who was not permitted to give words to the dreaming, he hadn't known anything but that restlessness. It was a feeling that was only shored up by Declan's behavior. If Ronan became more alive as they crept toward winter solstice, Declan became less so. His eyes developed bags. His moods got short. The brothers did not fight then like they did when they were older, but the seeds were already sleeping in the cold soil.

That particular winter had been unseasonably warm, and a few days before Christmas, Aurora sent the boys outside to kick a ball around. To Ronan's delight, the brothers discovered that the dun-colored fields around the farmhouse were lousy with starlings. Hundreds, perhaps thousands. When the birds first saw the brothers emerge from the house, they lifted up in a great swath of dark dots in the sky, like music notes on a page, but they quickly landed again just a few yards farther away.

This was much better than kickball. For quite a while they instead played a game of *who can get closer to the flock*.

Ronan won. This was partially because he was shorter than Declan and thus more clandestine, but it was also because he wanted it more. He was fascinated by this flock of flyers, this many-headed entity that was not tied to the ground. The birds were individuals, but when they lifted off, it was together, in something even more magnificent than they could ever be on their own. Ronan didn't have words for how they made him feel, but he loved them. He wished he knew how to explain it to Declan.

"I'd like a bird army," he said.

Declan's lip curled. "I don't think that would be very interesting."

"You're never into anything. You're the most boring person I know."

Declan retrieved the ball. The game was clearly over.

Without warning, Ronan ran directly into the flock. There was a brief moment of stillness and then they all took off at once, surrounding him.

It was so much like a dream. Wings upon wings upon wings. Too many birds to count. Too many voices to pick out individual sounds. He raised his arms. Ground and air seethed with birds, hiding both so thoroughly that it didn't seem entirely impossible that he had left the ground with them.

Imagine flying, he thought. *Imagine flying while awake. Imagine dreaming while awake—*

Then the birds had gone and he was just a boy standing on the ground. He was not flying. Being awake was nothing like dreaming. His older brother was a few feet away, the ball tucked under his arm, looking at him with an expression of vague irritation.

Ronan had never known such agony, and he didn't even have words for it.

A few nights later, on the shortest night of the year, Ronan dreamt of the birds, only now they were ravens, not starlings, and there were fewer of them. They were gathered in the field in a purposeful way, studying something in the grass. They were muttering to themselves: *make way, make way, make way.*

When Ronan approached to investigate, they scattered. In the grass where they'd been, he found a blond-headed baby.

In the dream, Ronan knew without being told that this was a new brother.

The baby smiled at Ronan. His hands were already outstretched for Ronan to pick him up. He was so, so happy to see him.

Ronan knew without being told that this brother would always be happy to see him.

"Hello," he told the baby.

The baby laughed.

Ronan laughed, too, and the awful feeling that had been inside him since that game of kickball dissipated. He scooped this new brother out of the grass.

And then he woke up. When he did, Matthew Lynch was still there, squalling and brand-new, in the hallway outside his closed bedroom door.

But the thing was—Ronan hadn't known. He hadn't known Matthew was dreamt. That Matthew was *his* dream. He couldn't remember how he'd explained it to himself at the time, but it must have been good and thorough, because all he remembered of that time was his delight at having a new baby brother. He hadn't remembered the circumstances around it until Declan had cornered him during a particularly destructive time in high school and given him the story. Niall Lynch had given Ronan stories, too, but they were always rewards. This was a punishment. A warning.

"You dreamt Matthew," Declan said. "Don't you get it? If you get yourself killed, you're ending his life, too."

"I don't think I did," Ronan said, but he knew he had. He'd just been pushing the memory away as hard as he could. It had been made easier by the fact that Matthew hadn't appeared right next to Ronan when he woke. Instead, like Ronan's dreamt forest, he'd appeared some distance away.

It had also been made easier because Ronan didn't have words, back then, to talk about what had happened. He wasn't allowed to.

"I was there," Declan said. "I know what happened. Saying it didn't happen doesn't make it real. You've got to keep this under control. His life relies on you."

Ronan had lived with that weight since then.

No more, he thought now. The ley lines would be powerful again. Matthew would have a life of his own.

"This will have to do," Bryde said.

They'd been charging away from Boston for a few hours when Bryde pulled over abruptly. There was nothing remarkable about the stopping place. It was simply a one-track gravel road that led into a wooded picnic area with a rotting bench.

Ronan stared around at their surroundings again, trying to decide if, in his misery over Declan, Adam, and Hennessy, he had badly misjudged how far they'd traveled. He could see a lake glistening through the dense trees. Everything continued to look very New England to him. "We're still in Massachusetts, aren't we?"

"Connecticut," Bryde said. "But yes, you're right. But something is happening. We need to free Ilidorin's line now or we might not be able to. That's what the trees are telling me. This is the best place I've felt so far for the energy. I'd like more, but I don't think we can wait any longer to dream something for the dam. We won't make it all the way there."

"Before what?" Ronan asked.

But Bryde just threw open the car door. Crisp cool air flooded in. It was a lovely day. It was the sort of day that caused people to put coats on dogs and take long scenic walks. It was the sort of day it had been when Ronan had last visited Adam at Harvard. It was the sort of day that Ronan would have used to repair fences and siding if he had been back at the Barns.

It was also the sort of day for Ronan and Bryde to sit in the dried leaves behind the car, leaning up against it, unfolding their dream masks. Chainsaw flapped up to a tree above them and waited.

"What do you feel?" Bryde asked.

Strange. It felt strange to do this without Hennessy. After this, Ronan vowed, he'd go back for her. He'd fix this. He'd fix her.

But that wasn't the kind of feeling Bryde meant. Ronan put his hands onto the ground to feel the ley line, but that made him think too much about how Adam sometimes did that when he was scrying. He draped them over his knees instead as he listened.

The ley line was there. Not overwhelming, but present. Sufficient. He could feel its low, slow pulse trying to sync with his heartbeat, or vice versa. "It's all right. I've never been to the dam. How are we supposed to know how to destroy it?"

"I know what it's like. I'll show you in the dream."

"And you want us to dream something here to destroy it way down there?" But Ronan answered his own question. "It has to be something that can travel."

"Yes," Bryde agreed. "Like the dolphins for the transmission line. Like the sundogs you sent to save your brothers."

His voice had no bitterness. Declan had tried to get them killed, but he didn't spit the word *brothers* at Ronan. Instead, his voice, if anything, became softer on that word. Soft on *brothers*. Hard on *sundogs*. The entire sundogs episode felt like a very long time ago. Ronan and Hennessy had been in Lindenmere, Ronan's dreamt forest, trying to banish the Lace from Hennessy's mind with the help of Bryde, who had been just a voice to them at that point. Bryde had disappeared in a hurry as the Moderators began to move in on other dreamers, and Ronan had received that fraught call from Declan that Matthew was in danger. Ronan still remembered the absolute terror he'd felt as he begged his forest to use the power of the ley line to produce the sundogs. He remembered how he'd sped across the state toward Declan and Matthew, the exact opposite of what he was doing now. And he remembered clearly arriving to find his dreamt sundogs had done what he'd asked. Saved his brothers' lives.

The exact opposite of what Declan had just tried to do.

Declan hadn't been so worried about Ronan's ability when Ronan was hidden safely away until needed.

Bryde said, "We don't have much time."

Ronan didn't know if he could stay focused with his thoughts as they were now. He wasn't thinking about the future. He was thinking about the past.

Bryde said, "I'll do my best to focus the dream. It will be different after this. Last push."

They dreamt.

In the dream, they were at the dam. Because it was Bryde's dream, it was vividly rendered. Ronan could see it, smell it, feel the unseasonably warm breeze on his skin. They were walking. He could feel it as if he were awake. The bite of his boot on the zigzagging walkway the two of them followed. The echo of their steps off the back of the low concrete visitors' center, which they passed. The tickle of gnats swarming from the overgrown dry brush. The buzz of a stink bug woken by the heat.

Ronan would have been hard pressed to identify how it was any different from waking life.

"What do you feel?" Bryde asked.

"Don't ask me that while we're dreaming," Ronan said. "It fucks me up."

They had come to a viewing area at the end of the walkway. Wordlessly, they leaned on the railing to look at the vast white dam. The scale of it was difficult to hold. On one side was the glittering blue water of the artificial lake, and on the other, hundreds of feet below, held back by the curved dam, was more glittering water, the choked Roanoke River. All about were mountains. The lake looked odd somehow, the water strange as it climbed the slopes, although Ronan couldn't understand why.

"They're drowned," Bryde said. "These mountains were never meant to have water up to their chins; picture this as a river valley instead. The dam did this. There are towns beneath that lake, if you can imagine. Beautiful, isn't it? Like a cemetery. How would you destroy it?"

For quite a long time the two of them stood there as Ronan studied the dam and thought of what the smallest, easiest dream would be to destroy it. Before he'd fallen asleep, he'd been imagining something strong enough to bust through the dam itself, but that now seemed unacceptable. This was more water than he had pictured. All of these gallons would have to go somewhere, and who knew how many houses and roads had been built downstream of this now.

He didn't want to kill anyone.

So it would have to be something gradual. Something with a bit of warning. Not a lot. Just enough to let people get out of the way. Not slow enough for them to stop it. Inexorable, unfixable.

His heart was beating hard in his chest. Just a few days ago he'd been contemplating how he felt about destroying a trash dump, and here he was figuring out how to take down a project that surely had cost billions of dollars and taken years to build. The electricity it generated was used to power all the vacation homes he could see dotting the mountains. Probably. Ronan didn't know a lot about how electricity worked.

He thought about how wonderful it was to dream in Lindenmere, where the ley line was good, where Lindenmere was focusing him, where everything was as he liked it. He imagined what it would be like to make that even better. He thought about the little Aldana-Leon dreamers. He thought about Rhiannon Martin's mirrors. He thought about Matthew. He thought about himself, what it would be like to live without fearing he would manifest rooms of murder crabs or bleed to death from nightwash.

He also thought about how Declan was worried that this was something he couldn't come back from.

"It is frightening how fast the world sickens," Bryde said. "Decades ago it seemed like we had years. Years ago it seemed like we had months. Months ago it seemed like days. And now every day, every minute, every second, it is harder to be a dreamer. It's so noisy. Even here in these mountains, it is so noisy. How they shout at us all, even in our sleep. Soon there will be no place for the quiet things, the things that undo themselves when they have to shout. Soon there will be no place for secrets, the secrets that lose their mystery when they are uncovered. Soon there will be no place for the strange, no place for the unknown, because everything will be cataloged and paved and plugged in."

Ronan thought about Adam's gloves set upon his shoes in the mudroom.

He thought about wanting to feel like he had been made for something more than dying.

"I know you are two things," Bryde said. "I know you are of both worlds. That will never change."

"What if it's too much?" Ronan asked. "I don't know if I want to do it."

"You do."

"You can't just say I do. You don't know what I'm feeling."

Bryde's voice was very, very soft. "I know you've already made this decision. You made it long ago."

"On a hoverboard floating in the air? After Rhiannon Martin was killed?"

"Further back than that."

"When we decided to go with you?"

"Further back than that."

"No," said Ronan.

"Yes."

All of Ronan's frustration burst out of him, so strongly that the dream shivered with it. The air shimmered. The lake simmered. He was tired of the lessons. The games. The riddles. For some reason, he suddenly remembered the long-ago Christmas starlings bursting around him as Declan watched. That agony again of wanting to fly and being unable to explain it to anyone else.

He was suddenly either very afraid, or very furious. He snarled, "You can't know when I made the decision!"

"I can," Bryde said softly. "Because I know when you dreamt me."

36

What is real?

You make reality.

Just like that, Ronan was in the worst dream again. The dam was gone. The lake was gone. The warmth and clarity of Bryde's dream was gone, replaced with Ronan's old nightmare. He was standing in the bathroom of the Barns and there was a Ronan in the mirror. Behind him, Ronan could see the reflection of Bryde standing in the doorway.

"No," he said.

Bryde said, "I only came because you asked me."

"No."

"Don't say no. You know. You knew."

"I didn't know."

"You knew," Bryde insisted. "Deep down, you had to know. You had to ask for it, or it wouldn't have happened."

The dream changed. It was Lindenmere now. They were surrounded by Ronan's massive trees, standing in the clearing where he had heard Bryde's voice with Hennessy that day. The dream was impossible to separate from reality. The details were perfect. Every lacy fern. Every growing patch of lichen. Every mote of dust and insect gleaming in the air.

"No," Ronan said again. "They knew your name. They knew the rumors."

"You dreamt the rumors."

"No. I can't do that. Only you can do that sort of stuff. The orbs—"

"You dreamt it into me."

The forest was alive with sound. Distant wings. Claws. Talons. Mandibles. Even after all these lessons, Ronan was no less likely to corrupt a dream than when he'd brought the murder crabs out at Adam's dorm, when push came to shove. "Why are you doing this?"

"Why did you keep Adam out of your dreams?" Bryde asked. "You were sure he would know. You wanted to pretend."

He frowned, just a little, and Ronan could feel that he was mentally driving the encroaching claws and talons out of the dream. Effortless. Controlled where Ronan was not.

"I didn't want anything," Ronan said. That was a lie. The dream threw it back at him. He thought he might throw up. "You knew about Hennessy. I didn't know about Hennessy."

"I know what Lindenmere knows," Bryde said quietly. "I am both of you."

Oh, God. Now Ronan was playing it all back in his head. He was going over everything Bryde had taught him. He was trying to recall the first time he'd seen Bryde. The first time he'd *heard* Bryde. He was trying to remember how he'd decided the game of finding him was worth playing. The promise of another dreamer had been so tantalizing. The promise of another dreamer who'd actually known what he was doing had been even more tantalizing. He could have generated that in a dream, just like those talons and claws. He'd wanted a teacher. He got a teacher.

No.

Ronan tried to think if Bryde had ever told him anything that Ronan himself didn't already know, that Lindenmere, as a forest situated on the ley line, able to see other events along the ley line, wouldn't have known.

Oh, God, Bryde getting his information from the trees, Bryde often knowing what Ronan was thinking before he spoke. Ronan looking at Bryde and thinking he looked familiar, or something, and shying away from what he actually already knew. The rabbit hole kept leading down. He couldn't find bottom. He was still falling.

The dream was now an Irish shoreline. An ancient hawk flew over the black ocean. Ronan could taste the salt in his mouth. Cold shot through him, a damp cold that made it all the way to his bones. It didn't feel like a dream. It felt like reality. It felt exactly like reality. Ronan could no longer tell the difference between them.

Bryde said, "You wanted me."

"I wanted someone *real*."

Reality doesn't mean anything to someone like you. Bryde didn't have to say it. Ronan already knew it. He knew everything Bryde knew, deep down.

"It's harder than I thought," Bryde said. "Being out here. I thought it would be simpler. I thought I knew what I wanted. But it's so much louder. It's so, so much louder. I get . . . confused."

Ronan's heart was breaking.

"Your quest," Ronan said.

"*Your* quest," said Bryde.

Ronan closed his eyes. "You're just a dream."

Bryde shook his head. "We already know what you think about that, because I told you. What do you feel, Ronan Lynch?"

Betrayed. Alone. Furious. He felt like he had nightwash even though he didn't. He felt like he couldn't stand to look at Bryde for one more second. He felt like he couldn't stand to be in his own head one more second. He felt like he couldn't tell if he had ever woken up from that worst dream.

The black ocean boiled and then burned. Ronan's mind boiled and then burned. Everything could burn if you hit it hard enough.

"Nothing," Ronan said. "I can't feel anything."

The grass was also burning now. The flaming waves had lapped the pebbly shore, which caught fire, and then the ascending cliff face had caught fire, and then the strange flames had wicked over the edge and caught the dirt and then the grass. The fire whispered to itself as it did its work. Its language was secret, but Ronan got the gist. It was starving.

Bryde said, "Right now, Hennessy is trying to dream something to shut down the ley line for good. Can you feel her? We can go stop her, or I can go stop her, or you can try to stop *me* and let the ley line be shut down and kill all of this. Either way. You have to make a decision. Is this my quest, is it your quest, or is it nothing? For once in your life, stop lying. Stop hiding behind me. Ronan Lynch, what do you want?"

In the dream, sweet Aurora's voice came through gently. She was telling Ronan he had to bury it.

He took a deep, shuddering breath. The fire was burning everything except for them.

"I want to change the world."

37

When the ley line disappeared, it was a very nice day. All of New England was experiencing an unseasonably warm afternoon, but it was a good kind of unseasonably warm. Not warm enough to make all the conversations center around anything unpleasant like climate change and the growing price of avocados. But warm enough that residents could shed their coats and gloves and get some of the ol' steps in, take the kid for a walk, knock the spiders off the badminton set in the garage.

Days like this, they said, *remind you what it's all about.*

Three Zeds were dreaming busily on this unseasonably warm afternoon and thus not able to enjoy it. Two of them, Bryde and Ronan Lynch, slept just a few yards away from a car that was very difficult to see. They had not been dreaming long, but already dried oak leaves had flickered from the woods around them and lit upon their clothes. There is a certain wrongness to seeing leaves settled on a body. It is not the same as leaves drifting over a rooftop or a fallen log. It makes one anxious to see it. It is wrong. Opposite.

The third dreamer, Hennessy, dreamt on an oversized beanbag in a small room in a tea shop. Two women watched her closely. One of the women, a woman so old that numbers no longer felt relevant to describe her age, gently brushed her fingers across Hennessy's forehead as she slept. The other woman stood watchfully at the door, her hands on a dreamt sword with the words FROM CHAOS etched on the hilt. She was ready to swing it at once should Hennessy wake with a nightmare instead of a dream to save them all.

"I don't have a good feeling about this," the woman with the sword said.

"It will be all right," the old woman replied, brushing her fingers over the dreamer's forehead again, but her hand was trembling a little.

The people who loved the dreaming Zeds were also unable to enjoy the warm afternoon.

Adam Parrish, who loved Ronan, sat on the floor of his dorm room alone, a single candle lit, his tarot cards stacked face up beside it. He stared into the flame, throwing his mind out into the dreamspace. He was trying to reach Ronan Lynch, but it was like a phone that kept ringing and ringing. This was a dangerous game, but he kept trying. He let his mind wander a little farther from his body each time.

Ronan! Ronan! But instead he kept catching glimpses of Bryde. Everything felt hot. He could smell smoke. He *was* smoke, drifting, drifting.

Oh, Ronan, what have you done, he thought miserably. *What are you doing?*

Matthew Lynch, who also loved Ronan, had gone walking. Not wandering like a dream, but walking like an ordinary teen, with purpose. While Declan was occupied with secretive errands, Matthew had set up an appointment with a local school for a tour. He was going to finish high school. He'd decided. He didn't know what he was going to do afterward, but until then, he was going to take Jordan's advice and start treating himself as real until Declan did, too. It was a very stuffy school office, though, and he could see the day through the tiny window next to him. It was hard not to wish he was out there instead.

He found himself quite suddenly thinking about fire. He wasn't sure why. He touched his cheek. It was hot. The school hadn't adjusted their heating for this unseasonable day.

Declan Lynch, who also loved Ronan, was cornered in his own apartment by a handful of extremely pissed-off Moderators. They had just lost three Zeds at a rose garden and had no Visionary to provide further leads. They had not immediately decided how they were going to use Declan to get their hands on Ronan, but they *had* decided they would grab him first and then figure out the finer points later. He was all they had.

"I'm no good as leverage," Declan told them. He thought about the gun he'd taped to the bottom of the kitchen table. It was four feet away, but might as well have been four hundred. Even if he could somehow get it, what was one gun against a room full of them? "As far as he's concerned, he thinks I just tried to get him killed."

He couldn't help but think about how Bryde's little dreamt orb would have let him walk out untouched. How Ronan's sundogs spilled from the bottle would have emptied this apartment instantly. Such power. Such power for just a very few people to hold.

Oh, Ronan, he thought, suddenly angry that his brother could never see the bigger picture, the long game. *What are you going to do now?*

Jordan, who loved Hennessy, was walking from her studio to Declan's apartment, head down, eyebrows furrowed, reading a news story on her phone. It was about a massive Boston street race that had sent seven drivers to area hospitals in critical condition. The chief of police had given a statement urging drivers to remember that life was not a video game or a movie franchise; actions like this had real consequences. She wondered if the play against Bryde had worked; Declan wasn't picking up his phone.

I wish you were dead, Hennessy had told her.

Jordan's cheeks felt hot as she walked. Fiery. Her chest ached and burned. She didn't know why Hennessy had to be like this. If they were still living together, they would have talked it out by now. Hennessy would have calmed down, gotten sad instead of mad, and eventually just gone limp, giving up. They would have once more reached equilibrium. Well, not *they.* Jordan was rarely the emergency. Hennessy was the emergency.

Hennessy, thought Jordan, *why didn't you give me all your memories?*

None of them guessed the fate of the afternoon was currently playing out inside the minds of the dreaming Zeds.

The Zeds moved inside a shared dream that jerked from one thing to another.

First it was the Lace, jagged and hateful.

Then it was the Smith Mountain Dam with a slow, sentient fire picking away at its base.

Then it was the Game, with each Zed in a different car jockeying for control of both the race and the dream.

It was a studio, it was a farm, it was a parking lot dumpster with opera singing sweetly, it was a teen girl in a gallery looking for Hennessy, it was a fire dragon exploding over a car, it was a bullet in a woman's head, it was Bryde crouched next to Lock's body in a featureless field.

"This game of yours," Bryde said to Lock's body, "this game of yours will only end in pain. Take a look. The rules are changing. Do you understand? Do you understand what we could do? Leave my dreamers alone."

"Bryde," Ronan said, but Bryde didn't attend.

"Thanks for the focus. I couldn't do that without you here," Hennessy said. She stood by the invisible car, watching Bryde plow through his lines from the memory. "God! Remember when you told me to kill my clones? And then we basically ran away with yours?"

She knew about Bryde. She knew because the dream had presented the knowledge to her without remark, as dreams sometimes do. The knowledge was this: Bryde was a dream. Bryde was Ronan's dream.

"How are you doing that to him?" Ronan asked.

Hennessy narrowed her eyes at the horizon, where smoke billowed. "I heard him tell that Moderator a clever thing at the rose garden—did you hear him? He said he didn't play mind games. He just turned the sound down on the stuff that didn't matter. Why didn't he teach us *that* shit? That's shit I can use. I'm using it now! He gave us such a hard time about what was real and what was a dream, but he was talking about himself, too, wasn't he? He doesn't know what he really is any more than we do. What's real now, Bryde? What do you *feel*?"

Bryde didn't attend. He was still moving through the memory.

"Of course he has a stake in all this," Hennessy said. "He told you he wanted to keep Matthew awake without you? He meant *he* wanted to stay awake. Fucking oedipal, man."

"Shut up," Ronan said. "What's your big plan here? Shut down the ley lines to keep away the Lace?"

Hennessy popped finger guns at him.

Then she reached into her pocket and pulled out a silver orb. It was possible to tell, in the way of dreams, that even though it looked a lot like Bryde's silver orb, it was not at all the same. It pulsed its intentions through the dream.

Its intention was this: Stop the ley line.

"So what now?" Hennessy asked. "We, like, battle forever? Is that going to be how it is? I try to make this thing that will shut down the line and you change the dream so I can't remember what I was doing and round and round and round?"

The two Zeds eyed each other. The dream pulsed with unspoken feelings, but none of them were malice. Really, there were just two. One dreamer was feeling *I need this to stop everything* and the other dreamer was feeling *I need this to start something.*

And the other Zed, the Zed who was also a dream, kept going through the motions. He was walking toward an Airstream trailer that had just appeared in time for him to walk to it. Hennessy was somehow re-creating the memory perfectly for him, everything taken in with her artist's eye and thrown back at him. She was very powerful when she was doing that.

On the horizon, the smoke continued to billow. The Smith Mountain Dam was there in the middle of these cornfields, being taken down slowly but surely by the unruly, otherworldly fire. Eerie dark herons circled above it, looking wispy as the smoke trail from a candle. They were ready to scoop up the fire and carry it wherever Ronan needed it to go. They would make the journey from Connecticut to the real dam in Virginia in very little time at all. Ronan was somehow holding the intention of the fire intact while also holding a conversation with Hennessy and also quietly shaping the dream into something else in the background without anyone noticing. He was very powerful when he was doing that.

"The Lace isn't here now," Ronan said. "As long as we work together, there's no Lace. I can keep it away forever. We can take a break from what we're doing. Hennessy, I found you before. You were drowning. I came looking for you. I wanted to do this with you. Do you remember? Don't make me beg."

Hennessy held the silver orb in front of one of her eyes and squinted, like it was a pirate's eye patch. Both of them could sense it. It was not so much a presence as a non-presence. It was an absence of potential. It was a TV with the cord yanked from the wall. She didn't say anything. Hennessy always had something to say, but she didn't say anything.

"You fuck everyone this way," Ronan said. His quiet changes to the dream were now visible to him, although still hidden to her. Slowly, birds were gathering behind her. Hundreds. Thousands. The fields were lousy with them. As he twitched his fingers by his side, they twitched, too, a gathering storm. They had a single intention built into them too: Get the orb from Hennessy. Destroy it so that Ronan could wake without it. Destroy it so Ronan could wake with his dam-destroying flames instead. "Have you thought about the consequences? You can't deal so the whole world has to instead?"

"I'm the rubber and you're the glue, Ronan Lynch," Hennessy replied. "What's funny is—Bryde's you, and he's still more right than you are. You're still thinking like a non-dreamer. At least I'm thinking like a forger."

She pointed behind him.

Ronan just had time to look and see that the real Hennessy

stood there, holding another silver orb in her fingers. This one was even stronger than the other Hennessy was holding. It was not just the absence of sensation. It was a blanket of nothingness. It was noise-canceling, sound-deadening, pressure-relieving, stain-lifting, subscription-canceling, and his birds were pointed at the wrong Hennessy and the wrong orb and—

Hennessy woke up in the middle of the teahouse.

"Liliana," said Carmen Farooq-Lane.

"I know," replied Liliana.

They both looked at the little silver orb cupped in Hennessy's paralyzed hands. They had not seen it appear. Instead, their minds bent and folded on themselves. One part of their brains tried to tell them the orb had always been there. The other part remembered that it had not.

The rule of dreamt objects is this: If it worked in the dream, it worked in real life.

Hennessy's orb worked in the dream.

It worked in real life.

The effects upon the unseasonably nice afternoon were immediate.

Dreamt birds dropped out of the sky here and there, pinging off windshields and onto the sidewalk before coming to a rest, sleeping. Dreamt dogs suddenly slept at dog parks, much to their owners' surprise. Cars veered off the road and into each other, their dreamt drivers suddenly staring into space.

A nanny pushing a pram outside a converted church in downtown Boston found herself pushing a child who could not be woken.

Social media lit up with reports of power outages as wind turbines mysteriously dozed to stillness.

At Logan Airport, a landing aircraft completely missed the runway and careened toward the bay. Air traffic control shouted to an unresponsive pilot before turning its attention to the radio reports of other planes dropping out of the sky across the globe.

In a very stuffy school office, Matthew Lynch put a hand to his burning-hot cheek.

"Are you all right, honey?" asked the school secretary.

"I'm sorry," he muttered, and then he fell fast asleep.

In Declan Lynch's apartment, Declan Lynch watched in astonishment as Lock stopped speaking midsentence and fell to his knees, followed by two of the other Moderators. In the shock, he leapt for the gun beneath the table. Ripping it from its place, he pointed it at one of the three remaining Moderators.

"What's going on here?" Declan demanded.

But the others, too, swayed against each other. They were asleep before he got his answer.

Their sleep *was* the answer.

In a Connecticut picnic area, Bryde sat up, shaking leaves off his body and memory-cobwebs from his mind. He reached into the pocket of his gray jacket and looked at the sweetmetal he had stolen off Lock weeks and weeks before. It was not very strong, but it was enough. For now.

He looked then to Ronan Lynch, who still slept, leaves across his face.

"Wake up," he said, but Ronan did not.

On the sidewalk in front of Declan's apartment, Jordan stood with her head tilted back, listening to sirens wailing. In front of her, a bird plummeted thoughtlessly to the sidewalk with a surprisingly quiet *flomp*. She crouched beside it. It was a beautiful little thing, jeweled and impossible. She touched its chest softly. It was not dead. It was fast asleep.

Her heart was beating very, very fast.

She could feel the ley line sucking away from her. Away from everything. It was like feeling the air leaving a room. It was like that day all those weeks ago when Hennessy had dreamt an entire ocean into the room and she'd suddenly found herself inhabiting a world that wasn't meant to support her. One couldn't argue with an ocean. Either you had an oxygen tank or you didn't.

At the end of the sidewalk, the door to the apartment building burst open. Declan stood in it, his jacket half-pulled on, his keys dangling in his hand. She didn't need to be told that he had been coming to look for her. She could see it in his body language, in his face.

"Jordan," he said. "You're—"

She could see another bird falling from the sky, a larger one, at the end of the street. It set off the car alarm when it hit the windshield.

With wonder, she said to Declan, "I'm awake."

She was very, very awake.

It really was a nice day.

END OF BOOK TWO

ACKNOWLEDGMENTS

David: you accompanied me as I painstakingly planned the perfect heist over a series of months and then scrapped it for a completely different one with eighteen fewer steps. This is a metaphor. Thank you for the metaphor.

Sarah: you patiently held the canvas as I threw paint at it, splattering you, the walls, the floor, the ceiling, bystanders. You always just sighed and handed me another tube of paint when I ran out. This is a metaphor. Thank you for the metaphor.

Ed: you're my sweetmetal, baby. This is a metaphor. Thank you for the metaphor.

ABOUT THE AUTHOR

Maggie Stiefvater is the #1 *New York Times* bestselling author of the novels *Shiver, Linger, Forever,* and *Sinner.* Her novel *The Scorpio Races* was named a Michael L. Printz Honor Book by the American Library Association. The first book in The Raven Cycle, *The Raven Boys,* was a Publishers Weekly Best Book of the Year and the second book, *The Dream Thieves,* was an ALA Best Book for Young Adults. The third book, *Blue Lily, Lily Blue,* received five starred reviews. The final book, *The Raven King,* received four. She is also the author of *All the Crooked Saints* and *Call Down the Hawk.* An artist and a musician, she lives in Virginia with her husband and their two children. You can visit her online at maggiestiefvater.com.